The Man
I Loved
Before

BOOKS BY ANNA MANSELL

How to Mend a Broken Heart
The Lost Wife
I Wanted to Tell You
Her Best Friend's Secret

The Man
I Loved
Before

anna mansell

bookouture

Published by Bookouture in 2020

An imprint of Storyfire Ltd.
Carmelite House
50 Victoria Embankment
London EC4Y 0DZ

www.bookouture.com

ISBN: 978-1-83888-624-0
eBook ISBN: 978-1-83888-623-3

For Maggie: from a casual conversation on the sofa in December 2018, to a real-life book we can hold in our hands, March 2020. Proof that hard work, self-belief and patience pays off. X

Chapter One

Dear Ben,

There are some things I have to tell you. Things I need to own so I can move forward with my life. But they're things that you may not want to know. After all, you left, as well you should have. I neither deserved nor appreciated you - at least, not the way you wanted me to. Not the way you had every right for me to. I wish I knew why I behaved the way I did, I wish I could put it all right, but sometimes, it's just too late...

Chapter Two

'Isn't thirty-eight a bit old for dating apps?' I suggest.

'Too old? You know Nicky Sales is getting married next year because of Tinder.' My best friend Leanne barely looks up as she swipes and types on my phone. I'd given it to her to get me on their new WiFi, but she apparently saw an opportunity to take my life into her own hands.

'I'm just not sure. I'm trying to nurture a gentler phase in my life after the last few years. You know how crap it's been. I think I just want to exorcise some demons and be happy. Learn to love myself.'

'Alright, Yoko Ono,' she says, cynically. 'Exorcising demons suggests you're going to start unpicking all that's gone off and I'm telling you now, no good can come of reliving the bad stuff.'

I shift uncomfortably because it's almost like she can see the state I got in when I wrote the letter to Ben. I hadn't anticipated how painful it would be, how much I'd relive all the moments I felt I wanted to say.

'Don't get me wrong,' she continues, not looking up. 'I'd like to see you love yourself, even the messed-up bits. Because if you've not messed up in life, then you're not living it right. But I also know you. Loving yourself won't happen overnight. Maybe a bit of positive male attention might help in the meantime.'

'Is that not the very opposite of what I'm supposed to be doing?'

'Who says what you're supposed to be doing? Also I'm not saying you need a man to make you happy…'

'Right!'

'But maybe a bit of flirting and a few dates might make you realise you're not a total lost cause.'

'Flirting and dates? Oh God. I can't even…' Leanne ignores me, so I raise my eyebrows at my brand-new, tiny goddaughter instead. Elsie Alice. She lies in my lap and doesn't respond. She probably doesn't have an opinion on Tinder. She's three weeks old but still a bit scrunched up, like, if she could, she'd climb straight back in the womb and nestle there for a few more months. I can relate to that. A womb is safe and away from reality. It's warm. You can mostly sleep. Nobody requires you to be a grown-up. Or join Tinder.

'You might meet the man of your dreams.'

'I don't think I'm ready.'

'You may not feel ready, but I'm here to tell you, you are. This is exactly what you need, the motivation to move on. Let's face it, you've never been that good at realising when it was time.'

I've known Leanne for years. Since school, though we didn't hang out much then. But we've been inseparable since meeting back up at work a couple of years ago. Recruitment. A job she got out of way before I did and, frankly, I wish I had followed her lead. At least then I might not have got the sack. She's seen me at my best and worst and whilst she has no problem in telling me if she thinks I'm being an idiot, she also seems to accept that mostly I'm not a bad person.

'Maybe you're right,' I say, uncertainly.

'It may not be the perfect solution, but something's got to give. Like I say, you can't keep looking back, Jem. So, what shall I say about you? In your profile bit. We need something funny, something sharp and sassy. Something that will make you stand out from the crowd.'

I smile. 'That I'm doing this under duress? That my life is a mess and I should probably be avoided at all costs. That I am broke, single and living back with my mum?'

'You can't start with that. You need to be open, but not too open. You need to seem keen.'

'How keen?'

'Keen enough to shave your legs before you go on a date.'

She looks pointedly at the bit of ankle poking out of my jeans, so I pull my leg out of view. 'I will shave my legs if and when I want to. It just hasn't really been a priority of late, is all.'

'No. I can see that.'

'In case you'd forgotten, there's not been much call for a shaven leg round these parts. And I've been a little busy here, helping you. Besides, Elsie Alice doesn't care about the state of my leg hair, do you, baby? Hey? No. No you don't.' I tap my finger from her chin to top lip to nose. Something I always do to babies and for some weird reason, it usually makes them laugh. Not this time. 'Nothing. Tough crowd.'

'She won't be laughing for weeks yet.'

'She could at least smile.'

'She's not a performing monkey! Right, I've said you're: *often wrong but never in doubt.*'

'Wow! Thanks.'

'It's a joke.'

'It makes me sound high maintenance!'

'Alright, what would *you* put?'

'I don't know. That I like reading, watching TV, and holidays abroad?' Leanne mock yawns. 'See! This is why I don't do dating apps, what the hell are you supposed to say? Maybe it's time I was single for a while.'

'You've been single for a year, Jemima Whitfield. And, whilst there's nothing wrong with that per se, I think you feel stuck, don't you?' I half nod, mildly irritated by her powers of observation. 'This could be a little kick-start.'

'But don't you think I need time to process it all? And what about Mum? She needs me.'

'She's on the mend, Jem.'

'In theory. But everything feels so raw. Since Ben left, at the risk of sounding over-dramatic, I feel like life has gone from bad to worse.'

'It went bad to worse a year ago. And now it's getting better. You're just testing the waters, that's all.'

'What does an almost forty-year-old, recently bankrupt, emotionally unavailable woman have to offer anyone?'

'You are only two of those things – thirty-eight is not almost forty. Not in my book anyway, I'm not owning that until I absolutely have to.' I scowl at her. 'It's exactly why I think this would help though, love. Give you some confidence that you are worthy, that you have something to offer.' She breathes in. 'Make you stop obsessing over Ben.'

'I'm not obsessing over him.' This is a lie and she'll know it. I never stopped thinking about him, despite everything that went on. All that I did. All that's happened since he left. I should stop hiding and beating myself up for past me, and all the things she did. It's time to acknowledge my flaws, own them, then move on. Be new. Be better. Be the person Leanne seems to think I can be. 'I wrote him a letter.'

'Who?'

'Ben!' Leanne looks at me and it's a bit like people who peer over their glasses, except she doesn't wear glasses. 'I thought it would be cathartic. Put some ghosts to rest, you know? I put everything in there. I told him everything.'

'Everything?'

She sounds surprised. I suppose because I've told her so many times that I just don't want to talk about it. And because she knows it all, she's never really pushed me to open up further. Just suggested that at some point, it might be a sensible option. But I can't. I don't want to. It's hideous and just reminds me what a terrible person I've been.

'Have you posted it?'

'Of course not! I'm not stupid.' Elsie Alice wriggles, so I pick her up, resting her against my chest. She nuzzles into my neck and for a second I close my eyes and imagine what it might have felt like to have my own small person wholly and solely reliant on me. I think probably I'd be a terrible mother. Leanne does it so well, but I'm just not that selfless. I snap myself out of the unnecessary daydream. 'Ben always had this thing about writing things down then burning them.'

'Ben did?'

'Yes. He said it helped. You write stuff down then you burn it. It's supposed to rid you of guilt and trauma.'

'Could work.'

'Can't make it any worse.'

'No.'

'So, I went back over everything. Wrote it all down. Hated on myself a bit then folded it up and popped it in an envelope. I'm gonna pick up one of those mini garden incinerator thingy's from Geoff's DIY, the ones that look like a metal bin with a chimney. I'll burn the lot on the patio. Maybe, after the smoke has gone, I won't be a terrible person any more.'

'There, you're all set. Let's get swiping,' she says, not passing me my phone back. 'And you are not a terrible person. You are my brilliant best mate who makes good tea.'

'You want tea?'

'I kind of want tea.'

I roll my eyes but don't really mind Leanne's request. Let's face it, she gave birth to a giant, tiny baby and has struggled to sit down ever since. She winces when she walks and cries whenever she breastfeeds. Something about her uterus. I grimace a little at that bit. But I *am* interested in Leanne's mental health and wellbeing, so tea is a small price to pay. Besides, I need her to be okay. I need her. 'Right, tea coming up. I think you might be required to feed,' I say, handing an increasingly agitated Elsie back to her.

'Probably. Doesn't stop eating, this one. You make tea whilst I feed her, and swipe for the future love of your life for you.'

Chapter Three

From the kitchen I can hear her, in between complaints about her uterus, or breastfeeding in general, shouting out about people she's finding. 'Oh, nice.' Or 'I'd ruin him!' Before I hear a, 'No way!'

'What?' I shout, spilling milk on the side.

'Isn't that the lad from school, the one from a couple of years above who used to follow Fleur Andrews around like a lost puppy?'

Fleur was Leanne's best friend at school. She was cool and beautiful and everyone fancied her. I wipe the milk up and head through.

'That's deffo him. Look.' She holds my phone up for me to check and I peer at it. 'Mitch! That's his name. Mitchell... Black! Failed his GCSEs, so had to hang back and do another year.'

She zooms in on the photo.

'Christ, Mitch Black. Yes. That is him.' I get a second to study his face before she pulls it back to take a closer look herself.

She cocks her head to one side. 'I was never sure about him really, but he does look good.' I make a noise that was supposed to sound indifferent, but I think comes out a bit eager. 'Oh yeah?' she says, grinning at me. 'You like a man that's grown into his face, don't you? That weathered, lived-in look.'

'Weathered and lived-in? He's not Alan Rickman.'

'No,' she grimaces. 'Mitch Black looks pretty hot.'

'If you like that sort of thing,' I say, holding my hand out for my phone. 'And there was NOTHING wrong with Alan Rickman, I'll have you know.'

'Hmmm. He could be your very own Alan Rickman. Only better. And alive.'

I'm about to point out that I still grieve the loss of one of my favourite actors but she's not paying attention and has, instead, swiped right before handing back my phone. My mouth drops open. 'No way, you did not just do that.'

'If it was left to you, you'd be moping around single and morbid for life.'

'I wouldn't, I just need time. And besides, didn't you say Mitch Black was weird?'

'No. I said I wasn't sure about him. Which I wasn't. But that was over twenty years ago. We all change. Besides, Ben left yonks ago, you need to get out there.'

'Need? I don't *need* anything.'

'We all have "needs",' she says, labouring the point.

'Needs I can satisfy perfectly well by myself, thank you very much. I don't need a man.'

'You don't. Of course you don't. But that doesn't mean to say you actively can't have one.'

'What? Mitch Black from school?'

'If he swipes right, too?'

'I think I want to die.'

'Not before he's swiped right, you'll not!'

I groan, dropping into the chair opposite her, just as Mum sends me a text.

I assume that letter in your room was for posting. So nice to see you two have been in touch. I've popped a stamp on and dropped it in the box. Give my love to Leanne. X

My heart stops. 'No, no, no, no!'

'What?'

I cough, trying to restart my pulse, apparently to no avail. 'The letter… Mum's posted the letter…'

'What letter?' Leanne leans away from Elsie Alice so she can blow across the top of her tea. 'I *will* drink this whilst it's still warm!'

'The letter. THE letter. The LETTER!' I get up and pace to the window.

'Oh no… not—'

'The one I was going to burn later. So nobody had to read it.'

'Where was it?'

'In my room. Mum goes in sometimes if she's putting a wash on and hasn't got enough of her own stuff. She saw it on the side.'

'But… shit.'

I spin to face her, hands on head. 'Oh God, this is bad. This is really bad. I thought things were bad before, but this is…'

'Bad?'

I grab my bag. I plant a kiss on Elsie's forehead, which means my nose brushes Leanne's boob. 'Sorry.'

'Don't worry. Most action I've had in months. You too, I'd imagine. Tinder could sort that!' I shoot her a look because now is not the time. 'Okay, don't panic. Go. See if you can get it back. It's all going to be fine.' I blow her a kiss and run out of the door. As it slams behind me, I just about hear her shouting, 'DON'T PANIC!'

Too late. I'm panicking.

Chapter Four

I drum my fingers on my steering wheel, looking up and down the street for a glimpse of the tiny red van driven by the postman that has the key to open the post box that contains the letter. If I can just get it back. If I can just... I look up at the sky as if cursing the universe.

Am I a glutton for this kind of punishment, just really unlucky, or am I entirely and wholly deserving? Is this karma in all its glory? Come on now, Jem, pep-talk time. Be realistic. Is this the worst thing that's ever happened? Is it worse than the time you emailed your boss with some juicy gossip when you meant to email your colleague? Is it worse than the time you meant to text someone you were flirting with but accidentally sent it to the next-door neighbour who happened to share the same name? What can I say? There are too many Daves in my phone. Is it worse than when you left a voicemail on what you thought was Leanne's sister's phone slagging off the boyfriend she had before she met and married Andy, but instead it was Leanne's phone you called? I mean, sure, it all worked out in the end, but at the time?

Is it worse than the love of your life leaving you? Or losing your house? Or job? Going bankrupt? All in the space of the last twelve months.

On balance, I fear this leapfrogs all the above.

I poured everything into that letter. I apologised for every awful thing I did to him; some of which he knew, much of which he didn't – because I am a horrible human being who totally did not deserve him. And like I said to Leanne, it wasn't really a letter for Ben. It was for me. Something to release me from my demons. Demons that have so far seen me stuff up lots of the good in my life and encourage – indeed positively welcome – some really stupid, bad stuff. Stuff that I should have been grown up enough to walk away from. Stuff that has pissed all over multiple bonfires in my life... and by bonfires I mean friendships, relationships, jobs.

Oh Jesus, he cannot read that letter.

And that is why I'm sat by the post box on Highfields Road. Outside the old post office I used to spend my pocket money in – a bag of penny chews and some of that fine pink sherbet stuff I used to like... what was it called... American Cream Soda! That's it. American Cream Soda. A quarter of it for ten pence. Scooped out of a paper bag on sticky fingers. Occasionally shared amongst friends when I was feeling generous. Or wanted one of their strawberry bonbons.

I digress.

Yes, that's why I'm sat outside the post office, waiting for the postman to arrive so I can try and intercept the letter and burn it in the back garden like I had every intention of doing in the first place. Before Mum, bless her beautiful heart, saw it on the side in my room and placed a stamp on it. A stamp from the many (many) packs she has in her purse – 'just in case' – and dropped it in the letter box before, I imagine, passing a few moments chatting with Vic, the guy who lives next door to the old post office in what used to be the greengrocer's. Vic who has twitched his curtains several times, watching me watching the post box in the £500 Vauxhall Tigra the Official Receiver gave me the funds to buy when my bankruptcy went through. It wasn't a Tigra he specifically said I could buy; he really meant any car that might get me from A to B in the hope it would get me a job. I merely went for the Tigra because I once had one as a company car and thought it might make me feel a little more like I hadn't entirely failed at life.

The postman's running late. It's 11.05 a.m. He was due at 11.00. My palms are sweaty and I am hungry after skipping breakfast, but this letter can't go. I cannot ruin things for Ben all over again by showing my face in a life that he explicitly – and perfectly rightly – cut me out of. A letter that says I love him. Have always loved him. Might always love him. A fact that will mean nothing to him. Nor should it. He found the strength to walk away and somehow I let him. But I did not intend to open up old wounds. Especially not wounds like these.

Chapter Five

My bag starts vibrating on the passenger seat and my heart rate spikes. I dig out my phone, the only thing I have taken from my pre-bankruptcy life. If I can just keep paying this monthly phone bill, without any help from Mum, I have a chance of restoring some dignity in my life. Speaking of the devil.

'Mum, hi.'

'Hey, love, I was just wondering if you were going to be back for lunch? That skate needs eating and I thought I was going to be back, but it turns out I'm not.'

I shudder at the thought of skate. I've never been a fan of fish, but skate is the worst. 'Erm, yes, I should be. Why, where are you?'

'Oh, I booked a last-minute Pilates session with Clare.'

'Did you?'

'Yeah, well, she had time. I had time… We all had—'

'Time? Okay, great. Good for you. That'll be nice.' Mum's new-found passion for all things health and wellbeing has come as something of a surprise, but then I guess cancer treatment can do that to a person. She was diagnosed nine months ago. It was a shock, but the hospital got on it straight away, surgery, treatment, all booked in within weeks. I moved in to care for her, maybe that's why the house repossession didn't smart quite as much. Maybe. Either way, we've both changed.

'Thanks, love. I need to pop in and see June too, so I guess I should be back around two. Ish. Unless we pop out for coffee. You know how she likes a coffee. Anyway, if you can make sure you eat it, that'd be great.'

'Right. Okay. Do you not want some saving?'

'No, no. Percy's playing up.'

Percy's the name she gave her stoma. The cancer treatment left her with barely any bowel and a brand new bag on the front of her tummy. She'd been determined they wouldn't take so much away that she would need one but was oddly calm when she learned they'd had no choice. I think she was just relieved to still be alive, to be honest. 'Oh right. Okay.' I picture her sat on her spot on the sofa, gazing out of the bay window, across the fields, towards the dual carriageway. 'Well, I'll get off then.'

'Was Leanne okay?'

'Yeah, yeah. She was fine.'

'You still there? Send me a photo of that little Elsie Alice.'

'No, no. I left. I'm not there.'

'Oh, that wasn't long. I thought you said you'd be there all morning.'

This is where it gets awkward. Do I confess or say nothing to protect her from the inevitable guilt she'll consume herself with if I tell her what dragged me away? I glance through the rear-view mirror, there's no sign of the elusive little red van. I stifle a sigh. 'I came out to get a few essentials. She's low on shopping. Thought it'd be easier if I got them in.'

'Ahh, you should have said. I could have done it when I went to post your letter.'

Mention of it brings me out in a cold sweat. Again. 'Well that would have been out of your way, wouldn't it?'

'No, no. I was down at the Civic Centre. I needed cup hooks from Geoff's DIY.'

'Geoff's DIY? You should have told me, I was going there on my way back.'

'Were you? Oh, I didn't realise. I just thought I'd put some of those new mugs up above the kettle. That'll look nice, won't it?'

'I assumed you nipped round to the old post office.'

'No! God no, I avoid there. Vic always collars me for a chat and he's lovely and all that, but very lonely and I can only say no to a cuppa in his day room so many times.'

'So you went to the civic?'

'Yes, to post your letter. Then I went to Geoff's DIY. Actually, I stuck my head in the charity shop too. Picked up a lovely Marky Sparks blouse with the label still on. Never been worn. Fifty pence. Bargain!'

As she chatters about her shopping, I scrabble for my seat belt, overturning the key in the ignition, which makes my engine do that painful screechy please don't turn me on any more thing. 'Cup hooks. Blouse. Lovely!'

'I want to get organised. In the house. You know?'

'Great, yes. That'll be good. Lovely. Look, Mum, I need to… Can I call you back?' I bite my tongue. It's not her fault. It's not her fault. I just assumed. What is it they say about to assume? It makes an 'ass' out of 'u' and 'me'? 'Look, I'd better go, Mum. My hands-free kit is in my bag on the back seat.'

'Okay, love. Drive safely. Send me a photo of the baby when you get back to Leanne's. They grow so much at this age.'

'Yep, will do.' I strain to look over my shoulder whilst holding her on loudspeaker, pulling out just as the postman arrives. At the wrong bloody post box. 'Say hi to Clare.'

'Pardon?'

'Clare. Pilates. Say hi to Clare.'

'Right. Yes. Okay. Don't forget to eat the skate.'

'Okay, no. No problem.'

'Love you!' she shouts as I drop the phone into my lap just in time to avoid the police car that passes in the opposite direction.

Shit. Shit, shit, shit. I fly down Highfields onto Hollins Spring. I narrowly avoid a Vauxhall Cavalier that cuts the turning as I make my way onto Gosforth Drive; roads I know explicitly. Every semi-detached, every topiary bush, every blind parking spot and old schoolmate's home, it all goes by in a blur as I race to the Civic Centre and hope more than I've ever hoped for anything in my life before… I hope that I get to the post box before the next collection is made.

Chapter Six

Of course I didn't get there before the next collection. I mean, why would I? That would just be too easy.

Shit.

Okay. What do I do? What do I do? In any other circumstance, I'd probably call Mum, but she'll be mortified about what's happened. Leanne though, Leanne'll know what to do. She's the sensible one of us both, practically a bone fide grown-up, she'll tell me exactly what to do. She'll know what to say.

'Well, if I was you, I'd do something perfectly rational like withdraw any savings you might have and move to another country, just to make sure you never have to run into him again. Mind you, since he's moved, it's not like you can just pop round his house any more.'

She underestimates me. Ben may have relocated a massive six hours' drive from here, but if needs must… 'He can't read that letter, Leanne. He can't!'

'Well, why the bloody hell did you write it then?'

'I told you. I was going to burn it.'

'I still don't really understand why though. Ah! Wait a minute! You were procrastinating.' Leanne is well aware that I am not entirely loving the freelance admin company I've set up in a bid to ensure I can afford to live. It's why I've been more than happy to help out with Elsie, or drop Leanne's older boy, my godson Harley, off at school since Andy, her husband, started working away all week – basically any excuse to get away from my desk and avoid what little work I actually have on. 'I've told you, just put your bum in the chair and get on with your work. New clients will come. Interesting projects will turn up.'

'If I was going to procrastinate, spilling my guts onto Moomin letter paper is the very last thing I'd do. I can literally think of a million more appealing options. So stop judging and tell me what I do about it?'

'Well…' She thinks. Hard. 'You want to move on, get over things, find a new future, right?'

'I really do.'

'Well, first off, you're gonna have to stop beating yourself up for being a dickhead.'

'Thanks.' Such a way with words.

'I mean it, Jem. This self-flagellation has to stop. Focus on you. On life. Get out there, reconnect with people. You've had a rough year. Most would have keeled over by now, but you? You're here. Somehow, you're still standing. That's why I set you up on Tinder… well, that and for a bit of vicarious living because Tinder came out after I met Andy and I've always wondered a teensy bit what it was all about. Look, don't panic about it. Shit happens. Let go and move forward. Has Mitch messaged you back yet?'

'Not that I've seen? Would I see?'

'You'll get one of them push notification whatsits.' As she says it, my phone dings in my ear and I glance to see the Tinder logo. *You've got a new message from Mitch.* 'Oh my God. He's literally just responded.'

Leanne squeals. 'Yes! I knew this would be good for you. What's he say?'

'I don't know. I've not read it. I'm talking to you about getting a letter back in which I told my now-ex, and soon to be very-very-ex – when he reads the letter – everything he didn't need to know. Christ, I was just venting!'

'Jem! That's what I'm here for. You are supposed to vent with me, over a bottle of Bombay Sapphire.'

'I'm still off the gin.'

'Oh.'

Leanne is well aware that this is wholly and entirely her fault, given that it was at her house, last year, just after Ben had gone and I was a mess. That night will forever be known as the night of the 'gincident'. That is to say, after several drinks and a takeaway, Leanne made me the longest, dirtiest, strongest gin (and allegedly tonic, but a court of law would question the evidence) known to woman. As such, I spent the rest of the night on the tiled floor of her conservatory extension, wishing myself dead. The only reason she didn't find me there in the morning was because I had a sliver of wherewithal to move in case it was in fact Harley who toddled in to find me flat out amongst her (wilting) orange trees.

'Hey, what if I asked the post office to locate it and give it me back? Do you think they would?'

'Oh, probably. If you asked them nicely with a cherry on top.'

'Really?'

'No! Of course they won't!' My despair finds new levels. 'Look, chuck, I think you need to chalk this one up to experience.'

'I can't do that, Leanne. I *have* to stop him reading it.'

'Even if you managed to be at his house as the postman arrived to deliver it, you'd not be able to persuade him to hand it over. They have a legal obligation to deliver all mail in their sacks.'

'Do they?'

'Okay, I've no idea if it's a legal one. But I think it's unlikely they'll give a letter over to a desperate woman begging them for mercy. I can't help wondering if I should have read this letter before you sent it. Censored it. Like in the war. Your behaviour suggests this was a bad move, Jem.'

A wave of nausea, not unlike the one I experienced that night on Leanne's conservatory floor, washes over me. I think she might have a point.

There's a rustling of hand over receiver. 'I'm on the phone to Aunty Jem, Harley. What? Now? Okay, hang on, sweetie.' The phone rustles again. I hear my godson in the background. 'Good boy. Come on then, up you go.' She's panicking. 'Hurry, hurry, that's right, good boy... oh. Oh shit.' Then a wail. 'Okay, no problem. Don't worry. It's fine. Come on now. Here, no! Not there, mind that! Jem, I've got to go. Nursery are insisting I potty train before they let him move up to the next group but he just took a wee on the staircase.'

She hangs up. In my car, alone, no moral support on the phone, the panic hits a new level. Defcon 1. I need to be proactive. Take back control. I look at my watch. 11.35. If I set off now, I could be in Cornwall by 8 p.m. I could try and get a room in that pub in the town where he lives now. The Sloop. Except that it's August and there are probably no rooms available there or anywhere else for that matter. And I promised Mum I'd eat that skate. Christ! Why did he have to move so far away? I told him I'd leave him alone. Why did he need so much distance between us? Derbyshire to practically the furthest point away in southwest Cornwall. It's excessive. We could just as easily have avoided each other if he'd moved to Eckington, or Nottingham, even Derby. But Cornwall? That was supposed to be our retirement plan, not his escape route.

I wouldn't have even known where he was, but he and Mum had stayed in touch a little bit. Which would be weird if it wasn't for the fact that she was basically the one that kept him standing when he lost his mum and dad. That time I was supposed to be there for him and instead… well, I can't think about that now. I can't think about any of it. And neither can he. Which is why I need to stop that letter.

Chapter Seven

The woman at the counter looks at me, unimpressed. 'It's just that I didn't mean to send it yet and I really need to get it back. So that I can fix the thing I got wrong. And then I can resend it afterwards.' I strain to see past her and into the back, not sure why I really think I'll be able to spot my letter amongst the many thousands that are clearly being sorted here. 'It was my mum, she was trying to help. Not that I'm blaming her, obviously. I just... I *really* need the letter back.'

'I'm afraid I can't help you,' she says again, mouth pinched, fingers clasped tightly before her. 'You'll have to make contact with the recipient.'

'I can't make contact with the recipient!' I don't mention the fact that that's because he's not talking to me. And he blocked me on Twitter.

'Well, I'm sorry, there's nothing else we can do.' She forces a smile then looks beyond me in the queue.

'Right.'

'Sorry.'

'It's okay. It's not your fault.' Hands on hips, I gaze down at the floor. My Converse are looking well and truly battered. A bit like I suspect my face does now. This is not good news.

'Is there anything else?' asks the woman, exasperated. 'It's just that... there's a queue.' She points to the people stood behind me. One scrolls through her phone. One talks on his. Another is staring at me with a grin on his face. Is that…?

'Still causing hold-ups wherever you go?'

Mitch Black. Mitch Black from Fanshawe School. Mitch Black of Tinder and Tinder messages. If I had died when I wanted to, back when Leanne swiped right, this wouldn't have happened. He's smiling. He looks a little older than the photo he put up on Tinder; there's maybe a smidge of grey in the hair now, some deeper lines, though Leanne put up one of me from about five years ago, so I'm in no place to judge.

The woman behind the counter clears her throat and I spin round. 'Sorry, I'll just…' I shuffle out of the line, knocking a fire extinguisher as I go. 'Shit. Sorry. It's fine. It's all fine.' I clumsily bend to replace it and my bag swings down from my shoulder to smash me in the face and Mitch is now stood in front of me. 'Mitch! Hi! Blimey!'

'Some things never change, eh!' he says, grinning, helping me grab my shoulder strap and placing it back on my shoulder. 'You always were a bit of a calamity at school.'

Rude.

'How are you, Jem Whitfield?'

I don't rub my face where the bag struck but it does hurt a bit. 'Me? Oh, you know, yeah. Good. Great! Wow, how the hell are you? Fancy…' He checks the queue over his shoulder, carefully moving back towards his place. I automatically follow. 'Yeah, I'm good thanks. Really good.'

'Great. You look well.'

'Oh, thanks.' I might have looked better if I had at least expected to bump into him in the post office. I'd have drawn on my eyebrows. Mascara'd.

'So.'

'So?'

'You swiped right.'

'Oh, ha! Yes, I did, well, my mate Leanne did.'

'Oh?'

'No, I mean, I probably still would have. If she hadn't.' Would I?

'I messaged you.'

'Yes. I saw. I've not read it yet though. Busy. Very busy.' I wave my hand over my shoulder as if that makes it clear I've been busy but probably demonstrates I'm having some sort of crisis.

'Fair enough.'

'What did it say? The message.'

'Well, it said hi. And thanks for the swipe.' He grins, insanely confidently. Though I guess with a face like that, not much phases. 'I reminded you that the last time we saw each other we were signing our school shirts at the end of the year. I drew a cock and balls on most of them, so, sorry about that.'

'Ha! Did you?' I laugh, loudly. Like an idiot.

'I also said I'd love to go for a drink.'

'Oh, did you? Well, I mean… that could be nice, you know… if you fancied me.'

'What?'

'It!'

'Oh.' Mitch grins, running his hand through his hair and I'm momentarily distracted from letter-gate. I also hate myself. 'So look, I'm not very good at this.' He can't be worse than me. 'Tinder, I mean. I only signed up today. Don't really know what possessed me.'

'Same! Well, Leanne signed me up. I'd never have! God knows who's on these things.'

'True. Though… us, for one thing.'

'Right. Yes.'

At this point I wonder if I could sneak out, delete the Tinder app and take Leanne's advice. I wonder what the weather's like in Playa?

'So what you up to?' he asks, moving forward in the line.

'Oh, you know, just...' I motion a hand in the direction of the woman behind the desk. 'Well, to be honest, I was trying to get hold of a letter I posted before I was ready to post it. Really could do with getting it back. I didn't mean for it to go at all, to be honest. Mum posted it.' Why am I still talking? 'She was trying to help...' Why is he looking at me like I've gone mad? 'Bless her.'

'I sort of meant in life, what are you up to in life?' He shuffles forward again, the queue getting ever shorter like sand through Her Majesty's Post Office timer. 'Apart from Tinder.'

'Oh.' I let out a nervous laugh, then flick my hair. 'Well...' Where do I start with that one? 'You know—'

'Next!' The woman behind the counter bellows, making me jump.

'Hang on.' Mitch goes to the counter, weighs his letter then passes it through the little window. After paying and having a quick joke with the woman, he turns to face me and my stomach flips. 'I've an hour spare now. If you're free? Do you want a coffee? I've heard The Forge is pretty nice. I've never been. I actually lived away until last month.'

'Oh, have you? I didn't realise.'

'Yeah. Which means I've totally lost touch with everyone. Come on. Coffee? My treat.' I must give him a look of suspicion because he quickly puts his hands up. 'Just coffee. I promise I won't draw a cock and balls on your blouse.'

This makes me do one of those snort laughs nobody means to do, so I try to cover it up with a cough. 'I'd love to, but I have to go... I need to...'

'Don't tell me. You're going to hunt down this letter, track it until it reaches its intended recipient and intercept it before they can read it?'

I feel myself prickle with the scarlet hives I know will now be forming across my chest. When he puts it like that, it does sound ridiculous. Certainly more ridiculous than just going for a coffee with him. 'Well... I mean...'

'God, I was joking. Wow. You really don't want that letter to be read. Let me guess, a letter to an ex?'

The hives creep from my neck to my face and I surreptitiously wipe a sweaty palm down my jeans. Leanne would be furious to know I'd turned coffee down so I could drive to Cornwall. On a Friday in August. Like no sensible person ever would. 'It's complicated.'

'Isn't it always?'

I suppose I could do coffee. Before I go.

'It'd be lovely to catch up.' He stuffs hands in his pockets and looks all boyish at me. My knees go a bit weak and I'm irritated by how bloody basic I can be.

I imagine the traffic. I picture the queues round Birmingham, Bristol and Bodmin. It's gonna take me forever to get there and the longer I put it off, the more chance there is of it getting posted through Ben's letter box.

'I mean, you know... You did swipe right,' he says, with a wink.

Leanne did, I don't say for a second time. 'It's just that, well, I really need to go and do this.'

'Right.'

Is he crestfallen? Do handsome people ever get crestfallen? I really shouldn't be walking away. 'I'd love to. Truly. Some other time, maybe? If you still want to?'

'I might hold you to that.'

I feel guilty. And confused. And I can see Leanne's face in my head. 'Okay. Hold me to it. I would really love to.' I back away, bag clutched to my chest. 'We'll catch up soon. When I'm back.' I throw a wave over my shoulder and practically sprint out of there. At my car, the remote central locking fails and I swear, fumbling to get the key in the lock.

'Here, let me.' Mitch, appearing from behind like some kind of genie, takes the key from my hands, our fingers brush. He unlocks the car easily, like I probably could have if he hadn't, then hands me the keys. 'Look, I sense you've got something going on. I like you, but I don't want to chase if you're not ready. I mean, the whole Tinder thing, maybe you weren't really up for it?'

Leanne would kill me if she knew I might have messed this up. 'Oh, I didn't mean to give you that impression.'

'It's fine. We all have baggage of sorts. Maybe you just need to sort some stuff out before you're ready to date? I understand.' He passes me a piece of paper with a mobile number written on it. His handwriting is neat, structured, controlled. I wonder when he had time to even write it. Does he have his number in his pocket just in case, for situations like this? Is that how men with a face like his operate? Why do I keep noticing his face?

'Here's my number. In case, when you're ready, you fancy that coffee. Just text me. After you've tracked down your post.' He smiles and through the crinkle of his eyes and the slightly cockeyed grin, I can see Mitch Black from school. The lad who stayed back a year to resit his exams and always seemed to be just hanging around. The lad who got a moped when the rest of us still had to travel everywhere on foot. The lad who somehow seemed like a grown-up, way before any of the rest of us. The lad who I guess I always noticed, but never for a second thought would notice me. 'I'll call you.'

I stuff his number into my pocket as he tips an imaginary hat then wanders off across the car park, hands in pockets. I thrust the key into Petula's lock, forgetting he'd already unlocked it before unceremoniously opening the door.

A text rings out on my phone. *Don't forget the skate.*

Chapter Eight

If skate tasted of anything, I'm certain that now, as I shove a world of useless clothes and socks into my bag, it would be repeating on me.

'You *boiled* it?' shrieks Leanne, who's currently on FaceTime as she feeds and I pack.

I root round the pile of clean washing I've not yet hung up, pulling out T-shirt and jeans. 'I don't know how you cook it. I just whacked it in the microwave.'

'Surely it was awful.'

'It was as tasteless as such culinary prowess deserves. Not that any of that matters now.' I gaze at the clothes, some hung, some in a pile of scrunched-up tops and trousers that may or may not need a wash. There's a clean pile on the side that Mum brought back up earlier. I keep telling her she doesn't need to do my washing but she insists it's to help weigh the drum down or some such. I love living at home, for now, after all she and I have been through it feels like really precious time, but I really wish she wouldn't keep doing my washing.

'I can't believe you're doing this,' Leanne says, switching boobs, wincing in the process. 'Are you sure it's sensible. I mean – ouch, you little bugger – if you let things take their course, what's the worst that can happen?'

'Well for starters, Ben could read it. Then, secondly, Ben could read it.'

'Yes, but so what? He'll read it then never speak to you again. That fact's already written.'

'Look, forgive me, but I've decided I'm doing this. I didn't call for you to try and talk me out of it, I called because you're my best mate and I wanted to tell you. And also because I need to know what to take. It's twenty-five degrees. Do you think I'll need a jumper? Wind chill. Off the Atlantic?'

She rolls her eyes, presumably at my inability to function as a grown-up without nominating someone else to make certain, basic, decisions. It's a fair response as I get on my own nerves too. 'I think you need your head read is what I think. How long are you even going for?'

'I don't know. Definitely overnight so I'm there for when the postie gets there in the morning.'

'Sure, because it would be madness to do a six-hour journey then just come straight back. Doing it in twenty-four hours though, that's not mad at all.'

'Well, it all depends. I mean, if I see him and he's prepared to talk, maybe I'll stay longer?'

'Jem, he said he didn't want to see you.'

'I know.'

'Ever.' She tries to say it gently but it still smarts.

'Yes. That too. But this is different. I dunno, maybe I should talk to him. I think it might be time I put the ghost to rest, you know?'

'Ghost resting is important, I grant you that. But only if it doesn't upset the person you're trying to feel better about in the first place. And only if you're prepared to then stop wanging on about it all. Otherwise

it could be considered a veiled attempt to try and get back with him.'
She looks at me, pointedly.

'It's not that.' Her eyes widen. 'It's not!'

'Have you heard back from Mitch?'

I zip my bag up, hiding my face.

'You have! What did he say?'

'Jesus, Leanne! How did you know?'

'Because you tried to stop me seeing your face and reading your eyes. Honestly, don't take up poker.'

'Just a minute.' I jog out of my room under the guise of getting my toothbrush and paste, but in fact to buy some time.

'Don't go buying time!' she shouts after me.

'What?' I protest, slinging the last bits in my front zipper and checking that the plastic handles on my market-bought weekend bag can carry the weight of clothes for every eventuality.

'Come on then, when are you seeing him?'

'I've already seen him.'

'Good God, Jem! What time did you leave me?' She looks over her shoulder at the clock on her kitchen wall. 'This was not a chance to hook up at the Whit Moor Travelodge, you were supposed to be going on a date.'

'I did not hook up there, or anywhere else for that matter. What do you take me for?'

She raises her eyebrows and I opt not to argue that one.

'I went down to the post office to try and catch the letter. He was in the queue behind me.'

'Woah! No way. That's serendipity, that is!'

'Is it?'

'Million per cent. You both swiped right. Then moments later you're thrust into the same room. The stars are aligned, Jem. This could be it. You could be about to start a relationship with the man you're going to marry!'

'Hang on a minute! You've just had me shagging him in a Travelodge, now we're getting married. Do I get a say in any of this? I don't want to get married. To him or anyone. Never have, you know that.'

'Okay, but that doesn't mean to say you can't live happily ever after, does it?'

'Of course not. But happy ever after for me is functioning as a grown-up. Not making bad choices any more. Being me and liking it.'

'Yes, I know. I know it is.' I drop down onto my bed, exhausted. Leanne pauses a second, giving me a breather. Eventually she says, 'So what did he say?'

I think back to the meet-up and cringe inside. 'Nothing much. We had a sort of awkward conversation in which I made a fool of myself. He invited me for coffee. I said I'd like to but couldn't do today. He gave me his number.'

'Well, that's perfect then. You can call him. Or text him. You can plan something else. Did he seem weird? Stalkery?'

'No! He's not a kid any more.'

'None of us are, Jem. None of us are. So, did you fancy him?'

'I don't know!' Surprisingly enough, I totally did. 'I don't think I fancy anyone at the moment. I think I'm a bit distracted. I mean, he looks nice. Older than the photos. I dunno, it was a weird situation. I can't really say what I felt 'cause I was actually working out how long it would take me to get to Cornwall.' Whilst also fancying him.

'How long it'll take you to get to Cornwall? Too long, that's how long.'

'Yes.'

'Is there nothing I can say to persuade you this is a terrible idea?'

'No. There isn't. I need to do this. I know it seems mad, but I have to.' I don't tell her that until just this second, there was every chance she could have persuaded me not to go. I don't tell her that I had been wondering whether to just leave it all and call Mitch for that coffee. I don't tell her that he mentioned something about baggage and reinforced my thinking that I have to do something to cut the ties even if I am worried this is not the thing to do. I need closure. For Mitch? For me? Whichever, I need closure.

Leanne sighs, sticking Elsie over her shoulder and rubbing her back, expertly tucking her boob back in her top. 'You better drive carefully.'

'I will. I promise.'

'When Harley gets back from nursery, I'm going to tell him where you're going and he will expect a present upon your return.'

'Healthy parenting.'

'If I can guilt you into returning home safely, that's what I'm going to do.'

'Okay. Okay.'

'Let me know when you get there.'

'I will.'

Elsie lets out a burp that contradicts her tiny size. 'Oooh, clever girl. Well done! That was from your boots, eh?'

'Talk later.'

'Love you, bye.'

Chapter Nine

I jog down the stairs but now I've decided I'm definitely going, nerves have crept in and I lose my footing, sliding down the last three steps. I try and recover like it was all meant to happen, before remembering there's no one here to see, so rub the small of my back and take a deep breath. I probably need to be extra careful if I'm going to make it down in one piece. To Cornwall, not the stairs.

Bag in boot, I return to the hallway looking for a pen from the pot of many that sit beside the house phone that Mum never uses since she got her iPhone. ('It does those calls where I can see your face, Jem!') I hover my hand over the pad. What to say? If I tell her the truth, she'll freak. If I lie, she'll just check up on me via Find My Friends in any case. I do need to go before Mum gets back though. Before she tries to talk me out of driving three hundred miles on a whim.

Mum, give me a bell when you get back X

Dropping the latch, I close the door and jump in my car. I plug my phone into the hands-free kit ready for when Mum calls and set off, fear nestled in the pit of my stomach.

*

Two and a half hours later and desperate for a wee, I pull in at Gloucester Services. 4 p.m. and still no call from Mum. Which is useful on one side as I do now see how ridiculous this all is. I could totally have just gone for coffee with Mitch.

I pop Ben's name into Facebook on my phone, as I've done so many times before, scrolling through recent posts. He never blocked me on there for some reason, for which I'm grateful; unfriending me hurt enough. Such a tiny thing, some might say inconsequential. It's just Facebook, it's just social media, it doesn't mean anything. But it did. It meant we couldn't even be friends. It meant that I'd done that much damage that the man I know loved me more than anyone ever has before, couldn't even connect with me via an app. It meant that even though we had three years and a whole load of good times, the bad far outweighed them and the love we shared had no place in his life.

The love we shared.

Did I share it? Or did I abuse it?

I get a notification on my own Facebook. A friend request. Clicking on it takes me to Mitch Black's profile. It's the same photo as on Tinder. I scroll his feed. A few comedy sketches posted from YouTube, they make me laugh. Some photos of a lads' holiday in Reykjavik from a couple of years ago by the looks of it. The About Him page is sparse, which is no help when you're social media stalking someone. Just as I'm about to accept, I notice he's made a comment on one of my videos. Are we scrolling each other's feed at the same time? Is that weird or a teensy bit romantic? Like in a film where two people are in love with one another, but the other doesn't know. Cue music section. Something slow and moody. Except I'm not in love with him. And he's commented on the video of me singing karaoke down the Green Dragon one night, filmed by a howling Leanne. I read what he's put:

Wow. You can really sing. Well... you can sing... well... you can... never mind. Maybe we should replace coffee for a pint and karaoke. I'd love to see if you sound this bad in real life. ;)

The part of me that wants to be offended by his lack of appreciation for my vocal talent is overshadowed by the part of me that laughs at his lack of airs and graces. Normally, when you see someone you've not seen in years, you at least try and pretend not to be laughing at them. It was awkward before, at the post office, but that was me. This feels confident. Self-assured. It's refreshing... dare I say, attractive. It's like he doesn't feel the need to make an impression. He's comfortable in his own skin. If I look back, I guess I do remember him being like that at school. Down to earth. Funny. Warm. He wasn't like some of the other lads who were either testosteroned to the eyeballs or head in a book. He was just regular Mitch Black. Always had a smile. Always had a laugh. Never seemed to have anything bad to say about people. Never laughed at my cheap trainers or knock-off shell suit. He just hung around. Did his thing. The Mitch Leanne remembers isn't the same one I recall. I make the photo larger, scrutinising his face. He has definitely grown into it. It'd be hard not to like him... from a purely aesthetic point of view...

You're on. Beer. When I'm home.

When I'm home. When I've let go of some of this bloody baggage. You can't move forward if you're still looking back...

Chapter Ten

Before I inhale the sausage roll I bought from the services, Mum calls. 'Hey, love, I just saw your note.'

'Ah, thanks for calling. You okay? You've been out ages.'

'Oh, yes, fine thanks. Just… a busy afternoon. Anyway, where are you? Are you around tonight? I fancied snuggling up to watch a movie. I've been looking, *Bohemian Rhapsody*'s on download, you said that was really good. I bought us some Rioja. Thought we could watch it together.'

I click my seat belt on, buckling up before giving her the news, as it were. 'That would have been lovely. The thing is… I've had to pop out. For a few days.'

'A few days? Where are you?'

'Now?' Brace. 'Roughly junction eleven on the M5. Westbound.'

'Heavens to Betsy, Jem. Where on earth are you going?'

'I know, I know.' Honesty. Come on, Jem, honesty. 'Okay, so… that letter you posted for me…'

'Yes.'

'Well, I wasn't planning to post it.'

'What do you mean?'

'I was going to burn it.'

'Whatever for?'

'It's a long story. Fact is, it was not meant to actually get to Ben.'

'Right… I see…'

'I know. Like I say, long story. I just thought I'd pop down and see if I can get to it before the postie delivers it.'

'*Pop. Down*? You're kidding!'

'No.'

There's a pause. I can imagine her, mouth open, confused, staring out of the lounge window.

'But, it was there. On the bed. With his name on. I assumed you'd finally got over yourselves and worked things out. I thought you were just waiting for me to get his address.'

Mum always did think it was a bit of a tiff. That we'd sort things out. That we were meant to be together. She had no idea what really happened, or that I was pretty much to blame. I didn't think I could cope with 'fessing up when it happened and now I'm just too ashamed. 'No.' I don't ask how she thinks I'd be unable to ask him for his address if we'd actually sorted things out.

'Oh God, I'm sorry, love. I just assumed. Oh, Lordy, I'm so sorry!'

'It's fine, it's fine. Well, it's sort of fine. I mean him reading it isn't fine. That's not fine at all. Hence me tracking it down.'

'But… really?'

'Really.'

'Sorry, Jem. I know this must be big for you to be doing this, but… it's ridiculous! Can't you just let him know? Ask him not to open it or something? I mean, I can call him if you like. Explain it's my fault. If that's less awkward.'

Sure, getting your mum to sort out your mistakes. That's less awkward. 'No, no, Mum. Thank you, but it's fine. This is my mess, I need to sort it.'

'What about your car? How on earth is your car going to get you all the way to Cornwall?'

With a protective hand, I stroke the velour passenger seat of my twenty-year-old pride and joy. 'Petula is just fine. She can manage this journey and then some.'

'Even if she can, what about the fuel? It'll cost a fortune. I'll have to transfer some money across, you can't pay for fuel there and back. Jem, I thought you'd calmed down. I thought you'd stopped doing stuff like this!'

'Like what?'

'This spontaneous stuff.'

She means being reckless. That was always her worry, that I was reckless. She called it spontaneous to my face but I overheard her talking to someone else once, reckless was the word she used.

'It's important to me, Mum. It's not about me being spontaneous, or any other word to describe it for that matter. In fact, if anything, it's the opposite.'

There's a pause on the line. She'll be staring at the fields that lead to the dual carriageway, more fields beyond it. She loves that view. She gets lost for hours, just thinking, staring at the view, marvelling at the trees that look like an elephant and its baby. Eventually she says, 'I can't believe you've just upped and gone like this. Did you eat that skate?'

'Yes, Mum.' I half laugh, though mostly because I'm tired and teasy, not finding any of this remotely amusing. 'I ate the skate.' I push the sausage roll out of sight, suddenly nauseous.

There's another pause. She's moving about. She'll be pacing the parquet flooring. 'I could get a sleeper train. I think I can get on it at Chesterfield. I'd be there by the morning.'

'I don't need you to get here.'

'Or I could ask Pauline if I can borrow her car. It's just come back from a service so I know it'll be fine.'

'Then there'd be two cars in Cornwall. Mum, I don't need you to be here. Just… chill. Please. Enjoy an evening to yourself for once. When did you last have that? Since I've moved in, I'm always there cramping your style.'

'I like you cramping my style. We've had a lovely time, with you cramping my style.'

She's right. Despite everything, we have had a lovely time. 'Mum, I love you. Go have a bath. Ease those muscles after Pilates.'

'Pardon?'

'Go. Relax. I'll be fine.'

'Give me two rings when you get there.'

'I will. After I've put the big light on.'

'Love you, Jem.' She sighs, despairing.

'Love you too, Mum.'

She hangs up. No doubt she's still pacing the parquet with added muttering to herself. Probably trying to work out if she really should just wait until I get back, or if she could get on a train and meet me. And I love her for that, but it's about time I stood on my own two feet. I need to prove to her that I can. In fact, perhaps more importantly, I need to prove to myself that I can.

Chapter Eleven

I expected the traffic round Bristol to be terrible. By the time I left I was ripe to hit peak commuting time. But I sort of hoped that by now, things might have eased up a little on the A30? I mean, I know it's Friday. In August. But why, in all that's holy, am I essentially parked up on Bodmin?

Nor do I like the fact that there's not a single room to rent anywhere. So even if I do ever make it to St Ives, I predict a night sleeping in my car. Can a thirty-eight-year-old woman still get away with that kind of behaviour? I'm just going to have to hope I arrive before the pub closes so at least I can have a drink, relax a bit before bunking down on the back seat. My phone dings a text from Leanne.

Any tips for getting toddler wee out of a loop pile carpet? X

I recoil. I have no tips. The closest I've ever got to something similar was trying to get wax out of a rug. Sadly, I used wrapping paper instead of brown paper and ironed a Christmas scene into my Habitat Penrose. Cost me a fortune, that rug.

Nope. Soz luv. X

The traffic crawls forward so I start Petula's engine, relieved to creep a few metres. The sun is setting up ahead and the sky has gone a mad pinky yellow. I should really be sat on Porthmeor Beach for this. Not in a clapped-out Tigra on the A30. Sorry Petula.

How's the journey? Are you there yet? You'd better be since you just texted back. X

I gaze out at the Moor, the wild ponies, a couple of big hills out to my left.

No. I'm parked up on Bodmin waiting for the traffic to shift. It's the journey from hell.

'You should probably just turn back round, you know,' Leanne says as her opening gambit when she calls.

'Pack it in. I'll be there before midnight. Probably.'

'If you were here, you could have bathed Harley and read him a story. Or gone out on a date with Mitch.'

'Mum wanted to watch *Bohemian Rhapsody*.'

'So that's three options that are all considerably better than being stuck on the A30.'

'True.' The traffic gains pace. 'Christ, I've just changed gear for the first time in about an hour.'

'Impressive. I just expressed a tiny amount of milk so Andy can do the night feed. Look at us, winning at life.' She makes me smile, in spite of myself. 'Are you sure you're okay on your own? Do you need me?'

'Yes, Leanne. I absolutely need you. You, the piskie permanently attached to your mammaries and Harley by your side. Please. Come quick. Use your womanly charms to tackle me out of my doom.'

'Don't be facetious.'

'Bet you can't even spell that.'

'I've just pushed a tiny human out of my nethers; I don't need to enter into a spelling bee to prove how great I am.'

'God, you women who've had babies, we know you're incredible. But I once sneezed and broke wind at the same time, something I imagine you've no chance of doing without an unpleasant side effect, so now who's amazing.'

There's a beat before we simultaneously collapse into fits of giggles.

'Look, the traffic is moving properly now. I am almost there. I always need you, but yes, I am okay on my own. I'm going to do this, Leanne. I am going to make this right. It's all part of the process. I am finally being a grown-up. I am sorting my life out. I no longer need you or Mum to bail me out. I promise.'

'Well… okay then. If you're sure. Keep me posted. Tell me everything that happens and do not do anything stupid, okay?'

'I won't. I promise. I love you.'

'Love you more. Bye, bye, bye.'

As anticipated, it's an hour later when I sweep down St Ives Road, past Tregenna Castle, past the hotels and new-builds, snatching glimpses of the bay between buildings. It's almost dark. Lights twinkle from shops and restaurants. As I come down the high street, festoon lighting leads the way. The streets are busy, holidaymakers wandering from dinner to home, tired toddlers wrapped up in buggies, sleepy children being piggybacked by parents. And as I turn the corner at the lifeboat station, there it is. Home. Home in all its inky blue-black skied beauty. I don't know why it always felt like that, we holidayed here a couple of times a year. But it was always our dream to make the move, one day. A little cottage on a backstreet. Open windows at bedtime to hear Mother Meor's roar. Early mornings woken by the gulls. Long, quiet winters with no tourists and all the space. Busy, frantic summers with no space, but all the holiday vibes.

How did I get to a point where I could mess up my future as significantly as I did?

Yawning, exhausted, eyes like pissholes in the snow, I pull into a parking space and switch off Petula's engine.

I made it.

Chapter Twelve

Somehow, I managed to get the energy to take the few steps from car to Sloop – reputedly Cornwall's oldest inn, right on the harbour front. It was late by the time I got in, most people having eaten and gone. There was a bar stool spare, right up near the bandit machine in the back bar. And that's where I've just spent the last hour and a bit, trying to dull the pain of being here without actually meaning to be here. Not really. Not properly. Not for a holiday, or a house-hunting trip or because I live here. But because I feel like I have no choice. So now I find myself, last one standing, leaving the pub into the night. I've rejected the offer to carry on at The Ferrets pub with some of the Sloop bar staff and stumble out of the bar as they bolt the doors behind me.

It smells of beach and seawater. The tide laps against the slipway and everything in me wants to go for a swim. A float in the briny. Wash away the miles and the stress. Embrace the fuzz that comes from mainlining two pints of Ghost Ship and multiple St Piran Flag vodkas.

Falling onto one of the picnic benches outside the pub, I pull off my shoes then sway down to the water. It's deliciously cold to begin with. A contrast to the balmy evening. The festoon lighting stays lit all night and casts a warm glow along the harbour stretching from the lifeboat round to Smeaton's Pier. Above, the silhouette of a few lonely gulls catching thermals draws my eye. Ben holidayed here every year as a kid and introduced me to it within a few months of us getting together. I fell for it instantly. This was our dream. To move here, to have this on our doorstep. He was going to try and get work on the boats, I was going to write. Living out of that little backstreet cottage. We hadn't considered the fact that these now sell for more than I could sell a lung for, but details like that were unimportant as we lay cuddled up in his bed in the flat he had round the back of the civic up in Dronfield. Back in those early days. Before I ruined it all. He should have been here with me, letting the water tickle our toes after a night down our local. And instead, I am about to spend the night in the back of Petula before trying to bribe a postie into not putting that bloody letter through his door.

Trying to unlock my car, the alcohol making my aim a little off, I smile at the memory of Mitch helping me with the door earlier on today. I pull out my phone and the scrap of paper he left his number on, tapping it into a new contact.

Was good to see you today. Even though you do look like your older brother. Or your dad. ;)

Within seconds, he's responded.

I'll have you know I look nothing like my brother or my dad. I take after my mother's side of the family. You can tell that by the 'tache and sagging boobs.

Wow. An attractive thought. I type back, smiling, pulling a picnic rug up to my neck and shuffling down into the seat. *Hey. Guess where I am now…* but instead of a text back, he calls.

'Tell me, Calamity Jem, where are you now?'

I gaze, fuzzily, at the car park. Empty bays surround me, a gull pecks at a bag that peeps out of industrial bins lining the back wall by a phone box and the (now locked) public toilets. 'Paradise,' I say, sleepily.

'Where's paradise for you?' he asks, gently, and the sound of his voice makes my eyes close, comforted.

'I'm in St Ives.'

'Cambridge?'

'Cornwall!' I laugh. 'St Ives, Cornwall. I've just had an absolute skinful in the pub and now, 'scuse me.' I hiccup. 'Now, I'm snuggling down in Petula.'

'Who's Petula and what does she think about you snuggling down in her?'

'Petula is my car. On account of the fact that she's purple.'

'Are petulas purple?'

'I've no idea. What even is a petula? Purple petula. It's allitre… allotter… alliteration.'

'That's easy for you to say. How much did you say you'd had?'

'Not enough!' I drawl.

'So, I assume the letter you accidentally posted was destined for St Ives then?'

I swallow a sadness that overwhelms me. 'You got it.' My eyes are tightly scrunched because I will not cry. 'And tomorrow morning, I shall intercept it and make sure, hic, that Ben doesn't read it.'

'Are you okay, Jem? You sound…'

'I'm fine. I'm fine. Just tired. It's a long way. I'd better go. Sleep. Hey!'

'Yes?'

'Night, Ben.'

'Mitch.'

'Shit. Sorry. Yes. Night, Mitch.'

'Good night, Calamity Jem.'

Chapter Thirteen

A knock on the window startles me awake and my heart leaps into my throat. I fumble with the key to turn on the ignition enough to open the window, wiping dried spit from the side of my mouth because, obviously, I'm immeasurably attractive. 'Hello?' I groggily manage, my head banging.

'This is not a campsite,' says an officious-looking man in a parking attendant uniform.

'I know, I know. Sorry. I just… I couldn't find anywhere to stay then I sort of fell asleep. I didn't mean to…'

'Well, you can't stop here unless you're going to pay for parking and in which case, you need to do that now. In the machine.' He nods in the direction of a black machine by the gate to St Ives Sailing Club. 'Or on your phone.'

I look down at my phone, now resting between the seat and the centre console, a knee move away from dropping between the two and being all but impossible to retrieve. I shove my hand beneath it to save the fall, scratching my finger in the process. 'Ouch!'

'Which would you prefer?'

'Pardon?' I say, sucking on the side of my pinky.

'Phone or machine?'

'Oh, right. Okay. Machine. I think. No, phone. I don't know.' My head hurts. I am not yet awake. He requires decisions that I don't think I'll be capable of until at least two coffees and possibly something that includes bacon.

'You'll have to do one or I'll have to give you a ticket. This is your heads-up. I have a few other cars to check on first. You have five minutes.'

He saunters off, peering in car windows, checking the little machine that hangs around his neck. I root around in the glove box for change and painkillers. Finding a couple of quid for the car park and an empty packet of Nurofen. The me that finished this pack and didn't replace it is an idiot.

Climbing out of the car, I stretch out, my neck clicks and my stomach waves with hunger. The gulls are noisier this morning. There's a squabble over at the bins and a small fluffy browny grey thing – that is supposed to be a gull chick but looks like a medium-sized cat, such is its size – hops around Petula's tyres. 'Shoo. Go on. There's nothing there.' I wave my arms until my head hurts again and opt for sloping steadily off to the ticket machine instead of fighting the good fight with starving birds. Three hours. That should do me for now. Three hours to track Ben's house down and see what happens next.

Parking attendant satisfied, with a ticket stuck in pride of place in my windscreen, I pop a polo mint in my mouth for freshness and, grabbing handbag and phone, head up Fore Street. Starlings sing-song the morning as I follow Google maps along the cobbles in the direction of Street-an-Garrow, the road Mum's phone book told me Ben now lives on. Shopkeepers lazily open up, hanging postcard racks outside, opening doors wide, smiling as I pass by. A young woman with a pink-flowered headdress loads box after box of rich red strawberries outside the deli, singing a good morning to someone she knows, before sharing a joke and a scream of insider secrets that I sort of wish I was party to. A woman changes books over in the window of the bookshop and the church bell rings. God I bloody love it here.

I grab a coffee from Scoff Troff – which was my and Ben's favourite breakfast café, on account of their scrambled eggs being the best we've ever tasted – before winding my way up the high street towards his house. Each step I take chips away at my mood. My love for this seaside wonder is fast being replaced by the fear that, in being here, I've just made another cataclysmic decision. My heart rate quickens and my mouth dries, though that could be last night's vodka. And there it is. The house he now lives in. A slightly bent, terraced cottage with low windows and a tiny door, just like the ones we always liked. Did he sell a lung?

The blind is shut downstairs, though upstairs is wide open, light on. I swallow. Suddenly terrified. And more than a little regretful about all events that have led me here. The second to last time I saw him it was as though I was a stranger to him, he was so disdainful, almost disgusted by me. Which, the benefit of hindsight tells me, was entirely justified. I had been out with my work colleagues. We'd been chugging Prosecco like the international shortage was entirely down to us. We had just won some team company competition and the big bosses were encouraging us to get absolutely off our faces in celebration. I had promised him I wouldn't drink that day because the following day he wanted me to go with him to his nan's funeral. He hadn't wanted me to be green around the gills as they buried the last woman in his family. He wanted me sober and alert and there for him, as was his right. But I couldn't manage it. I wasn't coping. I felt pressure from all directions, pressure to perform, pressure to be the strong one, pressure to pretend I was okay when in truth I was anything but, yet I couldn't possibly explain any of it to him because to explain that would be to explain everything. I couldn't do that to him, I couldn't do it to me. So instead, I was three bottles down, hanging, and inappropriately dancing with my boss's brother because what harm could it do? Turns out quite a lot.

I could reel off a host of excuses, a load of reasons as to why I did what I did, but not a single one of them would make any of it better. The truth was, I messed up. When he had specifically asked me not to. And this time, unlike all the other times I'd let him down and he forgave me because he understood that I had something of a self-destruct button that drowns out sense and logic, this time, it was too much. Even for him. The most generous, loving, caring, incredible man I ever met.

'Morning, it's 'ansum, isn't it,' says a woman dragging a shopping trolley behind her.

'It's beautiful,' I agree, gazing up at the denim-blue sky. And as I look back down, the front door to Ben's house opens. A woman walks out, a baby in her arms. She pulls a buggy out of the door, placing in the baby who gurgles and giggles as she talks to it. She is tall. Stunning. Fresh-faced and wide-eyed. She is everything I am not and maybe they're just friends. 'I'll see you later, babe,' she shouts. 'Love you,' she adds and I wilt a little.

Ben's face, tanned and beautiful, leans out of the house to kiss the woman and I dart into a doorway, just out of view. Their kiss is soft, they linger, she touches his face like I used to do and my heart breaks.

Chapter Fourteen

I dart away from the house, dropping down to my feet in an alleyway. Someone walks past, so I pretend to do up shoelaces I don't have. Casual.

I always knew he'd move on. It's not really a surprise. And yet seeing it with my own eyes is… well, it hurts more than I imagined it would. It stings, right in my chest. That could have been me. Everything about that scene could have been me, if I'd wanted it.

I pull my phone out. I need to speak to Mum but her phone just rings. What would she say? If I could speak to her now? After she'd said she told me so and that I should have stayed at home to watch *Bohemian Rhapsody*. She'd probably tell me to stand tall. To quit being a victim… which in this instance is fair, because I am not the victim… and then she'd tell me what food needed eating that she's got out from the freezer and that I'd better hurry home or it'd go off.

My phone rings in my hand and though I'm disappointed it's not Mum, there's an odd sensation to see that it is in fact Mitch. I think I'm pleased to hear from him. 'Hi. Hello.'

'Morning you. How's your head?'

I pinch the bridge of my nose. 'Gah! It's fine. You know, well… a bit tender.'

'I'm not surprised. You sounded three sheets to the wind last night. I can hear gulls in the background. You're still there then?'

'I am. Yep. Still here.'

'Done what you needed to do?'

'Not yet.'

'You okay?'

'Course! I'm in St Ives! What's not to be okay about that?' I push myself back up to standing, turning my back on the street.

'I don't know, I've never been.'

'It's beautiful. It's the best! Blue skies and turquoise sea. Cobbled streets and—'

'—great pubs?'

'Exactly. You'd love it.'

'Maybe I would.'

There's a stiltedness in our conversation, I'm not quite sure why he's calling. 'I should go,' I say.

'Right. Yes. Okay. I was just… checking up on you.'

The fact makes me smile. 'I'm fine. Thank you. There's no need.'

'Fair enough.'

'No! No, I don't mean it's not appreciated. It is. Thank you. I'm okay though. I'll be back in my car and heading home very soon.'

'You are hardcore. Or mental. I'm not sure which. Let me know when I can get you that coffee. Or beer.'

'Yes. That'd be good.'

'Have a pasty for me. Drive safely, eh?'

'Will do. Talk soon.'

'Bye.'

He seems to care. Which is nice. Maybe I can appreciate that now. Someone checking up on me, someone giving a damn. Before, it always frightened me. Terrified me. I don't know why, or where it comes from. Mum always said rejection, from Dad walking out when I was a kid.

She said I grew needy overnight. Said I needed acceptance and craved attention, love, but when I got it, I'd wriggle away. I've always wriggled, but I don't want to any more. Is it too much, too soon, to hope that I might get a second chance to appreciate someone kind and respectful?

And how long until I stop wishing I'd learned my lesson before Ben got fed up of trying?

I turn back to his house – just in time to see the postman delivering a letter. No! No, no, no, no! 'Excuse me?' I call after him. He's shuffling letters for the next address, dropping stuff through the letterbox, eyeing me suspiciously.

'Sorry to bother you… excuse me, erm, what did you just post there? To number ten?' I'm trying to hover out of view of Ben's, should he come out the door.

'Erm… a letter.'

'Yes, but what? What was it?'

'Sorry, do you live there?'

'No. But I need to know what you posted.'

'I'm not at liberty to say. Sorry.'

I do a little dance of frustration then try and turn it into something much less desperate and weird. Failing. The postman is now turning away from me, shaking his head. 'I know maybe you're not supposed to say anything, so I'll just ask a question.' I walk after him. 'Nod or shake your head, that's all you have to do. Then officially, you've said nothing.' He pauses, a bunch of letters in hand. I'm in! 'Were any of the letters you posted, handwritten, in a blue envelope…' I pause, aware how ridiculous the next bit sounds '… with a picture of a Moomin in the corner.' The postman stares at me. 'You remember them; those cute white, Swedish things?'

'I know what a Moomin looks like!'

'Great!' I clap my hands in delight, then glance over to Ben's again. 'I mean, okay. So, did any of the letters you posted have a Moomin on them?'

The postman shoves a load of letters in a letterbox and moves on to the next address. 'There was only one letter.'

'And?'

He sighs. 'Yes. It had a Moomin on. Now, please, I have to get back to work.'

'Thank you. Thank you!' I say, disproportionately relieved to know it's there. Then I pull up short. Ben has the letter. It is now sitting on the floor by his front door. Unless he's already picked it up. And if he's picked it up, has he opened it? Does he recognise my writing? He always said it was distinctive. Should I knock, try and explain myself? Or should I walk away like he asked me to do the night before he left?

Chapter Fifteen

I'm sat on a bench overlooking the harbour. There's a gentle breeze and I should probably leave. I should go before I bump into him. And yet being here makes me feel closer to him. Just for a moment. I could almost forget everything that's happened. It could be like nothing ever changed. We still share ice cream in front of the telly, both in our pyjamas. We still laugh at every episode of *Parks and Recreation*. We still bicker over who makes the better Yorkshire pudding. (Me.) Nothing's changed. Until I remember the letter. I need to speak to Mum.

Her phone crackles and rings before she picks up. 'Mum? Mum, can you hear me?' Her signal is coming and going. Or maybe it's mine. 'Mum, where are you?'

'Pardon? Jem? Where are you? The signal's not very good.'

'I know, Mum.' I check my phone, I don't think it's me. Full signal.

'Did you get the letter?' she shouts.

'No. No, I didn't. His postman delivered it when I wasn't looking.'

I'm not sure if the pause in conversation is because she feels sad about the fact or because her signal is so poor. 'You should come home, love,' I hear her say. 'Come home.'

'I will, Mum. I am. I just...' I take in the view for what I guess will be the last time. It's not my place any more. Boats lean to one side or another, the outgoing tide left them to rest on the sand. 'I love it here, Mum.'

'I know you do. I know, love.'

'I don't want to leave.'

There's some background noise. Voices. 'I know. But you need to. At least for now. Look, I have to go, love. Come home. We can watch *Bohemian Rhapsody*. Come on.'

A stunning blue greyhound runs the width of the beach, hind legs pushing it forward at speed. A gull swoops down, narrowly missing a toddler's ice cream. Fishermen tend to boats, waiting for the tide to return. People walk behind me, chatting, laughing, taking selfies with the harbour as a backdrop.

My eyes fill and spill onto my cheeks as a breeze whips up and my hair catches in the tears. I could be back with Mum by teatime.

No good can come of second-guessing. What's done is done. So what if he reads it. I can't do any more than I have. Yes, he'll hurt. And God, I wish it wasn't so. But it is. When we were together, I always felt everything he felt: joy, disappointment, excitement, sadness. That stopped when we met up, days after his nan's funeral, and he told me he was leaving; I could taste his defeat but somehow, I no longer felt it. He'd always believed he could help me be the best version of me. He never said as such, he never suggested I was anything other than brilliant, yet I know. He respected me. Even the worst bits. The self-destruction. He knew where some of it came from, I guess I'm a fatherless cliché, determined to reject before being rejected, or unable to reject for fear of rejection. A nonsensical, complex, impossible combination that always saw me making the wrong choices at the wrong times, terrified by the outcome of either case. 'Protection,' he used to say. 'It's for protection. If you hurt you first, nobody else can hurt you after.' I'd never known anyone who understood me better than me. Apart from maybe Mum and Leanne. A man though, I'd never met a man that understood my complexities. Who forgave me my choices. Who saw through the bravado and didn't want to hurt the vulnerable child I was still capable of being. 'I am not your father. I am not your previous boyfriends. I am not the person who wants to strip you of *you*. I love you. Because of all of who you are and everything you're capable of.'

Somehow, I could never believe him.

Somehow, the demons spoke louder than he ever could. They told me I wasn't worth it. That nobody could possibly love me as truly as he did. And that even if someone did, why did I think I deserved it. Him.

And I proved him right.

I close my eyes, turning my face to the sun. A cloud passes in front of it, casting a cool shadow across my face. I dig deep, push my hands on my knees and stand.

And there he is. Ben. In front of me. His frame casting the shadow across me, not a cloud. And I can't speak, I don't know what to say. I'm lost.

Chapter Sixteen

'Didn't expect to see you on my commute to work.' He nods down at the boats in the harbour, carrying a bag of his tools. Is he working on the boats, just like he always wanted to? 'I thought I saw you earlier. I tried to kid myself it wasn't, that you'd never come all the way down here when you knew I didn't want to see you. Then the post arrived.'

'I…' I stop before coming out with something untruthful or lame. Instead, I look to my shoes because to look at him hurts. I want to sit down, not sure if my legs can carry my weight with him stood before me.

'I recognised your handwriting and then I knew it had to be you I'd seen. Though, if you were planning to come down, I don't know why you had to write too.' He turns to rest against the railings. The sea, clear to the sand below it, glistens in the morning sun. The tide has come back in just enough for one of the fishing boats to tack out, leaving a gentle ripple in the creamy, flat waters. 'The envelope, the Moomins, that's from the pack I bought for you, isn't it?' I nod, my head pounds. 'You were supposed to write, then burn. That's what we said, didn't we?'

'Yeah. That was the plan.'

'Apart from the one you posted.'

'I didn't post it. Mum did. I left it on the side in my room. She was trying to help.'

He shakes his head as if he expects nothing less. As if I am so incapable of anything, I can't even get that right. 'How is she?'

'Mum? She's good. Amazing, in fact. Doing really well. Thank you. Your card, she appreciated it.'

'Good.'

'I know you mean a lot to her.'

'She means a lot to me.'

We fall into silence. He watches the world before him, his attention drawn to a small concrete jetty to the left of where we're stood. A woman takes her curly-haired child down it to look at the fish caught in a small pool left at the edge of the harbour wall by the tide. The child squeals with excitement, pointing and clapping with glee. Her smile is broad, open, joyous. As they chat, enjoying the moment, no photos, just watching and being, living for what they can see, I detect a delicate Black Country lilt. Ben watches, smiling gently as the pair climb the steps, calling out for Daddy to come see. And now he's looking back at me. He's studying my face and it hurts my heart. 'Sit down,' he says and my legs all but give way as I fall into the bench, leaving just enough room so we don't touch. I couldn't bear it if we touched.

'So, what does it say?'

'What?'

'The letter.'

I pick at my fingers, uncertain where to start.

'Actually. Don't. I don't know if I want to hear it.'

'I was trying to do what you suggested. Write it all out. Offload, you know?'

'Right. So probably better I don't know then, eh?'

I'd love to disagree and the fact I don't is clearly all he needs to know he's right. He breathes out, folding his arms. 'Why are you here then, Jem? I said I didn't want to see you so why did you come? What were you doing at my door?'

'I was trying to get the letter back. Before it was delivered.'

'Wow. The contents are *that* bad?'

'Well... I mean... you said you didn't want to see me. Or hear from me.'

'Yet here you are.' He lets out a sigh and I wish I could reach out and rest a hand on his. 'I've lived here almost a year now.'

I remember the day he left. I didn't see him. But I knew he was driving down with all his belongings in the back of his Saab 93. I went to Leanne's. She cooked cheese on toast and we did jigsaws with Harley. I cried because I already knew what I'd lost. 'Do you like it here?'

'What do you think?'

The child and her mum are back with the dad. I can see where she inherited the curls. And the smile. And even though I don't want children there's something about the three of them there, a tiny family team, that makes me wonder, what if things had been different?

'I was about to go.'

'Lucky I caught you then.'

'Is it?' It's the first time I can look at him. We hold each other's gaze and it takes everything in my body not to tell him I still love him. 'You said you never wanted to see me again, I don't imagine me being here is quite what you wanted.'

'No. It's not. Because seeing you reminds me what I had to walk away from. It reminds me what I've lost.'

I want to ask him to tell me what it was he walked away from. I want to hear him tell me what he lost. I want that glimmer of feeling I used to get knowing he loved me before it got too much and I couldn't cope.

'It reminds me why it's taken so long to find the strength to get up every day and not spend my whole time thinking about you.'

'But you've moved on. I saw her. I saw you both.' I pause, wanting to ask who she is and what she means to him, but it's not my right to know. 'I saw the baby,' I add, quietly.

Ben lets out a long sigh. 'I don't know what it is about you, Jem Whitfield. Everything in me knows you're bad news. And that's why I didn't want to see you again, that's why I moved so far away. I had to break us. I had to cut the connection. Yet here you are, a year on, sitting beside me, and it's taking so much willpower not to reach out to you, you look so broken. I should be angry with you. I am on some level. I should be annoyed that you'd go against my wishes, and again, I think I am, but…' He shakes his head, rubbing his hands through his hair.

'I haven't come to cause trouble. Or to upset you. I was trying to do the right thing and, to be honest, I probably made a bad call. But I've changed in that respect, you know? I can own it. I'm working really hard. I'm being accountable.'

'Hence the letter?'

'Well… I don't know about that.'

He laughs to himself. 'I don't know if the gesture was worth it, you know. I mean, Christ, at this time of year, it must have taken you forever, cost you a fortune. Where did you stay?'

'In my car.'

'Comfy.'

'Not really. Thankfully I'd had a drink or two in the Sloop, so think I probably didn't really notice.' He turns to face me, studying me. I can't even… 'My head's banging now!'

He nods, slowly. Eventually, eyes fixed on the horizon, he says, 'I think it's time you went home.' He stands.

'Is it?'

He holds his hands out to me, pulling me up. We hold on to one another for a second before he lets go and steps back, collecting his tools. 'Maybe in another life, things would have been different.' He plants a gentle kiss on my forehead before turning to leave.

My heart is in my throat. I'm confused. I'm overwhelmed. 'Ben!'

But he carries on walking, head down, tools in hand. I watch him until he disappears into a crowd of people, then away, down the slipway onto the beach. He shakes hands with a fisherman before peering at a boat engine, life carrying on as if we'd never met.

Chapter Seventeen

It's past six o clock. I left St Ives mid-morning. Is that a World Record for quickest trip ever? And for what? I mean sure, I picked up a flaky pasty from St Ives Bakery. Traditional. But it's a long way to go for lunch, however good the pasty was. (It was good. The best... Ben's favourite.) Point is, it was a wasted trip. I didn't get the letter. I saw Ben and was reminded, as if I needed to be, that I made the biggest mistake of my life letting him go. And for a brief moment, seeing him, I thought there might be hope. I thought he was softening to me. It really felt like we might be able to talk. Until it changed. Until he walked away. Which of course he would, he's in a relationship. They have a baby. He's not that kind of man. And now I don't know if he'll read the letter, and worse, there's nothing I can do about it if he does.

I'm knackered. I feel stupid. That was the last impulse decision I'll ever make. From here onwards, it's time to consider the facts. It's time to be careful. To take my time and do things that feel right. I've got to listen to my gut. I've got to trust instinct.

Mum sits in her chair by the window as I wrench on the handbrake, apologising to Petula for being so clumsy.

She's at the front door, arms open wide by the time I'm out of the car. 'Hey, love.' She pulls me in for a long hug and I'm weirdly relieved to be back.

'There's a lamb casserole in the slow cooker with your name on it.'

My belly strains with all the food I've comfort eaten on my journey home, topped off with a McDonald's from the drive-through up Chesterfield.

'It's been cooking all day,' she adds.

'It's a slow cooker. That's what they do.'

She rolls her eyes at me. 'Daft sod.'

I decide to leave the incriminating evidence of breakfast, lunch and tea in Petula for now. 'I love your casserole, thank you. I really appreciate it.'

'How was it?' she asks, taking my handbag and hanging it over the bannister.

'I don't know. Long. Fruitless.'

'Oh, love.' She sniffs, taking a tissue out from her sleeve to dab her eyes.

'Mum. Don't. It's fine. I'm fine.'

'I know, love, I know you are. I just feel bad. Responsible.' She sniffs again, wiping her nose then thrusting the tissue in her tabard. 'I just... I'm glad you're home.'

'Hey, I am okay.' She sniffs again. 'Mum? I'm okay.'

She nods. 'Okay is all well and good, but I want you to be happy. It's all I've ever wanted for you, Jem, and you deserve it. We all deserve it.' She sniffs again, she studies the carpet before her, flicking a bit of fluff with her black cat slippers. Then she sighs.

'What? What is it?' I say, as she shakes her head. 'Come on, out with it, what's up?'

'Nothing.'

'Tell your face,' I joke, as she would have to me, if I looked like her right now.

'I just feel sad for you, for what's happened, that's all. It's my fault.'

'No, Mum. It's not. It's not your fault.'

'And all that petrol.'

'It's not your fault.'

My phone dings a text as I give her another hug to try and convince her. Despite everything that's happened in the last twelve hours, my belly warms to see it's Mitch, checking if I'm home safe. Like Ben used to. I reply with a thumbs-up emoji, I'll message him properly later. Mum pads back to her chair, dropping into it, pulling her apron off and a pink velour cushion across her belly.

'I won't do it again. Take something from your room, I mean.'

'Unless it's dirty pots. You can take dirty pots down.' Mum laughs a little. 'Actually, don't worry about it, I'll bring my own pots down and pop a lock on my bedroom door instead.'

'Jem!'

'I'm kidding. Honestly. It's fine. Eeeh, I don't know, maybe I shouldn't have written it. I was being selfish. Ha. Newsflash.'

'We're all capable of being selfish, love. That alone doesn't make you a bad person because you're also really great.'

I flop into the chair opposite her. Me and Mum. Together. In the lounge. In our respective places. My favourite spot. My safe space. 'Eurgh, come on then.' I stretch my arms above my head and my back clicks, which gives some kind of odd relief. Who needs a chiropractor?

'*Bohemian Rhapsody*?' I ask because I don't want to talk about the trip any more. 'What's it on? Amazon Prime or something?'

Mum starts nodding as I reach for the remote control but her nod soon changes to a shake of the head followed by tears. 'Mum, for God's sake, please! It wasn't your fault!' I chip, feeling immediately guilty.

Mum shakes her head, wiping her eyes. 'It's not that.'

'Then what's up?'

She sniffs, wiping her face. She moves to sit up tall. 'I need to tell you something.'

Chapter Eighteen

'What? What is it?'

Mum shakes herself steady, clasping her hands until her knuckles turn white. Something she only ever does when she's trying to be brave.

'Mum?' My breath slows. 'You're scaring me.'

'I don't know how to say this, so I'm just going to come out with it.'

I clench my own hands.

'It's back.'

'What is?' I ask, even though I think I probably know.

Mum studies her fingers. That feeling of dread in the pit of my belly creeps in. Not the usual one I get when I've been an arse, but the real one. The one that matters. The one I had for most of last year until she had her op. A group of girls scream and laugh as they go past the house like I would have done with Amy and Catrin and Kate, once upon a time. We'd walk and laugh and chat. We'd spend nights at the park at the end of our road, swinging and eating ice lollies. Clandestine meetings with boys I wasn't supposed to be seeing. Gossiping. Free. A world away from this. Now. Being a grown-up is shit.

'I saw the doctor. Something's not been quite right.'

'You didn't say! Why didn't you say?'

'I didn't want to worry you. I thought it was just that I'd been eating the wrong thing. Not looking after myself as well as I might.'

She always blames herself. I hate that she does that. 'And?'

'They ran some tests. Basic stuff. They had to give it time because it's supposed to grow so slowly.'

'Right…'

'Well… it might not be entirely doing what they expect. I get the impression that the operation wasn't as successful as they'd hoped.'

I think back to the conversation I had with her surgeon after it. It was all so blurry, the emotions, the stress of it all, I can remember some of what he said but did I miss the bit where he told me that? Did they even know? 'I thought they got nearly all of it. I'm sure that's what they said.'

'Yes. They did. But what's left…' She reaches for a clean tissue from the little pack inside her handbag at the end of the sofa. 'It's growing again. Faster this time. They say it's… unusual…'

'But it can't be. That's not how it behaves.' I jump up, as if my standing will make this all different. 'That's why we were going to be okay. Because it was rare and slow, and they got it and you were going to be fine. It isn't aggressive. They said that, Mum. They said that!'

'I know, love. I know.' She tucks her feet up beneath her, all folded in on herself. Small. Protected by the cushion and her crossed arms.

'So, what's changed?'

'I don't know. They don't know.' She wipes her nose then stuffs the tissue up her sleeve. 'That's where I was earlier today. And yesterday. When I said I was with Clare. In fact, when I posted that bloody letter I was on my way to the doctors. I've been struggling with food, things not digesting properly. My cough has got worse.' That much is true. And I had wondered about it but she kept putting me off. She said it was cheese. Mucus. Something that made my knees go a bit wobbly, so I didn't push her on it. I should have pushed her on it. 'Dr Fairleigh referred me. I went to the hospital and they did a scan. They've checked in with the specialist and… it's definitely back.'

'What are they going to do? What happens now? They can operate again, right?'

Mum shakes her head. 'They're not sure. Not without another visit to Basingstoke.' Basingstoke Hospital, so far away, but the only place that can treat the rare kind of cancer she has. 'They want to keep me in overnight in the first instance, do their own scans, work out what's happening and see if there's anything they can do.'

'Okay. That's great. So, we go back. They'll sort it. It's going to be fine.' Mum wipes her eyes. 'Mum, it's going to be fine. You're going to be fine. You have to be.' I move to sit beside her, pulling her into my chest. 'I mean, who's gonna cook me casseroles if not?'

Mum falls asleep on the sofa. An unfair review of a really great film in my view. I watch her, studying her face, whilst also wondering how I could possibly fancy Brian May. IMDb gives me all the answers and I spend a good ten minutes googling Gwilym Lee by way of distraction from what I'm really feeling. But no amount of objectification can take away the sick feeling. This is bad. This is really bad. And I should have been there. She should have felt able to ask me to go with her to the doctors. I shouldn't have gone to Cornwall. Christ, I've been so obsessed with the contents of that bloody letter. Maybe I'd have noticed something was up if I hadn't been. I pour the last of the wine from the bottle she'd bought. She wasn't fussed about drinking in the end. I polished her glass off whilst sobbing over Freddie Mercury.

Cancer. Fucking cancer! She can joke, as she so often has, about this rare form. About how special she is. *One in a million* because that's as few people who are diagnosed with it. *I'm like Audrey Hepburn* because it's the same cancer she had. But the humour, the lightness, it changes nothing. It's back. That can't be good.

And as it's back, that means I need to step up. And I can't do it like I did last year. I can't play at it. I have to focus. Ben made me have a realisation this morning, he's moved on. I have to, too. I have to be strong. Stronger than I've been before. For me, for her.

I can't bear the idea that she's going to die and, even worse, that she might go before she sees that I'm okay. She worries about me. She can't do that any more. She's enough on her plate. It's time I pulled my finger out my arse and got on with my life.

I text Leanne to let her know I'm back. Then I remember Mitch's message, checking in. And I don't know what he is to me, or what he could be, but maybe sometimes life throws things your way to see if you can cope and, at the same time, maybe life has a way of bringing people into your life when you just might need them the most. I mean, I don't want to put too much on whatever this could be with Mitch, that's not fair on either of us, but maybe it's time to stop being so frightened all the time. Mum's not frightened… at least, not so as she'd let me see. If she can face this without fear, I can sure as hell face my life the same way.

Chapter Nineteen

'Get right on it, I say!' Leanne shrieks. I've agreed to go out for drinks with Mitch and whilst I was expecting her to be pleased about it, I had not anticipated the backslapping and overall head nodding approval. We're walking through a complicated route of interconnecting alleyways to take us from her place over to the nursery school for Harley. I'm pushing a sleeping Elsie and Leanne is enjoying what she describes as 'total freedom', because she's not got a child attached to her boob, hip or hand. 'I still think you're crazy for going all the way to Cornwall to establish the facts necessary for you to move on, but you did, and you have, so now you can.'

'What?'

'Move on. There're no ties. Nothing keeping you connected to Ben.' I go to interject something about feelings but she cuts me off. 'You're entitled to move on as well. It reached the end. It's sad. Maybe you made some mistakes. We can't dwell on the past, you've gotta start looking forward. This is why I set you up on Tinder, to get you out there, to meet people. That you already know Mitch, well that's a bonus, isn't it?'

'I don't know, is it? I sort of hate that everyone knows everyone round here. Maybe I should widen my search field, meet someone in Sheffield.'

'Oh yes. That's very wide.'

'Don't be sarcastic.'

'Jem, it's time. You're not marrying him. You're not getting a cat together. There is nothing to be frightened of. He has just invited you out for a drink. For God's sake, go. And enjoy it. Be open to whatever happens.'

'Whatever?'

'Well, maybe not whatever. It's worth holding… a few things back, you know, if you think you might actually like him.'

'I don't know what I think really.'

'So, don't cut the poor bloke off before he's had a chance to show you what he can offer. You may end up just as mates anyway.'

'I don't need more mates.'

'Of course you do. You pissed most of them off. What if I was run over by a bus tomorrow, what would happen to you then?'

'Please don't get run over by a bus. I'd feel obliged to move in with Andy and raise your children as my own and whilst I love them all, I think we both know that couldn't possibly end well.'

'I suppose so. I'll avoid buses.'

'Besides, I'm gonna need you these next few months.'

'Why? What else is up?'

'It's Mum.' I haven't said this out loud until now. Even talking to Mum, I haven't had to say it. We've got the shorthand. 'Her cancer's back.'

'No…'

'Or maybe it never went away.' We come out of a ginnel right outside the school gate. All my life I've lived here and I still get lost trying to navigate my way through the estate.

'Is she okay?'

'She's being brave.'

'Are you okay?'

'I mean, I should be, right? Given that she sort of is.'

'But you're not.'

'I'm crapping myself.'

We hang at the back of a group of mums sharing stories, laughing with each other. I'm grateful to Leanne for not thrusting me into the mêlée. Some of the women I recognise from school. One of them is good mates with a girl I used to share a house with.

'To be honest, then it's probably a doubly good time for the Mitch stuff,' says Leanne, tucking one of Elsie's toes back into the pram.

'How so?'

'Well, if you've got more heavy stuff with your mum, you're gonna need some light. There's only so much of that that I can offer, what with all this.' She motions towards Elsie and nursery.

'Is that the right reason to start dating him?'

'Of course not. The right reason is 'cause you like him. But you do, I can see it.'

'He makes me feel strange.'

'Strange?'

'I don't know how to explain it. It's like, butterflies, I guess.'

'Well, that's good then, isn't it? You want butterflies with someone new.'

'I suppose so.'

'Look, it's understandable that you're a bit hesitant. You've had a heavy year with your mum. You're still carrying some Ben baggage. You're allowed to feel a bit uncertain about things, but feel the fear and do it anyway, right? Isn't that what they say?'

'They also say something about frying pans and fires.'

'Mitch isn't frying pan or fire. He's a new opportunity.' The doors to nursery open, and parents move forward to collect their small people. 'Don't stand in the way of your own happiness, Jem. You've done it all your life. You're the self-destruct queen. Fear swallows you whole then spits you out. Don't let it…' She joins the queue to pick up Harley who launches himself at her from the doorway, and she swings him round, showering him in kisses. She takes him by the hand, suddenly no longer desperate for the freedom she mentioned before, and he toddles beside her chattering. I follow them, listening to his nonsense stories, admiring how she takes everything he says seriously, how she hears it all. How she chats back and affirms his three-year-old successes. She is the kind of mum I would have longed to have the capacity to be but know it's just not in me. And she's the kind of friend who's only ever had my best interests at heart, even when I didn't always reciprocate.

Maybe she's right about Mitch. She's always been right about everything else… not that I'd tell her. I don't need that kind of smugness in my life.

Chapter Twenty

'So, what brought you back then?' I ask, sipping at the large Sauvignon Blanc Mitch bought me, despite my protestation. Apparently it saves him going back to the bar too often.

'It was my mum. Mainly. Me and Abby weren't getting on well anyway, I don't know what happened, we sort of unravelled. She changed. Maybe I did, it's difficult to say. It was hard, and we hurt one another, trying to get things right, trying to work our way through stuff. It was pretty clear she no longer wanted to try and then Mum was given weeks to live and I just thought it'd be mad to stay where I was and miss out on whatever time we had left. I came back in April, Mum died at the start of May.'

'Shit.'

'Yeah. It was. It is.'

He sips at his pint. He's composed. Remarkably so, given what he's saying. I wonder where that strength of character comes from, that ability to talk about what must be the most painful thing in his life.

'I mean, I'm lucky. I got to be there for her. There was nothing left unsaid, there are no regrets.' He half smiles and I wonder what it really feels like to talk about it. About her. Now she's gone. 'It's just hard to believe it sometimes, you know?'

I don't. I don't know. And I don't want to know.

'Who knows how long it takes to adjust,' he says. 'Or if you ever do. Like, we barely spoke on the phone; we'd text, usually. Then when I visited, we'd talk. She was never a fan of phones, which was fine, I didn't mind. And yet now, I've lost track of the number of times I've picked the phone up to call and tell her something.' He shakes his head, sadly, and I can't imagine what it would be like to not be able to just pick up the phone. Or text. Or sit on the sofa and watch a film whilst she falls asleep… 'Like the other week, when I dropped the last of her clothes at the charity shop, I went to call her and let her know. It's stupid.'

I shake my head. 'It's not.'

'It's just an autopilot thing. Weird, really.'

'Clearing her stuff must have been hard.'

'Yeah. Awful. But necessary. And it's strange, when I go past I sometimes see an item of clothing in the window, or a pair of her shoes on display. Like today. What should be painful and horrible is oddly reassuring: a tiny pair of animal-print boots.'

'They sound incredible.'

'They're down the cancer research shop if you fancy 'em.'

'Hmm. Might be a bit weird.'

'Yeah. I guess so. Dunno why she had 'em. She never wore animal print. Yet she had them. They were hers. And seeing them there, it's weird, but it's nice. Almost like she's around and I can give her a wave.'

'Until someone buys them.'

'Yeah… I didn't think it through…' He half smiles again. 'Maybe you *should* get them.'

'I don't know if I could do that…'

'I wouldn't mind.'

'No, not the shoes. I mean… clear my mum's stuff out.'

'You have to. If there's nobody else to do it for you, you have to. And even if there had been, I don't know that I'd have wanted them to. She was my mum. I wanted to make sure that I honoured her, honoured her belongings. I didn't want to just scrap it all without making sure I'd checked it. I'd come across little notes she'd written. Affirmations and stuff. If someone else had done it, I might never have seen them. I wouldn't have them now.'

'That's beautiful.'

He sighs. 'Not all of them. One of them was a shopping list. Must have been from years back. It included condoms.' He shudders.

'Awks.'

'I know, right? Oh, I don't know. At some point I need to decide whether to get the house on the market or stay there myself. I can get work wherever I am, computers see, it's easy, but I don't even know if I want to really. She's everywhere and nowhere and that really fucking hurts. Plus, I don't know where I want to be. It's not like I love it here.'

'No?' I say that, but I sort of agree. It's not that there's anything wrong with Dronfield. With the exception of the rickety train bridge that definitely has trolls living under it, it's a perfectly lovely town. But it was never the plan to stay. And there are memories around every corner. And if my mum wasn't here, I don't know if I'd want to stay either.

'I suppose I just never saw it coming. Being back here. Single. Parentless. Well, essentially parentless.'

'We'd have bloody loved being parentless back in the day.'

'Ha! You're right. I could have played Spice Girls on full blast!'

'Now you're taking the piss.'

'Spice up your life is a lyrical masterpiece.'

I belly laugh. 'Go on then, late nineties music: Aguilera or Britney?'

'Britney!'

'Wrong! It's Aguilera.'

'Actually, we're both wrong. It's Shakira all the way.'

'Oh, boys! You're all so bloody obvious.'

'What can I say? I like breasts that are small and humble.'

'Hahaha! Anything more than a handful's a waste, is it?'

He clinked my glass and knocked his back. 'Come on, sup up. Don't leave me hanging!'

Chapter Twenty-One

He's back with more drinks and I finish up my first wine having decided, whilst he was at the bar, that my breasts are neither small nor humble. What if he doesn't fancy me?

'Cheers,' he says, clinking my glass. He looks at me and once again, my belly flips a bit. 'And thanks, for listening.'

'Ha. You're probably the first person to say that to me.'

'Really?'

'Yeah, I've not really been all that good at listening in the past. But this is part of the new me.'

'Well, I don't know what the old you was like, but this version is alright... I reckon.'

Maybe it doesn't matter about my breasts...

He leans back, hands cradling his head. 'So what else do you want to know? What can I tell you?'

'What about your dad? Do you still see him?'

'Nah. Not for years. Not since he left.'

'Oh, yeah. I remember that now. They split up, didn't they, your parents?'

'Yup. Worst time of my life, fourteen. I was supposed to be getting inappropriate erections and taking an unhealthy interest in a Freemans catalogue.'

'Lingerie pages?'

'Obviously. Instead, I was judge and jury for Mum and Dad's marriage breakdown. Which is a cheery thought.'

'Sorry. I should have stuck to Shakira chat.'

He lets out a groan. 'Eurgh. Probably. Right then, Jem. Save me. Save me from myself before I twist into a pit of despair. Or find Spice Girls' "Mama, I love you" on the jukebox.'

'God no!'

'Exactly. Come on then.' He grins. 'Tell me about you. Tell me what life has thrown at you these past few years?'

'Oh sure, put the pressure on me to change our mood. Maybe I would like a bit of music after all.'

'If it's Aguilera, I'm leaving.'

I narrow my eyes and half smile in a way that would definitely be seen as flirting, but stop because I don't think I'm very good at it.

'Tell me what you've been up to then, key things since school?' he asks.

'Ha! Where do I start? I too was not getting inappropriate erections or poring over the Freemans catalogue.'

'No? We both missed out!'

'I see that now.'

'So, if not that, what else do the cool girls do?'

'Cool girls?' I belly laugh. 'Of all the words you could use to describe me, cool is not one of them.'

'Of course it is!' He laughs. 'You are. Well, you were, anyway. Maybe that's all changed.'

I nod, sipping at my wine. 'If I ever was, I'm deffo not now. But thanks, I shall laugh at the very idea for many days to come.'

'Okay.' He grins again, his eyes crinkling at the sides. 'So, what makes you not cool then?'

'Apart from the elasticated waists on my trousers and the fact that I wear trainers because I'd be arse over in any kind of heel?'

'That's not uncool, that's just practical.' If Leanne could hear him now she would definitely agree, she loves an elasticated waist. I reckon she'd like him. 'So… presumably you're single?'

'Given that I'm on Tinder.'

'From what I understand, that's not always a given.'

'Oh, right. Yes then. I'm single. Very. No gossip to be had there.' It's possible the last bit comes out more forcefully than I intended.

'Okay, clearly love-life chat is off the table. Tell me about work then. Weren't you in recruitment at one point?'

I wonder how he knows, has he asked around after me? Scrolled through my Facebook? Is that a good sign? That he likes me? Whatever the answer, it gets a bit hot in this taproom as I think back to the morning I lost that job. Two weeks after Ben left. I was a mess, pretending I was fine. I walked into the office in a new suit I'd bought from TK Maxx the night before because late-night shopping was preferable to going back to my place where Ben very much would not be. The suit was hot pink and pretty sharp. I think I almost felt strong, confident and in control, oblivious to the fact I was about to get fired. As I casually whipped off the form-fitted jacket my boss presented me with an email I'd mistakenly sent to him instead of Julie, my work colleague. The email in which I gossiped about bedding a contract business analyst we'd just placed at HSBC. £500 a day he was on. We spent the night in the Wig and Pen, celebrating his placement, on me. Before he took me to the Ibis for a quickie, which was horrible. And he wasn't Ben.

But I didn't have to go home, so I rolled with it anyway. Then he left in the middle of the night, leaving me to foot the bill.

A new suit from TK Maxx could not get me out of that one. Form fitted or otherwise.

'Yes. Recruitment. For a while. Was glad to get out though.'

'I had a mate in recruitment, always sounded very boozy.'

'Very. Which, don't get me wrong, was fun. And you could earn decent enough money. I bought my first house 'cos of that job. Just up from Climax.'

'The nightclub? Didn't it shut?'

'You've not seen it?' He shakes his head. 'Fishing tackle shop now. They couldn't be arsed changing the name.'

'Wow.'

'I know, right.'

'I thought you lived with your mum, though?'

'Ah, yes… I don't have that house any more.'

'You sold it?'

Of course. Having once had a house and now not having a house. And living with your mum. 'Not exactly. If you were after inspiring success stories, I'm afraid you knocked on the wrong door.' He cocks his head to one side. 'It was repossessed three months ago.'

'Oh. Shit.'

'Yeah… about the same time I went bankrupt.'

'Ah.'

'Didn't I do well?' I force a grin, trying not to let the feeling of shame swallow my mood like it normally does. 'It's all a bit embarrassing really. I've kind of made a hash of things.'

'It happens. None of us are exempt from that.'

'No. Shame really.'

'I guess it doesn't take much for everything to go pear-shaped.'

'You could say that.'

Three months in fact. That's all it took. I lost my job, spunked my savings up the wall in a fit of *how dare they fire me, how dare Ben leave me* idiocy. It was a dark time. He doesn't need to know all the details.

'I had no work, no savings, and I had been living very much beyond my means. Mum was ill and I was trying to hold things together and care for her. It didn't take long before people were chasing me for money I didn't have. I wasn't in a great place. Just couldn't see how to fix it. So, I filed for bankruptcy, posted my keys through the letterbox and went back to Mum's, where I was practically living by then in any case. Not my finest hour but there we are, I guess. So now, I do a bit of admin for people. Like, online secretarial work.'

'Interesting?'

'Not really.'

'Pays the bills?'

'Not really.'

'So why are you still doing it?'

'Aaahhh... why *am* I doing it.' I give his question a moment's thought because nobody's really asked me that before. Leanne's just glad I'm being proactive. Mum's proud I'm still standing. Am I doing it for them? 'Partly to prove I'm capable of being a grown-up and partly because I don't know what I want to do. I don't know where I want to be. And it's handy because I get to work from home which...' I pause. I can't evade this with more Shakira banter. 'My mum's still not well,' I say, draining my glass.

'Oh no.'

'Yeah. I mean, she was bad, then she got better – or so we thought, and now it seems… well, it looks like things have taken another turn.'

'I'm so sorry. Do you want to talk about it?' I shrug, because maybe I do. He drains his own glass, reaches for mine and stands. 'Let me get us another. Then you can tell me everything. You know, if you want to.'

'No, no. It's my turn. I'll get these.' I reach into my bag, wondering how much I've got in my bank account. That trip to Cornwall turned out a smidgen more expensive than I anticipated.

'Put your money away. Let me. Might as well put the inheritance to good use.' He's joking I'm sure, I guess sadness does that. 'Look, I can afford it and I'd like to.' I fight back a sudden lip quiver because I feel sad for him and embarrassed for me. 'Same again?'

'Same again. Thanks.'

Five hours. That's how long we spent together, and it flew by. We didn't stop talking. I told him everything about Mum and even managed to find humour amongst it all. Then we talked about other stuff, I can't even remember what. I laughed. He did too. It was light and easy and fun. He walked me home. We chatted more, sat on my doorstep, whispering so as not to wake Mum. And then he stood, and there was that moment of whether or not to kiss someone and I sort of wanted to, but sort of didn't because I've always rushed into everything in the past. And as he walked down the drive I kinda regretted being standoffish because I don't think I want him to think I'm not interested, even if I still don't know what this is. Or if I'm interested in a romantic way. Or how I feel about anything… anyone… at the moment.

I've never been one for uncertainty when it comes to men… Maybe it's a good sign. This is different to anything I've known before.

Chapter Twenty-Two

I scrabble around on the bedside table in my box bedroom, searching out an Alka-Seltzer to drop into the glass of water that (it now appears) drunk me managed to organise last night before stumbling into bed. I don't think I realised I'd had that much. I mean, yes, a fair bit, but enough to feel like this? Was it the fresh air? Sitting outside talking? The lack of food?

As the tablet fizzes, and I try to focus my eyes, I tap out a text to Mitch, managing nothing more than, *Ouch, my head.* As is form for him, I'm learning, no sooner does he read the text than he calls.

'You've got to be kidding,' he says, laughing.

'I am very much not kidding.' I try and shift myself to sitting so that I don't pour Alka-Seltzer down my front.

'We didn't have that much!'

A memory of me slamming a glass on the table before downing it seeps in. 'I think it could have been the tequila slammers.'

'We didn't have slammers!'

'Eh?'

'No. You suggested them and I said no 'cause the last time I had tequila I was violently ill and vowed never to touch the stuff again.'

'That's so weird. I could have sworn we had at least three.' It wouldn't have been unusual, let's face it.

'Well, unless you necked them when I was in the loo, then no, we did not do slammers.' Did I do that? Surely I didn't do that. 'We left after our fourth large wine, I walked you home, we almost fell over laughing about the first time you shared a bed with a man and wore head to foot pyjamas and socks as he paraded in a luminous green thong.'

I sip the Alka-Seltzer, grimacing. I did do that… 'If I'd had salopettes I'd probably have worn them over the top.'

'Thanks for the sexy image. I'll bank that one for later.' Is he flirting with me? 'So, are you going to do what we said?'

I search my sensitive brain for a hint as to what he's on about. 'Um…'

'Oh my God, you really are a mess,' he says, laughing.

'Alright, you, less taking the mickey, more enlightening me, please.'

'You were going to get back in touch with Kate. See if you could arrange coffee.'

I have no memory of this whatsoever, but the fact he has brought my old schoolmate up suggests I really did open up last night. 'Ah, right. Yes. I really should.'

'It'll be fine. Didn't you say a year has passed? More than that, eh? She's married now. She should be happy, so she surely won't still be holding it against you. And like I said last night, from what you hinted at, you were in a bad place. It's no more your fault than hers.' Christ. How much did I tell him? 'Invite her for coffee. Tell her you're sorry. What can go wrong? At least with this one, you don't have to chase anything to Cornwall.'

Please God don't let me have told him everything about Ben. 'True.'

'Go on. Feel the fear and do it anyway. You'll be better for it.'

'Okay,' I say, uncertainly. 'Okay, I'm going to message her.'

'Good work. I'm proud of you.'

'Thanks. I think.'

'And hey, I meant what I said last night.' I don't say anything, hoping he'll expand. 'I'm here for you. I get it. This stuff with your mum, it's not going to be easy, but you have me on the end of the phone, or in the pub, or wherever, whenever… however you need me. Okay?'

'Okay.'

'Any time. Day or night.'

'Thank you.'

'Now go. Be brilliant for your mum. Be brilliant for you. Let me know how you get on with Kate.'

My heart swells in a combination of *oooh, I fancy him*, and *wow, it's good to have people who have your back* way. At least I think it's my heart and not my stomach complaining about being empty after last night's overindulgence. I try sitting up, my head spins. Maybe he's right about Kate. Maybe I pushed her away because seeing her happy and in love was too painful for me, especially at that particular time. I've always found it hard, when others are moving on in life, and that particular time was the worst. She was the last one of my mates to marry and, for me, everything was colliding, collapsing. I've always felt judged, even though I probably wasn't being. I've always felt left behind, like somehow I'm less of a person for not – in Kate's case – falling in love, getting married… having a baby.

Not showing up at her wedding though, that was… eurgh, I shrivel at the memory of that time. All that was going on. I mean, it wasn't actually her wedding day. It was weeks before when it all happened really, but still, it was shitty. I was shitty. I could make all the excuses – I have about all sorts for the last year – and though I appreciate Mitch telling me that sometimes we make choices to protect ourselves, something Ben always said too, I can't escape the fact it was crap. And I really do want to make amends with her.

I open the Facebook app on my phone, searching her name. And there she is. Ash blonde hair, pixie cropped. Kate Pinkerton. Grinning at the camera with adorably dimpled cheeks. She's a mum now. There's a tiny version of her, clinging to her arm in the profile photo, can't be that old. I scroll her page, careful not to accidentally like anything because that would be weird. She posts photos mainly. The occasional news story relating to the charity she works for. There's a post wishing her other half a happy first anniversary. Where did this last year go?

A knock on my bedroom door makes me guiltily close down Facebook. 'Come in.'

Mum peeks her head around the door with a smile before entering fully, mug of tea and a plate of toast and Jaffa Cakes in hand. 'Thought you might like these,' she says, handing them over, then perching on the end of my bed. She smiles at the bedspread, running her hand across the face of a Forever Friends bear. She bought me the bedding for my fifteenth birthday when I was obsessed with all things Forever Friends, despite it not being particularly cool. (Proof if proof were needed for Mitch!) Of course, I'm now so attached to it and the memory of the years I'd come back to stay for the odd night here and there, even though I had my own place, that I won't let her replace it with the new grey cotton bedding she bought me last month. I keep telling her she doesn't have to buy me stuff. 'Good night?'

I nod. Which makes my head hurt. Did we really only have wine? 'Lovely, thank you.'

'Where did you go?'

'The Green Dragon. Just had a few drinks.'

'A few,' she says, wryly, nodding at the spent Alka-Seltzer pack.

'Yeah… well, I don't know quite how many. Mitch just told me not as many as my head is suggesting, but I didn't have much to eat for tea so maybe that's the problem.'

'Oh. You've spoken to him already this morning?'

She's got that look in her eye that mums have when they think you're pretending not to be interested in someone you are in fact gagging for. 'He called me. We are just friends at the moment. Do not overthink this,' I warn. Wondering who in fact I'm warning. 'He's not long out of a relationship.'

'Didn't you say you met on Tinder?'

'Well, we saw each other's profiles, but we were actually at school together. And then we met up in the post office.'

'Right.'

'I said don't overthink it.'

She puts her hands up in submission. 'Who's overthinking it? Not me.' No. Me neither. Probably. 'It's just nice to see. I want you to be happy.'

'I am. Thank you.'

'Of course. That's fine.'

'Besides, he's had a rough time lately.'

'Oh?'

And now I wish I hadn't said that. Like I always wish I hadn't said something about someone who's died of cancer because it always makes me wonder how that makes Mum feel. 'He split up with his girlfriend. Ended up back here.'

'Right. Oh, and didn't his mum die a while back too?' she says, as matter-of-fact as you like because this is Dronfield and everyone knows everybody else's business.

'Erm, yes. I mean, I don't think it was that long ago but, yes, that too.'

'You see, that'll be good for you. Having someone who knows what it's like.'

'Mum! You're not going to die.'

'Well, we all die someday, love.'

'Yes. But not you. Not yet.' We fall into a slightly awkward silence that is entirely of my doing. 'Sorry,' I say, reaching for her hand.

'Hey, love. It's fine. We're both working our way through this. There's no rule book. No guide.'

'No. Which is a bit crap really, isn't it?'

'It's all a bit crap. A lot crap. But we will not let it define us, right?'

'Right.' I nod.

'Anyway, on that note, can you sort out a new playlist for us? My Basingstoke Hospital date has come in, so we need a new road trip selection.' The drive takes the best part of four hours. She retrieves an appointment letter from her back pocket. 'Can it not include anything by The Wanted? But I do like that new song from Little Mix.'

'Only a woman with cancer could make such a request and get away with it,' I say, which makes her laugh and I know we're going to be okay.

'Now, if you'll excuse me, I'm going to love you and leave you. Marjorie is taking me to lunch and you will, I am sure, have work to do.'

I stretch and tighten my legs, toes pointed, hands above my head. It feels restorative. 'You're right. I do. Enjoy lunch. Thanks for the toast.'

She shuts the door as I open up Spotify. Shakira's the first thing I put on it.

Chapter Twenty-Three

It only takes a few hours to get on top of my workload, such as it currently is. I really need to try and get some new clients or get a proper job. Part of showing Mum that I'm on it. That I'm being a grown-up. Except that how can I get a proper job if I'm going to be toing and froing to Basingstoke with her again. Last year, along with the general appointments, I was there for two weeks, living on site in the family accommodation whilst she underwent her op. Eurgh, the family accommodation. I can't even think about that.

'Do you want a cup of tea?' shouts up Mum who's been back twenty minutes and hasn't stopped clattering pans since she walked through the door. God knows what she's doing down there.

'Please,' I shout back over the din.

I bring up Kate's Facebook page again. Since this morning, she's posted a photo of her baby and their dog. She's got one of those Cockapoo things, by the looks of the tan-coloured blur that appears to be chasing something around the garden. Nice. She always liked dogs. And babies. I wonder how old it is – the baby, not the dog – I'm no good at guessing but it's small. Bigger than Elsie, but maybe not that much.

I open Messenger. It's just coffee. It'll be fine. She might say no, but she might not, and I won't know if I don't ask. Breath held, I tap out the invite:

Hey, Kate. I know this is a bit out of the blue, but I'd love to catch up. Have a chat. Maybe over coffee? Whenever suits you. It would be lovely to see you, it's been too long. X

I click send before I can reconsider and, as I head downstairs for the cuppa, I wonder if I should have said something more apologetic in my message. Would she really want coffee with someone who basically just stopped answering her calls?

'So, Sue has booked you into the family accommodation. She said she'd do what she could to get you back in the same room you had before,' says Mum about the super-efficient nurse administrator at Basingstoke. 'She thought you might appreciate the familiarity but couldn't promise as it depends if it's being used when we get there.'

I hope Mum can't see that the idea of staying there fills me with literal dread in the pit of my belly. Even watching back-to-back *Sex and the City* from when it was good can't make up for the hell of that place. 'Bless her, that'll be great,' I say, pouring milk into the half-made cuppa she's got distracted from.

'She's made my appointment for the afternoon so we don't have to stop in the Apollo Hotel the night before.'

'Ahh, that was the best bit.' I nudge her. 'Do you remember that woman you shamed out of the jacuzzi?'

'It's not catching!' she cackles, reliving the moment she shouted after the woman who couldn't wait to escape the jacuzzi when Mum told her she had cancer because she was irritated by her tone. 'Gosh, wasn't I awful?'

'Yes. And also a little bit funny.'

'She just had that way. I couldn't get on with it. Coming in. Complaining about how busy it was. How she was a member and couldn't even get a parking space. Asking us what we were doing there. How dare she.'

I adopt the woman's tone. 'Sixty pounds a month, I pay for that membership.'

'Ah, money to burn. Please herself. So, I was thinking we could leave around nine, when the traffic has died down. If we need to stop off, we should still have a bit of time, but hopefully we can just get there. My appointment's at two-thirty.'

'Okay. Sounds good.'

'Sue said that we'd see that lovely Mr Faux first.'

'You're not supposed to fancy your consultant, Mum.'

She swipes at me with a nearby tea towel before winking because she totally fancies her consultant. 'He'll run some tests. They'll see us the next morning. Hopefully that'll be it and we can come home.'

'Cool. Sounds great. A road trip. We can Thelma and Louise the hell out of it.'

'I look terrible in a headscarf.'

I agree. We know this because she tried them in several different ways when she thought she might lose her hair. I bought her a wig from Amazon instead. Thankfully she never needed it because she didn't look much better in the rainbow dash, multicolour, cosplay wig I bought her for giggles. 'Some people just can't carry off headgear that's not their own. You want pasta for tea?'

'No. Not hungry really.'

I turn to face her because if there's one thing I know, she may not be able to eat as much as once upon a time, but Christ, she's never not up for food. 'I went out with Marjorie, didn't I? We had one of those afternoon tea do's at The Manor House. It was lovely. They made me a special selection of sandwiches that I could eat. And they used a jam in the sponge cake that didn't have seeds in it. There was so much of it though, I'm stuffed! There's a doggy bag over there, if you want to finish it.' She leans against the kitchen worktop. 'Stuffed and shattered actually. I might take a book to bed and have an early night.'

I check the kitchen clock. '*Now*? It's not even four o'clock!'

'Of course not now, no.' She looks around at the pots and pans she's pulled out of the cupboards. 'I thought I'd give these a clean and sort through first.'

'Why on earth...?'

'Oh, I don't know. It's been waiting for yonks. I've still got loads of stuff I need to sort, love.'

It's not the first time she's said that. She's a hoarder, but has been slowly and steadily working through cupboards and rooms these last few months. Taking stuff to the tip. Giving things to charity. Now I know what she's been doing: clearing her stuff, getting organised, making sure she doesn't leave a mess. I want her to leave a mess. Or not leave at all. I also want her to feel like she's in control of her destiny and maybe this is part of that process, however I feel about it. 'Do you want some help?'

'No, love. Go on, you go finish whatever you were doing. I'll get this sorted and give you a knock before I go to bed.'

I must give her an uncertain look because she shoos me out of the room as she puts her apron on and crouches down to start bleaching the cupboard.

Chapter Twenty-Four

'So, when do you go?' checks Leanne, and I know she'll have the phone in the crook of her neck as we talk, so her hands are free to put the date on her family calendar in the kitchen. She biro'd an extra column with my name on it back on New Year's Day.

'Erm, a week today. Driving down on the Tuesday, hopefully home Wednesday.'

I've taken myself back to the Green Dragon for a small wine for one tonight. Thought I'd leave Mum to have some quiet for her early night and I needed to escape after being in the house all day.

'Well that's not too bad then, is it,' Leanne says.

'I guess not, no.'

'Do you want me to come too? A bit of moral support? I can crash in your room.'

'Don't be silly. It's fine. I'll be fine.'

'Andy's still working down in London, but the kids could have a cheeky sleepover at Nancy's.' Her mother-in-law loved having them whenever possible.

'Elsie's too little for that yet, isn't she?'

'Well, maybe, I mean I could try and wean her to a bottle but she can be a picky little bugger. I could bring her; she'd be no trouble. We can watch a film and pretend none of it's happening.'

I laugh. 'It's fine. I'll be okay. It's one night.'

'If you're sure.'

'I'm sure. Mitch offered too, which is sweet. Both of you are lovely, but I'll be fine.'

'Did he? That's nice. How is he then?'

'Oh, you know, he's okay.'

'How did it go? Your date.'

'Was it a date? I don't know, we just had drinks and talked. We talked for hours.'

'In a bar, after both having swiped right on Tinder – it was a date, Jem. So, what did you talk about?'

'God, all sorts. How it's been hard for him with his mum, and before that, splitting up with Abby, his girlfriend.'

'Abby?'

'No one we know. They met at work, I think. They were together for about six years.'

'What happened?'

'Dunno. I think they just outgrew each other. It happens, doesn't it?' She mumbles an agreement. 'Anyway, he was lucky, or so he says, he got a heads-up his mum didn't have long left and he could be there for her. I think he's struggling a little to adjust to his new normal though.'

'I can imagine.'

'But hopefully I can help a little, too. You know, I don't know exactly what he's going through but I get some of it, don't I?'

''Course.'

'And we talk. It's easy. We have a laugh, which is good. I need that and I'm certain he does too.'

'That's nice then.'

'Yeah. And hey, guess what I did today?'

'What?'

'I messaged Kate.'

'Kate, Kate?'

'Yeah. Mitch persuaded me it would be a good idea. All part of the new me.'

'I like the old you. So should he.'

'He does. I think. And the new me is very similar to old me, she just feels less guilt.'

'Is this about Ben again? It better not be about Mitch, he's got no place to be laying any guilt on you!'

'No! He's not. It's all me, just getting my shit together. And with Kate, I just want to own the fact I let her down.'

Leanne and Kate never really got on. Leanne always thought she was snooty. A bit above herself. I think I used her judgement to justify my behaviour.

'I know you feel you let her down, perhaps you'd have been able to talk to her if things had been different. Kate isn't perfect either, remember.'

'I know. None of us are. But I would like to see her.'

'Fair enough. What's that, Harley? You've dropped a sock down the toilet? Jesus.' She mutters the last bit under her breath. 'Look, I'd better go. I'll talk to you tomorrow, okay?'

'Okay. Love you.'

'Love you, bye.'

I reach for my book, smoothing the page out where I'd got to. It's warm out, the beer garden is busy, despite it being a Tuesday. It means the lounge is quiet and a bit fusty. Which I quite like. It feels secure. I read, sipping at my wine, feeling almost content.

'Now then, Jem. How are you?' I look up to see Mark, the landlord. 'Bet your head was banging this morning, wasn't it?' He laughs and his paunch lurches up and down, the buttons on his shirt straining on a par with the shame I feel but don't quite understand. I'm about to ask what he means when he diverts his attention to a punter. 'Yes, mate,' he says, grabbing a pint pot and chatting as he pours before disappearing out the back.

I knock the last of my glass back, saving the page in my book until I get home later. Getting up to leave, I scan around where I was sat to make sure I've not left anything behind, walking into someone as I leave. 'Oh, sorry!'

And there she is. Stood in front of me for the first time in a year. Kate Pinkerton.

Chapter Twenty-Five

'Oh wow! Kate!'

She stares at me, lips pursed, dimples hidden.

'How funny, seeing you today of all days. Well, 'cos I messaged you earlier on. Don't know if you saw it or not? It was on Facebook, I know sometimes life happens and we miss messages on there. I just don't have your mobile number any more.' I colour because I only don't have it from deleting it in a fit of spitting my dummy out. 'I lost loads of numbers. A few months back. You know how it can be…'

'I suppose so.' She moves past me to let one of her friends get through the door. 'Lime and soda please, Sue.'

'Wow, it's so nice to see you. You look amazing.'

'Thanks.'

I look down at my book, noticing she too carries a book. 'I was just having a read, with a drink. Bit of peace and quiet, you know?'

'Right. Sure.' I look at her book again, hoping we might find some common ground. 'I'm out with my book club.'

'Oh! I'd love to join a book club.' She nods at me tightly. I wait, hopefully, for an invite to join them. I'm nothing if not optimistic. 'What are you reading?' I try, eventually.

'*Hollywood Wives.*'

'Oooh, Jackie Collins? I used to love a bit of Jackie Collins.'

'We always read Jackie Collins.'

'Oh, that sounds amazing. Jackie Collins and Jilly Cooper, my teenage favourites. Do you remember that time I asked for *Polo* for my birthday and Dean Summers bought me a piece of paper with a Polo sellotaped on, with a note beneath it, Jilly Cooper's Polo.' The memory makes me laugh almost as much as it did the day I opened it. 'Gosh, Dean Summers. What a crush I had on him. Haven't seen him for years.'

'No.'

She's still staring. She's rigid. I'm flailing. 'Right.'

'You said you messaged me,' she said, with a sigh.

'Right, yes, I did. The thing is, you see, well, it seems an odd thing to say now that we're stood here like this, but I was kind of hoping we could have a drink, a coffee, a catch-up.' She frowns at me as if I've just made the most ridiculous suggestion. 'I know, it's been ages. And I guess… oh, sorry, excuse me.' I move out of the way for someone else coming through the door, the woman smiles at Kate who points to where her Jackie Collins mates are sat. 'It's a big group,' I say, smiling over at them.

'Yeah. It is.'

'I guess – what's not to love about talking all things Lucky Santangelo whilst drinking wine with your mates?'

'Indeed.'

'Well.' I gaze around the pub, now under no illusion about her mood. 'I wouldn't want to keep you from the group, you know…'

She lets out a spiteful laugh, one of those that suggests I'm not about to leave unscathed. 'What? Is that it?' I go to say something but realise I've opened my mouth without any idea of what words might come out of it. Kate on the other hand… 'We don't see each other for a year. The last time we spoke was to arrange the final fitting for your bridesmaid's dress.' I wish the ground would open up. 'A fitting that you didn't turn up to.' It wasn't really supposed to go like this. 'But I suppose that didn't matter seeing as you had no intention of turning up for the wedding either, did you?'

This was a bad idea. I mean, I probably definitely deserve every word, every ounce of her anger and upset; her eyes glisten and that makes me feel even worse yet. All I want to do is run away. Fast. And not look back. And possibly never read Jackie Collins again. In fact, that coffee seems like a really stupid, terrible idea. Why did Mitch encourage me? Why did I go along with it?

'Were you ever going to let me know?' she asks, her voice small.

I could have avoided this if I'd just stayed at home.

'I can only assume not, since I heard nothing. I just had to guess the fact, given that you stopped taking my calls. And my texts. And even when I rocked up at your place because I was genuinely worried that something awful had happened, that you'd done something awful…'

I remember her coming round. I remember how I felt that day. I remember the guilt.

'… you couldn't even be bothered to answer the door. I saw you, Jem. I saw you shift out of view when I came to the window. Which is essentially the only proof I had that you weren't hanging somewhere, or bleeding out of your gut surrounded by packets of paracetamol.' Ouch. 'Seeing your panda socks sneak out of view is the only reason I knew you weren't lying at the foot of a bridge on the A61 somewhere up near Gunstones.' She stares at me. The glassy eyes and sadness has been replaced the more she talks. A sort of cold anger has taken over as if she's remembered exactly what I put her through, and exactly how she felt. If hatred had a look, I'd say it was this one, now, the look in Kate's green eyes as she burns a hole in my resolve. 'Hey, girls,' she shouts across the pub, taking me by the hand and dragging me across to them. As if things weren't already really, really, awful. 'Do you remember I told you all about the bridesmaid who ghosted me just before the wedding?' They each nod, staring at me with a mix of looks that range from confused to accusatory. 'Well, this is her. This is Jem Whitfield.' She holds my arms up like I'm a winner. I feel nothing like a winner. 'We were really close. Had been for years. She was going to be my chief bridesmaid. The one person I could rely on, on my big day.' She lets go of my arms and it's a split second before I realise, leaving me standing, arms aloft, midriff exposed, no Jackie Collins book in hand. 'The same woman who decided she didn't have enough about her to tell me she no longer wanted to be there for me.' Her anger splits and, for a second, I'm fairly sure she wants to cry again. 'On my big day,' she says to me.

My throat goes sore as I try my very hardest not to cry. And not just because everyone in the pub has surely seen my flabby belly.

'I got your message earlier today, Jem. And thanks, but no thanks. I have no interest in meeting you for coffee. I have no interest in hearing whatever lame excuses you've come up with to justify your behaviour. You let me down in the biggest, most unforgivable way possible and there is nothing you can say or do to make that better. Now, if you'll excuse me.' She sits down amongst her friends, sitting upright as the one to her left reaches out and squeezes her arm whilst scowling in my direction. I hug my book into me, working up the muster to turn and leave even though somehow my legs have stopped working. 'You're a leech, Jem Whitfield. You suck up peoples love for you, you suck up all their good faith, you take every last bit of patience and you spit it out without a care for how it makes them feel. I was done with you then and I am done with you now.'

She runs out of steam for that final sentence, leaving her to take a sharp breath in before biting her bottom lip. I can see how hurt she is and can only imagine it's as hurt as I feel now. I stand and stare, somehow unable to move away, until somebody else arrives at the table, and I'm forced to move to let them sit down. So I turn, aware that of the few people now in the bar, all are trying not to stare at me, but totally watching my every move. I do my best to hold my head high and leave with any shred of dignity I may have left. And I walk like that until I get into the churchyard over the way and, pulling my T-shirt down, casting my book to one side, I collapse onto a bench in frustrated tears.

Chapter Twenty-Six

Oh God, oh no, oh God. I'm sat on a bench in the bit where they keep people's ashes after a ceremony in the church and a trip up to Hutcliffe Wood Crematorium. Somewhere amongst the markers and flowers, Kate's grandad's ashes presumably lie, maybe with some carnations left by her mum, because I seem to remember her saying they were his favourite flower when I stood here with Kate, on the day of his funeral. She held my hand, sobbing, unable to breathe and I just waited until she was ready to say how she felt. Then I gave her a Trio, like the ones we used to nick from his biscuit tin on our way home from school, and she cry-laughed then ate it. I don't suppose a Trio would help now. Even if I could track one down. It's a crime they ever stopped making them. Especially when you can still buy a Blue Riband.

Was her anger justified? I mean, I know I'm an idiot. I know I messed up. But did I deserve a slating like that, in front of everyone? Even if I did deserve that, nobody deserves to have their muffin top exposed for all to see.

I'd like to ring Leanne but one mention of what Kate just said and I'm pretty sure she'd jump in her car and come kick her head in. Which would be embarrassing for all of us because she's a lover not a fighter. And I'd like to ring Mum but she's knackered and stopped fighting my fights in the playground when I was seven owing to an unfortunate incident with a boy called Neil. And I can't ring Mitch because I only spoke to him earlier on and I don't exactly know what's going on with us yet, but I'm fairly certain that at my age I should be able to handle myself with a little more dignity than was just displayed.

It's at times like this, I'm reminded how nice it is to be at home. There's something about my childhood box room that feels comforting. That I can't quite stretch out in my single bed is unimportant. That I can't fit all my clothes in the sliding-door wardrobe Dad built when it was my nursery. After they'd wallpapered the room, ceiling and all, in flowery paper just because it was called 'Jem'. Wallpaper I painted over with Denim Blue when I was thirteen and thought I knew better. Turns out I didn't. And Denim Blue paint takes about fourteen layers of Dulux Wheat Dream before it stops showing through.

Still. Wheat Dream walls and sliding cupboard doors. It's mine. It's always been mine. And nothing and nobody can deny me that.

Unsteadily, I get up, winding my way through the path, down the steps and out the other side of the churchyard so that I don't have to walk past the pub again. In fact, I may never go there again. Which makes going to Dronfield pubs tricky, since I was kicked out of the Sidings for cheating in the pub quiz and an ex-boyfriend still works in the White Swan. I make my way home, past my old infant school, where I was best mates with a girl called Philippa until she moved away and for some unfathomable reason, not long after Dad had gone, I told everyone she'd died. Now *she'd* have a valid reason to shame me in front of a full pub.

I walk along Scarsdale, past Kate's grandad's old house. I nip up Wilson Street remembering Rachel. My best mate – after Philippa – in the Juniors. She had a dog called Dina and her mum used to send us to the corner shop for milk and cigarettes. I dropped Rachel when I got to senior school and found new friends that I thought were much more interesting and exciting than her. Kate was one of them. I walk up a little side street, thus avoiding the house on Hallowes Lane that a friend of a friend had a house party in. I drank her parents' home brew before vomiting all over the daffodils, because I was fifteen and could no more handle home brew than the Mad Dog 20:20 my mates were drinking. I pass the house I used to babysit at and steal the kids Easter eggs. I pass the back road I used to kiss somebody else's boyfriend in. I pass the shops where Vic lives and the post box that never had that bloody letter in it anyway. By the time I get home, I have relived so much of my youth I can barely breathe for self-loathing and reach for a bottle of sloe gin that Mum put to the back of the cupboard when she realised neither of us really liked it. Everything hurts. My heart hurts. And I don't know how to stop this. I don't know how to make things right. I don't know why I made all those awful choices. Mum always blamed Dad. She said that his rejection started it. I was about eleven. No age is good for a parent walking out but eleven was particularly crap. Hormones were kicking in and everything felt confused and frightening. Not helped by the fact that after he'd gone, somehow he worked it so that his parents wanted nothing to do with us either. Mum always said it was her they cut out, that they'd always disliked her, but whatever their reason, it hurt me as much as Dad leaving, if not more. It vindicated him. Mum always tried to make up for it. She worked so hard to be Mum, Dad, grandparents, her own parents long dead. She tried to fill the gap I felt each birthday. Each Christmas, when friends would reel off the list of gifts they'd been given from every member of their family, from siblings, to grandparents, to aunty and uncles twice removed. Each weekend when she was working, she'd pay for me to do exciting things: workshops and day trips, anything to fill the void.

But I don't think it helped. I didn't want any of those things, I realised years later. I just wanted to feel loved. And when you feel unloved, you do more to get attention, and the more attention you seek, the more unlovable you become. A self-fulfilling prophecy dictates your past, present and future. Somehow, Mum's love alone, was not enough.

Yet now, I don't think I could live without it.

Chapter Twenty-Seven

When I wake the next morning, an empty bottle of sloe gin is the first thing I see. I can't quite focus, the time on my phone fuzzes in and out of view. I think it is 9.45 a.m? Thank God I don't have a proper job that requires actual timekeeping. There's a knock at the door. I wait, listening out for Mum's footsteps. The doorbell goes again and there's still nothing from Mum. The radio isn't on. She always has the radio on, wherever she is in the house. If it's not Radio 2, Peak FM is usually singing out a combination of Pink, John Parr and one of several songs by runners-up on the *X Factor*, Mum usually singing along, badly. Not least because she knows none of the words for anything except the John Parr one. She met him once. Got his autograph on a serviette in the Hobby Horse pub up near Meadowhall. Apparently their mac and cheese is to die for.

Mmm. Mac and cheese.

The doorbell goes again, but by the time I've overcome the swell of morning after the night before, the postman has gone. There's a load of letters on the mat, a 'Sorry you were out' card on the top. I scoop them up, sorting them into a pile on the phone table before a rise of bile swells up in my chest at the sight of a blue Moomin envelope. Returned to sender. Unopened. And I can't tell what's worse – that he sent it back, meaning I needn't have gone all that way to Cornwall after all, or that he thought so little of me, he couldn't even be bothered to read it. We met. We talked. Was that still not enough? Except it's not my right to judge or be hurt, not really. I didn't write it for his forgiveness, I wrote it for my own. That I'm not there yet, that's not his fault, is it?

Sun streams through the window, highlighting an old school photo. I see fifteen-year-old me, newly permed hair because I wanted to look like Gloria Estefan except that I never looked like Gloria Estefan. I suppose it could have been worse, I also liked Sinead O'Connor. I see Kate with long bob and straight fringe, the girl I used to hang with when we were teenagers. So much of life has happened and I can't imagine fifteen-year-old us having any clue how things would pan out. It seems such a long time ago. *She* seems such a long time ago, even though we only fell out a year ago.

Mitch texts me with the name of a song he was trying to remember when we were talking yesterday and to see his name on my phone makes me smile for the first time since I left the pub last night. So I text him back. *What you up to? Do you fancy a walk?*

'So what? She just laid into you?' asks Mitch, throwing a stick for Pip, his mum's dog as we wander through Kitchen Wood. 'In the middle of the pub?'

'Yep. No holds barred. I mean, don't get me wrong, I'm not looking for sympathy. I've no doubt I deserved every word she said, but it was still pretty humiliating.'

'Well of course it was, she had no right to do it so publicly.'

'I turned my back on her when she needed me most.'

'Yeah, but what else was going on? What couldn't you tell her? There had to be something for you to feel the way you did.' I shift uncomfortably. 'You know she always used to blank me in school? I think someone once told her I fancied her and from that day forwards she decided I didn't exist. I think maybe she's just not very nice.' He picks up a long thick twig, stripping it of some smaller branches and moss before handing to me to use as a walking stick.

'It's generous to frame it that way, but I don't know. She's definitely not faultless, but I'm not either, I do need to own that.'

'Okay, maybe you were both to blame. Maybe you were right and she *was* lording it a bit. Maybe she was terrified; she was about to get married, that's a scary thing.' He gives the dog a treat and sends it on its way again. 'Still think she's mean.'

'Maybe.' I wander over to a fallen tree, sitting on the trunk as we watch Pip excitedly jump in and out of the brambles, through fallen trees, around the dried-up stream, tail wagging. The sun peaks through the leaves every now and then, dappling the ground, and my face as I turn to embrace it. 'Leanne says I should stop beating myself up about things.'

'Leanne is probably right.'

I nod and just about manage a smile as we fall into a comfortable silence. We sit there for a while, just listening to the birds, feeling the warmth of late August sun as it bleeds through the canopy. This was always my happy place at school. When we were out for study time, supposedly to prepare us for the GCSEs I largely failed, we'd all come here. On my sixteenth birthday, me, Amy, Kate and Catrin walked down here with sandwiches in our rucksacks and freedom in our hearts.

'He sent the letter back,' I say, eventually. Mitch turns to face me. 'The ex. It arrived this morning, returned to sender. Unopened.'

'That's a good thing, isn't it?' He tries an encouraging smile. 'You said all along that you didn't want him to read it. Those were your exact words to me. And he hasn't. So, take this as a win, for God's sake, in amongst everything else right now, take it as a win!'

'I know. I should.'

'And yet?'

I take it out of my pocket, staring at my writing. Staring at his, beside it, almost touching. 'I think, probably, I actually wanted him to read it and then forgive me. I think I wanted him to see through what happened and tell me it wasn't my fault. I think I wanted him to call me up and tell me he doesn't hate me for it. I mean, I'd have been amazed if he had, all things considered, but I really wish he had. I shouldn't need his forgiveness to forgive myself, and yet… I do.'

Mitch lets out a long sympathetic groan. 'Oh, Calamity Jem, what are we going to do with you?'

'What?'

'Do you really need other people's acceptance and love so much? Can you really not find it inside yourself, without anybody else?' I shuffle my feet, exposed. 'Give it here.' I look up, sharply as he thrusts out his hand. 'Come on, give it here. I'll read it.'

'No. No, I can't.' I get up and start walking. Pushing brambles out of my way with the walking stick, letter grasped tightly. I've told him plenty, granted he didn't smart at any of it. But this? No. No, thank you. That'll be a nope.

'Come on. I won't judge. I promise I won't judge. You want someone to read it and tell you everything's okay, so let me. Let me see what's so big and scary that you can't let go. And when I've read it, I promise you I'll turn to you and give you a big hug.' I clearly look unconvinced because he catches my hand, holding it as we walk. 'Hey, I'm not Ben, and maybe that's for the best, maybe he isn't the man you think he is. But I am me. And I'm here. And if opinion's matter, then mine is as worthy as his.' He rubs his thumb down mine. 'I promise you I won't judge. We've all been idiots. We all make mistakes.'

'I'm not sure…'

He blocks my way through the kissing gate out of the woods and into a field, Pip scampers between our legs. 'Maybe this is exactly what you need. Someone to see your truth, however ugly it will be. And then love you anyway.' I cough. 'Well… you know what I mean. At least platonically.' He moves slightly from the gate, but not quite enough to let me escape what has suddenly become a little bit awkward and not quite the nice walk through the woods I was hoping for. 'We're friends, Jem. Would Leanne judge you?'

I think for a second. Unsure if to admit that she knows most of it, if not the detail then the basics. 'She'd think about it long enough to make me sweat, and then she'd pull me into a hug. She'd tell me she loved me anyway and we'd go to the pub.'

'See. So why can't I do that for you?'

'She's my best friend. I've seen her vomit down the side of a Mini Metro, before pretending to her parents that she was totally sober. She has to love me. I know too much.'

'Try me.'

He fixes his eyes on mine, my heart rate spikes. If this is to be anything, Mitch and I, secrets can't stay secret. Lies need to be owned. My past doesn't have to dictate my future any more. He whips the letter from my hand and though I go to protest, it's not quite enough to stop him reading…

Chapter Twenty-Eight

Dear Ben,

There are some things I have to tell you. Things I need to own so I can move forward with my life. But they're things that you may not want to know. After all, you left, as well you should have. I neither deserved nor appreciated you - at least, not the way you wanted me to. Not the way you had every right for me to. I wish I knew why I behaved the way I did, I wish I could put it all right, but sometimes, it's just too late.

I've often wondered how much you knew and chose to ignore, versus how much I'd got away with lying about. Like the time I kissed George Newman at his house-warming party after you and I had a row. I justified it by telling myself I thought we were over. Or that George came on to me. I was lying to myself as much as you. I was so hurt by our row, I was so frightened that it meant the end for us, and where most people would fight, something in me couldn't. I pretty much rolled over, accepted my fate.

Except it wasn't my fate, was it. You came back. We talked. It was just a silly row. I'd been so frightened of losing you I made the worst choice. You'd think I'd have learned my lesson after that but there were more lies...

Chapter Twenty-Nine

'I can't, I'm sorry, I can't.' I've snatched the letter out of his hands, stuffing it into the safety of my pocket before he can try and get it back. 'Sorry, I just… I can't.'

'You snogged his mate. Come on, Jem, it's really not that bad. You'd fallen out, it happens.'

'Is that all you read?'

'You didn't give me much chance to read the rest.'

'It gets worse. And I can't.'

'Right.' He starts walking off, kicking some leaves for Pip, who finds a pile of mud in the field far more interesting.

I jog to catch up with him. 'Wait!' He pushes on, quicker than I can keep up with. 'What's up?'

'Nothing.'

'Mitch, slow down,' I say, almost unable to keep up with his sudden pace. 'Mitch!' I reach out and just grab his arm. He spins around, almost angrily, making me step back a little. 'What have I done?'

'I thought we were friends.'

'We are!'

'Friends trust each other.'

'I trust you.' He looks at me uncertainly. 'I do! This isn't about you, it's me. It's my fears, I just… I'm not ready.' The sun's gone behind a cloud, dropping the temperature in the woods until I shiver. He kicks the ground. 'Mitch, please. I'm sorry.'

We stand in silence, for much longer than I'd ideally like before, eventually, he says, 'Come here', and pulls me into a hug. His arms are strong around me and my heart is pounding so hard I wonder if he can feel it. 'I'm sorry, you just reminded me of Abby, that's all.'

'What do you mean?'

He lets out a long sigh, his chin resting on my head. 'She used to hide stuff from me. Keep things secret. It was like she never trusted me and it turned out, I shouldn't have trusted her.'

'No?'

'No. She did all sorts behind my back. Other men. Spending my money. Pretending to be something she wasn't. I was a fool, missed all the signals for years. She made me look an idiot. I guess, maybe it was just echoes, you know. You not trusting me. It made me panic. What if you're like her?'

'I'm not! I'm not like her at all.'

'I think I know that really.'

'Oh God, I'm so sorry. I didn't mean to, I just—'

'Hey, it's okay. It's fine. I forgive you.' His arms are strong and he smells a little bit of Kouros body spray, which should, technically, be horrible, but takes me straight back to being fifteen and in the woods with the first boy I ever loved and I can't help but swoon a little. 'Whatever else is in that letter, I'm sure it can't be that bad,' he says, so quietly I could be mistaken for missing the words. 'We all make mistakes. We're human.' I daren't look at him. I daren't move or breathe or speak. I can't go back to the words in that letter, I can't relive it any more. 'Jem?' he says, moving me so he can look at me. I shake my head, his face blurred through my tears. 'Please, don't keep secrets from me though, yeah? I can't do that, I can't cope.'

'Of course not. I'm sorry, I mean. I won't. And I will tell you, in time. When I'm ready, just... please bear with me.'

'You don't have to be frightened of me judging you.'

'I know, I know I don't. And I can't tell you what that means to me.'

'So you'll tell me everything?'

'I will. Soon. Just, give me time.'

'At some point in life, you have to forgive yourself for the mistakes you make, don't you?' I nod my head, a tear escapes and he rubs his thumb across my cheek to wipe it clear. I'm so grateful he's here. 'Come on, you need a drink,' he says, and the weight that lifts from my shoulders sees me crumple into his hold. 'You don't have to be this person, Jem,' he says, his breath hot on the top of my head. 'This letter doesn't have to define you.' And so close are his choice of words to what Mum said the other day, I am floored. Flawed and floored. And he is holding me up. Strong. Unwavering. No judgement. 'Come on,' he says, my hand in his, striding through the kissing gate without pause. 'Let's go to the Talbot.'

'Thank you,' I say, placing a pint of beer before him.

'You didn't have to get these.'

'I wanted to. It's the least I can do.'

'You okay?'

I nod. Because I think I am. Because I'm exhausted, I feel like I could sleep forever, but there's something about someone having read a bit of what I wrote and still standing before me that gives me hope. Something about us having our first disagreement and the world not imploding, maybe it calms me. I mean, it didn't at the time, but he's still here. Whatever this is, me and him, we survived something that maybe in the past I'd have freaked out about. Closed down. Shut myself off from. And for me, for my future, it makes me think this could be different, that I'm different. 'You have no idea how much I appreciate what you just did. You're right, I made mistakes. We all make mistakes. I don't have to be defined by them any longer.' He nods, seeing me. Getting how I feel. 'I didn't think anything could make me feel better and yet somehow, you have.'

'Is that because I asked you to buy pork scratchings as well as a pint?'

'Oh yes, the pork scratchings!' I get them out of my back pocket, where they now, because I've sat on them, more likely resemble a pork crumb. 'I really am sorry if I made you feel uncomfortable, Mitch. I think I'm not very good at relationships sometimes.'

Mitch sips at his pint, the sun obscures his view of me, so I shift to block it out and stop him squinting. 'We're mates,' he says, simply, ripping the packet open with his teeth. 'That's what mates do.'

Mates? Is that all we are? But what if I want more? Am I misreading his signs, the way he held me in the woods? How upset he was at the idea I might have been keeping something from him? Is that how he is with all his mates or is he playing it down now? Have I ruined any chance there might be?

I gaze into my own wiping condensation from the side of the glass. 'If I hadn't been in the post office last week, we might never have met up.'

'You messaged me on Tinder.'

'Leanne did.'

'Oh yeah.'

'I think I'd have deleted the app. I mean, not because of you,' I add, quickly, because I don't want to upset him again. 'Because I didn't know if I was ready to meet anyone. For anything. And yet, I already feel like I can't quite imagine my life without you being here, and you've only been around for a hot second.'

'A *hot* second, you say?'

My cheeks flush. 'You know what I mean.'

'I guess true friendship doesn't consider little things like time.' He nudges the last full scratching in my direction and I snaffle it, gratefully.

'Do you believe in serendipity?' I ask.

'I do.'

'Leanne thinks us meeting at the post office was serendipity…' I cough, embarrassed. 'She thinks that maybe the universe is doing its thing.' It's the most I've said, perhaps fuelled by the last couple of hours and the sun and the beer and the fact that I see it now – I like him. I really like him. And he makes me feel good about me. I don't have to be frightened. 'Maybe we were always destined to bump into one another. I don't know, maybe I needed you, this, us…'

'Maybe we bumped into one another when *I* needed someone.' I feel myself colour a little at his suggestion, the newness of this… whatever it is… the intense look in his eye. 'Seriously, I've been rock bottom. I've got a bank account full of cash, I've got a house, a car, a dog, and yet, I feel I have nothing. But, here you are, and I'm able to be a friend. To support you. Let you buy me beer and salty snacks. Maybe *you* are what *I* needed, not the other way around.'

'Maybe none of that matters.'

'Also true.'

We smile at one another and I realise his eyes are a deep, deep brown. So deep you could be forgiven for thinking they're black. 'Do you have any contact with her?' I ask, randomly.

'Who?'

'Abby.' He shakes his head. 'Didn't you say she called you, after your mum died?'

He shakes his head again, frowning. 'She never called me. She's had nothing to say to me since the day I told her I had to come home. Which just happened to be the same day I found out she'd been seeing someone else behind my back. Now that's serendipity.'

'Oh! I thought you'd said she called and tried to get you to go back?'

'Nah. She doesn't want me back. She's moved in with a new fella. Not even the one she was screwing whilst living with me. Greg, he's called.' He enunciates every letter in his ex-girlfriend's new boyfriend's name. 'I feel sorry for him, to be honest. I don't think people change. She'll do to him what she did to me but you can't tell someone that when they're in a new relationship, can you? I tried calling her, to talk through logistics, who got what, bills that needed paying and so on. She wouldn't pick up.'

'God. Her and Ben should talk!' As soon as I say that, it feels off. Wrong. Ben doesn't deserve my judgement after everything I put him through.

Mitch shrugs. 'Let's just say it's a good job I have the inheritance. I can clear it all and leave the whole relationship behind me. I guess we're probably both better off without them.'

'Maybe.' Total agreement is, if I'm brutally honest, a stretch just yet. And I want to be honest because this thing with Mitch is the most honest I've been with a bloke in years.

'Well, I think we are. I'm quite happy on my own for now,' he says and there's a tiny part of me that hears the on my own bit louder than the rest of what he just said. 'I don't need the complication. I don't want the games that come with relationships.'

'Relationships shouldn't come with games,' I say, repeating words Ben once said to me, bruised. I've put him off. I've said too much.

'No. True. But those relationships are rare. The ones that are game-free. I'm happy being me, sorting the house out, getting a plan of action together.'

'Sorting it out? Are you selling up then?'

Mitch laughs to himself. 'I told you I thought I would the other night! Christ, we're going to have to get the important stuff out of the way before we start drinking, you know. So that you remember.' He necks his pint. 'On that note, another one?' He doesn't wait for my reply and I watch as he jogs into the pub for his round. He's solid. When he runs. Like he does it a lot and nothing wobbles. Like his thighs are the kind that wouldn't look out of place amongst a rugby line-up. Not that I want to think about his thighs. Or a rugby line-up, for that matter. Not when I'm already sweating in this heat. And he's just said he's happy being on his own.

Pip sits up, flaps his ears, then cries a little at the sight of Mitch's retreating back. 'Crikey, what happened there?' I ruffle the fur on his head, wafting my T-shirt to cool off. 'It's okay, he'll be back in a minute. Come on, settle down.' Pip sniffs and licks at my hand with a tiny tail wag against the concrete, before he shuffles to lie down beneath the bench, out of the sunshine. Dogs. I could have a dog. Babies, not so much, but dogs? That I could probably just about manage. They'd be easier. Less reliant.

One day.

Chapter Thirty

I can still smell Kouros from the last hug Mitch gave me as he bid me farewell down by the Civic. This time, as I weaved up Gosforth Drive, I didn't analyse every road, house and significant place. Well, apart from a wistful memory of losing my virginity at a house on Garth Way. Back bedroom. Color Me Badd on the radio. 'I Wanna Sex You Up'. The romance.

By the time I've made it home, I don't hate myself. Which is a novel state of affairs and I might even quite like it. I stumble in the back door, my head hot from too much sun, my shoulders red raw, but I don't care. Maybe I'm okay.

'I've been calling you!' says Mum, her head poking out from another cupboard.

'Oh, sorry!' I pull my phone out to check it, seeing five missed calls and a text. 'Damn, sorry, Mum! I didn't hear you calling. I must have knocked the silent switch without realising.'

'Oh yeah. Not because you were off with Mitch and didn't want any interruptions,' she says, winking.

'No!' I catch sight of myself in the painted mirror above the toaster. I've gone pink. I think that's the sun too. Mum is grinning at me, on all fours, by a cupboard again. 'Are you okay? What's wrong?'

'Nothing's wrong with me, love.' She brushes off her apron, standing, sniffing in my general direction. 'You smell like you could do with a cuppa.' She points at the kettle, so I fill it up.

'Ben sent the letter back.'

She pauses, her shoulders drop a little, but she keeps faffing with stuff in the cupboard. 'You okay?' she asks, pulling out a couple of pretend-crystal sherry glasses before pushing them to the back of the cupboard. 'Do you want to talk about it?'

She has such genuine concern in her voice, which, by God, I love her for, but now is not the time. Despite all the things she's got going on she still whittles about me. 'I'm fine, Mum. Honestly. I just went out for a walk with Mitch to clear my head. We talked.'

'A walk. To the pub?'

'No. We walked through Kitchen Wood first actually. I've not been there in years, it was bloody lovely.'

'So what about Ben?' She passes me teabags.

'What about him?'

'Did he say anything? Has he read the letter? Do you feel better?'

I drop some bread in the toaster, pushing milk and butter on the side as I dig around the back of the fridge for some marmalade.

'Back, left,' Mum says, directing me straight to the Golden Shredless she bought me because it's always been my favourite.

'I do feel better. Weirdly.'

'Why weirdly?'

There's something that stops me sharing what Mitch did. I don't think it's 'cos of the Kouros or the rugby image. I think it's just 'cos it's mine. It feels authentic. And I'm not quite sure what to do with that really, because it's also alien. He'd read some of that letter. He said I should forgive myself.

'I don't know. Maybe I just needed to get the letter back. Drop it in the incinerator and watch the smoke twist into the sky. It's time to move on, Mum.' The toast pops up. 'Oh my God, how good does toast smell?' I pick it out, burning the tips of my fingers. 'Oooh. Ouch.' Blow. 'You eaten?' I slather it in butter before taking a pre-marmalade bite, my mouth watering at the taste.

'I've eaten, yes, thanks.'

She looks tired. And is she going a funny yellow colour or is that these godawful lemon blinds she insisted we put up when I first moved back because *it's like living in sunshine, Jem!*

'You want some help with those cupboards?' I ask, as she opens a new one, slumping at the amount of lidless takeaway containers that tumble from behind the door. 'I don't know why you keep them every single time.'

'It's waste, Jem. We can't just landfill the evidence of our Saturday nights in.'

'True. Though I fear that cupboard is like our own miniature landfill.' Behind her, I peer inside it. 'Have you really still got that mug from when Charles and Diana married?'

'It was commemorative. I bought it 'cos it was the same year you were born and I thought you might like the history of it. You drunk your first cups of tea out of that mug.'

I wince at the memory of unnecessarily milky, two-sugared tea. 'I'm probably not going to use it any more though, am I? Can barely fit a thimbleful in that tiny thing!'

She picks it out of the cupboard, smiling at it sadly. 'Time flies so fast.'

'Stop! Come on, give it here.' I reach in, taking it from her with a nudge to her hip because melancholy isn't allowed. 'Cats Protection love this kind of tat. Pop it in that box and step aside, I can see you need someone with a bit less sentimentality to make any headway in these cupboards.'

I shovel the last of my toast in, wiping crumby hands on my jeans before bending down to survey the hoarding evidence. Mum backs away, perching on a kitchen stool by the makeshift breakfast bar that we only ever use for wicker baskets full of cables and plugs and the sort of stuff you don't really know what to do with so hide in a wicker basket.

'Go on then. Pull it all out. Let's see what we want to keep and what we can sling.'

I find another couple of commemorative plates and mugs from various royal weddings right up to Harry and Meghan. 'I had no idea you were such a royalist.' She shrugs non-committally, so I place them all carefully in the cardboard box with a wry grin. Then I move my attention to pile after pile of vintage plates. White ones with that blue willow pattern on them.

'They were your nana's,' Mum says, fondly. 'Her pretend posh set. If you look closely, you'll see where the picture has slipped because it was a transfer not hand-painted.' I pick through a couple, finding some that are perfect and several that are fuzzy and misshapen. Which makes me like them all the more. 'They're all fakes. Your nana wanted the proper willow stuff but couldn't afford it, so bought these off Dronfield Market. She bloody loved 'em. Brought 'em out every Christmas.'

'Well, you can't get rid of these then.'

'What am I going to do with a thirty-two-piece fake willow dinner set?'

'Bring 'em out for Christmas!' There's a pause, then she gets up and heads out into the dining room and through to the lounge. 'Mum?' I call out after her but I can hear her, sniffling. 'Mum? What's the matter? Mum!' I take her in my arms, pulling her close. Her head barely reaches my chin and she feels tiny. Belly aside, there's not much of her any more. I don't think I'd realised, beneath the shoulder pads and bulky cardigans she wears, even though it's peak summer. 'Mum, come on, what's the matter?'

'What if I'm not here for Christmas, love? Eh? What if I'm already on borrowed time?'

'Mum! You can't think like that, not yet. Not now. We can't be defeated. Just because it's back, it's going to be fine. They're going to sort it. You've got bags of time yet! You can't go anywhere. We've got stuff to do. You've a bucket list that we've barely scratched the surface off.'

'I had lobster the other day.'

'Ooh, was it good?' We've both always wanted lobster.

'It was bloody gorgeous!'

'There you go. And there's still another fifty odd things to do yet. And you are definitely not going anywhere until we've been to Knowsley Safari. Leanne says she wants to take Harley and we can go through the monkey bit in her car, not mine. Not having them nimble-fingered little bleeders nick Petula's rubber beading.'

Mum laughs and sniffs at the same time and I realise how quickly the tide can turn. How this afternoon it was me, in Mitch's arms, desperate for reassurance. And here, now, it's Mum's turn. And for maybe the first time in our relationship, I've made it. I've done it. I am being the strength that she needs, when she needs it. Did Mitch help me get here? Is it because of him that I feel like I can finally do this? I can be the daughter she deserves. I can get my life together. And she's going to be fine, she just is. 'You're going to be alright you know, Mum. I promise.'

'You can't promise anything.'

'I can. And I am. So come on. Wipe your face. Stand as tall as your skinny legs will carry you. We have a cupboard to empty. We have fake blue willow to wash and dry and put back in the cupboard in time for our massive Christmas dinner. Okay?'

She nods.

'Okay.'

Chapter Thirty-One

The house is quiet. Mum's gone off to her Pilates class. To her real one, not the fake one she used to hide the fact she was at the doctors. She wasn't sure about going back but I think I managed to persuade her of the benefits. Not least the hour to herself without having to listen to me complain about work. Or lack thereof. Three clients I've got at the moment. Three clients who require a combination of typing work, a bit of social media updating, and one who thinks that the thirty pounds they pay me to trawl through their bank statements and tick off every direct debit payment they've received is both profitable and interesting. In fact, that particular job is the one I hate the most. When those statements come through, I sigh. Heavily. Because apparently switching it all to a spreadsheet to auto check in five minutes is not effective. Still. It's work. I am grateful, I am happy, I am at one with my life choices.

That's the new mantra Leanne suggested I repeat. She bought me rosary beads from the hippy place down the lanes in Meadowhall… the least hippy place on earth, but still. At least I can say yes, I've done it, to the text she's just sent me.

Have you done your mantra?

God, I love her.

'Yes, I've done my mantra,' I declare when she picks up my call. 'Have you done yours?'

'If only. Not had a chance to scratch my arse yet this morning. I've done four loads of washing; the house looks like a laundrette 'cos the line's already got the bed sheets on.'

'You wanna take the weight off your slingbacks, love. Shall I pop over this afternoon, give you some respite?'

'Obviously I'd love that but it's the annual water-birth baby gathering so I'll be out with Harley and Elsie all afternoon.'

'This is the one where you all had babies at the same time and are now inextricably linked for all eternity?'

'That's the one. Christ knows what we'll talk about. They're all very good mums who do not leave all the washing to the last minute and who probably still cook every meal their child eats from absolute scratch.'

'You don't need that kind of negativity in your life.'

'I know, right. One of them can't make it because she's skiing and I swear to God she offered her apologies by pointing out that it was essential her son learned to ski. We live in Dronfield. Sheffield ski slope's not even going any more. We're not living in Val d'Isère.'

'Nope.'

'Anyhow, that's not what I was ringing about. It's my great-aunty Vi's ninetieth this Saturday and it turns out they're having a big do up at the Miners Arms. Apparently someone told me but I forgot because of children and life, and do you wanna come?'

'Well, as inviting as you make the whole affair sound, whilst I'd love to because I adore Aunty Vi—'

'Who doesn't?'

'I'm supposed to be seeing Mitch.'

'Tell him you can't! Tell him this might be Aunty Vi's last and you're on duty with the open sandwiches.'

'If it's potted meat I am definitely not on open sandwich duty.' I recoil.

'Of course not. We've got cheese, ham, and egg mayo.'

'Eurgh. Egg mayo.'

'Worse, hot egg mayo. Hot egg mayo that's being kept at room temperature by the strip lighting in that function room.'

'Oh God. Don't.' I grimace. 'My twenty-first birthday party was in the Miners Arms function room. Half the party went off with food poisoning because Mum made the egg mayo sandwiches too early and it was July. And red hot. And nobody ate the egg mayo until they'd either drunk too much and didn't care or smoked too much and ate everything in reach.'

'Like you'd be able to remember anyone's twenty-first birthday party, least of all your own. Bets on you were three sheets to the wind before you even got there!'

'That may or may not be true, but I do remember snogging Tony Parker up against the fire doors.'

'Oh my God! I had forgotten about him! You were obsessed.'

'Nah, he was,' I chip back.

'Why don't you bring Mitch along? You know, if you can't live without him for a night.'

I give a sarcastic laugh. 'It's not that I can't live without him. It's just that he bought us tickets to see a show at the Lyceum on Saturday evening.'

'What show?'

'I've no idea. It's a surprise.'

'You hate surprises.'

'I know. Can't be ungrateful though, can I?' I was quite taken aback when he said he'd got the tickets. I've never said I like the theatre particularly; I mean, there's nothing wrong with it as such, I've just not had much experience of going. 'Do you have to dress up? For the Lyceum?'

'Well, I don't suppose you have to go full-on evening dress. No need to drag out the taffeta. Why don't you dress smart casual and swing by us first? The party starts at four. Bring your mum too, if she's up for it. Aunty Vi would love to see her, and I would too, for that matter.'

'I guess I could. Yeah, okay, let me check with Mitch and Mum, but I think that sounds like a plan. I'll text you to confirm. You know. For the buffet.'

'You're basically just coming for the buffet, aren't you?'

'Possibly.'

'Well, whatever your motivation, it'll be nice to have you there, and to see Mitch for that matter. I want to check out this person you seem to be spending so much time with. Make sure he's not still a weirdo.'

'He's not a weirdo!'

There's a pause and I can practically hear her working up to the stealth enquiries. She'll be acting nonchalant in the kitchen, pretending she's not about to sniper me with a question. 'So, is Saturday a date-date, or just another let's go out and chat and be mates date?'

'I don't know.'

'Oh, for God's sake, of course you know.' I imagine her dropping a hand on her hip in exasperation.

'I mean, I like him…'

'Like him how? Like, like ooh, what a lovely new friend, or like, like phwoar, I'd love to rip your pants off?'

Such a way with words. 'I don't know.' I laugh. 'It's hard to say. I like him, but I don't know that he's ready for anything new.'

'He was on Tinder, what more evidence do you need?'

'Seems to me, Tinder's just for hooking up. I've had more dick pics than I care to remember.'

'Show me!'

'I've deleted them!'

'Boring.' I roll my eyes, even though she can't see me. 'Alright, so you don't know what he wants, but what about you? What do you want?'

'I don't know. I'm trying not to be frightened because I like him, but I don't want to make another mistake.'

'Who says you will?' I think about the awkwardness that arose over the letter and how we had to sidestep that. 'Look, Jem, maybe swiping right was a metaphor – for you to start saying yes, and moving on with your life.'

'*You* swiped right!'

'Well, let's not overanalyse. Look, do you fancy him?'

I pause. Because whatever I say to this question will be brought up as evidence for all eternity. My God can she remember a fact. The thing is, I do fancy him. I really fancy him. He's hot and charismatic and really seems to get me. He makes me feel a bit fizzy inside when we talk, or meet up, or when he texts. But I've been in love with Ben for so long… even when I was screwing things up, I loved him.

'You've taken too long. Which means you totally do.'

'What science is that based on?'

'The science that says, I am your best friend and I can read you like the proverbial. You would like him to do rude things to your nethers and you are pretending that is not the case because you don't want me to know. Which, frankly, is offensive. I am your best friend. I can be trusted.'

'Didn't you once tell Victoria Williams that I loved her brother?'

'I was fifteen and you were drunk on Bacardi. Besides, we weren't really mate mates then. I would never... EVER... tell Victoria Williams anything any more.'

'That's because you don't like her.'

'Correct. She reads *Hello!* magazine without an ounce of irony.' We both laugh, but I still don't answer. 'Look. I'm not going to ask again. I shall simply scrutinise your body language when you turn up looking smoking hot for his benefit at Aunty Vi's do.'

'Okay. But whatever you think you do or do not see, say nothing. I like him. I don't want it to get all confused and messed up. I am a broken woman, Leanne. I do not need complication.'

'You are not broken. And complication or no, we all need a bit of sex. Love you, bye!'

She's gone, cackling, before I can counterclaim. God, she's infuriating.

Chapter Thirty-Two

'You nearly ready, Mum?' She's running late, having lounged in the bath with a book and The Beatles blaring out of her new, upstairs Echo Dot. Because why not have multiple Amazon smart devices dotted round the house, so they can cater to your every whim.

'I'm coming. Hang on, I'm coming. Alexa – stop!'

She clatters down the stairs, out of puff but beautifully made up. 'Mum, you look gorgeous.'

'This old thing?' she says, looking down at the navy-blue jersey dress, dolled up with a sequin bolero jacket and a touch of makeup on her cheeks. 'Thanks, love.'

'Come on.'

'Are you sure you don't mind me tagging along. I can get a cab, or I can drive myself.'

'Of course I don't mind.'

'Mitch?'

'He doesn't mind either. So long as you're okay getting home later?'

'Of course. What show are you seeing?'

'I still don't know. He won't tell me.' I checked online. There are two options, one is some kind of political drama type play with an incredible cast but it looks a bit dry, the other is some musical on a UK tour after a stint in the West End. I don't know if I'm up for either really. I always feel so out of place in the theatre. Never sure I entirely belong… or know what's actually going on. I blame a visit to see an operatic version of *Romeo and Juliet* with school. Shakespeare and Italian opera… I didn't have a clue!

Mum perches on the arm of the chair, watching out of the window for Mitch to arrive. 'I think that's lovely, that.'

'What?'

'That he's making it a surprise.'

'I hate surprises.'

'You hate not being in control.'

'That too.'

'Maybe it's time to relinquish a bit of that. Let someone do nice things for you. Let him spoil you a bit, you deserve it.'

'Do I?'

She shoots me a look. 'We all deserve nice things, Jem. You are not the exception. And look, don't worry if… you know…' She stares back out of the window again. 'If you decide to stay out…'

'Mum!'

'What? I'm just saying. I won't worry about you.'

'I'll be back tonight,' I say, pointedly, because she's been suggesting she'd be fine if I didn't come home since we indulged a mutual craving for eggs Benedict down at Lawries on the bottom road. The very idea of it was utterly preposterous until I went to get ready earlier on and her words leaked into my psyche and totally freaked me out. What if I do want to stay out? What if I do want to spend the night with him? We're just mates, aren't we? That's not even on the cards, is it? Does he like me like that? I can't tell. I'm out of touch. With me, with my feelings. With his…

Which is exactly what this neurosis became when I got dressed and could only find a fairly average pair of M&S pants and a bra that doesn't match. Which is why I will not be stopping out tonight. I've rushed into things so often before. I've not even thought about it beforehand, just done it and wondered afterwards if I even enjoyed it. I've not cared if my underwear was matching, but this time, this time, I think I do. I think… maybe I want it to be at the right time. In the right place. If anything is going to happen, it has to be different to the past. I will not mess things up by having casual sex in the back of his car with mismatched, ageing underwear.

'In you get, Mrs Whitfield,' says Mitch with a big grin on his face. 'Jem can go in the back, you get in the front next to me.' Mum giggles, obliging.

I open my door, ungainly clambering into the back seat owing to the heels I found at the back of the wardrobe. A pair I've not worn in years. Mitch gives them a wry look. 'I thought you didn't wear heels?'

'I don't,' I say. 'And that less than graceful arrival is why.'

'Go back and put your trainers on then, we've got time.'

'I will not put trainers on with this dress. It's vintage Biba from the second-hand shop. Vintage Biba and trainers equal no.'

'Whatever you say. Just don't come crying to me if you fall over and do yourself a mischief.' He winks at Mum.

The car reeks of flowers, a massive bouquet rests behind me on the parcel shelf. 'Good grief, have Interflora got anything left?'

'Haha, nope. Wiped them out of the lot. Let's hope Aunty Vi doesn't have allergies.'

'Ahhh, that's so sweet of you,' says Mum.

I nestle my clutch beside me, turning back to take a sniff of freesias and lilies and goodness knows what other flowers there are in there. I'm no horticulturist. 'You didn't have to do that.'

'I know I didn't. But it's always nice to bring a little something when you're gatecrashing a party.'

'You are not gatecrashing. You've been invited. You're my guest.' He nods, his eyes still focused on the road up ahead. 'And we're not stopping long anyway.'

'We can stay as long as you like.'

'What time does the show start?' asks Mum.

'Not 'til seven thirty. We've plenty of time. We can chat, you can have a drink, maybe even a dance.'

I shake my head. 'I don't do dancing.'

'Well you should,' he says, holding my gaze in the rear-view mirror. 'You look lovely, by the way.'

I smooth out my dress feeling noticed. Maybe he does like me.

Chapter Thirty-Three

I've barely taken a step inside the door when Leanne launches herself at me. 'Jem!' she says, squeezing me tight. 'You look amazing. Is this for Aunty Vi or the theatre?' she asks. 'The theatre…' she says again, as if by theatre, she means something else entirely.

'It's for *me*, actually,' I say, squeezing her back. 'I dress for me.'

'Sure thing. 'Course you do.'

I poke her in her side, right where she's most ticklish, and she jerks out of my grip with a giggle. 'Oi, you! Touchy!'

'Is Andy here? I've not seen him for months.'

Leanne rolls her eyes. 'No, Elsie Alice's temperature sky-rocketed this afternoon, so he offered to stay home with her. Any excuse to avoid a family gathering, he's probably got his slippered feet up in front of some rugby replay, wine open, Calpol on standby.'

'Ahh, is she okay though?'

'She's fine. And I'm just jealous. I'd forgotten how much I hate leaving the house of an evening. I could be in my pyjamas right now, you know.' She adjusts her dress with a grimace.

'Come on then, where is she?' I glance around the sea of people to try and spot Great-Aunty Vi.

'She's propped up in a corner with a ginger wine and some beef crisps until the buffet comes out.'

'Standard.'

Mitch, having taken Mum to hang her coat up, has now arrived beside me. 'Mitch! Oh my God, how long has it been?'

She flings her arms around him and I can just about see him smile at me, between the flowers, over her shoulder. 'Oh, I don't know. Barely any time at all, looking at you!'

'Don't be fooled. I've got a bulldog clip at the back of my head,' she jokes, sucking in her cheeks, making her face look thinner and younger.

'You're kidding. You've probably just got one of those ageing paintings in your attic.' Leanne raises her eyebrows at me, clearly enjoying the flattery. 'Now, is there anywhere I can put these?' He extricates himself from her, holding up the flowers. 'Just a small token for… Vi, is it? Aunty Vi?'

'Great-Aunty, yes. Ahhh, thank you.' Leanne sniffs at them. 'God, she'll be delighted. They're gorgeous. I was just saying to Jem, she's over there. She'll be thrilled to see you both.'

'Great. Come on then, Jem.'

'Yes. Coming.'

'A joint gift, is it?' says Leanne, as Mitch leads me off to deliver the flowers. I give her a good-natured glare and she winks in response before greeting Mum with just as much excitement as she did Mitch and I, dragging her over to see Harley who is knee sliding across the dance floor.

Aunty Vi spots me coming through the crowd and necks her ginger wine before unsteadily standing to give me the kind of hug she's always given me. One of those nana hugs where you're completely consumed by their love and the not-so-gentle aroma of Lily of the Valley. 'Jem, love, you look gorgeous. How are you?'

'I'm really good thanks, Aunty Vi. Happy birthday.'

'Oh, thank you. I didn't want any fuss.' That will definitely be a lie. 'But you know what this lot are like, any excuse for a party.' Leanne's family hate a party. They have always had them because Aunty Vi insists on family gatherings. 'Still, I'll manage. You know.'

'Of course. You're a trooper. So, this is Mitch.'

'Mitch, hello. Gosh, you're handsome. Tell me you're finally going to get our Jem to settle down, she really needs a good man and you look like a good man.'

Mitch laughs. 'Only the best for Jem, eh?'

'We're just friends, Aunty Vi,' I steam in, possibly a little overzealously.

He looks at me, head cocked slightly to one side. 'Yes. Friends.'

'I've heard about you young people and your friends,' she says, winking. 'Friends with extras, is it?'

'Benefits,' says some woman sat beside her who I've never seen before.

'No benefits round here, more's the pity.' He winks and I flush. 'We've only just met up again, knew each other back at school. We're just… getting to know each other, isn't that right, Jem?'

I nod, shyly. Confused because he wanted to be single the other day and now we're getting to know one another. Am I misreading signals?

Aunty Vi eyes up the flowers. 'Are those for me?'

He laughs good-naturedly. 'They are for you. Happy birthday!'

'Oh, you shouldn't have.' She pulls him in for a big hug, planting what looks distinctly like a classic wet kiss on his cheek, letting the woman beside her take the flowers to put them somewhere in water.

'You look like you might need a drink, too.' He nods to her empty glass. 'What you on?'

'Oooh, I like this one, Jem!' she whoops. 'Ginger wine and it'll all be fine,' she says, dropping back into her seat and nudging the woman sat on the other side of her.

'Coming up.'

I follow him to the bar. 'Good lord, you never told me I was going to be eyed up by the octogenarian.'

'Eh, she's ninety now!'

'A noctogenarian. Is that the right word?'

'No idea.'

'Me neither.' He laughs. 'Is she always like that?'

'Pretty much. Hey, let me get these drinks.'

'Put your money away.'

'You bought flowers. And the show tickets.'

He turns to face me. 'So?'

'Well… I just…'

'You don't need to spend your money. Christ, it's not like you've got much, is it?'

He laughs and I'm sure it wasn't meant to sound harsh, but it bruises a little. I'm probably being hormonal. Oversensitive. After all, the more I look at the state of my 'business', the more I wonder what the hell I'm playing at.

'What you having?'

'Vodka and Coke, please.'

'Two vodka and Cokes and a ginger wine, please,' he asks, then turns to me and strokes my arm, just gently, for a second. 'You really do look lovely.'

'Even though I can't walk in these shoes?'

'Even though you can't walk in those shoes.' He hands me my drink and the first sip seeps straight into my veins, making every ounce of nervous energy leak out of my bones. 'You'll just have to hold on to me, won't you. Wait there, let me take this over to Vi.'

I watch him nip through the dance floor, occupied by a few girls spinning to the music, delighting in their skirts as they poof out with the energy of their twirls. Some of the younger kids, including Harley, are entranced by a decidedly sweaty entertainer who's twisting a pink balloon into something concerningly phallic. Mitch delivers the wine, chats a little more with the women at the table, making them all laugh.

Leanne sidles in behind me. 'He's very charming, isn't he?'

'I guess so.'

'Smooth.'

'Mmmhhh.'

'I can see you watching him.'

'Shut your face.' I spin round.

She holds her hands up. 'Just saying. I notice things… you like him. So I'll be watching him too, he's got to measure up to get your loving.'

'I'm in charge of who gets my loving, thank you very much.' She sticks her tongue in the side of her cheek and I push her away before Mitch gets back.

Chapter Thirty-Four

Two and a half hours and numerous drinks later, I'm sat at a table in the corner of a room, two vodkas lined up and a plate of buffet food in front of me. I love a buffet. All those tiny sausage rolls and bowl after bowl of crisps. I can lose myself in a buffet, I've always found that. If I'm ever at a party with a trestle table covered in a tablecloth and be-doilied plates, you can guarantee I will have truffle-pigged my way through every one to load up a plate of delights. They should offer a buffet on the NHS. It'd save them a fortune on antidepressants.

'You want more?' Mitch asks, finishing the last slice of miniature pizza on his plate.

'Shouldn't we be going?' I ask, lovingly gazing at a prawn vol-au-vent before shoving it in my face.

'What? Drag you away from your friends and the bar and all that lovely food up there. I'm sure I've just seen tiny Cornish pasties arrive.'

'Won't be as good as a real one but I'd be happy to give them a go. What time is it though, half six? We'll be late.'

I'm suddenly assaulted by a small person with a vice-like grip and a snotty nose. 'Aunty Jem,' comes a small voice and I know it's my godson.

'Hey, Harley Farley Chocolate Barley, how are you? Have you been watching the magician?' He holds up a bag of Haribo sweets and I try and snatch it from him.

'No! They're mine.' I pick him up and blow a raspberry on his belly 'til he calls out for mercy. 'Oh, alright, you can keep them. Hey, Harley, this is my friend Mitch. Mitch, this is my brilliant godson.'

Harley smiles widely, and my heart melts. As far as kids go, he is one of the coolest. 'We're gonna have to go soon,' I say, offering him a crisp.

'Why?'

'We're going out. To the theatre. You know where we went to see Peppa Pig?'

'We don't have to go,' says Mitch. He puts his hand on mine. 'In fact, let's stay. You're having a nice time, aren't you?'

'Of course I am.'

He squeezes my hand then takes it away. 'So then. Let's stay. Maybe you and Harley can have a dance, we can both get more buffet and you can carry on with the vodka.'

'But what about your car?'

'I'm happy to drive. Look' – he checks over his shoulder, lowering his voice – 'I know you're not wanting to dwell on anything, but I also know how hard things are with your mum.'

I glance up at her, unsteadily dancing with one of the kids. Something has made her laugh and she's coughing. I don't like the coughing.

'I've been there, remember. What I wouldn't have given for times like this. A family party with seemingly unlimited buffet and a cheap bar and your best mate and her boy around you.' Harley puts on his best, most sweetest grin and I feel like they're tag teaming me. 'You can't disappoint this one, now can you?'

Mum bids the little girl farewell, tottering back over to a table with some of her friends. Mitch winks at me, warmly. 'Okay, okay. Yes, it's nice to be here. Yes, it would be lovely to stay. Are you sure you don't mind?'

He fixes me with a look. 'I'm certain. Certainly certain.'

'Oh! I love this song!' Harley jumps off my knee and grabs my hand over to the dance floor.

'Thank you,' I say to Mitch, taking a swig of my vodka.

As I'm pulled past Leanne, she grabs hold of my hand. 'I can see you…' she says, pointing two fingers to her eyes, then at me, '… and him…' She waves at Mitch who waves back. 'You'll be shagging by Tuesday,' she predicts with a belly laugh before 'twerking' her way off the dance floor like only a hurtling-towards-middle-aged mum ever could.

Chapter Thirty-Five

'Your mum looks tired,' Mitch says, coming back from the bar with another drink. I've collapsed into the rough velour of a bar seat, exhausted from all the dancing. Which is exactly why I don't dance. 'I think I'll see if she wants a lift home.' He goes over to talk to her.

Two minutes later, he's back. 'She says she's had enough. You stay here, I'll get her coat and drop her home. I'll be back in twenty minutes.'

'No, no. I'll come. It's fine.'

'Stay. Honestly. Let me get her home, then maybe I'll drop my car back and jog over.' He leans into me. His breath heavy on my cheek. 'Watching you with all that vodka, doing all that dancing. You've rather whet my appetite. Maybe we could throw some of our own shapes.'

'Throw some shapes? A rave just called. It wants your big box, little box back.' I wink. 'And like I told you, contrary to this evening's display, I don't usually dance.'

'Clearly.'

I wipe my brow, probably taking my eyebrows off.

'Look, I'll take your mum, then I'll be back. Don't go anywhere. Maybe rest a while. Save some energy for me.'

He disappears into the crowd, taking Mum by the arm as he goes. I watch until I can't see him any more and wonder if it's vodka making me want to feel closer to him, or just because he is being so nice. So kind. Those flowers, they were such a lovely thought. And now, taking Mum back because he can see she's tired, it's so sweet. So attentive. And I've never let anyone be like that before. Ben tried, for so long, and I always ignored it. Disrespected it even. Maybe this is my second chance. Maybe I could get it right this time. I could appreciate someone giving a damn. Maybe I'm in a better place to respect it. I am over making mistakes. And… I've learned my lesson. If there is anything I can take from what happened with Ben, it's that I can't keep disrespecting myself and others the way I have for so long.

I do a bit more dancing with Harley before my neckline feels like I've been jiving in a sauna and cool air is needed. 'I'm just nipping outside,' I say to Leanne, picking my drink up on the way past. She gives me a nod, having just danced so hard to the Spice Girls that she put her back out on the dance floor and can't properly move.

I flop against the wall outside the pub, taking a lungful of August night air. Eyes closed, I imagine what it might be like to be leant against a wall outside a Cornish pub, the air being so different to here. There's a faint smell of the bins in this part of the car park and not a note of seaweed. Instead of a seagull, two magpies fly above. One for sorrow, two for joy? I salute them, as I always do, before necking the rest of my drink.

'Still on the sauce then?' comes a voice. I turn to face the person who has just interrupted my attempt at a Cornish daydream to be met with a look of pure hatred from Ben's best mate, George Newman.

'George.'

'I'd have thought you'd have stopped by now,' he sneers. 'You know, what with all the trouble it gets you in.'

'What are you talking about?'

'Well, I reckon Ben'd still be here if you could have put him before your love of anything that numbs your self-induced pain.'

'Excuse me?'

'You. Drink. It makes you do bad things. Like come on to people you're not supposed to because your boyfriend had a moment's clarity and tried to leave you.'

'That was not my fault, at least, it wasn't just me. It takes two…' I run out of steam because I know he's right. However much I hate the fact. I did come on to him. I was drunk at the time. Ben and me falling out was never a good enough excuse and that's why I wanted to own kissing George in the letter. Own it in real life. I just don't want to own it in front of him when he stands here being all pompous and superior.

'Yeah, you can't justify it, can you? *Sometimes* it takes two, *sometimes* though, it just takes one. One drunken, stupid girl who thinks she can get away with it and only did because I was not about to tell him and hurt him the way you had. Thank God he finally saw you for what you really are. What was it that finished him off in the end? He never would tell me.'

I fold my arms, tightly, partly to try and stop my heart from leaping out of my rib cage. 'There are lots of reasons a relationship breaks down and I don't have to talk about any of them with you.' My heart now clatters in my chest. I feel sick. A taxi pulls into the car park forcing George to step aside. 'Who even are you to come up to me and say these things anyway?'

'Your ex-boyfriend's best mate. The one who would pick up the pieces every time you were a dick.'

Mitch gets out of the cab, peering at me suspiciously. I try and force a smile but he throws cash at the driver then slams the door shut as George takes a step closer to me, leering. 'You know, you're a waste of space, Jem Whitfield. I always thought it and I was so glad when Ben finally caught up. But because of you, my best mate now lives hundreds of miles away. That's how far he had to go to escape you. That's how awful you are.'

'Woah, hang on a minute, mate.' Mitch has forced his way between George and I, and there's something comforting about the sight of his broad back and his chest, puffing up in defence of my honour. 'Do you wanna carry on talking?'

George puffs up in response, taking a step towards Mitch, and realising what was initially comforting could turn into something entirely stressful and inappropriate at Aunty Vi's birthday party, I jump in between them. 'Just leave it,' I say, over my shoulder to Mitch. 'He's angry. It's fine.'

'Doesn't give him the right to talk to you like that,' spits Mitch.

'Nice, Jem. You got yourself a new sucker to—' but before he can finish his sentence, Mitch has pinned him up against the wall by the scruff of his neck and I'm pulling at his hands to try and free him.

'Get off him, Mitch, please!'

The men stare at each other, testosterone apparently burning through their veins.

'Please, leave him alone. For me.'

Mitch lets go of George's shirt with a final shove against the wall. George readjusts his clothes, smoothes his hair down and slopes off up the steps into the pub.

'Are you okay?' Mitch asks, turning to face me, taking me by my shoulders. 'Did he touch you?'

'No, he didn't touch me! Christ, Mitch. I can handle George Newman.'

'I'm sure you can, but you don't have to. I'm here.'

I adjust the straps on my dress, frustrated and embarrassed. 'I don't need you fighting my battles. I made my bed. I can lie in it.'

'I can't help it if I don't appreciate people I care about being spoken to like that, can I?'

He sounds like an injured bird. Unappreciated. We pause. Staring at one another. He's not quite so puffed up as he was. I should be grateful.

'I need a drink,' I say, going back inside.

Mitch catches my arm. 'Hey, I'm sorry. If I got that wrong, I'm sorry. I was just trying to defend you. You're vulnerable. I can see that.'

'I'm fine.' He lets go, his eyes drop to the floor and I immediately regret being so defensive. 'Hey, look, sorry. I'm sorry, I appreciate it.' I search out eye contact. 'I appreciate you.' Tentatively, I reach for his hand, he doesn't resist. Through the window behind him I see Leanne has noticed something's gone off. I wonder how long she was watching. 'Come on.' I lead him into the pub behind me, our hands clasped together, and we don't let go until we're through the pub and I free mine to open the door of the function room, painting a smile on.

Chapter Thirty-Six

Two hours, many drinks and a lot of dancing later (because apparently, now, I *do* in fact dance), I think Mitch and I are back on an even keel. The last orders bell sounds and I fetch my purse. Leanne texts Andy to check up on Elsie whilst stroking Harley's head as he sleeps on the bench beside her. She adjusts her boobs and I know they'll be straining under the pressure of not having fed for a few hours, probably made worse by wondering if Elsie is okay. It reminds me how selfless you have to be to have babies and I wonder if mothers are born that way or if they learn it?

I need another drink.

'Last orders?' I shout to them, straining to be heard over music that has now got quite a bit louder and I don't know how Harley can sleep through Taylor Swift or Katy Perry or whichever American pop singer is being played on full volume. Mitch and Leanne shake their heads.

'Two vodka and Cokes, please,' I say, swaying sweatily into the bar. I can't remember the last time I had such a full-on night. I don't remember ever dancing as much, for so long, even back in the day when me and Leanne would go into Sheffield and dance the night away in Kingdom or Republic or, if it was student night, despite neither of us being students, The Leadmill. With the exception of Kate the other day, I can't remember the last time someone made me feel as small as George did earlier, yet as tall as Mitch makes me feel now. What a combination. It's like someone just put me in a box and nailed the lid down just as I've rediscovered freedom and music. I am not that person. Not any more. George can think what he likes but I've changed. I'm changing. There's no beauty in perfection. If I was that bad, Mitch wouldn't like me, would he? And he does, I'm sure he does. I feel it. I see it when he looks at me. And it terrifies me but excites me, too. When did I last feel that?

Drinks in hand, I stumble over to Mitch and Leanne. Mitch places his hand on the small of my back. 'Steady on.'

'Blimey, I'm jiggered,' I say, necking the first vodka to quench my dance-floor induced thirst.

'For someone who doesn't dance, you have got some moves, Calamity Jem.'

'Calamity?' asks Leanne, dropping her phone into her bag.

Mitch laughs. 'You must have noticed, there's always some kind of something following her.' Leanne cocks her head, agreeing though not entirely enthusiastically.

I give my (sweaty) hair a flick. 'I guess you've either got it—'

'Or you've had enough drink to make you think that you've got it,' chips in Mitch, before he falls about laughing.

'And that there is why I don't dance!'

He pleads he's just joking, pulling me towards him by my hips.

'I saw you watching as I taught that teenager how to do the running man. Jealousy is an ugly trait, my friend.'

Leanne narrows then rolls her eyes. 'I should get him home,' she says, gently, stroking blond hair from Harley's forehead. 'Daddy's back off to work tomorrow afternoon, so it'd be nice for Harley to be awake enough to spend the morning with him. He's danced his socks off, little thing.' She gazes at him, so full of love for her small person and once again I'm forced to wonder what it's like to love someone so completely, so unconditionally. The idea terrifies me.

'You want me to call us a cab?' asks Mitch, standing. He looks tall, tired, gentle.

'I think I'd like to walk.'

'Okay. We can walk.'

'You don't have to come with me, I'll be fine on my own.'

'Let you weave your way home on your own after the skinful you've had? Not likely.'

'I'm fine!' I plead, losing balance on the chair as I reach down for my handbag.

'I can see that,' says Mitch, shaking his head at me with a smile.

Leanne feeds her arms into her cardy, gathering her bag. 'Go on, let him walk you. Me and H are getting a cab, you can't go off on your own.'

'And I don't mind,' Mitch says, standing. 'I quite like a late-night wander through the streets.'

'Weirdo!' I say, knocking back the last of my final vodka and catching Leanne's watchful eye.

'Shut your face, you.'

'Oi! Don't you start! Or I'll give you a bit of George treatment.'

'What? You're gonna pin me up against a wall?' There's a beat between us, my heart rate quickens.

'Well, I don't know what you two "friends" are talking about, all this up against a wall business, but I think I'll leave you to it.' She pulls me into a hug though I'm still staring at Mitch. 'Aunty Vi had a bloody lovely time, thanks for coming.'

'Wouldn't have missed it for the world,' I say into her hair.

'Thanks for coming, Mitch.'

'My pleasure, it was nice to be able to bring Jem and her mum.'

'Yeah. Lovely of you. Thank you.' She turns back to face me. 'When do you take your mum to Basingstoke?'

'Tuesday.'

'Will I see you before you go?'

'Not sure, I'll try. I need to do a few bits of work before I go, make sure I don't get behind.'

'Okay, I'll probably talk to you tomorrow at some point anyway. Come on, Harley, come on, sleepyhead, time to go.' He rubs at his eyes, barely able to open them. 'Ahhh, so sleepy! Come on, baby, you just need to walk to the cab. Just outside.'

Mitch stands. 'Come on, little man, climb on. Let me give you a piggyback.' Harley does exactly as instructed and my heart is warmed by the sight of Mitch being so lovely and borderline dad-like.

Chapter Thirty-Seven

Half an hour later and we're slowly wandering up the hill back to mine. The moon is full, casting a pool of blue-white glow before us. 'Gosh, it's beautiful, isn't it?' I pause by the gate to the park, the sky full of stars.

'It is,' Mitch says, leaning against the stone wall. But he's not looking at the stars. And I daren't look at him because I think my lady parts might explode. Which may not sound very sexy, but let me tell you, the walk and the chat and the watching-him-with-Harley and the smell of him (Goddamit Kouros and your teenage hormone-inducing scent), it's all got a bit much. 'I had fun tonight.'

'Did you?' I've just applied a coquettish tone to my voice because I am an obvious idiot fuelled by vodka, should I stop myself? I mean... I know what I want. 'I'm sorry about the George stuff. And us missing the theatre.' I move in between the gate entrance, closer to him, our groins probably only centimetres apart. If Leanne could see us, she'd be judging with her eyebrows.

'Hey, it's fine. It's forgotten. And you were having a good time. I was hardly going to drag you away from that, was I?'

'I know but—'

He takes my hand, just briefly, squeezing my fingers. 'Honestly, it's fine.'

Electricity surges through my body. Out of the corner of my eye I see a shooting star and take that as a sign that now is the perfect time to lean in and kiss him because it's hot, and I'm a bit drunk, and I realise I like him. I really do like him. And I fancy him, too. I fancy him a lot. So I kiss him. Full force. My breath heavy, my hands reaching inside his shirt to realise he is significantly more ripped than his wardrobe would ever let on, and Jesus, I am so hot for him right now.

'Hey, hey…' he says, catching the words between my kisses.

'Come back to mine. I need you, I just…' I kiss him again, and at first I think he's kissing me back but then he stops and he takes my hands, which are now realising how incredibly perfect his bum is. Like, tight and taut and fuck me… Actually, fuc—

'You're drunk.'

'I am.' I lean in again.

'So, we shouldn't…' He pulls back, out of my reach, flexing his jawline in a way that makes me want him even more.

'I'm fine though, I know what I'm doing.' I really know what I'm doing and now I'd like to show him.

'Not like this, I'm not sure…' He links his fingers through mine, holding my hands to his (incredibly well-defined) chest. 'I like you.' He lets out a low growl, looking up at the sky, which is quite a sexy thing to do under the circumstances. 'But, we shouldn't. I can't.'

'Right.' And just like that I wonder if I could die of unfulfilled lust combined with acute embarrassment. 'Sorry… I just… sorry.'

'It's fine. I'm sorry, God, I'm sorry.'

I start walking across the field wishing I hadn't made that choice because the moon's gone behind some clouds and I can't see (to avoid) the dog poo that's bound to be all over the grass, but obviously I can't turn back and go round the path because that's like leaving a room in a huff then having to go back for your coat.

'Jem!' he calls after me. 'Please...' He catches me up, taking hold of my hand, spinning me to face him. We look at each other as the moon comes back out of the cloud and the fact this will be giving me an attractive Insta style filter on what is undoubtedly a slightly drunken, too much dancing, rejected face, does not go unnoticed. His eyes flick from mine to my lips, then back to my eyes. Slowly, he leans into me, this time not taking his eyes off mine. Our lips brush and touch and I inadvertently let out one of those movie sighs before realising he is just giving me a peck. And now he's leading me through the park in the direction of my house. And I don't think we're going to have sex tonight after all. 'I like you, Jem,' he says, as we reach the bottom of my drive. Mum's drive. Whichever. 'I really like you. But this... like this... it's not right.' He leans in again, brushing my lips with his, again, before planting a gentle kiss just to the side of my mouth in possibly the hottest non-kiss I've ever actually had. And that includes those times I was perving over Ben when he was in the shower and I was in his bed, reliving what we'd just done.

God. Ben.

Ben.

'I'll call you tomorrow,' says Mitch, turning to walk back in the direction we just came.

Hot. Confused and suddenly, very, very drunk, I lock the door behind me and stumble up to bed.

Chapter Thirty-Eight

'Is this everything?' I hulk Mum's massive bag into my boot.

'I think so, love.' She's fussing about at the bottom of the staircase, fiddling with curtains and shuffling bits of scrap paper that sit beside the house phone.

'Are you sure?' I peer into the boot, wondering if I can just about manage to squeeze my tote bag with a pair of pants, a T-shirt and my toothbrush rammed into it. 'It's just that I don't think you remembered the kitchen sink?'

She puts her hands on her tiny hips. 'You never know what you might need.'

I peer at the collection of bags, noticing the one she carries her curling tongs in.

'Planning on a night out?'

Mum rolls her eyes at me, heading into the lounge for a sweep look around. I follow her, shoving my tote bag on my shoulder, remembering to dash into the kitchen to get my phone charger just as it rings. I cancel Mitch's call. As I have done each time he's tried calling since he walked away the other night.

'Get that if you need to, love?'

'No, it's fine. They'll leave a message if it's important.'

'Right,' she says, nipping into the downstairs loo for what must be the tenth or eleventh time since I said we should make a move, about an hour ago.

My phone dings out a text.

Hope the journey isn't too bad. Call me if you need anything. X

I hover over what to say in response but he texts again.

I miss the sound of your voice. Xxx

He misses my voice. I keep avoiding talking to him because I'm embarrassed, confused even. Does he like me? Was he being polite? *I miss the sound of your voice* though, I mean, you don't just say that to anyone. I wouldn't say it to Leanne. I might say I miss her face. I do if I don't see her for a few days. Or like that time when she moved to Bath and I barely saw her at all. I missed her face a lot then. But her voice? That's… too intimate. Maybe I didn't make a total tit of myself. I mean, sure, I made something of a tit, let's say seventy per cent tit. But if he can text that, he can't think I'm one hundred per cent, can he? I just wish I knew what to say. I've answered his texts. The one the next morning after I ignored his call to check I was okay, where I told him I was totally fine, just swamped with cooking dinner for Mum and some of her friends. It wasn't a lie – I was cooking dinner. I just could probably have talked to him as the roast potatoes parboiled. Or while the gravy simmered. And I could certainly have spoken to him when they'd all gone and Mum and I were watching *Antiques Roadshow*; there wasn't even any decent jewellery on it.

Then the next day, when he called again, and I clicked it silent before messaging that a big project had come in. I scrolled Amazon Music, making the playlist for today's journey with Mum instead. I then answered his text later that day, because he had directly asked me if I was ignoring him. I said *No, of course not, why would I ever?* It was just that I'd been in a meeting with a potential new client (wow, business was really taking off!), then I was having an early night ahead of this morning. Again, I didn't lie, I was in bed by half past eight. Except that was mainly so I could binge watch *Killing Eve*. But the truth is I still cringe every time I think of how bloody blatant I was at the park gate.

Though I miss his voice too.

'Right, come on then? We're not going to get there hanging around here all morning. There you go.' Mum passes me a leopard-print scarf, before running an identical one around her neck, then her hair, then her neck again, expertly tucking it in until she looks like a movie star.

'What are you doing?'

'I'm doing what you said. I'm Louise, you're Thelma.'

'What?' Mum spins me around, scooping my hair into the scarf, whipping it round the same as hers. 'Mum?'

'Thelma and Louise. I know this is different. I mean, you're not exactly meek, and we haven't killed a man, but to hell with it,' she says, which is shocking because Mum never swears. 'Let's road trip the crap out of this journey. You got the playlist?'

'I have.'

'The Wanted?'

'No.'

'But Little Mix?'

'I'm afraid so.'

'Then come on, get these sunglasses on.'

'But Petula doesn't have a soft top.'

'Open the sunroof! Let's cruise to Basingstoke.'

'It's not quite the Grand Canyon…'

'We're not quite Susan Sarandon and Geena Davis.'

She's right. Nobody has ever mistaken me for either of those two women. I take a look at myself in the mirror, cats-eye glasses were never really my thing.

Mum climbs into the car. I take my phone out, tapping a message to Mitch, *I'll call you later* then join her.

Chapter Thirty-Nine

The road trip was less *Thelma and Louise* and more silent movie as, by the time we'd got on to the M1, after indulging in a drive-through Starbucks, Mum was silently staring out of the window, hands gripped tightly round her skinny Frappuccino. I told her to go full fat. The nurses at Basingstoke had all said, go full fat the last time we were there. Something about replacing the lost energy with sugars to keep her going. She even turned down a Cherry Bakewell.

In fact, the first thing to lift her mood was arriving at the hospital to realise that they'd assigned her to one of the rooms normally reserved for private patients and she was delighted at the prospect of an en suite on the NHS.

I was, as Sue promised, assigned the same room I'd stayed in before, which I know was supposed to be a gesture of care and familiarity *'at this difficult time'*, but walking over from the hospital to the relative apartments brought back all the sick feeling and darkness from when we were here before. When I'd whiled away her eight-hour operation by shopping for dungarees I'd always wanted and an upgrade to my mobile phone.

I'd been feeling pretty depressed about it all, treating myself to some retail therapy whilst my heart basically went on pause until I knew she'd made it through. Four and half hours in, I got a phone call from her consultant explaining that they'd done the major part of the op. That they'd not been able to get all the cancer and that they'd had to fit her with a stoma. I joked that she'd be furious and would definitely want her money back, which I mainly said because the relief she was still alive made me want to cry and I was not about to do that in a Basingstoke shopping centre.

I was optimistic at best. As soon as Mr Faux hung up, I fought through a student invasion of Primark's casual-wear department so I could at the very least cry on a bench in the mall. And that's what I did. Slumped in a leatherette sofa by a pop-up donut stand; stunned, exhausted and relieved… until I realised the music tannoy was playing 'Everybody Hurts' by R.E.M. and I felt like I was in a Richard Curtis romcom, so laughed at the ridiculousness of it all, then ate five donuts for a pound.

No time for retail therapy this visit.

Which is good. I've no cash. Not only is business not booming, as Mitch no doubt now mistakenly thinks, business is on its arse since one of my clients has taken her work back because her daughter *wants a part-time job and this'll be perfect.* So I'm now down to two clients. One of which being the one with those blessed bank statements that need to be digitised. And the other on shaky ground after the husband of the husband-and-wife business team suggested he and I went out for a drink. Once upon a time, I might have gone because I had no moral compass. But this time I picked my phone up to tell Mitch, before remembering I was avoiding him. Which also reminds me that he texted again.

Don't want to call, in case you're busy with your mum. But just wanted you to know I'm thinking of you. X

I tap out a thank you and drop my phone in my bag. I need to focus. If only to stop me calling and asking him to come down and stay in the accommodation with me.

'Right, Mum,' I say, having dropped my bags off in my room and picked up a bacon, lettuce and tomato sandwich from the café. 'What's the plan?' Mum had unpacked her bag into the patient station beside her bed. Three books sit on a to-be-read pile on the chair beside her. 'How long are we going to be here for?' I ask, flicking through them as Mum surveys the hospital TV channels.

'Well, hopefully only tonight but you never know, and I wouldn't want to get bored.'

'No, well, that's fair enough.'

'I can leave whatever I don't read,' she says, landing on an old episode of *Escape to the Country* and I know for a fact I'll be taking these to the communal coffee table cum patient library before we leave tomorrow.

'I'd love to live in the country,' she says as the presenter guides some house buyers through a Cotswold stone cottage in Castle Combe.

'Bit of a stretch for the bucket list, that one,' I say, reading the blurb on a Jackie Collins and wondering if Kate's book group have read it. 'Mind you, if we win the lottery, we can always do it then.'

'Oh, I must put it on for this week—' but the door swings open before she can finish her sentence and in walks Mr Faux.

'Mrs Whitfield.' His coat billows, his entourage hover behind him. 'I'm sorry we have to see you again so soon.' He perches on the side of Mum's bed and she shuffles to one side for him, fixing her hair and smile. The effort, however, sets her cough off, which is probably not the look she was going for. Mr Faux waits patiently, watching her, until she's popped a Halls Mentho-lyptus lozenge, which somehow, as usual, lets her breathe. She needs to survive just to keep Halls in business.

'That cough's pretty bad,' he says, when she's finished.

'This? Oh, no. It's fine. I had a cheese sandwich. Cheese always sets me off.' She waves a tiny hand dismissively. I don't remember the cheese sandwich.

'She does cough a lot,' I chip in, because she's a bugger for playing everything down. 'It's definitely got worse.'

Mr Faux nods, saying something I don't understand to one of the women stood beside him. She makes a note in Mum's paperwork.

'So, your doctor thinks the symptoms have returned quite aggressively then.' Mum nods and I stare at her because she never used the word aggressive with me and what does that even mean? 'As we said before we did the debulking, your tumour markers are high. We anticipated that, whilst the disease ordinarily tends to be slow growing, it's possible yours wouldn't behave that way.'

'What does that actually mean?' I ask, immediately wishing I hadn't because what if Mum doesn't want to know. She's staring at Mr Faux.

'It means that we need to do various scans and tests to establish what is actually happening before we can determine our next course of action. It means that...' he takes a breath and I automatically brace myself against the high backed, NHS chair I'm wedged into '... it might be that there *is* no next course of action in terms of treatment or surgery. I am sorry but if the tests tell us what I think they will, then we may need to prepare for the likelihood that we're looking at a care package for your symptom management.'

Shit.

His words hang heavy in the room. His entourage look poker-faced. He focuses wholly and entirely on Mum and I'm not sure if it's Mr Faux in particular or just consultant surgeons in general, but they're so perfunctory when delivering facts that take your breath away and I can't process it. I don't understand. This isn't what we came here for. This isn't the news we were waiting on. She's going to be okay. I promised her.

Mum fiddles with a bit of tissue she's pulled out of her sleeve. Her hands visibly shake.

'If you can't do anything, how long have I got?' she asks eventually, sitting up tall like she did the other day, and I now realise that's her brave position. The one she adopts when she's fixing her face to give or receive information that she or someone else isn't going to like.

He pauses. For a discouraging length of time. 'We can't say. Yours looks to be a particularly special case.'

'You mean she's being awkward?' I laugh, trying to keep things light, which under the circumstances is messed up and I can't believe I'm making jokes.

Mr Faux smiles. 'Humour is good. You need to keep your sense of humour.'

'Oh' – Mum looks from him to tissue to me – 'we can manage that, can't we, love?' And I can tell by the pitch of her voice that she's not as calm as she wants me to believe. I want to tell her she doesn't have to be calm, or brave, or any of the other things she's digging deep for, and yet I don't want her to be anything else because if she loses it, I'm going to, too.

'We can always manage humour. It's our default. If you can't laugh you've got…' I can't finish the sentence because nothing is what I'll have when she's gone.

'So.' She shoves the tissue back up her sleeve and clasps her hands. 'Is it years? Months?' She swallows. 'Less?'

Mr Faux moves up the bed slightly. He takes Mum's hand. 'At this point, it's incredibly difficult to be accurate, Mrs Whitfield.'

'Oh, come on now, please, call me Val.'

He pats her hand. 'Let's do some tests, let's try and mark the regrowth, let's talk after that.' Then he stands with a sharp intake of breath that puts an underline on the prognosis chat. 'Okay, let me have a quick look at your belly, then Dr Wilkinson here will start the tests and by tomorrow morning we should have a better sense of where we're at. We appreciate you coming in. Each time this disease acts differently, we can better understand it. You're really helping our research.'

'Well, that's good, isn't it, Jem? We might as well be useful as we're here. What with this en suite room and all you people's time. Got to pay our way, eh, love?' She shuffles down the bed so Mr Faux can do what he needs to and I get up, staring out of the window into a courtyard below because I can't quite get my head around what just happened and I don't want her to see the fight I've got going on with my tear ducts, and I suppose I want her to retain whatever modesty she has left.

A pigeon pecks at crumbs it's found beside a bench. I focus on its efforts, allowing my life to momentarily become nothing but me, the pigeon and somebody's leftover lunch crumbs. I wonder if a house in the country comes with the care package?

Chapter Forty

Ten long minutes later the room falls quiet as Mr Faux shuts the door behind him. I lean against the wall, staring at the ground as Mum reaches for her Jackie Collins. She looks up and down the page as if trying to focus on where she'd got up to until she gives up, slamming it shut and says, 'Bollocks.'

Now, under any other circumstances I'd probably point out that she isn't a swearer but as it is, and because I've lost words and sense and control, I simply nod.

'In fact, Jem, I'd go as far as to say, fuckety bollocks.'

We sit for what must only be a second but feels like forever because my head is full of questions and fears. What if this? How come that? I don't know what to say, or where to start. I want to be sad, and angry, and shouty but it's so surreal it doesn't feel sad, or angry, or shouty, it feels… numb, strange, detached from reality, it feels unreal. I pick up the book that now rests in her lap. 'You know, you'd better get on with some of that reading or you'll die before you find out what happens.'

Mum looks at me, her eyes fill with tears and I briefly wonder if that was a step too far, until she fights the emotion and puts on a mischievous grin. She slaps me, playfully. 'They'll have libraries in heaven,' she says, sniffing everything back.

I sniff too. 'Assuming that's where you end up.'

'Where else? I am the very model of a heavenly woman. Besides, I reckon I could get Peter on my side dead easy.'

'You think?'

'Yeah! He's a bloke.' She wipes her eyes, shakes her head a little. 'I'll just flash my cleavage and stroll straight in.'

I let out an involuntary cry laugh. 'You do realise you've put women's lib back a few hundred years.'

'I'm dead. Don't judge me.'

We laugh, then fall back into a sudden heavy silence and once again I don't think either of us know what to say.

The rest of the afternoon was a circus of nurses and tests. Mum was prodded and poked. She told everyone that she'd named her stoma Percy. She complained that she hadn't had a decent curry since they'd lumbered her with him. She proudly showed off how well her nails were doing despite how poorly they kept telling her she was. She had bloods taken, the bit I really hate because I can't stand needles and blood and so made my excuses to grab a peppermint tea at that point. When I got back, she was chatting up the cleaner. A northern bloke who laughed with her as he ran one of those dust-buster cloths around the electric cable casing that was supposed to look like a dado. 'Your mum's brilliant,' he said to me as he left and she beamed, proudly. The tea trolley came round and Mum was delighted to learn she could eat, though a little less chuffed when she realised it was jacket potato and cheese but the jacket had been microwaved not baked, even though she can't eat potato skin any more. She was, however, thrilled to learn they were still dishing out the jellies that she'd basically lived on when she was here the last time, and savoured every last mouthful like a kid enjoying a lolly.

She booted me out at 6 p.m. because someone else had come in to palpate her belly and after that she wanted to settle down and watch the soaps. 'Go on, love. I'll see you in the morning.'

So here I am. Sat in the hollow room that is tonight's accommodation. It's like the worst kind of student digs you can imagine. A cheap wardrobe and desk along one wall. A mirror above the desk that catches my reflection when I really don't want it to. There's a tiny bathroom to one corner and in the other, a single bed that has one of those plastic hospital mattresses, two flat pillows and a sheet. A sheet! If I'd remembered this fact, I'd have brought my duvet. What I wouldn't give for some Forever Friends comfort right now.

As if on cue, my phone rings out and I leap on it because talking to someone is preferable to falling into the kind of pit of despair the room invokes. 'Hello?' I drop to lie down on the bed, eyes closed off from the room.

'Hey, it's me.'

The sound of Mitch's voice doesn't make me as nervous as the idea of it had become over these last few days. 'Hey you.'

'Are you okay? How's your mum?'

The question makes my heart lurch. 'Causing mayhem. Chatting up cleaners. Enjoying the luxury of an en suite room.'

'Wow, they pulled out all the stops for her.'

'She's very special, don't you know?'

'I do know.'

I keep my eyes closed and imagine myself in my bedroom, chatting to him as I have done many times.

'And you? How are you? Are you okay?'

His question brings me brutally back to the room. 'Am I okay?' I sigh, shifting myself up on the bed. I see my reflection, all dark circles beneath the eyes, hollowed out cheeks that once were full and bright. I don't know if I remember the last time they looked full and bright. A year ago? Two? Maybe a bit more. 'I'm standing,' I say because it's about as much as I can manage. I pause, he doesn't try to fill the space. 'I hate it here,' I whisper. 'Like, I don't want to seem ungrateful, I know it's free and all that, but…' A shadow appears as sun briefly lights up the room before presumably a cloud pitches it into early-evening grey. 'If rooms were Harry Potter characters, this would be a Dementor. It literally sucks all life out of you, leaving the really bad bits stuck to the wall for the next guest to absorb. I feel like I'm carrying one hundred people's fear and, frankly, I've enough of my own.'

'What have they said?'

'It's not good.'

'Oh, Jem.'

I think back to our chat in her room. 'She may not get to finish her latest Jackie Collins.'

'Eh?'

'Never mind. It's shit really. It's all shit. But you know that.'

'It is. And I do.'

'Where are you?' I ask, because I want to imagine it.

'I'm at home. Just finished my tea.'

'What did you have?'

The phone rustles as, I guess, he's moving about. 'Pasta and pesto because I couldn't decide what to have and, apparently, I cook like a student now.'

My belly rumbles. 'I'd love some pasta and pesto right now.'

'It'd be cold by the time I got there.'

'Drive quicker.'

'You want me to come down?' he asks and I want to scream *Yes!*

'It's fine, honestly. I'm okay,' I lie.

'I can. If you need me.'

'I know you could, and I appreciate it but no, I'm okay. I'm fine.' I get up, pulling thick blackout curtains closed. 'I will be fine. I just need to get my head down and sleep.' I glance over at the three bags of Doritos and medium-sized vodka bottle I picked up from the shop on my way back, smuggling it in because there was someone in the communal kitchen and I didn't want to speak to them, or let them see that I was one of the few people in the world who loves a lime-flavoured Dorito… or let on that I planned on getting smashed tonight.

'When do you get back?'

'Tomorrow, late on, I think. If things go to plan.'

'Okay. So… erm…' He stumbles over words and I can hear him moving around again. 'Maybe we could go out for a drink? I mean… not tomorrow,' he adds, quickly. 'In a few days. When you're ready.'

'That'd be good. I'd like that.'

Has he noticed we've gone a bit weird? Is it my fault? Is it drinks as mates, after I pushed things too far, or are we going on a date? Does it even need a label? Probably not now, at the moment, I've enough on my plate. But a drink would be nice.

'Call me tomorrow. When you can. Or tonight, if you need me.'

'I will. Thanks.'

'Bye, Jem.'

He hangs up and I feel empty. Alone. Like I want to call him back and talk to him throughout the night until the sun comes up just so that I don't have to face the night in this room, worrying. I reach for the vodka, the sound of the cap when I unscrew it is satisfying. I take a swig from the bottle, biting at the taste, before pouring it into a teacup from beside the tiny kettle and complimentary biscuits. Such glamour on the NHS.

I don't know what time I pass out.

Chapter Forty-One

The following twenty-four hours flies. My feet, heart and soul barely touch ground after we get back home. So when I open the front door to Mitch, I'm stunned.

'I know you said not to come over but I just… I needed to see you.' Mitch stands on the porch doorstep, concern etched over his face, a bottle of wine in hand. 'Thought you might want this.'

I look at the wine first, then up the stairs in the direction of Mum's room, where she's been sleeping since we got back home this afternoon. 'Come in,' I say, kind of relieved he ignored me being brave. And bizarrely not weirded out about seeing him for the first time since I threw myself at him in a fit of drunken, wanton lust. 'Just be quiet though, she needs to rest.'

'Of course.'

He tiptoes into the hallway, hovering until I direct him through to the lounge. He feels out of place in our house, to me at least. It's as if he doesn't quite fit in and I don't know why. Maybe it's 'cos it's rarely ever more than me and Mum and when it's not it's just other women in the house. I can't remember the last time a man stood here; Ben occasionally but Mum usually came to mine if we were all getting together. Before that? Maybe Mr Shaller, my junior schoolteacher, when he came to see Mum about me. I loved Mr Shaller. He was tall, broad, safe. The kids at school would tease me about not having a dad after he left because kids are dicks and Mr Shaller always leapt to my defence. Metaphorically and physically. I remember one kid, Edward something, he shouted it across the classroom. Mr Shaller jumped up, took two strides to the opposite side of the room – such was the length of his legs – and picked up the workbook Edward was supposed to be working on, bellowed his disapproval, whilst ripping the book in half and throwing it across the room.

'Were you at Dronfield Juniors? Do you remember Mr Shaller?' I ask, grabbing two glasses out of the cupboard in the kitchen, Mitch having followed me through.

'I was, yeah, and God, do I. He was a tank of a man and he terrified me! Why?'

'I dunno. No reason. He just… he came to mind.'

Red wine sloshes into the glass. I take a sniff, then shake my head. It's not right. What if she needs me? What if I have to drive somewhere, do something? It took me 'til nearly lunchtime before I could see properly today.

'You know what? I don't think I can do this.' I hand him the glass, flicking the kettle on.

'Do what?' he asks, uncertainly.

'Drink, I can't drink. I just… I don't know. I think I need to not. I think I need a night off. I mean, what if she needs me? What if…?'

'I get it. I do, but it's medicinal. I don't suppose it'd be the doctor's advice but shit, would I get it if you did. I mean, I did. When it was me. Christ, I drank so much. Worrying really, when I look back. But you do whatever you need to, to get you through, you know?'

'Well, Mum's consultant did say that I should definitely get totally wrecked every night, and in fact, ideally, he said I should have a few drinks during the day too, you know, hair of the dog and all that…' I force a smile. I'm failing at funny because I've spent all day trying, just to keep Mum going. 'Nah. I think, maybe I need a night off.'

He puts his glass on the side then steps towards me. 'Maybe I'll give it a rest too then.'

'Steady on. Your blood to alcohol ratio might dip.'

'It's fine. I'll make up for it when I leave. I always find drinking in total isolation is a healthy way to maintain the status quo.' He does one of those half smiles that people do when they're trying to keep your spirits up. 'Do you want to talk about it?' he asks, gently. 'I mean, you don't have to, just… I'm here, if you want to. I get it. I understand. I know what you're going through.'

'I know, I know you do.'

'And you don't have to be brave, for me.' Without warning, his words and the way he's looking at me and the touch of his hand on mine, the whole lot outs me completely and I unravel entirely, and from nowhere I'm consumed by all the feelings I've been ignoring since yesterday lunchtime. He wraps his arms around me as I collapse into him. As I cry, he holds me, he holds me up, he holds me close. He says nothing, just lets me weep into his very lovely shirt that I really hope I don't wipe mascara all over. He strokes my hair and I can hear his heartbeat, maybe even feel it against my cheek. Even when we were dancing the other day, we weren't as close as this. Even when we kissed the other night and I was grappling with his backside, we weren't as close. And with my eyes shut, I'm dizzy with emotions and the weight of holding it together from this morning's final meeting with Mum's consultant.

From the moment Mr Faux told her – that he was sorry, but there was nothing more to be done. From the moment he explained it had already been too far advanced in the first place and though they'd tried their best with the first op, they couldn't have anticipated how things might be as it grew. From when he ran through what the likely development of the disease would be and how they would manage that, but that ultimately, it would compromise her organs. How, in particular, he was concerned about a growth around her bile duct; as matter-of-factly as he'd told us everything from the moment we first met him. And that was why in certain lights, from certain angles, her skin was taking on a yellow shade. From the look on Mum's face as he left the room and I told her she had to cry because she couldn't pent-up the emotion as that would poison her system even more than the cancer already was; which is stupid when you analyse it, but I believed it when I said it. And from the sound of her voice when she tried to joke that her tears – from the moment we left Basingstoke, to the second we pulled up on the drive – were entirely my fault because I'd told her she *had* to cry and now the floodgates had opened and she couldn't bloody well stop. From the sound of her gentle snoring, minutes after climbing into bed, because she was so exhausted from the last twenty-four hours of bad news after bad news. Because this, this here, with her tucked up beneath a heavy quilt on a sweltering late-summer's evening, this was it. This was the official beginning of the end and I'm not ready. It's not time. It's too early. She's too young.

'I'm here,' Mitch says, as I look up into his eyes and I know that I want distraction. I want to feel close to someone. I want to get out of my head and into somewhere I don't have to think about the fact that Mum is dying. I want him to take me in his arms. I want him to lay me down. I want him to kiss me until I can't think of anything except how it feels. How he feels. Inside me.

'Shall I stay?' he asks and I nod because I've never wanted anything more. 'If I do, you can't make me drink alone.'

He holds my gaze. I feel his breath on my face. Our knees touch. I really could do with a drink. I just need to make sure I don't throw myself at him again, here. Now. On Mum's old couch from Ponsford. It cost her a bloody fortune.

Chapter Forty-Two

The light is golden, sounds are muffled. Mum and I wander up a pathway from the car park to the stately home we are visiting, her with a real spurt on 'cos 'there's cake at the top of the hill'. I take a photo of her, one of those live ones. When I play it back, her dress sways as she slowly takes left foot then right in search of Battenberg. She turns a corner, signalling me to hurry up and I drop my phone in my bag and go after her, but when I get to the café, she's not there. I search around, desperate to find her, calling out her name yet I can't hear my own voice. Then something jolts me awake.

I'm not in bed. My back and hips are telling me that much. I manage a snatched glimpse at my surroundings to see the lounge, a cocoon of cushions, my duvet and... the dead weight of a leg over mine. Outside, a car engine starts up and pulls away and even that tiny noise makes my head pound. Light streams through a gap in the curtains and my eyes strain to see past dust dancing in the shaft of light, finally focusing on Mitch, fast asleep beside me.

Something like butterflies pitch and dive around my stomach. What happened? Did we...?

Eyes adjusting, I can see we're surrounded by every pillow and cushion from my room. Did I collect all these? I've a vague recollection of stumbling up the stairs, shushing myself as I giggled. My duvet lays widthways across us both, protecting only our modesty, for want of a better name. There are three spent candles on the coffee table beside me, next to a half-finished glass of something that gives rise to a swell of revulsion as I sniff at it. Vodka. The wine bottle Mitch brought over lies on its side, empty, taunting me. It's not feeling terribly medicinal right now.

I shift to try and sit up but don't want to wake him until I know what happened, until some memory returns. Which it does. Slowly. Moment by moment unfolding. We were drinking. He held me. We talked and talked. I spoke about Mum. Every tiny detail. Every last bit from the moment we found out something was up, almost two years ago, to coming away from Basingstoke yesterday.

Oh God. He asked to read the letter. I definitely said no again, but we talked about Ben. How much did I say? Why? Why did I talk about him? Except, maybe if I hadn't I wouldn't have got upset again. And maybe he wouldn't have told me that I had a right to believe I was worth something. That I was brilliant. That I was funny and smart and inspiring and then he kissed me. Oh God, he kissed me. Slowly. Unlike before. Like he meant it, like *we* meant it. And I remember feeling lost in him. Out of control. And I remember him making this pod for us to lie in. Here. Pillows and cushions piled high as if making us a safe space where nobody and nothing could reach us. I remember him pouring more drink as we kissed like teenagers. I remember feeling drunk on him. Drunk on lust. Drunk, probably, on wine and vodka. But we were even. We were both the same. Unlike back at Aunty Vi's party, this was us, together, drinking and talking and feeling and kissing. I remember him laying me down, one hand in the small of my back as he moved to rest against me, almost on me, and the weight of him was everything I wanted and needed. I remember...

'Morning.'

His voice is groggy and it sparks the butterflies to leap into my throat. I gaze down at chipped nail polish.

'How are you?'

'My head hurts.'

He reaches up, letting his lips rest on my forehead. 'Me too,' he mutters. 'I told you not to open that second bottle.'

'Was that my idea? Christ,' I groan. 'Water. We should have had water?'

'If only.' He brushes hair from my eyes, and part of me wants to escape. My head is spinning, not just from the hangover, but his proximity. I feel energy fizzing, spinning, right where our heads touch. 'I'm sorry.'

'What?'

'I'm sorry. That shouldn't have happened.'

Shit. Oh God, what have we done? What have I done?

'I promised myself I wouldn't.'

'Right.' I move away from him. Why am I such an idiot? Have I not learned my lesson? Could I not just have stuck to the plan to drink tea instead of getting all needy and lusty. 'Sorry, sorry, it's my fault.'

'No! No, it's not. And it's not because I didn't want to, Jesus, you've no idea how much I wanted to.' He pauses, looking down at me. 'You've no idea how much I want to…' He kisses me again before sighing and pulling away. 'It was so hard to walk away from you the other night. In the park. But you came on so heavy and I didn't want you to think I'd taken advantage. And then I thought I'd blown it because we didn't talk for days and I missed you, I needed to hear you, but I didn't want to make you feel bad or frighten you off, then I knew what was going off for you and I just wanted to be by your side. I needed to see you. And maybe it's selfish, but I needed to know you were okay. I gave myself a talking-to before I knocked on your door. Do not sleep with her I said.'

'Right. I mean… if it helps… I think I'm probably glad you didn't listen.'

'Are you?' I pause, then nod. 'Because I would totally understand if you feel you don't need this in your life, right now.'

'This?' I ask.

'Us? A complication? I mean, maybe we should just be friends. You've so much going on right now.'

'Maybe that's why now is a good time. A distraction.'

He leans in and kisses me and I melt into the floor, consumed. Before I hear a key in the front door and we jump apart as Mum calls out, 'Good morning!'

She drops her keys in the bowl by the door, appearing at the archway into the lounge. 'I thought you two might want bacon.'

'Oh God, Mum. I…' I pull my legs beneath the duvet wishing it was bigger. Wondering how I missed the fact she'd got up and gone out. Surely after yesterday she'd be in bed, for ages. I was going to take her a cuppa up. I was going to make *her* a bacon sandwich. 'Sorry, I… we lost track of—'

'No, no… please don't explain,' she interrupts, eyebrows raised and a fleck of mischief in her eye. 'Lovely to see you again, Mitch.'

'Erm, yeah, and you, Mrs Whitfield.'

'Oh, please. I've seen you without a top on now. You might as well call me Val, eh?'

'Erm, right. Val.'

'Well, I'll let you two get up. And maybe get dressed too. You like bacon, Mitch?'

'Well, yes. But, please, can I make it? You sit down.'

'What? And see you two try and casually get up and sort this love pit out whilst I recline on the sofa?' She's grinning, enjoying the whole moment far too much. 'As hilarious as that would be, no. I don't think so. You sort yourselves out. I'll be in the kitchen when you're dressed. It's time for pop quiz.' And with that, she disappears into the kitchen with an 'Alexa, play BBC Radio Two.'

Chapter Forty-Three

Half an hour later, Mitch and Mum are recounting old school stories at my expense and I am trying to remember that this is a good thing. They're bonding. I don't have to be sensitive around him. He isn't out to get me. It's fine.

'And you know I heard she always got out of science by telling them some story.'

Mum is staring at me, eyes wide, head cocked to one side. 'I did hear that when it came to dissecting animals, she always said she couldn't do it on ethical grounds,' she says, smirking.

'How did you know that?' I ask.

'Mums know everything, it's their job,' Mitch says. 'Mine always said I mostly tripped myself up by saying stuff I thought was innocuous, but that always exposed some kind of mischief.'

'I mean, really, ethical grounds? Oh yes, dead ethical, our Jem.' She's belly laughing. Actually laughing from her boots. As Mitch talks, Mum sparkles. She looks better than she has in weeks. Months even. She's rejuvenated by his presence as she nibbles on the edge of her bacon sandwich, still giggling. 'I've always said how ethical she is. By the way, how is that mass-farmed pig bacon, love?'

'Mum!' I look down at my sandwich, its appeal briefly jaded.

'Did you ever have to dissect the daffodil?' Mitch asks.

I nod, colour creeping into my cheeks. 'I told them I had hay fever. I pretend sneezed in between every word. I hated science.'

'I reckon Miss Drake will have just let you go in the end, anything to stop the disruption,' says Mitch, amused.

'And incessant fake sneezing,' Mum adds.

He smirks at me over his mug of tea and I try to laugh along because it's not his fault that I am suddenly a bit rubbish at having the piss taken out of me.

'Where did you go?' asks Mum as she puts her barely touched sandwich down.

'I dunno. Drama. The common room. Up to the shops. It's no wonder I failed my exams, is it?' I pick at my sandwich, feeling like a failure.

'Hey, you're proof you don't need all those exams to make a success of life, isn't she, Val?' Mitch moves to sit beside me. It's the closest he's been since we packed away our makeshift bed and I hid in the bathroom trying to take control of my face and hair. 'No qualifications, yet a booming business. In charge of her own destiny. I think you're bloody amazing.'

'She is. She always has been.' There's a pause. 'So,' Mum begins, tentatively, and that's never a good sign, 'what does all this mean for you two then?' Oh God. She flaps her hands in the space between us. 'You two "friends"…'

'Mum! I mean, I don't think we need to label us, this I mean—'

'Labels or not, I think maybe we've moved past the friend zone, haven't we?' Mitch peers at me, his eyes glinting. The part of me that is a little bit excited at the look in his eye and the prospect of a repeat performance of what happened last night, not least so I can remember every detail, is also a bit perplexed because is this not a weird conversation to be having with your mum?

'Well, I'll tell you this much, kids. Life is too short to hang around. You two have clearly had feelings for each other from the get-go and it's nice to see you with a smile on your face, lady. I've been really worried about you.' She looks at me pointedly and I know exactly what she's talking about, even if she doesn't want to say it in front of Mitch. 'It's good. You're happy.'

'I'm also dying inside, Mum.' I immediately regret my choice of words and I suspect she sees it.

'Don't be so dramatic. There's only one of us round here who's dying and you do not see me crying into my bacon sandwich.'

'I don't see you eating your bacon sandwich.'

'Look. It's almost eleven o'clock and I have things to do. Mitch, if you are remotely interested in my daughter, and I can see you very much are, you will pick her up later for dinner or some such. Make a nice evening out of it. And if it's all the same to you two, if you insist on having sex on my carpet, can you please make sure I don't have to find you entwined the morning after. You've put me off my breakfast.' She pushes her plate out of reach, grabs her tea and newspaper and retreats upstairs to her bedroom.

Mitch and I are stunned into silence. At least we avoided the sofa.

Chapter Forty-Four

I've been distracted all morning. I keep catching myself gazing out of the window like Mum does. The sky is blue. Electric. No vapour trails, no clouds. Mum has been in her room all morning, reading. I've called out, checking if she wants a drink or food, it's always a no. Her door is shut too. She was bright this morning, chatty and full of life with Mitch but it's as if she used all her reserves and wiped herself out. Or maybe she's just processing the prognosis. How can you even begin? How can you think about things knowing there is nothing anyone can do to save you? I mean, I know we all die. I know it can happen out of the blue, at any moment, and yet that's not how any of us walk through life, is it? We don't sit with the knowledge that our death is in reach.

They wouldn't say how long, she asked a few more times, they couldn't be certain was all Mr Faux said. I googled it. Which was a bad call. Because although some people said it was six months or twelve, or more in some cases, from the moment the patient was put on a symptom management plan to the moment their loved ones passed, all I could see were the ones who died within weeks or months. And each one so different. There's no consistency to it. The range of things that finally cause the end is too broad. So, what do I do? Panic about every little symptom? Mum's stoic, I know she'll take it in her stride, when she finally comes out of her bedroom with brave painted on. But me? I don't know if I have her strength.

All she has said is that it's nice to see me with a smile on my face. And I think it is too, but my head is full. One minute it's all Mum, fear, questions, worry. Then it's Mitch. His lips on mine, his touch, his smell. My heart is torn between the thing I fear the most… and Mum dying. She's always said I shouldn't be afraid to love. As a kid, she'd say it. I was fifteen. I had a holiday romance with a marine I met in Ibiza. God my heart broke, shattered, when he eventually said he couldn't see me any more. He was being practical. It could never have worked, but I wasn't sure I'd ever recover. Mum said it first then, 'Never be afraid to love.' And I've remembered it always, yet somehow, I don't know if I've truly lived by it. I think I've always kept something of me hidden. A part of me that nobody sees, not even Ben. And I did love him, I know I did, but I think I also know I only loved him as much as I allowed myself to, there was always something I kept back because to give fully makes me vulnerable. Now, I don't even know if could let go…

I really shouldn't think about it. I've got work to do. These bloody bank statements. What should only be an hour-long job has so far taken me almost two and I'm still not done. Life's distracting. Mitch is distracting. Not in a way I've known before. He's different. Arresting, maybe. Not sure. I feel different with him, maybe he sees the part of me I've always tried to hide.

Mum likes him. I can see that. She'd love to see me settle, to know that I'm okay.

He told me to be ready for 7.30 p.m. He told me to wear something nice, but not too nice. What does that even mean? He won't tell me where we're going again. It should probably be exciting. I think I've perhaps got too much on to be excited. And I just keep thinking about Mum.

My phone rings and I leap on it, mildly disappointed to see it's Leanne. 'Jem, where the hell have you been?'

'Good morning to you too.'

'I called and texted last night. Didn't you see?'

'No? Sorry, I've been distracted since I got back.'

'You said you'd call, I was worried.'

'I've only been back a day,' I point out, irritated. 'I didn't know you'd texted.'

'You read my message!'

'Did I?'

'Well, according to my phone.'

If I did, I've no memory of it. Too busy drinking and talking and sexing. I don't mention that though. If she's been worrying about me, she'll tut.

'I was just checking you were back.'

'Sorry, yes. I am. We are. I got distracted, sorting Mum out. Then Mitch turned up.'

'Oh, did he?'

'He was worried. Wanted to know I was okay.'

'Oh, right. Nice of him. So, what's happened? How's your mum? What have they said?'

I feel guilty I've not told her. Mitch knows everything yet Leanne, my best friend in the whole world, didn't even know I was back. 'It's not good. I mean... that's an understatement. A lot has happened...' I look out of the window to the electric blue sky. I see the tree elephant and its baby. I gaze disdainfully at the statements on my bedside cabinet-cum-desk. 'Are you in for a bit? Can I come over?'

'Of course. Harley's gone on a trip with nursery 'til later anyway. It's just me and Elsie.'

'Okay, I'll be there in ten.'

I fold the corner down on the form I've got up to, barely halfway through. Some things can wait.

Chapter Forty-Five

I knock then let myself in, pulling mail out of the letterbox and dropping it on the side table. The theme tune to *Loose Women* comes on from the lounge and Leanne shouts, 'Flick the kettle on, Jem.'

'Tea or coffee?' I ask, opening the cupboards for mugs.

She pads through to me, Elsie over her shoulder, fast on. 'Coffee, please. Barely got any sleep last night and I'm functioning on Kenyan Taste the Difference.'

'Eurgh! Sounds awful. I don't know how you cope. I'd be a wreck if I didn't get my sleep.' I go over to give her a hug and kiss Elsie on her tiny milk-drunk forehead.

'You cope. You have to. It's amazing how well you adjust when the babies arrive, it's like your body pulls up its braces and cracks on with it.'

'Yeah. Okay.' I'm unconvinced.

Leanne leans against the worktop, picking at a few cashew nuts from a bag on the side.

'Have you eaten?' I ask. 'Can I make you something?'

'I'd bloody love a crumpet with blue cheese!'

'What the hell?'

'I know, right. Filth. But good filth. And when these little bleeders are drinking you dry of all goodness, you need to stock up. Besides, I couldn't eat it when I was pregnant, could I? Can't get enough now.'

'Crumpet, blue cheese and coffee coming up then.' I wince.

Busying myself in her kitchen feels good. Familiar. Whilst Andy is away during the week, I've all but lived here for the past few months, helping out with Harley when Leanne was heavily pregnant, supporting her with Elsie when she arrived. At the risk of sounding like it's all about me, it's made me feel useful. Needed. That's going to have to change though. Mum needs me. Somehow that feels less useful and needed and more scary and uncertain. Like I'm not sure I really know how to be the person she needs when she needs it most.

'Come on then. What's going on? You look… worried.'

'Do I?' Peering into the mirrored bit of the microwave, I pull at my eyes and forehead. 'I look old, is what I look. That's bloody Basingstoke for you.'

'So how did it go? What did they say?'

Whilst pouring the coffee and making her lunch, I tell her everything about our trip. She listens, like she always does, letting me speak before offering words of wisdom in amongst the sounds of sadness because when I recount it all like this, it really is pretty shit. And I realise why the consultants always sound so perfunctory because how else can you talk about it? You can't get emotional, it hurts too much, it's not useful, it achieves nothing. There's no silver lining, so no plus points to highlight. It just is what it is. 'It's a mess that won't get better and then she'll die.'

'Oh God, Jem. I don't know what else to say.'

'There's nothing you can say.'

'This is a stupid question, but… are you okay?'

Am I? I'm standing. I'm breathing. I'm not, to my knowledge, dying. 'Yes. I mean. I suppose. As much as you can be. Of course, no, too. I'm not okay in as much as it's the single most horrendous, distressing, stressful, upsetting and dark thing I've ever gone through, but, I don't know, trying to find something positive, at least I'm here. I can be with Mum. You know? I have time, I can care for her. Some people don't get that, do they? It's a privilege.'

I hand over her lunch, she takes a giant bite out of the crumpet, letting out an appreciative groan.

'Mum's being amazing. As you'd imagine. She said to Mitch this morning—'

'This morning?'

Shit.

'Erm, yeah.' Carry on, she won't notice. 'She said to Mitch that she was not going to spend whatever time she had left being dictated to by cancer.'

'That's your mum all over.'

'It is.'

'But how come Mitch was there this morning? I thought he came over last night?'

Nothing gets past her.

'Well, yes, he did…'

She waits, giving me a look with her eyebrows as I try to form the right words to describe what's going on but apparently I take too long. Her eyes narrow, then widen, before she breaks out into a massive grin. 'Oh, my God, you did not? You did! You had sex. You did the rude stuff. I knew it! I told you! I called it at Aunty Vi's. You've let him touch your lady bits. Ha!' She takes another bite of her crumpet. 'Excellent work,' she says, mouth full. 'If I didn't have crumpet in one hand and a sleeping baby in the other, I'd high five you right now. Come through here, tell me everything. I want details.'

I drop onto the sofa opposite her. She switches *Loose Women* off, so this must be important. She scoops up bits of runny cheese that have escaped through the holes in her crumpet, sucking them in whilst waiting for me to dish the dirt.

'Like I say, he came over last night. Wanted to check how I was.'

'I'll bet he bloody did, the dirty dog.'

'Leanne!'

'Go on.'

'We chatted. He brought wine. I said I wasn't going to have any then he pointed out how crap things were and that if I couldn't have a drink then, when could I? So, we drank it. Then...'

'Yes?' She licks her fingers, leaving the plate on the sofa beside her.

'Well, then we had sex on the lounge carpet.'

'Oooh, carpet burns.'

'Nope. Thankfully not.'

'I got them once. Nightmare. They take forever to heal. Still got the scars.' Leanne is trying not to jiggle as she laughs because Elsie's still knocking the zzzs out. She shifts her from shoulder to the sofa beside her, nestling her amongst a couple of cushions so she can't roll off. 'So' – she clasps her hands together, elbows on crossed knees – 'how was it?'

I was hoping she wouldn't ask this because whilst I can remember the kissing, oh, the kissing, and I can remember feeling the weight of him on me, the rest hasn't entirely resurfaced just yet. 'Well... I remember us drinking and kissing and talking. We made a sort of den, on the lounge floor... I remember getting vodka and us doing truth or dare.' I bury my head in my hands. 'Oh God, truth or dare shots. Christ, who knows what I bloody well said?'

'You can't remember?'

'No! I don't think I can. What if I said something awful?'

'And what about the sex? Can you remember that?'

I slouch down into the sofa with a groan, wishing I could bloody remember. 'I mean, I think it was great.'

'You think? Were you *that* hammered? Hang on, did he take advantage of you? I knew there was something off about him!'

'No! No, he wouldn't do that. He's walked away before, when he thought I was too drunk. He wouldn't. We were both drinking, it was a stress release. After Basingstoke, I just... I don't know... it sort of happened. It wasn't planned. I just can't quite remember it...'

'Who says romance is dead?'

'Anyway, what do you mean by there being "something off about him"?'

'No, nothing. I just meant from before, at school...' She stares at me, unblinking.

'Oh, Leanne, it's awful, isn't it?' The weird knot I've had in my belly seems to niggle even more.

'No, not awful. Just... well, not ideal. Is it?'

'I guess not.'

'So what now?'

'Well, we're going out tonight. On a date.'

'Where to?'

'I don't know.'

'You *need* to tell him you hate surprises, Jem.'

'I know.'

'Because otherwise it's a relationship based on lies.'

'It is not a relationship, and it's not based on lies! Christ, dramatic!' She folds her arms at the same time I do. 'We just sort of got pushed into it. Mum said we should go out, she just told him to pick me up tonight and that was that. There wasn't time to argue with her or plan where to go. He just said he'd sort it. I let him. It's nice.'

'I guess. And not so easy to tell your mum no right now, anyway.'

'That's what Mitch said.'

Elsie murmurs and Leanne leans over, stroking her face. She has the magical touch of a mum and Elsie settles straight away. Leanne peers at her for a moment, just checking if she's really back asleep. She's gentle with her. She sort of oozes kindness and warmth and love. I envy it, weirdly.

'You like him then?' she says eventually, reaching for her coffee. 'I mean… I've worried about you Jem, what with all that Ben stuff. I wondered if you'd be able to move on, I wasn't even sure with the Tinder thing, but I had to do something. You needed a shove. Was it worth it? How does he compare? I don't mean compare, I know you shouldn't compare but… well, you were broken after Ben. I know it's still raw.'

'It is.' The letter I wrote him is still on my bedside table. I don't know what to do with it. I should probably burn it like I was going to in the first place. 'He's moved on though, hasn't he? And I need to, too. I've needed to for a long time, you and Mum saw that before I did.'

'That's our job. But it has to be with the right person. I mean, I don't want you to rush into anything, it's a difficult time.'

'I know it is. But Mitch has been there, he knows what I'm going through. It's hard, you can't imagine it unless you've been there. And thanks to you giving me the shove, I've met Mitch and he knows. I needed to snap out of it, Leanne. The trip to Cornwall. The letter. All this Mum stuff, maybe it's making me realise how much I need to move on. I want Mum to see me happy, settled. And she needs me, now.'

'You need you too, Jem.'

'I know, I just mean, Mum stuff, it's major. It's not going to get better. You know?'

'I know. Hey, what was it you said to me when Harley was born? That I should look after me, so I can look after him. Same applies here, for you. You have to look after you to look after your mum. Mitch seems great, but…'

'But?'

'Just… take your time. You're important to me.'

'I know. You too. It's fine. It's all going to be fine. Let's face it, what's the worst that can happen?' I smile, sadly, because we both know the worst that can happen and we both know I can't escape it.

Chapter Forty-Six

I stand in front of the mirror, holding dresses up to me, discarding them on the bed. Leanne's words have echoed all afternoon, I need to be okay. I can't look after Mum unless I look after me. And I know it, all that stuff. In fact, it's weird to hear her shoot it back at me, but she's right. And though I'm not sure what this is with Mitch, I know it's something I've never had before, never felt before. And Mum wants to see me happy, settled, so I have to explore it for her sake as much as mine. I want her to know I'm okay. I don't want her worrying about me, about what will happen when she's gone.

The Moomin envelope catches my eye. I pick it up, flipping it over, running my finger along the scrawled biro mark that says Return to Sender. I don't know that the trip to Cornwall was quite the closure I was looking for but maybe this was. Return to sender.

A text message pings and I reach for my phone.

Wear the green, animal print dress.

Leanne has obviously been thinking about this date way too much. I gaze across at my wardrobe, rammed full of clothes, some on hangers, some stuffed in the bottom, crumpled, uncared for. The dress in question pokes out of the bottom of that pile.

It needs ironing.

Then iron it! You lazy mare. Call me tomorrow. I want to know all the gory details. Love you, bye.

Love you bye.

It's ten thirty. Mitch pulls up outside my house and turns off the engine. He turns to face me, pulling me in towards him.

'I had a lovely time,' I say, between his kisses.

'Me too.'

We kiss more. Like teenagers. It's not the first time I've sat outside Mum's house, snogging in a car. I didn't imagine I'd still be doing it at my age though. Funny how things turn out.

'You didn't have to pay for everything though, you know.'

'I know,' he says, before really kissing me, one of those deep full-on proper snogs. It makes my knees all weak and wobbly. 'You deserve to be treated. You deserve some loveliness in your life.'

I kiss him back, thoroughly intoxicated by the evening, by his attention. It started out with him arriving on my doorstep with cupcakes he'd made for Mum because he knows about keeping up her energy levels and thought she might like them. Then he drove me in his brand new shiny, fancy car that, whilst not being into shiny, fancy cars as such (and having no idea what it was other than shiny and fancy), has a heated, leather seat and I am down for heated, leather seats. We ended up at Rafters Restaurant in Sheffield and though I'd never heard of a Copper Maran Egg, when it's served with aerated hollandaise I can confirm it is properly orgasmic. As was the rest of the meal. Including the 'optional' cheese course at the end because Mitch said, 'How is cheese ever optional?' and despite my stomach straining at the drop waist on my (ironed) green dress, I was not about to argue.

We kiss more. My heart rate spikes.

'Do you want to come in?' I ask, breathless. I run my hand up his (incredible) thighs but find his hand stops me going any further.

'You should go in.' He takes my hand to his chest like he did when I threw myself at him up at the park.

'But...' I kiss him again, doing that stupid movie groan because I have not needed anyone this badly for a very long time. Not since—

'I think we should wait.'

'Wait? Don't you think that horse bolted last night?'

Firmly, he takes hold of both wrists now. 'It did. But... you're too special. I don't want to ruin this.'

'Right.' I sit back in the passenger seat. Bruised. Aching. A teensy bit shameful.

'Look at me.' He drops my wrists and takes my face by my chin, pulling it round to look at him. 'I mean it. You're special. I want this... I want you...' He kisses me in a way that makes the shame subside a bit and the butterflies return. 'I just... I want to do things right. I want to give us a fair chance. I want to take you out, treat you like a princess.'

'You may or may not have noticed, but I am very much not a princess.'

'But you could be.'

I resist reeling off all the reasons why I could not now, nor ever, be a princess. Not least because he might not want to have sex tonight – and I am definitely not feeling great about that fact – but I would like the chance to do it when I have all my faculties about me, when he is next up for it.

'I want to take it slow. We've both had a tough time. You're still having a tough time.'

That much is true, I guess. He's probably right. I've just never been very good at waiting. But maybe that's why this is different; he's different.

Mum hasn't left the porch light on so I pull my phone out of my bag to turn the torch on for walking back up the drive. 'Oh, no!'

'What?'

'My bloody phone!' I look up at the house.

'What about it?'

'I don't know. It keeps turning on silent. Or I keep knocking it, missing calls or messages or something. Look, Mum texted.'

'Oh! Is she okay? Do you need me to come in?'

'No, no. I think she's fine. She was just asking how it was going. She's as impatient as me.' I flick my eyes up to him and he smiles. 'It's fine. I suppose it just makes me worry. What if she hadn't been? I mean, the consultant said things can change really quickly now. A blockage, anything. She could be in real danger, really quickly. I could do without my phone playing up.'

'Is it under warranty?'

'What do you think? Are they ever? They always start failing when they're out of warranty.'

'Give her my number. Then at least when you're with me, she can contact you.'

'And what about when I'm not? I mean, we're taking it slow, aren't we? That's what you said. And I agree, you're right.' He takes my hand.

'You are right. You're important to me too. Taking it slowly is definitely the right thing.'

'It is. I know. Look, get in. Check she's okay. Drop me a text and let me know, yeah?'

'Okay.'

He leans across, putting my hand on his chest. He kisses me again and I try my hardest to be a bit passive to it, but he really does do something quite arresting to me. 'Thank you, Calamity Jem, I had a lovely night. You are… just what I need in my life.'

He watches me walk up the drive. He watches me unlock the door and go inside. He waves as I close the door. He leaves as I pull the curtain across wondering what I did to deserve him, after everything I've done before.

Chapter Forty-Seven

A week passes in a blur of text messages and phone calls and me desperately wishing Mitch would finally give in and let me climb him like a tree. Leanne thinks it's strange, but is, I think, quite impressed with him pushing for us to take our time. Mum keeps asking if I'm stopping out tonight, or if he's coming over. She said he could always stay, if ever I wanted him to. I can just see it now, me and him squished up in my single bed. It's not quite the kind of environment I want to entertain him in, if I'm honest.

That said, it's also not quite so high on my agenda as it was a few days ago. Mum's first appointment came through and we're here today, waiting for the first meeting with a Macmillan nurse. Now that's an appointment to kill your mojo. Macmillan. I mean, God, this is real. It's happening. It feels so weird, so surreal. Is that how everyone feels when faced with this kind of thing?

Mum sits in her chair, waiting. She's left the toast I made her but has knocked back her pills despite being deeply unimpressed by the variety she's now required to take. As we wait, she's browsing a Betterware catalogue that someone just shoved through the letterbox. There's everything from a remote control 'candle' to a pair of American tan tights that comes in in sizes XXXS to 'arse the size of Macclesfield'.

'We should get one of these,' she says, turning the page over after starring some product that I know will end up in the box, in the cupboard, never to see the light of day. Like that tofu press she bought. She doesn't even like tofu.

I'm dusting. Something she laughed at when she saw me. Which is probably fair enough because I'm not sure I've ever actually dusted before. That's a lie. I have. As a kid I'd get a great thrill out of dusting for some bizarre reason. Kids are weird. But as a grown-up? Nah. Dusting's not for me. Until today, because in this light, you can see how thick with dust the video recorder has got. 'How old is this recorder?'

'God knows. Got it when they first came out, so must be thirty years. They don't make stuff like that any more.'

'It's probably worth something. You should eBay it, then switch up and get a DVD player. Or just get rid altogether now we've got Amazon and Netflix.'

'Then what would I watch all my old box sets on?'

'They're probably all online now, nobody watches videos any more.'

'But I have them all in there, I don't need them online. And it'd be such a waste to just throw them away.'

I open the video cupboard.

'Look, there's *Friends*, *Sex and the City*, *Frasier*,' she says, reeling off her favourite TV shows.

'Did you not watch British TV in the nineties?' I browse the back of *The Golden Girls* collection.

'Of course I did. There's *One Foot in the Grave* at the back there.' She stars another item, folding down the page. 'I bet if you dig far enough back you'll find a *Brush Strokes*. I used to love that guy off of *Brush Strokes*,' she says, circling more useless (colour changing?) gadgets in her catalogue.

'She's late,' she says, slapping the catalogue shut with a tut as she strains to look out of the window. Tiny rainbows appear on the wall as the sun comes out from behind a cloud and catches a crystal she hung there when she was into feng shui, until she realised the entire house would need remodelling if she was really going to live her life by it. 'I hate it when people are late.'

'I can call them, if you like?'

'No, no. We'll wait. I mean, I've got other things I could be doing, but it's fine. We'll wait.'

A car pulls up and I stand to peer out and see. 'Next door's Joanne.'

'Ahhh. She's lost tons on Weight Watchers you know. I couldn't believe it when Pauline said.'

'Has she? Good for her.'

She looks at her watch, tutting out of the window. 'I suppose you never know, do you?' she says, with a heavy sigh.

'You never know what?'

'Well, if they've got an appointment before us. You never know if they're running late because someone is poorly. Or someone died.'

'Mum!'

'What? I mean, they're Macmillan nurses, aren't they? They're visiting because people are at the end of their lives.' She whispers that last bit. As if gossiping about people that aren't her. 'Very difficult job.'

'Yeah.'

'Still. Wouldn't hurt to be on time.'

We wait another hour before a woman pulls up in a battered Corsa, lugging three bags about her person as she meanders up the drive. She's got fizzy mad hair and wears layers of linen and round-toed shoes.

Comfort and ethical procurement over style. Maybe that's unfair. They're probably stylish to her. I'm judging. Stop judging. 'Morning, how lovely of you to come.' I bite my tongue to stop myself adding *over an hour late.*

'Morning, am I alright parked there?' She doesn't wait for my answer, or check if she has to take her shoes off as she wanders through into the lounge. I mean, it's fine, I could tell her we operate a 'shoes on unless you want to take them off' policy because it makes people feel more comfortable, but I don't get the impression she's here to chat. Not to me, at least. Which is fine. It's all fine. I'm fine…

'Morning, you must be Mrs Whitfield.'

'Please, call me Val.'

'Lovely to meet you. I'm Deni.'

I head into the lounge to see she's sitting in my space on the sofa. Which is totally fine. She can sit where she likes. She's here for Mum. It's all fine. 'Can I get you a drink at all?'

'Oh, that'd be lovely. Thank you. Yes. Tea, please. Peppermint if you've got it. Anything herbal really.'

'I'll see what I can find.'

Chapter Forty-Eight

I'm in the kitchen. Mum and Deni are talking about how she is and I want to be there to check if she really tells her everything or gives her the edited version she gives to most people. I flick the kettle on, popping to and fro to loiter, just in case.

'Jem and I call it fuckety bollocks. All this stuff. It's all a load of fuckety bollocks. Most inconvenient. I'm barely through my bucket list.'

Deni lets out a gritty laugh like someone who's smoked Marlboro Red since exiting the womb. 'Fuckety bollocks. I like it.'

'Yeah, well. You have to keep a sense of humour, don't you?'

'You do. The whole process will be a lot easier if you retain that.'

'Let's face it, it's all I've got left, eh, love?'

She glances over to me and I force a smile of agreement. 'It is. Well, that and your hair.'

'Yes!' she says. 'One of the lucky ones. It's a shame really. I was sort of looking forward to getting some wigs and acting out an alter ego.'

The kettle clicks off and I retreat to the kitchen wondering if there's any peppermint at the very back of the tea cupboard. We had some in, yonks ago, when Mum was on a health kick, just after her initial diagnosis. Until she was told that no amount of green tea and spinach was going to help her, and she binned the lot in favour of pulled pork

and a stout. Protein and iron, she said. Can't go wrong. How I wish
it had been that simple.

*

The meeting with Deni takes an hour. Mum plays the model patient.
Polite, agreeable, happy to be told what is in her best interest. Deni
talks about the amount of steroids Mum is on, suggesting she needs
to think about reducing them because they'll shorten her life. I made
a gag about the cancer doing that already, which made Deni laugh so
loudly I thought she was going to cough up a lung. We went through
a questionnaire in which she asked Mum how she was. You know. In
her self. Deni made notes about various bits of equipment she thought
Mum would need as she started to feel less able to get out of the house
and more likely to spend time in bed. Inflatable mattresses to stop
bedsores, a table with wheels to help her walk to the toilet and eat her
dinner off – apparently they don't advise you multitask this. She said
there might be space in the hospice if we wanted her to try and Mum
said she was stopping here until her dying breath and no mistake. I
tried not to think about that too much. Deni gave us a whole host of
forms to read and sign, including a Do Not Resuscitate form, which
is when I properly stopped larking about because it's all so bloody
grim. Humour or no, it's happening. I can't even get my head around
it but it's happening.

Deni stands. 'It's been lovely meeting you both, thanks for the
drink,' she says, offering me the cup back, barely touched. 'Shall I come
back in two weeks and see how you are? I'll bring those bits I've not
got with me today and we'll see how you're getting on reducing those
steroids. Thanks again for the tea, call me if you need anything before
I'm here next.' And out she swooshed, mad frizzy hair bouncing down

the drive with her. It was like a really slow whirlwind had just been in the house and whipped it all up into a terrifying future, frightening frenzy. I feel disconnected. Discombobulated. I've never had cause to use that word before but that's exactly how I feel, discombobulated.

Mum stands at the window, waving her off. She smiles broadly until she's out of sight. Then, she turns to face me, exhaustion etched deeply across her face, and says, 'Well, she could at least have apologised for being late.'

Chapter Forty-Nine

The doorbell goes and I leap up and run down the stairs to answer it, hoping Mum isn't woken. Pretty much as soon as Deni left she took herself off to her room. I went up with a cuppa for her and could just hear tiny snores coming from her room. I think the intensity of it all got too much for us both and we needed space from one another.

'Are you ready?' Mitch says, as I open the door, half looking over my shoulder.

'Oh! Hi! Uhm… am I ready?'

'To go out?'

'Oh, no, I didn't realise… sorry, I thought you were going to call or text or something.'

'I texted. Said I'd be here, now. I'm taking you to lunch.'

'Oh!' I look down at my comfies, which are not exactly appropriate for leaving the house in, never mind an impromptu date. 'Are you?'

'Yes! I did say. I'm sure the message sent.' He checks his phone, flashing it at me. 'Yes. I did. Sorry, I assumed no response meant you were getting ready. I didn't think… ahh, sorry!'

'No, no! It's fine. It's my bloody phone. I need to talk to O2. Or Apple. One of the kids in the Genius Bar. Maybe they could fix it. But that does mean going to "Meadowhell" and who wants to do that voluntarily?'

Mitch pushes past me, kissing me as he goes. 'Don't worry about it. I should have made sure. We don't have to go. We can stay here. What have you got in? Maybe I could whip us something up?'

'No, no, I'd love to go. It'd be nice. I mean, I should probably get changed first,' I say, picking at my T-shirt.

'I don't mind stopping in.'

I fling my arms around him. 'No. Please, let's go. Thank you. That's really lovely.'

He grins. 'Go on then. Get yourself ready. I thought we could take your mum down too. I checked with Ferndale and they have a couple of things I thought she could eat.'

'That's so thoughtful, thank you, though I'm not sure if she'll be up to it, I think this morning rather took it out of her.'

'Where is she?' He calls out, 'Val? Are you about? How do you fancy lunch down at the garden centre? My shout.' I hope he's not just jolted her from any sleep she needs but I don't say anything because he's being so thoughtful.

An hour later and we're sat at the table with our drinks and a wooden spoon with our order number on. Mum looks tired. It took her an age to get from car to café and she was so desperate to sit down by the time she made it, she didn't even ogle the cakes. I don't know what's happened to her, she's suddenly slowing down. Like, out of the blue. 'Busy, isn't it?' she says, glancing round at the other diners. Mostly women of a certain age with the occasional lap dog or shopping trolley. She glances down at the menu. 'Oh. It's O65s discount day, that's why.' She pauses, her shoulders droop. 'There's another thing I'll bloody well miss out on. All these years spending a fortune in this café or on Christmas decorations and I won't ever get ten per cent off a teacake.'

'You can't eat teacakes.'

'I could have. Before the fuckety bollocks. Percy put paid to that.'

'Percy?' asks Mitch.

'Her stoma.'

'Ah. Yes.'

'I'd pull the currants out if they gave me ten per cent off.'

I reach out and give Mum's hand a squeeze just as someone walks past with a teacake and she growls under her breath.

Mitch interrupts the moment. 'Hey, I've got something for you. Close your eyes.'

Christopher, the boy I used to play with when I was a kid, he was the first person to ever make me close my eyes like this. I did as asked and he put a spider in my hands. I opened my eyes, screamed, and the spider scarpered up the sleeve of my Angora cardigan. A cardigan knitted by Mum, the one and only time she knitted. Of course, being Angora, you couldn't get the bloody thing out and I ripped it off so quickly, launching it across the garden, that it landed in their compost bin just as his mum tipped the potato peelings in. I hated wearing it after that and was relieved when I learned what Angora was made out of and could use that as a reason not to keep it.

'Go on. Close 'em.'

Angora jumper in my mind, I nervously do as instructed.

'Hands out.'

Oh God.

He places a box in my hands. It's cool and rectangular. It has pointy edges and feels expensive. Mum lets out an 'ooooh' of appreciation.

'Open.'

A white box with an Apple symbol sits in my palm. 'What...?'

'I thought that, since yours is being a bit weird, you could... you know...'

I open the box to find a brand new, gold iPhone 8. 'What's this for?'

'For you. I know you're worried that your mum will call you and you'll miss it, so I thought I'd get you a special hotline just for her.'

Mum lets out an '*ahhhh*' before clamping her lips shut with thumb and forefinger.

'But this is too much! These are—'

'You're worth it. Your mum is worth it. Remember, I know what this is like.' Mum sniffs and pretends her eyes are watering, just because. 'It's got a new number. You can just give it to your mum. And me, if you like.'

'Well, of course I'd give it to you.'

'Whatever, it's fine. The important thing is that you have a phone that works for whenever and however your mum needs you. No missing calls. No missing texts. It's a new number. A new contract.'

'But I can't afford a contract.' Which reminds me I'm late paying this month's bill.

'I'm paying for it.'

'Mitch, you can't. That's too much. It's too much.'

'It's not. You need a phone that works. For your mum. If I can help with that, I want to.'

'That really is very lovely of you,' says Mum, beaming.

'It's fine. I just want to help.'

'But...'

'But what?'

I can't really answer. I don't know. It feels all wrong, I know he's trying to help and do the right thing, but it just feels... I feel bad. Of course I'd sort my phone out myself, if I had the money. 'I'm just a bit overwhelmed.'

'You're going to have to get used to being looked after, you know, and supported. That's what people in a relationship do.'

Mum is smiling from behind her fingers.

'Are we in a relationship?'

'Of course we are! If you'll have me?'

An older couple on the table beside us have clearly overheard and smile at us, then each other. I feel a bit embarrassed by how public it all is, but he's so enthusiastic and Mum's so happy and—

'Who's having the pie?' asks the waitress. I stick my hand up and she pops the plate down just as I whip the phone out of her way. Mitch takes it from me, putting it into my bag with a wink and a smile and I realise how lucky I am. And how unused I am to letting someone care for me this way. Ben tried so often, I rejected it so often. It's another thing to do differently.

Chapter Fifty

By the time we get home, Mum just wants to head back up to bed. Mitch hovers on the doorstep. 'You can come in, you know.'

'I shouldn't. I can't trust myself.'

'Do you have to trust yourself? I mean… we could…'

'No. No. Not today. Not like this. Not here. Let me take us away.' I go to protest but he cuts me off. 'Not far. I know you don't want to be away from your mum. Look, let me book us into a hotel somewhere. Hathersage. That's nice. And we can be back in half an hour if she needs you.'

'I do love Hathersage. Some of the pubs have B&B rooms, I think…'

'Leave it with me. Keep your weekend free.' He leans in slowly; his lips graze mine as he cups my cheek. We kiss gently, softly, like we're scared to really go for it, yet if he's anything like me right now, we could both totally go for it. This time it's his turn to groan. 'I should go. Before I change my mind.'

'You can change it at any time.'

'You are terrible. But I love you.'

We both pull back, aware of what he's just said.

'Sorry. Ignore me. That was… that was my groin talking. I didn't mean it… well, I mean…'

'It's fine. Don't worry.'

'No, really. That wasn't fair. I mean, you've enough on your plate. You don't need doorstep declarations to add to your emotional mix.'

'It was quite a nice doorstep declaration.'

'Yeah?' he says, running his hands through his hair.

'Yeah.' I nod, pulling him towards me and kissing him hard.

'I'm going. Before I do any more damage. Get your phone set up. Text me when it's done. Make sure it's turned up loud.'

He winks at me, turns on the top step and jogs down to his car and I am left with that dizzy feeling you get when someone new makes you feel like a kid and a woman all in one go. When you want to jump someone's bones but also run away a bit because it's all going really fast, even though you're supposed to have put the brakes on. I can hear Leanne in my head, telling me to be careful but open. Telling me to go for it so long as I'm steady, because nothing good ever came from running away. And I bite down on my bottom lip until it hurts a little so the butterflies go away.

I tap on Mum's door, carefully opening it to see if she's okay.

'Hey, love, come in.' She's got her headphones in, her old CD player rests on the bed sheets. 'I was just listening to Queen. My first boyfriend, a good while before I met your dad, he took me to see them, ooh, when would it have been, nineteen seventy-four-ish, I guess. I must have been about sixteen, seventeen? He was older than me. A journalist for a Sheffield paper. He had backstage tickets and I stood in the wings at Sheffield City Hall, they were incredible!'

'Wow. That's pretty cool. How did I not know about this?'

'God, I bet there's loads of things like that.'

'What was he called?' Mum looks blank. 'The boyfriend, what was his name?'

'Oh.' She smiles. 'Terry. He was called Terry Booth and I loved him.'

'You loved him?'

'I did. And he loved me.'

'Wow, Terry Booth. So if you loved him and he loved you, what happened?'

Mum moves the CD player to her bedside table. 'Oh you know, life got in the way. I got frightened. Your dad came along eventually. I was stupid.'

'Stupid? That's harsh.'

'I suspect life would have been very different if I'd married Terry Booth.'

'You wouldn't have had me, for starters.'

'Oh, you'd have still been here. You'd have just looked like him, and he'd probably still be around. We wouldn't have had to fight to survive on our own for all those years.'

I shift to sit cross-legged before her. 'You know, it didn't feel like a fight, Mum.'

'No?'

'Never.'

'Some of it was a fight, for me. The bills, the shame I felt, the need for you to be okay and I wasn't always able to be certain you were. Maybe that would have happened anyway; as you grow, you distance yourself from your parents, that's natural but...' She pauses to think. 'We didn't need him,' she says, eventually. 'I think that's what I always wanted you to know. He might not have wanted us, he might have left, rejected us, but we had to come to realise we didn't want him either. Not on his terms, not the way he'd have us live.'

I think back to the rows, the passive aggression, the constantly being made to feel like I couldn't say anything in case I got it wrong, in case

I said something stupid, or triggering. I guess that he wasn't violent made us lucky, but so much fear could stem from a look he gave, or a stern talking-to. His choice of words. His subtle pushing down of our spirits. His dominance so often just snuffed us out.

'You know what it felt like, after he'd gone?' I say, realising. 'It felt like we were a team. It felt like we could do anything as long as we had each other. It felt like you were free, and I could be free too because nothing and nobody was going to control us or shame us or make us feel like we weren't worthy any more. It made me feel like I learned who the real you was.'

'I think it was the first time in a long time that I could be the real me.'

'And I loved that. I mean, obviously Dad going was horrendous. And I don't know how long it took for us to truly get over it.' Or if I ever did. 'But I do remember you telling me we didn't need him. I remember I didn't believe it. But I also remember that you seemed relaxed. You felt warmer, somehow. And despite all that was going on, and how much I hurt at the time, we'd laugh, do you remember that? Whatever his leaving did to me, however much it shaped some of the choices I went on to make, I remember watching telly with our dinners on our laps, because we could. I remember going out and doing those workshops together, making rubbish pieces of artwork but we didn't care because it was fun, and we were together and when we got home we knew we could get takeout from the Happy Garden and nobody would complain about the smell.'

Mum smiles, her eyes glassy. 'I do remember. I remember it all. I could murder a Chinese.'

I check my watch. 'They're shut.'

'I know. Don't think Percy would like it anyway. And I'm knackered.'

I shift, getting off the bed. 'Come on, move down a bit. Let me plump up your pillows and tuck you in like you used to do for me.'

'It shouldn't be this way round.'

'Course it should. You did your bit, now I'm doing mine. That's how this works, it's the natural order.'

'It's a bit early for the natural order though, isn't it.' It's not a question, because she knows I agree. I shift her bedside table about so she can reach her water and tablets and the menthol lozenges. 'Mitch seems good. Kind. He thinks about you.'

'He does.'

'Ben used to think about you too though.'

I go to fiddle with her curtains, make sure no light can come in before she's ready to wake. 'He did, and I couldn't cope with it.'

'I always wondered what your dad leaving would do to you. I wondered how you would cope, I wondered about the lasting damage. And I know, Jem, I know it was hard. And I know you shut off to the pain. I know you missed him, even though he wasn't particularly nice to be around.'

'Funny how that goes, eh?'

'It is. But it's understandable. He was your father. You loved him, no matter what. You were a kid.'

'I was.'

'And that's why I've always told you—'

'To never be afraid to love.'

'He took so much away from us, Jem. Don't let him have that too…'

I turn to face her. Her eyes are closed, she's washed out. Thin. The last few weeks have definitely shifted things. And I can see now, that I'm caring for her. That she relies on me. And however much it hurts,

I am so grateful that I've found the strength to, at the very least, do that. I got that from her. Dad couldn't have taken that away.

'I don't know what happened with Ben,' she says, her voice almost as small as she is. 'I don't know what you wrote in that letter, but, whatever you did or think you did, whatever it is you've been seeking forgiveness for, you can't get that from anyone but yourself,' she adds, turning over. 'You have to forgive yourself, Jem. And you should because you're brilliant. Don't let anyone tell you otherwise, least of all yourself.'

Chapter Fifty-One

I pull her door closed, quietly letting it click shut, trying not to wake her. I've sat for the last half an hour, just watching her. Her breath is shallow. I kept watching her chest to make sure she was still breathing. I've studied her face, the woman I know better than anyone else in the world, the woman who's taught me so much, the woman who knows time is running out. There's a weakness I've never seen before, something in that feels wrong, it's anti-her and I don't know what to do with the taste it leaves. And the very worst part of it all is that I want this to be over. I want the pain to go. I want the bad stuff to finish, yet the only way that can happen is if she was no longer here and I don't want that either. I really don't want that. How can it be fair? Whilst Dad presumably still struts around wherever he may be, she is here, failing. There are people all over the world who deserve death more than she does and yet that's not how it goes.

And how bitter must I be to even think that in the first place.

That night I climb into bed, wired but tired. Conflicted again. A day that started out with the Macmillan nurse visiting, that moved on to lunch and loveliness, is drawing to an overwhelmingly sad close.

The Apple box sits on the side, beside a bottle of Chianti I found in the kitchen. I pour a glass, then reach for the phone, switching it on, getting set up. I tap out a text,

Hey you, phone set up, this is my new number. Thank you for this, for caring. I feel so much better to know that I won't miss a call or message from Mum.

I half expect him to call like he normally would but am sort of relieved to just get a message back. *You're welcome. Glad I can help. X*

I drop the phone back on the side, look disdainfully at my old one, then snuggle down into my bed, head just raised enough to sip at my wine as I let the day's events wash over my heart. I catch sight of the Moomin envelope on the bedside table. If I had a lighter, I'd burn it now. Here. In my room. I'd watch the flame swallow the words and I'd blow the smoke as it twisted. I reach for it, staring at my handwriting. It feels like such a long time ago that I wrote it. I feel different from the person who emptied her regrets onto the page. Was I honest? I feel like I was, it felt cathartic at the time. I just wrote and wrote. Everything I could remember I wanted to say sorry for flowed onto the page. But was it enough? Is it enough to leave the past behind me?

I turn the envelope over, peeking inside just enough to expose the paper. I see the blue curl of my letters and reach inside, pulling the letter out. It feels alien.

Then I read.

Dear Ben,

There are some things I have to tell you. Things I need to own so I can move forward with my life. But they're things that you may not want to know. After all, you left, as well you should have. I neither deserved nor appreciated you - at least, not the way you wanted me to. Not the way you had every right for me to. I wish I knew why I behaved the way I did, I wish I could put it all right, but sometimes, it's just too late.

I've often wondered how much you knew and chose to ignore, versus how much I'd got away with lying about. Like the time I kissed George Newman at his house-warming party after you and I had a row. I justified it by telling myself I thought we were over. Or that George came on to me. I was lying to myself as much as you. I was so hurt by our row, I was so frightened that it meant the end for us, and where most people would fight, something in me couldn't. I pretty much rolled over, accepted my fate.

Except it wasn't my fate, was it. You came back. We talked. It was just a silly row. I'd been so frightened of losing you I made the worst choice. You'd think I'd have learned my lesson after that but there were more lies.

Like the time an old work colleague knocked on my door at two in the morning. I guess I must have mentioned that you were away, working. He'd been out drinking with rugby mates and was hammered. He pushed his way into my house and I didn't resist because I knew him even though I felt uncomfortable. He asked if we could have sex and I said no but he didn't let up. He kept telling me how much he fancied me, how he'd always fancied me. He reached for my hand and placed it on him, he was hard. He told me it was a gift for me and I didn't know how to get him to leave. I told him all about you, I reminded him I wasn't single, he said neither was he and then pushed himself on top of me and though I consented, in as much as I didn't push him off me, I didn't really want to do it. I just felt like I had no choice. We didn't have sex, that much I managed to avoid. But we did other stuff, and I felt cheap and ashamed and dirty. And I felt like I'd let you down. I did let you down. I should never have let him in. I should never have let him talk me into anything. You asked me if I was okay the next day, when you got back. I was in the shower for the third time that day. You must have sensed something. I lied. I said I was fine because, as ever, I'm weak. Always weak...

The memory of that night makes me feel nauseous. I knock back the rest of my glass of wine to take away the taste I can still taste whenever I think about that night. Putrid. The shame in my belly when I saw Ben the next day and he pulled me in for a hug and I froze. I wanted to run away. But it was Ben. I should never have felt that about Ben. But I couldn't tell him either. I'd done it. I'd consented. I hadn't screamed and shouted and fought the guy off. I just went along with it because it felt easier than the alternative, and that's me all over. Never enough fight. Never enough strength.

I fold the letter up, my lip curling in disgust. I shove it into the envelope and bury it at the back of my bottom drawer. Today me would never let that happen. Today me is appalled at the old me. Today me pours another glass of wine and knocks it back in one before sinking deep into my bed and pleading for sleep to come quickly. Today me is exhausted of the noise in my head. The constant, judgemental noise.

Chapter Fifty-Two

I'm ticking my way through the bank statements for my client, Leanne on FaceTime beside me. 'What did you say?' she asks, because of course I had to tell her about Mitch's love declaration.

'I didn't know what to do. I don't know if he meant to say it or if it just sort of tumbled out of his mouth.'

'It's a bit soon, isn't it?'

'Does it matter? If that's how he feels about me? I mean, yes it's quick, but…'

'I guess you can't help what your heart feels.'

'Exactly.'

'So, what's holding you back?'

'I like him. I do. I really like him. He makes me feel… I don't know. It's like butterflies. It's strange. I don't think I've ever felt about anyone quite the way I think I could about him.'

'What? Not even Ben?'

My heart sucker punches at the sound of his name. 'I don't know. No. I don't think even Ben.'

'Wow. You loved Ben.'

'I did…' I drift off. For a fraction of a second I am back in Cornwall, the sun on my back, his arm resting across my shoulders as we both sunflower to the sky. 'But maybe only as much as I let myself. And I want it to be different with Mitch. He's thoughtful. He gets me. He doesn't judge. I feel like maybe I'm a better person because of him.'

'You don't need him to make you a better person, Jem. You're already great.'

'You know what I mean. Doesn't Andy make you a better person?'

'Depends if he's dropped his pants *in* the wash basket or just beside it! Look, you know what I'm going to say, don't you?' She strokes Freddie on her lap, not looking like a Bond villain because Freddie's a scruffy, three-legged black cat and she's in her pyjamas.

'To stop being frightened?'

'This is your time.'

'It's my mum's time,' I say, hearing Mum move about downstairs.

'Okay, yes, it's your mum's time. But you can't look after her if you don't look after yourself and if looking after yourself means allowing yourself to leave your past behind you and fall for someone new, and you're really certain he's a good guy, then maybe that's what you should do.'

'Do you ever wear those on the nursery run?' I ask, deftly changing the subject.

'My pjs? Of course I do. I like to shock the soccer mums with my laissez-faire attitude.'

'Laissez-faire? Yes, I've always had you down for not giving a shit.'

'Don't you try turning the tables on me. I see you. I see what you're doing. It'll not wash with me, my girl. Look, go on, get yourself to Hathersage. Enjoy some time away. Relax. Let him run you a bath. Let him treat you. Let him do that thing you like—'

'Leanne!'

'Just saying. I'm sure he would if you asked.'

'I'm going!'

'And tell me everything when you get back!'

I hang up, slinging my old phone on the bed. Which reminds me, the bill's due. I check my bank account to see I've not quite got enough in to cover it and I sink into the chair, wondering what the hell I'm going to do. I've a tiny bit left in my savings, may as well move the whole lot over, as I can't imagine when I'll next see any decent income. Shit. How did things get this bad? How did I let myself get into this mess? What is wrong with me?

The phone Mitch gave me is on the windowsill, all bought and paid for. It's brand new and doesn't have a smashed corner of the screen from when I was trying to bring all the shopping into the house in one trip not three. The two phones are like a metaphor for my life. One pristine, available, there for me and Mum. The other, a little bit battered and bruised and there's no cash in the bank to pay for it. The new phone definitely feels more appealing on that basis, for sure.

I send my new contact info to Mum so I can save it into her phone when I go down. Bubbles pulsate as she immediately types a response. I can hear Alexa streaming music from the 70s and I wonder if she's reminiscing.

Great. Mitch is so lovely. We're lucky to have him around.

And that she considers him around for us both makes me smile. So what if he loves me before I'm quite sure what I feel. I don't have to hide from that, I don't have to worry. I was just taken aback. She's right. He is a good man. And I deserve that, I'm sure I do. And very soon, I'll start feeling that too, right? Fake it 'til I make it?

I pull out my weekend bag from the back of the wardrobe and start throwing clothes into it. I'm going to enjoy this, the being spoiled, the being taken care of. It's all allowed. I don't have to run away.

But I'm definitely not going to ask him to do that thing that I like…

Chapter Fifty-Three

My head sinks into the pillow, my face hot, my heart racing. Mitch nuzzles into me, his own breath heavy. Whatever happened before, on Mum's carpet, in our love pit, can't possibly have been as good as the sex we just had, because surely, I'd no way have forgotten it. So focused on me, so generous, so all-consuming and free and dizzying. I mean, I've had it good before, now is not the time to compare, but somehow, this was different. Is it me? Am I different?

When Mitch said he was booking us a little trip away, I didn't expect it to be the honeymoon suite in The George. I had not imagined us dropping our bags in the room, lying on the bed and holding one another until I thought I might explode, at which point he got up off the bed and ran me a bath, undressing me and holding my hand as I climbed in, then talking to me as I soaked. I had not imagined him picking out a dress for me to wear, helping me into it, kissing me, up against the wall, with everything that he had, before taking my hand and leading me, breathless, to the bar downstairs to order champagne whilst we waited for our table. It was like I didn't have to think about a thing, I could just relax, give in to him to care for me. It felt strange at first, the control freak in me panicked, and yet he was so gentle, so loving. And it's time I stop trying to hold on so much that I never let go. Which is why it felt good to have him pull out my chair as I went to sit down, laying the serviette across my lap before bending down to kiss me on my forehead, then taking my hand in his as he sat down before me. I couldn't have dreamt of having my food ordered for me to see if he could guess what I might have liked and him getting it exactly right.

We took another bottle upstairs with us. He poured us both a glass as I lay on the bed. I took a sip, and he kissed me. The fizz of bubbles matching the fizz in my belly as he pushed me back onto the bed. His hand, slowly moving down my neck to my chest, brushing against my nipple, then down further still, his own breath catching, as he realised how much I needed to feel him inside of me.

And now I feel heavy and light at the same time. I feel whole, I feel safe. I feel like everything that has gone before can no longer cast a shadow over me because I'm in the moment and I'm happy and I'm drifting, weightless, content.

A shaft of light casts a golden pool from window to carpet. I reach for my watch to see the time. It's eight in the morning, the latest I've slept in since Mitch stopped over. I feel rejuvenated. Sleep was heavy, no dark dreams or memories this time. I turn to watch him, the sheet down to his waist, his chest rising and falling as he shallow breathes. I yearn to reach out to him, trace my finger from his neck to his waist. I want to pull him into me, feel everything I felt last night again and again until I sleep once more. I shift closer to him, I lay a kiss on his shoulder, before biting him gently. He doesn't open his eyes, but wraps an arm around me, pulling me in close. We're chest to chest, I drape my leg across him and feel him come alive. Eyes still closed, he pushes me back, lying on top of me, my legs wrapped around his. He rocks, gently, and I let out a soft moan gripping him closer into me. And then my phone rings, and I panic because it's the phone Mitch bought me. The one only he and Mum have the number for. He stops, instantly, reaching to pass me the call.

'Mum?' I ask, moving to sit up as he places a hand on my leg and waits to see what's up.

'Love, don't panic, but I'm in Calow Hospital.'

'What? What happened?' I jump out of bed, wrestling clothes out of my bag to find pants and jeans and my T-shirt.

'I don't know. I had a fall. My legs, they just gave way. I couldn't move. And I waited, I sort of hoped they'd come back to life and that I could move myself, get up. But it didn't happen.'

'So how did you end up in Calow?'

'I waited until this morning; I didn't want to wake next door. I didn't want to bother you.'

'You could always have bothered me, Mum. That's why you have this phone, that's why we didn't come too far away.'

'I know but—'

'There's no buts, Mum. Jesus!'

'It's fine. I managed to drag myself to my phone this morning. I called Marjorie, she came over, found the key in the back and let herself in. She helped me up then called the paramedic. They've just brought me in to check me over.'

'I'm coming, I'll be there as soon as I can.'

'It's fine, love. I didn't call for you to come over, I just knew you'd be cross if you came home to find I wasn't in and hadn't told you.'

'Mum! I'm not cross. I'm *worried*. I shouldn't have come away.'

'Nonsense, you can't put your life on hold, just in case.'

I lean against the same wall Mitch kissed me against, energy suddenly depleted. 'I'll be there within the hour.'

'Okay, love. I'm sorry.'

'What for?'

'Ruining your break.'

'You've ruined nothing, Mum. I'm just glad you called me eventually.'

I throw clothes and underwear into my bag, telling Mitch what happened as I race around the room trying to collect everything. 'I can't believe I wasn't there.'

'You're allowed a break, Jem,' he says, packing his own bag. 'You're allowed to have time off.'

'But I should have made sure she had everything she needed, or got someone to check in on her.'

'As if she'd have let you do that.'

'True, I suppose. Oh God, what if—'

'What if what?'

I don't really know what I was going to say, it just all feels so significant.

'You can't think about what ifs.' He comes to stand before me, his hands on my shoulders. 'Breathe. Okay. Breathe. Let me finish packing your stuff, let's check out and I'll take you straight over.'

'But we haven't had breakfast.'

'It doesn't matter. It's all fine.'

'Are you sure? I feel so bad.'

'Stop!' His firmness takes me aback. 'You don't have to apologise every time something happens to ruin our plans. Please, Jem, this is your mum. She comes first, okay? No arguments. No question.'

I nod. Tearfully.

'Come here.' He pulls me into his arms and I wish I could stay there because reality isn't nearly as warm. 'I'm here. You're going to be fine.' I nod into his chest, grateful. 'Let's go.'

We're downstairs. Mitch carries both bags. I'm flicking through the newspaper waiting for the bill to be settled, trying not to hop from one foot to the other. 'It's declined,' says the girl on reception for the third time.

'It can't be. I don't understand.'

'I'm sorry, sir. Do you have another card?'

He flicks through his wallet. 'No. I don't. But there's money in there, it must be your machine.'

'I don't think it's our machine, sir. I just processed a payment a moment a go.'

'Bloody hell.'

'Hey?' I say, rummaging in my bag for my purse. 'Don't worry, I'll sort it.'

'You can't afford this!' I look up sharply. 'Sorry, I just mean, it's expensive. It was supposed to be my treat.'

'Look, don't worry about it. It's fine. Let me sort it.' I just want to leave. At this point, I don't care who pays the bill. 'Here.' I pass my card to the girl, hoping that the money I transferred from my savings is enough to cover it.

'I'm so sorry. I can't understand it.'

'Don't worry, it's fine.'

'That seems to have gone through, thank you.' She passes me my card back and I'm relieved the money was there.

'Come on then, let's go.'

I grab for my bag but Mitch moves so it's out of my reach. 'The least I can do is carry your bag.'

'Don't worry, it's fine.'

'I don't understand it. I'll transfer the money back to you later.'

'There's no need. Come on.'

I jog over to the car, waiting for him to unlock it. He fumbles for the keys and I try to hold on to the moment before her call when everything was perfect and I wanted him to swallow me whole, not this moment now, where his floundering is making us late, and emptying my bank account, and it's fine, it's not his fault, I just really need to get to Mum.

Chapter Fifty-Four

The consultant sat before us has Mum's full notes in his hand. 'I'm afraid there's a few things going on. The fall was probably just due to increasing muscle weakness owing to your steroids. Not ideal, but a known side effect. I'm more concerned about your colouring, from the scans we did it appears as though the bile duct blockage has shifted and increased in size, which is now causing a major problem. I understand from your Basingstoke notes that Mr Faux had warned us this may cause a problem, but as this cancer can move around within your abdomen, they hoped it might do, relieving the bile duct without invasive intervention.'

'What does that mean?'

We're surrounded by the blue curtains that seem to make doctors think the rest of the ward can't hear your diagnosis. The ones they swoop closed as they whoosh in with files and people and no real answers about what is happening and how long it's going to take and what they're doing actually means. Or maybe that's just how I feel now, sat here, looking at Mum as she half smiles at me, clearly frightened.

'It's not going to move on its own, so we need to intervene. I've liaised with a colleague and though it's tricky surgery, owing to the extent of cancer mass, we believe there is a small section that is clear enough for us to fit a stent, something that will allow the bile duct to navigate past the blockage.' I suppose that's fairly self-explanatory. 'It's a risk, because you're weak, and it's not an easy area to access, but the procedure itself shouldn't be too difficult, once we get in there.'

'Do I *have* to have it done?'

'Well, no… you don't *have* to.'

'What do you think, Jem?'

I look at her: tiny, exhausted over being poked and prodded. 'I think you need to do whatever you want. Whatever feels right for you.'

'What happens if I don't have it fitted?' There's a sharp intake of breath from the consultant, he perches on the side of her bed. 'Just tell us how it is, please. We can take it, can't we, Jem?'

I'm not sure if I can, but obviously I agree. The consultant nods, reaching for Mum's hand and I button up as tight as I can because whatever he is about to say, this isn't good. And I didn't see it coming. I mean, I know they said things weren't great, but it's so quick, so… sudden. I'm not prepared. Can you ever be?

'If you were my mum, I'd tell you to have it done. The alternative is that the blockage rapidly gets worse. Honestly, it could be the difference between a few days and a few weeks, maybe months, if we can manage the rest of your symptoms.'

He's the first to be so explicit and it's like having the wind whipped from my sails. I can't imagine how it feels for Mum who gives a brave, shallow nod. 'Book me in,' she says, her voice fracturing.

'Great. Good call. I think this is the right decision, Mrs Whitfield. We can try and get it sorted this afternoon, if you're ready to go as soon as we can fit you in. We're just looking to juggle a few procedures around. All being well, I'll send someone for you within the next hour. Okay?'

'Okay.'

He looks at me with a bedside manner smile, then leaves, talking to one of the nurses on the way out. This time he leaves the curtain closed, save a small gap. I watch him walk away. I am stunned, silent.

'I'm so sorry for all this, love, I bet you were having a lovely time and there I go and spoil it.'

I turn to face her, refusing to let her see how scared I am. 'You didn't spoil it, Mum, it's fine. I'm just glad I can be here, I'm glad you called, though…'

'I know. I should have called sooner. I was just trying to do the right thing, you know? Not interrupt things for you. You've done so much these last few months, this last year, I am so desperate for you to have nice things in your life, nice people, a nice time.'

'I have those.'

'Yes, but… well, this with Mitch, it's new, isn't it? These are the best times, the most exciting. And they're important to treasure because when you've been with someone forever, the excitement goes. You have to make the most of it.'

'I am making the most of it. Not that I know what our future holds, or how long we'll even be together.'

'Of course you don't. But you like him, don't you?'

I nod. I think back to how cross I was in the hotel, how arsey I got over paying the bill. He must have been so embarrassed under the circumstances. He was trying so hard to make things nice. 'It's strange, Mum. I can't put into words what it is about him. I guess, as terrifying as it is, I feel like I'm getting a second chance at happiness.'

'Good. You should. You deserve it.' She lets her head drop back onto her pillow. 'I wonder how long it'll take for them to come get me?'

'I don't know. Hopefully not too long. There's activity out there.'

'Is there? That's good. And on a weekend. I'm honoured.' We both know that a weekend procedure means things really aren't good. Neither of us say as much. 'Is Mitch still here?'

'Yeah, he's downstairs. He said he'd wait for me. I told him to go, but he wasn't having it. Told me I needed him.'

'That's nice. You should feel like you can rely on him. I never could with your dad. Mitch is a good man.'

'Yeah... I think he is.'

'Mrs Whitfield?' A porter arrives suddenly at the end of her bed. His name badge says Stuart. He's tall and smiles kindly as he pushes the curtain around its rails. 'I believe we have a journey to go on. You up for the ride?'

'Blimey, that was quick.' Mum looks to me, there's fear in her eyes but she smiles as I lean in to give her a kiss. 'Come on then, let's get this sorted,' she says, patting my hand. 'First class, please, if that's alright by you.'

'It's the only class I'll push,' says the porter. 'No free tea and biscuits though I'm afraid, bit of a shame.'

'Do you know how long she'll be?' I ask.

'Not sure, did they say she was getting a stent? Maybe a couple of hours. Time for you to kick back and relax.' He says it in such a way that I suspect he knows most visitors aren't doing much more relaxing than the patients.

'Yeah, I'll go grab a coffee. Put my feet up.' Mum squeezes my hand. 'I'll be waiting. Just call me when you're back up, okay?'

'Okay. Will do. Love you, Jem.'

'Love you too, Mum,' I say, really quickly, so I can shut my mouth and bite my bottom lip really hard until she can't see that I'm not holding this together as well as I'd like. She fixes her own eyes forward, focusing on the ward door as Stuart pulls and pushes her bed, expertly navigating his way out of the ward and down the corridor.

I watch until she's gone. A final glimpse of her thinning brown hair and skeletal fingers holding on to the rail. Shit.

A woman in the bed opposite puts her book down and looks at me. 'I've been chatting to her. She thinks the world of you, you know.' I just about manage a smile. 'I reckon she's a tough old boot, your mum,' she says, kindly.

'She is,' I agree. 'Toughest old boot I know.'

I head downstairs to the main entrance. Mitch sits in the Costa Coffee nursing an empty latte as he reads a newspaper. 'Hey.' I drop into the chair beside him.

'Hey, Jem, are you okay? What have they said? Can I get you a drink?'

'Erm… I don't know. Yes. No. I don't know. They're fitting a stent. It's a blockage. That's what they said would happen. I don't… I can't…' I look up at the menu and over at the cakes and I can't eat anything, and I can't see because I'm crying and shit. 'I can't do this, I've got to be strong, I can't…'

'You don't have to be strong for me.'

'But if I let go, I don't know if I'll stop,' I say, standing, pulling my jacket around me. 'I can't afford to unravel… I think I need air. Can we?'

'Come on, let's take a walk?'

I nod, tears spill onto my cheeks. He pulls me into him, his arm around my shoulder, guiding me out into the blistering sunshine. And I just about manage to put one foot in front of the other, silently praying for this to all be okay because this is not the time for her to go. Not yet. Not now.

Chapter Fifty-Five

We find a bench beneath a tree that's leaves are thick, rich and green. I sigh, stretching out my legs before me, checking my phone to make sure the volume is up as high as it will go. 'Shit,' I say, realising it's dead. 'The battery. I didn't charge it. It never lasts more than a day any more. What was I thinking?'

'Your new phone's okay though, isn't it? The one I got you. That should have plenty of battery if you've barely used it.'

I reach inside my bag to see the battery still has 87%. 'Yes, thank God. Thank you. Thank you for this! I'll just, I'll call them, let them know the right number.' I fumble with the phone, dialling the ward number scratched on my hand from earlier. They take my new number, saying they've heard nothing yet but that I shouldn't panic. It can take some time. I hang up, turn the volume up high but keep it in my hand, shoulders hunched, neck sore. 'Oh God, I can't tell Leanne what's happening.'

'Do you need to?'

'Well, I don't need to. But I'd normally call her.'

'I'm here, you don't need to worry her at the moment. Focus on your mum.'

'I know. But I can't even text. Her number's in my old phone and I didn't give her my new number.'

'Well it's for your mum really anyway, isn't it? You don't want to get it clogged up with other people. Hey, don't worry about it. She'll understand. It's fine. Come on, she's not going to get cross about this, and if she did, well, you need to have words.'

'No, of course she wouldn't, I just… we talk all the time. She knows about Mum stuff. If she doesn't hear from me, she'll worry.'

'She'll understand.'

'Yeah, okay, yeah. You're right. God… I hate this. I can't think straight.' An ambulance siren kicks in as one passes us, racing out of the car park on a shout. A couple walk past, the man holding the woman's hand as she caresses a swollen belly. An old lady shuffles past us using a frame to steady her walk. I look down because I feel bad that I wonder how old she is and how she's still here, yet Mum may not make it past the next few hours never mind longer. I wonder how life is fair and then I feel bad because she might be someone's mum too and how dare I be so selfish.

I don't know how long it takes, or how many people pass us, or how many times Mitch asks me if I need anything, for me to tell him no, before the sun's gone in and a cold wind gets into my bones and my phone rings. I leap on the unrecognised number, terrified. 'Hello?'

'Jem? Jem, it's me.'

Mum's voice sounds funny, but I'm so relieved to hear her I could weep. 'I got the nurse to lend me his phone.' Of course she did. Impatient as ever. As if she'd have waited until she got on the ward. 'They said it worked, the stent. I'll be back up on the ward in about twenty minutes.'

A weight lifts from my heart and shoulders and I realise I can breathe. 'That's amazing, Mum. I'm so pleased. Okay, I'll be up in a minute. I'll see you there. Tell them thank you!'

I hang up, and let out a long, loud release of air and nerves and fear. 'Shit, that was… Fucking hell. I thought…'

Mitch stands, his frame masks the sun and I can look up at him and into his eyes for the first time since the hotel room this morning. 'You can't think anything, it'll eat you up. Are you okay?' he asks for the millionth time, now reaching for my hand and pulling me up to stand.

'I think so, yes. Jesus, that was…'

'Intense. Terrifying.'

'Yes, both of those.'

'Come on. Let's get you a coffee and then you can go see your mum. I'll wait back down in the coffee shop for you.'

By the time I get back up on the ward, the consultant is opening up her curtains and I've missed the post procedure talk. 'Excuse me,' I say, hanging back to speak to him before I see Mum. 'How did it go? Is she going to be okay?'

'It went fine, as well as we could hope. I'm afraid I can't promise it will make enough of a difference though, your mum…' He takes my arm, moving me to one side. 'Your mum is very ill. She's clearly strong and fighting to be okay day to day, but things are advancing quickly. We've upped her steroids to give her some strength for eating and so on, but that will undermine the strength in her muscles. She's going to need a lot of care, have the Macmillan team been in touch?'

'Yes… erm, yes. We saw someone. The other day, she was wanting Mum to reduce her steroids. And some other stuff. What's for the best?'

'Your mum needs to keep pain-free, she needs to eat for strength, she needs to be okay day to day. The medicines we're prescribing will do that. I'll talk to your doctor and they'll liaise with Macmillan, make sure everyone is aware. Okay?'

'How long will she be in here for?'

'To be honest, now she has the stent, there's no reason for us to keep her. She says she just wants to go home. Does she have anyone there?'

'Me. I live with her. I can care for her.'

'Okay, good. If that's what you both want, I'll sort out the necessary paperwork. Hopefully it won't take too long, under the circumstances.'

I hate that circumstances are used as a reason for special treatment, yet I'm so relieved at the prospect of getting her home. Of me getting home. I've never needed to be back in my own room, my own bed, so much as I do right now. 'Okay. Thank you, I mean, for everything you've done for her. Thank you.'

The consultant gives me a half smile then moves on. I take a deep breath before fixing my own smile and making my way back to Mum. 'Hey, how you doing? They say you can come home as soon as they've sorted the paperwork.'

'Yes, thank God. The woman over there is driving me mad and Liza Tarbuck's on at six.'

'Well, fingers crossed we can get back in time.'

'Yes, please.'

We pause; I don't really know what to say to her.

'Who knew the fuckety bollocks could get worse, eh?' she says, eventually, resolute. 'Is Mitch still here?'

'Yeah. Downstairs.'

'Get him to come up. He can entertain us. Distract us from all this nonsense.' She waves her hand around at the room. 'What's the point in having an attractive man at our disposal if we can't objectify him in a moment's darkness, eh?' Her smile is weak. Whatever she says now, she gets.

Chapter Fifty-Six

I climb into my single bed. It's still light outside. Mitch takes me in his arms, holding me close. He insisted on staying, told me that Pip the dog had gone to a neighbour's anyway, that it was fine, he was here for me. I'm glad I didn't fight it. I can barely keep my eyes open, despite it not being late. Mum is in bed in the room next door, her gentle snores oddly reassuring.

'I could never have carried her up the stairs you know, Mitch. Thank you.'

'Hey. It's fine. I'm just glad I could be here to help.'

'I don't know how we'll cope when you've gone back home.'

'I'll stay as long as you need me.'

'What? Here, in this single bed. It's hardly ideal, is it?'

He pulls me in closer. 'It's cosy,' he says into my hair. 'My place, it's too much of Mum. I feel happier here, with you.'

I imagine how his place might look, full of his mum's pictures, fixtures and furnishings. A place that he's inherited but perhaps hasn't yet had the strength to put his own stamp on. I get that. I don't think I could. Especially if he's selling it anyway. Yet, even still, this isn't right for a new relationship. Us here in my childhood bedroom. My body sags, disappointed. 'It's not how it was supposed to be though, tonight, is it.'

'No.' He shifts my face to look at him. 'And another night in the hotel would have been lovely, but your mum needs us.'

'She does.' Us. I'm not in this alone.

He adjusts, resting his head on his hand. 'Maybe we should think about moving her bed downstairs. Or making her a new one up somehow, in the living room, or the dining room even. So she doesn't have to climb those stairs, in case I'm not here.'

I lay back into my pillow, aware how much she'd hate the idea of us creating a bedroom downstairs, yet not having any alternative ideas. Would it seem like she'd given up? Would she feel we'd written her off?

'You could buy her a daybed. Pick one up from IKEA tomorrow, maybe. We can set it up nicely, get cushions or something. She can get up and about whenever she has the strength. Surely knowing she can just move to that would be better than her coming upstairs.'

'It would, I suppose. But isn't it taking her privacy away, her room? That's her sanctuary, always has been.'

'She's going to need 24/7 care soon, trust me, this is going to be the best thing for you both, I promise.'

I can't help feeling doubtful, only because I know Mum. I know how she feels about her own space, about her room. Her bed is just as she wants it. Her pictures are how she likes them. The view out of her bedroom is the one she's enjoyed from the first day we moved here after Dad left. Taking all that away seems so harsh and yet… Mitch is probably right.

'I know this is hard. I really do. You don't have to explain it to me; I've been there. But I'm here to help, to support you. We can get through this together. Okay? Leave it with me, I'll sort it.'

Any doubts I have must take a back seat. I know Mitch is right. 'Thank you, for this. For everything.'

'Hey, it's what I'm here for.' He kisses me. 'This is what you do when you care.'

'I know, I just… I'm not used to it.'

'Then the men before me have been shits and they didn't deserve you.'

'It wasn't their fault, not really.'

'No?'

'No. I guess I was just never comfortable taking help, being cared for. It feels weird, it makes me feel more vulnerable somehow.'

'That's crazy.'

I can't help but agree. When I look at things now, this, today. I don't know if I'd have coped without him. I mean, I've been through heavy stuff with her before, but this is different. There's a reality that everyone is setting us up for. The medical professionals all know what's going on and they're telling us in the most basic terms without explicitly saying, 'Your mum's going to die. Soon.' It's weird to know that's what they're all thinking, yet none of us can bring ourselves to say the words out loud. I guess it doesn't have to be said. It changes nothing. It's a truth better left in the back of our minds whilst we find our path through the days, weeks we have left. Surround ourselves with people that can help us, support us. 'Shit!' I sit bolt upright.

'What?'

'Leanne, I didn't call her. She'll be worried.'

'Why?'

'We talk every day. She'll wonder what's gone off.' I jump out of bed to dig in my bag for my phone, which still hasn't been charged.

'She knew you were away with me though, didn't she?'

'Well… yes.'

'So, she won't be expecting an update from you anyway, would she?'

'Well, I'd have texted. At least.' I plug my phone in, waiting a moment for the battery to charge enough for me to turn it on.

'Really? Even though it was a weekend away, just me and you?'

'We're very close.' I grin, cheekily. 'She'd have wanted all the details.'

'All the details? What's that supposed to mean?' He sits up in my bed, suddenly tight, wound up. 'What are we? Kids again? You don't talk details with your girlfriends any more, do you?'

'Well, not girlfriends, plural… just Leanne.'

He raises his eyebrows. 'Wow. Right. Good to know I'm being scrutinised.'

'What?'

'No, nothing, I just thought this was a grown-up relationship, I didn't realise that you have to tell your best friend all the gory details. What does she want to know? What we did? How it felt? What I'm like in bed? Do you rate me? Marks out of what? Five? Ten? Shall I measure my dick so you can text her length and girth?'

'Mitch! You're being ridiculous!'

'Am I?'

I swallow. Not sure how we suddenly got here, like this, him staring at me as if I'm some stupid kid. I pull down the T-shirt that barely covers my modesty. 'She's my best friend,' I say, quietly, stupidly.

'And who am I then?' He carries on staring before shaking his head, shifting off the bed nudging past me as he leaves my room. I drop onto the bed, stunned, not sure quite what just happened or what I did to trigger him. Not sure what to apologise for because I know it'll be me that's said the wrong thing, it always is, except that I just told it as it is. I mean, I wouldn't have told Leanne *everything* exactly…

And as the front door slams shut and his car starts up, pulling off the drive. I'm overwhelmed with a weight of sadness and fear that I've never known before. Because I don't think I can do this without him and now I don't know how to get him back.

I glance at my phone, should I call Leanne? Text her? Or should this be the start of me standing on my own two feet?

Chapter Fifty-Seven

When I wake the next morning, I can hear Mum's radio in her room. At first, I forget what happened last night. But it's not long from opening my eyes that I remember the look on his face. The way he stared, disbelieving. The way he judged my friendship with Leanne. Maybe he's right, maybe I'm too reliant on her, maybe we do act like kids sometimes. I guess we just get one another's sense of humour and there's no secrets between us. I've made such a mess of all other relationships bar the one with her that I probably do put too much weight on it. My phone is fully charged, but I've not switched it on. There'll be a message from her, I know it. But if he and I are in a relationship, he doesn't need to feel like he's second fiddle to her. He shouldn't have to worry that I'll be telling her intimate secrets. She surely doesn't tell me everything, she's got Andy. I'll call her later. She'll understand.

I pick out my other phone, the one from Mitch. I hover over a message to him before tapping a simple sorry. Maybe it all got too much for him. It's not long since his own mum died. He's still grieving, living with that pain. Maybe yesterday was too stark a reminder and whilst he's there trying to support me, I didn't once ask him how he was feeling. If he was okay. He must have spent so much time at Calow, sitting by her bedside. It must have been all kinds of trigger for his emotions and I didn't even stop to think. I delete the words sorry and steal myself to call him, but as the phone connects and rings, I hear a car pull up on the drive. His car. I run downstairs.

'Hey, hey, I was just calling you.'

'I'm so sorry, I don't know what came over me.' He scoops me up into his arms, holding me close to his chest and that dizzy feeling comes back where our heads touch.

'It's fine. I don't know what I was thinking either. It was a heavy day, yesterday, wasn't it? For both of us. I realised that after the fact, I'm sorry. I guess I was so consumed with Mum stuff I just didn't stop to think about you and what you've been through.'

He takes my shoulders. 'You don't have to. I understand. Honestly. I'm just sorry I flipped. I think you're probably right, I underestimated how the whole thing would affect me and I think it just hurt a bit, that I was there yet you still needed Leanne.'

'She's been my rock for so long, Mitch.'

'Of course she has. I get it. She is amazing.'

'She is.'

He takes me through to the lounge and we sit, facing one another, knees connected. 'But I'm here too, now. You can talk to me. I'm here for you.'

'But it's painful, all of this. It must be.'

'It is. But you're...' He winds his fingers into mine. 'Look, I meant what I said the other day. About not wanting to put all these heavy emotions on you when you've got all this on your plate already, but... I love you, Jem. I couldn't believe it when you popped up on my Tinder. I'd always liked you at school but you were so out of my league. And then when we bumped into each other like that, on the same day, I was like... How weird is this? Is it meant to be? I was terrified, I didn't want to believe what it might mean because I knew I had strong feelings. And then you had all that letter stuff, you just went off to Cornwall…'

'For closure.'

'I know. And that's good. I realised you needed to do that, that and the letter, it's all part of you moving on. But… I want you to move on with me in your life. I want us to journey together. I don't care that this is going to be hard, because I want to be there for you. Whatever you face, I'll face it with you. I'll protect you. You are special to me and I'm sorry I messed up last night. Can you forgive me? Please forgive me.'

'There's nothing to forgive, Mitch. I understand. Of course I understand.'

We hold each other's gaze for a moment before he leans forward and kisses me, so tenderly I might melt into him. 'You don't have to say it back, Jem. I wouldn't put that on you, but I love you. And I'm here for you. You're the most important person in the world to me and I will do anything I can to make this time with your mum the most special and beautiful time that I can.'

He kisses me again, my belly flips. 'I love you too, Mitch. I love you too.'

Chapter Fifty-Eight

'I thought we could celebrate,' Mitch says, popping a bottle of Prosecco and letting the fizz fall into two mugs because my mum appears to have got rid of the flutes. 'To us, to new beginnings.' He hands me a mug and though it feels strange to be toasting anything at the moment, it's quite nice to forget about the reality of life and just float in the nice bits. 'I think your mum likes her new bed, doesn't she?' he asks, peeking through at the daybed he set up for her this afternoon. We picked out soft furnishings for it, telling her it was all a surprise. She was a little taken aback but seemed to relax when I promised she didn't have to use it until she was ready. Like Mitch says, it's a plan B, there for if and when she needs it. 'Are we okay?' he asks, pulling me in to him.

'We're okay,' I say, clinking his glass. I tiptoe to reach him, kissing him like I really properly mean it because I'm so grateful for all the thought he put into sorting Mum out and how much I feel like I can stand because he's here.

'And it doesn't matter that she didn't sleep in it tonight, she can try from tomorrow, can't she?'

'Well, yeah, I mean, if she wants to.'

'Of course, if she wants to. I just think it'll be better for her. You know, less stress getting up the stairs. She can lounge around whilst we wait on her hand and foot.' He says that last bit with a smile on his face but I sort of want to point out that she's not lounging around. I don't though, obviously, I'm sure he didn't mean it that way. 'She seemed pretty good today though, didn't she? Considering.'

I move through to the lounge, tucking my feet beneath me as I settle into my normal chair. 'I think so, she's mostly just glad to be home.'

'Come here,' he says, beckoning me over to Mum's sofa. 'There's more room here, let's snuggle down, watch a film or something.'

It feels strange to sit here with him, in the spot Mum normally sits, but I do because he's right, there's more room. And it's just a sofa, not her sofa. My need to keep things as they are is fear based, I'm sure. He pulls one of her throws over us, topping up my fizz. He reaches across me, putting the bottle on the side, before shifting to lie on top, manoeuvring himself between my legs. 'Now don't you go getting all interested on Mum's sofa.'

'She'd never know,' he says, kissing me.

'She bloody would.' I laugh. 'That woman's got radar for all the things you're not supposed to do, especially when it comes to her sofa. Leanne had a dog, years back, Chien. I let it get up on the sofa when she came over to visit and I swear to God Mum took one look at it and knew there'd been a dog in her seat.'

'Impressive skills,' he says, working his way from my neck, down to my shoulder.

'Honestly, I'm telling you, she'll guess.'

'You don't have to make excuses you know, if you don't want to do this.' He lifts his head from my belly. 'We don't have to…'

And though a part of me can't think straight for everything that's going off with Mum at the moment, part of me wants to make up for the lack of that extra night in the hotel. 'You're very persuasive,' I say, moving down on the sofa.

'I can be, when I want to be.' He pushes his hand beneath my T-shirt, running his hand up the middle of my chest, before pulling me into his touch.

'Let's go upstairs,' I say, reaching down for his hand.

'But your mum, she's in the room next door.'

'What?' I whisper. 'Do you get stage fright?' I take his fingers into my mouth.

'Me? Not a chance. Not when it comes to you. You do things to me, you make me want you. I've never wanted anyone like I want you. Need you. That's it,' he says, shifting himself up, his arms either side of me. 'You make me need you. Now. Here.'

The ache I feel is sharply interrupted as the house phone rings. 'Leave it,' he says but I jump out from beneath him.

'I can't. It'll ring in Mum's room too and she's sleeping. Hello?' Mitch shoves his head into a cushion as I answer.

'Jem, it's me. Are you okay? I've been trying your mobile but couldn't get through, is everything alright?'

'Leanne, shit, I'm sorry. I was going to text you earlier then we got sorting some jobs out and time ran away with me.'

'What jobs? What's going on?'

Mitch reaches for his drink, knocking it back. I can see he's trying not to be irritated by the fact it's Leanne on the phone but I can definitely detect a bit of pissed offness. I can't blame him, it's not ideal. And he was definitely up for whatever he had in mind whether I'd have managed to get him off Mum's sofa or not.

'Look, sorry, now's not a good time.' A smile creeps on Mitch's face as he tops his glass up. He passes me mine, which I empty, handing it back for more. 'Can I call you back tomorrow?'

'Of course you can, but is everything okay?'

'Yeah. It's fine. I mean, well, no,' I add, because I realise I've not told her anything about Mum and hospital and the op and prognosis. 'I mean, we've had quite the weekend, but it's okay. Mitch is here. I'm okay. Mum is stable. I'll call you tomorrow, or pop round. Are you in?'

'All day.'

'Okay, I'll pop round. We can catch up then. Oh, hang on, the doctors might be coming at some point. Let me find out what time, when I can in the morning, then I'll message you and come over.'

'Okay, if you're sure you're okay. Just let me know if you need anything, yeah?'

'Of course. Will do. Talk tomorrow.'

'Okay, promise we'll talk tomorrow.'

'Promise.'

'Love you, bye.'

I catch sight of Mitch's face. I don't think he's irritated, but he definitely doesn't get it. 'Okay. Bye, bye, bye,' I say, hanging up.

'Now, where were we?' I ask, cringing at myself because I'm not in a romcom.

'You know what? Maybe the moment's passed. I'm pretty tired after all the running around this afternoon. And you're probably right, shagging on your mum's sofa seems a bit off.'

'We could make up a den again. She can't come down of her own accord and interrupt us this time.'

'She can't. But no, let's save it for when we're not quite so tired.' He must see my obvious disappointment. 'Hey, I love you. We've got all the time in the world, haven't we?' I nod. 'So it's fine. Here, finish this. I've got more in the car.' He kisses me hard, which is a contradiction to all the backing off he's just done. 'Gimme two minutes.'

He jogs out to his car, now a permanent feature on our drive. I adjust my clothes and shake out the frustration that's built up since we stopped what he started. I wish it were different, and then I feel guilty for thinking it. I mean, in any other situation, any other new relationship, we'd be at it all the time. We'd be sneaking to each other's places whenever we could. We'd be excited by the time we got to spend together. I'd be sharing it all with Leanne, and Mitch and I would be learning how to be with one another. The Mum stuff has sort of interrupted all of that, maybe we'll never get it back. And yet, maybe we've got something different, deeper forming now. He's here at the worst moment in my life, he's around, he's strong, he's helping. Some new boyfriends would run a mile at this situation and yet he hasn't once questioned what he's doing here. At least, not to my knowledge. He's stable, he's present, he's what some people might call a rock.

'I guess we have to seek the good amongst the shit,' I say, when he comes back in with two bottles of wine and a whisky bottle.

'We do,' he agrees, dropping his keys into the bowl on the side. 'I'll pop these in the kitchen.'

'Both of them?'

'Obviously not. Go on, find us a film. I'll pour the wine.'

And as I flick through the TV channels, it feels nice to hear him move about the kitchen like he's lived here forever.

Chapter Fifty-Nine

I knock on Leanne's door, like I haven't in years. Not sure what's stopped me just walking in but it's been days since we spoke properly and I feel bad. Weird, even. When she doesn't come, I ring the bell.

'What the fuck are you ringing the bell for? Just come in!' she says, Elsie hanging off her, Freddie the cat making an escape for freedom out of the crack she's opened wide enough for her to see me, not wide enough for the street to see her feeding. 'Put the kettle on, will you, I'm bloody parched. This one's been crying and feeding and crying all chuffin' morning and Christ knows what's the matter with her.'

'Teeth?' I offer, getting out mugs and milk.

'Too soon. Colic, probably.'

'Bless her. You want me to take her?'

Leanne offers her up immediately. 'Actually, bloody hell, yes. You can have her, she's faffing now anyway, give me a break. Honestly, I feel like she's permanently attached at the moment. So bloody needy. The total opposite to Harley. I could leave him on the play mat for hours whilst I cleaned or cooked or watched *Diagnosis: Murder* on catch up. This one? Not a chance. She clearly doesn't like Dick Van Dyke.'

'Harsh.'

'That's what I said.'

I sit at the breakfast bar, bouncing Elsie on my shoulder. She's a bit grumbly but Leanne doesn't look like she's gonna step in any time soon.

'Anyway, never mind me. What's been going on with you? I thought you'd fallen off the actual planet. I was really worried for the first two days.'

'I know, I'm sorry. Really, I am. It was just… it all happened so quickly.'

'What did?'

'Mum. Mitch and I went to Hathersage, to The George, the honeymoon suite, no less.'

'Nice!'

'Yeah. It was. Bloody lovely in fact, but then Mum took a fall—'

Leanne spins round. 'Shit!'

'I know.'

'Why didn't you call?'

'There wasn't time. Mitch and I paid up and left as quickly as we could. We were only there one night, he'd booked us in for two.'

'A pricey do, I'll bet. He must have been a bit annoyed at having to leave early?'

'No, he was fine about it. I ended up paying the bill anyway.'

'What?'

'His card was declined, we were in a rush. He'll pay me back, I'm not worried. It's just that we needed to get to Mum. Think he was pretty embarrassed really.'

'Right.'

She's making tea but studying me as I talk. It always makes me nervous when she does that. 'Anyway, we paid up, went over to Calow, and it all pretty much went to shit from there.'

'You okay with Elsie?'

'Yeah, I'm fine.'

'Come through.'

I follow her to the lounge, shifting into the corner of her massive sofa, tucking my feet under a giant cushion. Cosy. 'So, yeah, she had a fall. Her muscles are wasting away, it's the steroids.'

'Oh, no…'

'And then they noticed she was jaundiced, so ran some tests and found a blockage.'

'Shit.'

'They were great. It was weekend doctors, but they still managed to sort it.'

'Thank God for the NHS.'

'Totally. They fitted a stent, sent her home.'

'And is she okay at home? What have they said?'

'Well…' I move Elsie into the crook of my arm. She relaxes and a tiny bubble blows out of her mouth. 'It's not good.' It feels like an understatement but how else do I talk about it?

'How not good?'

I run my fingers down Elsie's velvet soft cheeks. A new life, so much ahead of her, the idea overwhelms me.

Eventually I just come out with it. 'Mum's not got long left.' And though I thought I was okay, in control of my emotions, as soon as I say it, my nose stings because I realise I've been trying not to cry for the last few days, even with Mitch, yet here, now, with Leanne, I don't think I can help myself. I put my tea down. I take a deep breath. 'I'm losing her, Leanne.' She moves beside me, Elsie tucked between us. She takes my hand and passes me a tissue. 'What am I going to do without her? It's so unfair. She's too young, I just… I don't want her to go yet.' Leanne pulls me into her arms and holds me as I shake and cry and everything about the last few days just floods out. 'I've been trying to stay so strong for her, be so on it and in control so she knows she doesn't have to worry, but I don't feel strong and in control.'

'You don't have to, do you?'

'I don't have to, but I don't want her to worry about me. And she would. If she could see me crack, she'd worry, and she's got enough on her mind. It's like Mitch says, she doesn't need the pressure.'

'She wouldn't expect you to be superhuman, Jem. You know that.'

I wipe my face on my sleeve, then my sleeve on my leg.

'What else has Mitch said?' she asks, gently.

'He's been amazing. He's carried her to her bed because she wasn't ready to stay downstairs, in the daybed he's bought and built for her. He's been cooking. He's been out to fetch things she really wants to eat. It's weird. A few weeks ago, she could barely eat a thing and suddenly she's wanting pulled pork and ice cream, all these things she's not eaten for months.'

'Well, that's a good sign, isn't it?'

'I don't know. Mitch said his mum perked up before she died and so I keep thinking this is it: this meal she's eating, this snack, it could be her last. Something could happen so quickly now that she'll just go and I'll get no warning. Like now, I shouldn't be here because what if something happens, but I needed to get out, just for a minute. I needed to see you.'

'Oh, love, I don't know what to say.'

'There's nothing you can say. It's fucking horrible, I wouldn't wish it on anyone.' I wipe my eyes again, gazing down at Elsie who is now flat out.

'You've got the magic touch. That's all I needed these last few days, you to pop round and sort her out.'

'That's probably all I've needed too. A cuddle. A chance to tell you everything.'

'So why haven't you 'til now?'

She passes me my tea and I move to make sure I'm drinking it away from Elsie's head. 'I don't know, time just… disappeared these last few days. And he is being so supportive, but Mitch and I had words the other night; I think it's brought back stuff for him with his own mum too and he felt that I was putting you first before him.'

'Really?'

'Yeah, I mean, he knows that's not the case, obviously. It's just that, with time being so pressured these last few days, when I have wanted to call you, it's been the first time Mitch and I have had a moment and I didn't want to upset him. He's done so much for Mum and me these last few days.'

'Which is lovely, that's great that you have the support. But he doesn't have to make you feel bad for talking to me.'

'No! He's not. It's me making me feel bad. I just, I'm so tired right now. So confused by everything. I suppose you were the person I thought I didn't have to please.'

'You don't have to please anyone at the moment, chuck. You just have to be okay for you and your mum.'

Elsie murmurs so I move her to the other side, shaking my dead arm into life. 'I know, I do know. It's just hard…'

We sit in silence. Leanne gazes out of the window. 'What's up?' I ask her, eventually.

'Nothing.'

'You're a rubbish liar.'

'No, it's nothing. I'm just… I'm worried about you, that's all. I can't imagine how awful this is for you. I wish I could do more to help. I mean… are you sure you're getting the support you need from Mitch?'

I pull back. 'Of course, why wouldn't I be?'

'Well, like you say, he's still processing his own stuff. It must be hard, he might not always be able to get it right.'

'He's got it right every time so far…' I try not to think about the other night and our falling out.

'Good. So he should.' I stare at her, she's not saying something. 'So what can I do, then?'

She says it in a weird way, like I don't need her or something. 'What do you mean?'

'Well, if Mitch has got things covered, what do you need from me?'

'Baby cuddles with this one. Patience. No grief over my lack of contact. Love me despite everything that I am.'

'Of course I love you *despite everything you are.* Somebody's bloody well got to.' She squeezes my hand and I blink back any tears that threaten again because there's no use crying over veiled sentimentality now and, besides, something's shifted between us. It's odd. 'Do you want food? Let me cook something for you. I bet you've not eaten properly for days.'

'I have, it's fine,' I lie, because despite all the cooking he's done for Mum, Mitch and I have mostly eaten crisps washed down with copious amounts of alcohol because it seems that's the only way either of us can get any sleep at the moment. Not that I tell Leanne this, she wouldn't understand. 'I have to get back anyway, I was only popping by to update you. Mitch wanted to pop out before he cooks tonight and I don't want to leave Mum on her own.' That bit is true. He said he'd cook for us all for a change.

'Okay then, maybe this weekend. Come over Sunday, let me do a roast.'

'I don't know what we're doing.'

'So you come. On your own.'

Mitch would love that at the moment. Can I just pop out whilst you look after my mum so Leanne can feed and water me? 'I'd love to, really, but I don't know what's going to be happening. With Mum, I mean. I feel like I can't plan ahead.'

'Well, maybe we could come to you. She can have a cuddle with Elsie. Harley can bring his joke book, she'd like that, wouldn't she?'

'She gets tired so easily.'

'It's fine, we don't have to stay long.'

'I guess...' My phone dings with a text from Mitch asking me when I'll be back. 'Hang on.' She watches as I tap out a five minutes to him. 'Look, let me call you. See how she's doing. We'll sort something, play it by ear. Is that okay?'

'Of course it's okay. Just...'

She stops talking as I stand. 'What?'

'Stay in touch, yeah? Don't let Mitch persuade you that you don't need me.'

'He wouldn't! For God sake's, Leanne, he couldn't, you're my best friend!' There's a spike of something between us. Something I've never felt with her before. A disconnect. 'I'm sorry. Just bear with me. It's weird, I feel weird. Things are happening so fast.'

'Okay.'

'I'm sorry it's not a longer visit.'

'Hey! It's fine,' she says, strangely. Then adds, 'I'm just glad you're okay and haven't shagged yourself into a stupor.' She half smiles at me but I feel like she's studying me too, judging.

'Chance would be a fine thing.' I hand Elsie back over to her. 'I'll let myself out, okay. You stay there. She's asleep, get *Diagnosis: Murder* on.'

'I might. Or I might just sleep too.'

'Sounds bloody lovely. Hey, thank you. I'm sorry I didn't tell you what's been going on until now. It's just really hard. I feel a bit pulled all over.'

'Yeah, I know. Look, just remember I'm here, okay. Whenever you need me. Yes?'

'Yes.' I give her a kiss, then sneak out so as not to wake Elsie. As I climb into my car, she's at the window, waving. Something's changed. And I don't know if it's me or her or both of us.

Chapter Sixty

'I don't know why you don't just jack in all your work at the moment,' says Mitch as he places a glass of wine beside my laptop. 'An old client of mine has asked me to pick up some work for him, they've got some analysis they need doing. I mean, obviously I don't need the money at the moment, but it can go into a pot for us and it's not like your work is paying enough to worry about, is it?'

'I know, and I hate it, but I feel bad. And I really need the money, however little it is. I wiped my savings out with The George—'

'Look. I'm not struggling for cash, am I? Mum left me plenty and I've got work coming in. I said I'd pay you back and I will! We've just been a little bit distracted with more important stuff, haven't we?'

'Oh, I know, I wasn't chasing it. I was just saying, sorry. It's just that my phone bill's supposed to have come out too, I'm bound to be overdrawn but I daren't look.'

'A healthy attitude towards money.' He sits on my bed, back resting up against the wall, feet and most of his legs dangling off.

'You'd think I'd have learned with the bankruptcy. I just don't think I can cope with it all at the moment. Lack of money on top of Mum stuff, it's too much.'

'Of course it is. And anyway, if they cut you off, it doesn't matter, you've got your new phone.'

'I have.' I stroke his leg as a thank you. I tick the final sheet clear, packing them back into the envelope to give back to my client. Job done. I'm thirty pounds up. 'Though, I'd like to at least be grown up enough to manage my own phone bill once a month.'

'Wow. Thanks.'

'What?'

'Nothing.'

'What do you mean, nothing?'

'Well, it just sounds a bit ungrateful, that's all. I tried to do the right thing with your phone, I was just trying to help. Your old one wasn't working properly anyway, was it? So why does it matter?'

I shift my knee to touch his and he moves away. 'It wasn't, no, but it matters because it's my independence. It's the only bill I have and I just want to try and keep on top of it. Everyone has that number too, you know?'

'Everyone? Who is everyone? The only people that ever call you are your mum, me or Leanne.'

'Well, yeah, but… look, never mind. Forget I said anything. I'm sorry, I was just… it doesn't matter. I'm sorry. It's money stuff, it always stresses me out.' He sips at his wine, face stony. I move beside him, leaning in against his hips. 'Hey, sorry. Forgive me?'

He eyes me suspiciously before saying, 'I always do.'

We sip at our wine; the house is quiet. Mum reluctantly decided to sleep downstairs tonight, something about not wanting Mitch to carry her up the stairs again. I think she's feeling weak and she'll hate that. She's not relied on a bloke since Dad left and having to do that now must be conflicting for her.

'So look, I was thinking—' he says.

'Dangerous.'

'What's that supposed to mean?' The stony look returns.

'Nothing! Sorry, I was just joking. Go on.' There's a pause and I hope he carries on because I don't want to fall out. I'm too tired. I'm too stressed. I'm too everything, really. Which won't be helping either of us. 'Sorry, go on.'

'I was thinking that it seems stupid, me and you squashed up in this room, trying to fit into this tiny bed of yours.'

'I know. It is a squeeze. You can go home at any point, babe. I would totally understand. Things have levelled out a bit here, with Mum. I can call you if I need anything. And your neighbour's probably had enough of dog sitting by now.'

'It's fine, she always used to walk him for Mum anyway. And I like being here with you.'

'And I like having you here.'

'So, why don't we move into your mum's room? Now that she's not going to be using it.'

I stop mid sip of wine. 'What?'

'Well, it seems stupid, that big room with nobody in it. This tiny room with two fully-grown grown-ups in it.'

'But, that's Mum's room.'

'Yes, but she's not going to be using it again, is she? She won't mind, she knows we're a bit cramped in here. She even said it today.'

'Yes, but she was trying to give you permission to go home, not move into her bedroom.'

'Permission to go home? Since when do I need permission?'

'You know what I mean.'

I lose words. I mean, on a practical level, I get why he'd suggest it, but emotionally? I'm not ready to move into Mum's room, she's not really ready to have moved out. Given half a chance she'd be back in there.

'Who's to say she won't ever need it back? She might get her strength back up. She's eating better, the doctors said that would help.'

He takes my hand. 'Jem, your mum's not going to get better.'

Breath leaves my chest because I know this, but I don't always need people to be so quick to remind me. 'I know, I mean I know that, but…' My bottom lip starts to wobble which is a bloody irritation because if I'm upset I can't argue this rationally, and I really want to because it's not right. Moving into Mum's room is so off the mark, I can't even… 'We're not moving into her room.' I pick up my phone, (my phone!) and check emails. 'Damn!'

'What?'

'My phone bill didn't come out. There wasn't enough in the bank. The George wiped me out.'

'For God's sake, Jem, I said I'd pay you back.'

'I know you did! But you haven't yet, and so I can't pay my phone bill.' His whole body turns stony this time. 'It's fine.' It's not. 'I'm just saying, I wasn't having a go.' I sort of was.

'Give it here.'

'What?'

He rummages in his pocket, the force of his movement spilling wine on my Forever Friends bedding. 'Careful!' I jump up to grab a towel, rubbing at the duvet. Fifteen-year-old me is furious. In fact, so is thirty-eight-year-old me.

'Give me your phone. The payment details. I'll pay the bloody bill.'

'I don't want you to.'

'So, what? You'd rather get cut off, would you? How would your clients contact you then, eh? You're being stupid. Just let me pay the bill.' He grabs the phone off me, my heart is racing, the sheet looks stained. He taps away at his own phone, a credit card resting on his knee. 'There. Done. Paid for. Happy now?'

'I didn't want you to—'

'Look, I get it. I owe you money, you couldn't pay your bill. I mean, we don't have to talk about the wasted money on theatre tickets, or the nice meals out, or the intention behind going away, do we? Let's just focus on the fact that you had to pay money out you didn't have because, for some clerical error reason, I couldn't manage it. If you'd not been in such a rush, I would have sorted it with another card.'

I stand up, heart now beating out of my chest because I don't know what the hell has got into him but I'm not okay with it. 'Mum was in hospital, how much of a rush did you imagine I'd want to be in?' He rolls his eyes. 'What the fu— tell you what, you sleep in here. Stretch out as much as you like. I'll be downstairs on the sofa.'

'Careful not to do anything your mum wouldn't approve of!'

My mouth opens, I'm stunned. I grab my phone from him, and give him a final, disbelieving look, before shutting the bedroom door behind me as firmly but quietly as I bloody well can.

Downstairs, I creep past Mum to the kitchen, flicking the kettle on. The whisky bottle from yesterday is almost empty. Spitefully, I swig the last of it, wincing at the peaty taste. Whisky was never my drink. I survey a collection of empty and full bottles of wine on the side, noticing that they're always one or the other, there's never a bottle with so much as a drop left in it. I grab a full one, twist open the lid and chug a good quarter of the bottle in one go. It feels good.

Chapter Sixty-One

It's four in the morning when I wake. I know this because there's a digital green glow emanating from the video recorder. I shiver, pulling one of Mum's throws over me, clutching it into my chest. I rub my eyes, trying to adjust to the darkness so I can locate my phone, distract myself from this tightness in my chest, the knot in my stomach, until I fall back to sleep. There's a warm halo glow coming from the dining room, is Mum awake?

I wrap the throw around me and tiptoe across the lounge to the dining room door. Mum's face is lit by a torch focused on her book. 'Mum?' I say, gently so as not to startle her.

'Jem, love? What are you doing up?'

'I was just… I couldn't sleep. What are you doing?'

'Same. Thought I'd try and finish this book in case they don't have that library in heaven.' She smiles, but it's not meant. It doesn't reach her gently lit eyes. It falls from her mouth too quickly. 'Come here, talk to me.'

I clamber on the daybed beside her, moving a cushion to wedge behind my back, feet tucked under her duvet. 'Is it comfy?'

'Not as comfy as my own bed.'

'I can try and get you back up there, if you like. Or wake Mitch, he'll carry you up.'

'No, no. It's fine. I think the energy of holding myself small for him to lift me, that's as exhausting as trying to climb the stairs myself.'

'You know you don't weigh anything any more, it's really no trouble for him.'

'I'm sure. Hey, what I wouldn't have given to be this thin a few years back.'

'Mum.'

'Oh, I know. I'm just kidding.' She pauses. 'It's getting harder and harder to find the humour in all of this, isn't it?'

'It is.'

She puts her torch face up on the table beside her. A shaft of light hits the ceiling and I stare at it.

'What were you two having words about before?'

I snap to look at her. 'What?'

'I could hear you, not what you were saying, just, words, tone. It didn't sound like the chat of a happy new couple.'

Her duvet is warm, I pull it up a bit further, finding her bony bum with my toes. 'Oh, I don't know. Nothing specific. It was my fault really, I missed paying my phone bill and took it out on him.'

'Really?'

'Yeah. Stupid, isn't it. I don't know what's wrong with me. These last few days, I've just been so short-tempered with him. So… snippy. And he's doing so much for us. He's so thoughtful, I don't know what's up with me. It's like I'm repeating history, pushing him away all of a sudden. It's what I do, isn't it?'

'But I thought you really liked him. You said this was different.'

'It is, in so many ways it is, and yet, somehow, I don't know. He told me he loved me the other day.' I neglect telling her I reciprocated.

'Ah. So you're panicking.'

'I don't know, maybe.'

'You know what I think about love, don't you?'

'I do. And I'm trying not to be afraid, but how do you stop it? It just feels so…' My first instinct is to say wrong, but that's so unfair on Mitch I stop myself. 'How do I get past this, Mum? This need to run away all the time.'

'I don't know, love. Not really. All I can say is that every time you run away, things bite you on the bum. I wonder if life keeps trying to teach you a lesson sometimes, and until you hear it, the lessons will get bigger and louder.'

'I can't keep making mistakes.'

She reaches out for my hand. Her fingers are like the bone Hansel hands out for the witch to kid her into thinking he's not gained weight from all her force-feeding. 'You know, Jem, I think you're pretty bloody perfect.'

'Are you drunk again?'

'Not me. That's your zone, that one. Don't think I don't notice how much you sink. That's why you're awake now, I'll bet.'

'Mum. I don't need lectures on alcohol.'

'I'm not giving you a lecture on alcohol… though I do sometimes wonder if I should. I am giving you a stern talking-to about you though, about what you think of you. And how you need to start living and loving and you'd better do it quickly because I can tell you this for nothing, my sweet, life is bloody short.' That last bit makes her hiccup in her breath because she's trying to be strong for me, but I can hear in her voice that she's not feeling it. 'Give him a chance. Let him love you. He may not be the one, The One, but he is your one, for now, and he's trying. Feel the fear and love him anyway.'

'But—'

'Be you. Be strong. Be everything I love you for. But be open too. If there is one thing I want for you in this life, whether it's now, or after I've gone, it's for you to be totally and unequivocally happy with yourself and your life and your choices. I don't want you to hide any more. I don't want you to try to forget or numb pain. I don't want you to think you're unlovable. I don't want you to push and kick and scream when the chance of happiness presents itself. You have every right to be as happy as the next person and you owe it to yourself to embrace that.'

'Mum—'

'And I am not about to lay a guilt trip on you, as I lie here, with however long I've got left to live. I will not tell you that I want to see you happy in my lifetime. That I want to see you settled whilst I am still just about up to seeing it and appreciating it. That wouldn't be fair.'

'Mum don't, please don't. I can't think about it.'

She squeezes my hand, gently, her face resolute. 'You have too, love. *We* have to.' She takes a breath, tapping our hands on her legs. 'This is happening, Jem, we both know it. I wouldn't have got this far without you, without everything you've done. And now it's my turn, whilst I've still got time left, to help you see what you are.'

'I want to see it.'

'I know you do. And I know other people can't be the ones to give that to you, you have to take it for yourself. But now's the time. See you from my eyes, from Leanne's, from Mitch's. See the Jem we see and stop giving yourself a hard time for the person you think you are, or were. That Jem has gone... and in any case, she was never as bad as you believed her to be.' Mum's breath runs out. Energy depleted.

'Here, Mum, come on, lie down. Enough of the life lessons, I hear you,' I say, tucking her in. She shuffles into place on her pillow, her tiny frame swamped by the bed. I lie behind her, holding her arms and listening to her breath, tears streaming. She doesn't do life lessons, my mum. It's not really her way. Funny how things can change when you think there's only so much time left to say the things you want to say.

'I love you, Jem Whitfield. You are the best daughter a mum could have,' she says, before drifting off to sleep.

And I am broken.

Chapter Sixty-Two

'Morning.' I place a tea on the bedside table and straddle Mitch on my tiny bed. He's right, this is ridiculous. We can't both sleep here.

He moves to lie on his back, taking hold of my thighs. 'Well, I suppose there's some benefit to a bed this size, you know, if you have to sit on me to wake me up…'

I lean down, kissing him, running my fingers through his hair. 'I'm sorry. Again. I am a total dickhead sometimes and you are definitely better off without me,' I say between kisses.

'And yet, here I am.' He kisses me back.

Fifteen minutes later and I roll off him, energised and exhausted in equal measure.

'I knew I was stopping here for a reason,' he says, not opening his eyes.

'You mean you're just using me for my body.'

'Well, if you will hand it to me on a platter.'

I slap him playfully and he grabs hold of my wrists, pulling me towards him. 'I'm sorry. Again. I know I'm being so difficult at the moment. I just… I've never been in a situation like this before. I'm not doing a very good job of navigating it.'

'It's not easy to navigate.'

'No. It's not. But you're doing so much to help me, to support Mum, and I'm not appreciating it, you.'

'Oh, I don't know. That just then was pretty appreciative.'

'That just then was an apology.'

'One of the best kinds.'

I manoeuvre myself off the bed, opening the cupboard to find something to wear. 'I'm taking Mum out. She wants to get some clothes, some winter stuff. That wheelchair they delivered the other day, she's decided she's prepared to give it a go, so if I can get it into the back of Petula, I can take her to Cole's, shopping. She loves a department store. We can have lunch, mooch about the clothes. I'll be home this afternoon.'

'You'll never get it in yours. Take mine. I don't need to go out and if I do, I can just use Petula.'

'She's very picky about who drives her,' I tease, pushing my legs into jeans I've found at the back of the cupboard that I'm not sure I can entirely do up.

'I will be very gentle with her.' He reaches down for his trouser pocket, pulling out his keys. 'Here, catch.'

'Thank you. You're the best.'

'I know I am. Now, leave me alone. I didn't sleep so well last night, then I was rudely awoken by some woman demanding sex. I'm exhausted.'

I roll my eyes, blow him a kiss and duck out to leave him be.

The Cole Brothers' car park in Sheffield City Centre is pretty clear and given that Mum's in the chair, I opt to park at the top, out of the way, with free space to try and unload the wheelchair and load Mum into it, hopefully without anyone watching to see if I foul it up.

'I remember parking here with you, when you were a baby. It was my first trip out on my own and I couldn't work out how to put the pram up. Wrestled with it for about fifteen minutes before some bloke noticed I was struggling and snapped it up in seconds. I was mortified. Felt like going home straight away and I would have if I could have worked out how to take the pram back down again.'

She grabs hold of my neck so I can move her from car to chair. It's surprisingly easy given we've never done this before. 'Food and coffee or shopping first?'

'Coffee, then shopping, then food.'

'Crikey, look at you with all the energy.'

'I know, right. Let's make the most of it whilst it's here.'

We down our coffees in record time and I wheel her through homewares to the lift for women's wear. I push her around the store, stopping for her to rummage through clothes rails, asking me to pick stuff out and hold it up for her to see. 'Too short,' she says. 'Too long.' 'That'll need a T-shirt underneath it.' 'Do you think it'll get caught in my wheels?'

Despite how picky she is, it's not long before we've got a pile of clothes to take to the till, and she doesn't seem to blink at the bill of £387.

'Christ, I think that's the fastest I've spent that many notes in one shopping trip.'

'You've obviously not been working hard enough at it then,' she says, handing me her purse to put back in her bag. 'Is there anything you want? Whilst we're here?'

'No, thank you.' I'm hooking the bags of clothes she's just bought over her chair handles.

'Ahh, come on. Let me get you something. My treat.'

'I don't need a treat.' I smile at the lady on the till, pulling Mum away before she can do any more damage.

'Why not? It's not like I can take it with me when I'm gone, is it?'

'Mum!'

'What? Come on, let me just get you a little something. A dress? A handbag? A new pair of shoes.'

'I don't need anything. Save your money.'

'How about perfume? You don't have any, do you? I've seen you sneaking into my room to steal mine before now.' It's true. I have done that. 'Come on, let's go downstairs and see if we can't buy you some perfume. That's a right proper treat that, isn't it.'

'Well, I guess it would be, yes.'

'Go on then, forwards. To the lifts. I'm not taking no for an answer.'

I laugh because it's clear she's having a great time and who am I to interrupt that just because I feel guilty at her spending money on me.

Two hours later, she's bought me perfume, some shoes, and a handbag I really fell in love with and totally did not want her to buy but she just wasn't having it. We've shovelled garlic bread and pasta at Zizzi's because she was desperate for some Italian, and lord knows how she managed to put as much away as she did but bloody hell it's nice to see her eat. And so we're here, back in the car park. I've managed to get her back in the car and am now just battling with the wheelchair, grinning to myself over her story about the pushchair.

'Hey, excuse me? Who are you?' A woman, wearing a green animal-print dress like one I have at home, storms across the car park in attack mode. I look behind me to see who she's talking to. 'You! I'm talking to you! What are you doing with my car?'

'Pardon?' I just about manage to drop the chair down flat and get it in the boot, catching my arm as I go. Shit that hurt.

'That's my fucking car. Who the hell are you? Has he sold it to you? It wasn't his to sell.'

'Who? I don't know what you're talking about. This is my boyfriend's car.'

She pulls up short. 'Oh, God, no. He hasn't. Has he? Already? Wow. That's pretty quick even by his standards.'

'Who are you and what the hell are you talking about?'

'Hi. I'm Lisa. Mitchell's ex-girlfriend.'

I shake my head. 'I think you may be confused. Sorry.'

She laughs, her face sour. 'Confused? I doubt it.'

'Are you okay, love?' asks Mum from the front seat.

'Yeah, I'm fine thanks. Just give me a minute.' I slam the boot closed and take a step towards the woman, which I immediately regret because she's taller than me and really bloody angry. 'Look, my mum's not terribly well. I have to get her home. I don't know what your issue is but please don't take it out on me. Now, if you'll excuse me.'

'Oh, I'll excuse you. For now. That's my car but I guess it's not your fault you've been suckered in. I'd watch yourself though. He's bloody good at getting under your skin and then you're blind to it, to him. I fell for it for three years. Until he wiped me out of all my cash and took my car. Thank God I kept my house. Hey, just keep an eye on your phone, don't let it out of your sight.' My body turns ice cold and the woman stood before me detects a chink in my armour. 'That's how it started with me. Fixing my phone so I thought it was playing up.

Then he buys you a new one.' I swallow and she shifts weight from one foot to the other. 'Oh. You already got the phone, didn't you?' She folds her arms, shaking her head. 'Just watch for him texting people on your behalf. Or making out you haven't done something? Or have been told something you've no memory of. You'll question yourself, he'll tell you you're crazy, he'll make out it's all you and you'll spend all your time apologising. Listen, I don't know what you think you're getting into with him, but he is not who you think he is and I'd be doing a disservice to womankind if I didn't give you the heads-up. Kicking him out was the best thing I ever did.'

I stare, stunned. A dog, locked in a car somewhere else in the car park, barks; the noise echoes.

'Whatever your name is, whoever you are, don't trust him. D'you hear me? He's a narcissist. He's not interested in you, only what you can do for him. And when he's done with you, you'll think you've gone mad because he will make sure you feel that way.'

'I think you're wrong. Or you're mistaken.'

'Yeah... I thought I was wrong for a long time. Turns out I wasn't. Only I didn't realise until he'd cut me off from my friends and made me pretty much wholly dependent on him. Just don't say I didn't warn you! I've got my dog, house and dignity back, tell him I'm coming for the car next.'

Chapter Sixty-Three

'Oh, look, love, he's mowed the lawn,' says Mum as we pull up on the drive. 'Bless him, oh and look, there's some new plants in the porch window. Dahlias look, your grandma liked a dahlia.'

I gently pull on the handbrake because whether it's Mitch's car or the woman from the car park, it's very definitely not mine. 'Nice, that's really lovely.'

'Are you sure you're okay? You were white as the proverbial when you got back in the car after talking to that woman. What was she saying?'

'Nothing, Mum, it's fine. I think I'm just tired. It's you, keeping me up talking all night.'

'Bloody cheek.'

I climb out of the car but Mitch has bounded over to Mum's side before I get a chance. Would he really be this keen to help and support us if he was the man that woman described him as?

'Hey, you, how was your trip?' he says to me, beaming across the car. I try and read his face, see something I've not seen before.

'Oh, yeah, it was—'

'We had a bloody lovely time, didn't we, love? I bought some new bits for me, she'll have to hang 'em up when we get in. And I bought my little girl a few bits too, which was a real treat.'

She clings onto his neck as he scoops her up out of the car, carrying her into the house, me following behind them. 'Sounds perfect. Just what you both needed.'

'Oooh, what's that smell? Have you been cooking?'

'Yeah, slow roast belly pork. That's your favourite, isn't it, Jem?'

'Her favourite, my favourite. Bloody lovely.'

'You're not hungry again are you, Mum?'

'Well, I wouldn't see it go to waste, put it that way. Can you help me to the daybed, love? I'm a bit jiggered after today.'

He carries her through, gently laying her down. The smell of food is amazing and by the looks of things, he's been cleaning all day. The place is immaculate. He weaves his arms around my waist from behind, kissing my neck. 'You've been busy,' I say, my shoulders tight.

'Thought it was about time I earned my keep.'

I'm still rigid, uncertain, confused. He's a good man. He's kind. I don't know what a narcissist is like really, but he's not one... is he? 'Is everywhere as immaculate as this?' I ask.

'Everywhere. I hope you don't mind, Mrs W, but I did a bit of tidying in your room. Changed the bed sheets and stuff.'

'Oh, love, you needn't have done that. Our Jem could have done that.'

'I wanted to. She's been so busy with work and looking after you, she's not had time for things like that.' I prickle because I probably could have made time if I'd thought about it. I just didn't think. And isn't it a bit weird of him to do it anyway? That's Mum's bed. Her sheets. Her room.

'To be honest, love, I keep thinking about that big bed up there and you two all squished into her single bed. You two should probably—'

'Mum, no.'

'Well, I don't need it, do I. It makes sense if he's sticking around, which if he's cooking and cleaning I very much hope he will.'

'I'm not going anywhere,' he says, holding me tight. I should feel good about it.

I wriggle out of his hold. 'Mum, that's your room.'

'Yes, but we all know I can't get up there. Go on, please. Just move a few things in there, make it feel like yours. Anything of mine you don't want, just pop it in the cupboard. Buy yourself some new bedding though, don't take that bloody ancient duvet through.'

'That's my favourite, Mum!' I think about the red wine stain. He knows how much I love that duvet. He didn't seem to care about the stain. I suppose it is just an old duvet.

'Yes. But it's also a single duvet for a single teenager. Go get yourself some decent stuff and take my card. The pin number's 1938.'

'Mum! You don't tell people your pin number.'

'Oh shush, nobody's here. Come on, Mitch, pass me my purse, will you, love?' He does as instructed and she fumbles to get her card, holding it out for me. 'Take it. And use it for food shopping too, there's bloody loads in there since I've been too ill to spend it all. Get some nice bedding and any knick-knacks you want for the room. Now, if you'll both excuse me, I need a bit of a nap. What time will tea be ready, love?' she asks Mitch.

'It's slow cooking, so can be on for one hour or five. So whenever you wake up,' he answers, grinning.

'Well, aren't you the bloody best? Go on, kids, out you go, shoo, I'll see you in a bit.'

And she turns over, slowly, taking the covers with her, letting her body rest into the daybed.

Mitch grabs my hand, pulls me out of the house and down to the car. His car? 'Come on, hop in. Let's nip up to the new retail place now, the one at Meadowhead, see what we can find?'

'Mitch, no, I can't. I've been out all day, I've got stuff to do and…'

He pauses, car door open. 'What?'

'I don't know, it doesn't feel right.' I want to tell him to slow down. I feel steamrollered, backed into a corner, by Mum as much as Mitch. And I want to ask him about the woman in the car park.

'Your mum said it, Jem. Didn't she? It was her idea. And I know, it is strange, I get that. But it does seem silly for us to be staying in your room when hers is so big and empty. Look' – he rests on the car roof, chin on hands, boyish look in his eyes –'you can bring your duvet through too, if it makes you feel better.' I must still look uncertain because he shuts the door and comes round to my side, pressing me up against the car. 'Your mum wants us to be happy, we have a duty to be that for her. She needs to see you're okay, she wants to see me help you be that. *I* want to help you be that. Let's not have a repeat performance of last night.' I look down at my feet, he catches my chin. 'Hey, I love you. She loves you. There is nothing to be frightened of, okay? I'm not going to hurt you.'

I stare into his eyes, wondering who the hell Lisa was and why on earth she'd say those things if there wasn't some semblance of truth in it. I wonder about him, about why he's so keen to stay, to move into Mum's room, about his apparent lack of need for his own space, about his dog. Was it even his dog? What did Lisa say? That she got her dog, home and dignity back? Is that why he doesn't need to get back and feed it, because it's not even his or his mum's, or whatever it was he said. And then my phone rings, and it's Leanne, and Mitch tells me to answer it before kissing me on the cheek and helping me into the car.

Chapter Sixty-Four

'How's today?' asks Leanne as soon as I pick up.

'Oh, it's been… lovely. Really nice.' I side eye Mitch who's buckling up as he reverses out of the drive. 'I took Mum to town, she wanted to buy a load of clothes. She was determined.'

'Ahhh, that's lovely.'

'Yeah, didn't think I'd get her in the wheelchair when they first dropped it off, but she was more than happy to sit in it when she realised she could get pushed about on a shopping spree.' I can hear myself talking: stilted, polite even. I don't feel like I'm talking to Leanne, she's a stranger.

'I love that. Bless her! You sound like you're in the car now, is she with you?'

Does she sound the same? Guarded? 'No, I just dropped her back. She's having a rest. I'm popping out with Mitch to get a bit of shopping in.'

'Oh, right.'

'Yeah.'

'All okay?'

I look across to him, he smiles, then focuses on the road up ahead. 'Yeah, all okay.'

'You sure? You sound weird.'

'No! No, not at all. Tired, probably.'

'Hey, don't you complain about tired until you've got two children tag teaming you through the night!'

'Oh, alright, you get the monopoly on sleep deprivation,' I snip.

'Hey, I was joking. Are you sure you're okay?'

Mitch reaches his hand across to my thigh, giving my leg a squeeze. His touch always gave me butterflies… it doesn't feel the same. 'Yeah, I'm fine. Like I say, just a bit tired. Look, I'm going to lose you in a minute, we're just heading down the dip. I'll call you later.' Mitch sniffs. 'Or tomorrow. When I get a chance.'

'Okay, love, no problem. I'd still like to pop up though, see your mum.'

'Yeah, maybe over the weekend?'

'Okay. Well, Sunday would work for us?'

'That sounds… yeah… I'll check with Mum and let you know. Okay, talk to you later. Or tomorrow. Talk soon. Love you. Bye.'

I hang up. Mitch looks across at me. 'Alright?' he asks.

'Yeah.' I drop my phone into my bag. I gaze out of the window as Dronfield passes by. The old church, the little Sainsbury's, the factories, the fishing tackle shop where the old nightclub was, the pub on the bottom road. How the hell do I talk to him about the woman I met? Should I even? It's probably nonsense, and he'd be hurt I could ever think she was right, wouldn't he? I've no idea who she is and yet I've listened to her.

My phone though…

Money.

I'm unsettled and I can't work it out. Is it me? Am I creating it? I should just bloody well ask him. Come out with it. He'll explain it all, I'm sure.

'Hey, let's nip to the pub first. I bet you're parched, aren't you? All that pushing your mum about and stuff. The weather's nice, let's get a gin and tonic before we go shopping. You can tell me about your day. Come on.' He pulls into the car park at the Bowshaw.

The sound of the dual carriageway rather takes the charm off the pub garden I'm sat in as Mitch comes out with drinks. It's not as warm as the sun would have me believe, either. 'Here you go. I got doubles.'

'You're driving.'

'It's only one double. I'll be fine.'

'Right.' I sip at my drink, tonic bubbles fizzing on my tongue. There's a niggle in my chest. 'A weird thing happened today.'

'Oh yeah?'

'At the car park. Some woman started yelling at me.'

'Really? What had you done?'

'Nothing! Nothing at all. She wanted to know who I was and why I was driving her car.'

He doesn't flinch. 'Oh?'

'Yeah. Said you took it when you broke up with her.'

'What? You saw Abby?'

My face screws up because either she was off her nut, or he is a bloody brilliant liar. 'Lisa. She was called Lisa.'

'Who the hell is Lisa?'

'I don't know. She said she was your ex. Said that was her car. Called you "Mitchell".'

He leans down to pet a dog that's wandered over to us. 'Can you smell my dog? Can you, oooh, you're lovely, aren't you?'

'I don't know how it'd smell your dog – you've not been home in ages. Are you sure your mum's neighbour is okay looking after it? Bring him to us if you like.'

'It's fine, she likes having him.' He turns his attention back to the dog. 'Do you like that? A little scratch under the chin, oh you do, don't you?'

'Mitch!'

He looks up sharply, the dog trots off. 'What?'

'Who was the woman in the car park?'

'I don't bloody know, do I? She sounds like a weirdo to me. No one calls me Mitchell. Could have been anyone. I don't know a Lisa. That is my car. What? Are you drunk or something? Is that what this is?'

'Course I'm not fucking drunk. It's the middle of the day. I've been driving.'

'Alright, bloody hell, calm down.' I suck in my cheeks because I've never done right well with anyone telling me to calm down. 'I don't know who she was or why she picked on you, but really, Jem, it's nonsense. In fact, I can't believe you'd take some random ranting stranger's word over mine anyway. How can we be in a relationship if you don't believe me? I mean, I worry about us sometimes, whatever this is. You, you're so… testy all the time. And you clearly don't trust me. I'm doing everything I can here, I am trying my hardest. And you know this isn't the way a relationship should start, it's not ideal but I understand. I'm prepared to make sacrifices for you, for us. I'm prepared to make allowances, but you've got to trust me.' He moves round to sit next to me, one leg on either side of my hips, his arms snaked around me. 'Jem, I keep telling you I love you. I wouldn't lie to someone I love. Forget this random madwoman in the car park. This is me and you. If we can get through this, with your mum, we can get through anything.

We're strong, me and you. We've got a future together.' He nuzzles into my neck. 'I've never felt about anyone the way I feel about you. I've never wanted to spend the rest of my life with someone, I've never wanted to grow old with someone. Until I met you. You're everything to me. You and your mum, you're my world. And I won't let anyone make you think anything different. Okay?'

I knock my drink back trying to feel what he says in my heart, trying to believe him.

Chapter Sixty-Five

I follow him round in a daze. He picks stuff up, duvets, cushions, he shows me fake plants and candles. He's affectionate. He loves me. I know he does. And it is all rushed, but that's because of life at the moment. If it wasn't for Mum, we'd probably have started very differently. We'd have dated, we'd have held hands and walked in the park. We'd have taken our time and got to know one another. It's not his fault that things are different for us. But he's certain about how he feels and I have to remember how bad I am at recognising what I want in life. I always do this, at the point things get serious, I panic. I act like a dick. I've got a track record. Things have to be different this time. I'm probably oversensitive and it's no wonder, what with everything that's going on.

He shoves things into the trolley. He's excited. I'm being stupid. I've got a chance at a second go here, a chance not to do to him what I did to Ben.

Ben.

'Do you think your mum would like this?' he says, holding up a jam jar with a fake posy of flowers. 'For on the little table by her daybed?'

'Maybe. It's pretty.'

He looks at it, deciding against it before moving on to lighting. 'We'll get her real flowers, that'll be nicer. She could do with a lamp though, couldn't she? Are there lamps in her room? I can't remember.'

'Erm, no, she just has a little reading light clipped to her bedstead.'

'Oh, yeah, that's right. These are nice, look. What do you think?'

I check the label. 'They're expensive.'

'It doesn't matter. I've got it covered. What about this one for your mum? It's simple.'

'It is.'

He puts two of the expensive lights in the trolley then a third, smaller lamp. 'It's one of those touch lamps look, so when she's not as strong, she'll still be able to turn it on and get it to whatever brightness she wants.'

I nod. I follow. He's thoughtful. We're lucky to have him.

So why do I want to go round to Leanne's and talk it all through with her? Get her take. I want to call her, go round. I want to hold Elsie Alice and Harley. I want to sink into her sofa. I want to drink tea and watch Netflix whilst we talk about nothing and everything and she can tell me what the hell I'm doing wrong, or right. But I can't, I've got to do this on my own. I've got to stop running to other people to sort out my problems. To help me make a decision. *For heaven's sake, Jem, stand on your own two feet. He loves you. That woman was confused. Don't mess this up!*

'Is that everything?' he asks, sieving through the contents of our trolley. 'Duvet, cushions, throws, lamps, candles. We could get these first and then think about what else you might want.' He pulls me into him. 'I can't wait to go to bed with you tonight. In our room. Together.'

And I think, in the very pit of my stomach, I can feel those butterflies again. The excitement. There's something there, I know it. I need to hear it. Feel it. I need to pull it up from the depths of my heart and embrace it. Care for it. Nurture it. Relationships are hard, especially under these circumstances. But I deserve this. I deserve to be happy with someone who cares for me. Someone who loves me. It's fine. It's all fine.

We get to the till, he loads things up on the counter as the assistant scans things through. He chats, makes charismatic small talk. The women around us beam. He takes his wallet out and pulls out a card to pay and several other cards drop out. I bend down to pick them up but he grabs them before I can, shoving them in his pocket.

'Shitty wallet,' he says. 'I need a new one. Hey, can you load those bits back in the trolley whilst I sort this out.'

'Of course.' I do as instructed. He smiles at me. I smile back. We're fine. It's good.

'There you go, thank you, that's great. Cheers.' And he's paid. It's all done. And he's pushing the trolley out of the shop, scooping me up in his arms as he goes. He chats and loads the car and opens my door for me, waiting until I'm buckled before shutting it and returning the trolley.

Look at everything he's doing. He's taking control to help. He's thinking about stuff for Mum because that's the kind of person he is. Sometimes I wonder what the hell is wrong with me.

Chapter Sixty-Six

'How cosy does this look?' Mitch rests his arms on my chest. 'Is it too early to go to bed? Would anyone notice if we just grabbed a bottle of wine and spent the rest of our night making out?'

I laugh and kiss his arm. I mean, it does look nice. It's still Mum's room, but it does look nice. And she did want us to do this.

'Who needs The George, eh?' He pulls me onto the bed, showering me in kisses. To begin with I feel suffocated until I remember to relax and then I can fall into him. And it's like we're teenagers, snogging on the bed like I used to with Jamie Potts. Kissing until I had stubble rash and could barely stand because it was so intoxicating. This is what you do in new relationships.

We're interrupted by a text from Mum on my 'mum phone'. The other one now pretty much constantly cast off in my bedroom because carrying two phones around was getting ridiculous.

Would you mind getting me some dinner? Legs aren't so good but I'm really hungry.

'Mum's hungry. Will the pork be ready?' He groans but shifts to let me go.

'It will. There's some mash to go with it. In the fridge. Just wants microwaving.'

'You're amazing.'

'Yeah? How amazing?'

I grin at him, pulling him on top of me and locking my legs around his waist. 'Very, very, incredibly, brilliantly amazing.'

He groans again. 'I suppose you're going to make me wait until you've fed your mum before you can really show me?'

'I am. But it'll be worth it.' I push him away with a bite on his bottom lip and he slaps me on the arse as I jump up to the door.

'I love you, Jem Whitfield,' he says, lying back, hands behind his head.

I pause, because I do love him, I'm sure I do. I just... he waits, fixing his eyes on me. And I remember what it was that attracted me to him: the older face of someone who's lived a bit. The face of someone you know isn't a kid any more, but you can still see a bit of the lad you remember from school. The face of someone who knows you have secrets yet remains by your side. No judgement.

'I love you too,' I say, leaning against the door to admire him and the room. I don't know what I was thinking. That woman before? She could have been anyone. I have to learn how to listen to my heart, how to trust my gut. And the nerves I'm feeling are perfectly understandable. I'm learning to let go, no wonder it's scary. But I can do it. I know it.

'I'll bring a few bits over from your room. I reckon your chest of drawers will look nice over there, look.'

'Great. Lovely. Thank you, Mitch.'

He shakes his head. 'No need. Honestly. No need at all.'

*

'How's it looking? Is it full on shag pad up there?' Mum tucks into the pork, making all the appreciative sounds whilst asking me highly inappropriate questions.

'Mum!'

'What? Christ, you might as well make the most of it. That bed's not seen much action. In fact, you two might be the first.'

'Mum, wow! Please.'

'Oh, lighten up. Enjoy the space. And tell him this is bloody gorgeous, it really melts in the mouth.' She starts coughing between mouthfuls and it fair takes up her energy, but between breaths, she is rattling, giddy. 'So, what have you done? How does it look?'

'Mitch picked out a few bits. There's the new duvet, new lamps. He picked out a few pictures that he wants to put on the walls, too. In fact, he really went for it. New curtains and everything… But are you sure you don't mind? I feel weird.'

'Jem, please. Don't feel weird or it'll make me feel weird too. I don't want either of us to overthink this. In fact, I want to see it.'

'Can you get upstairs?'

'Nope. I don't reckon. Can you take photos?'

'I mean, I guess I could…'

'Go on, do it now, I want to see how it looks.' She shovels slow roast pork in, knocking it back with sips of water. Her face is bright, happy, considering everything she looks quite beautiful. 'Go!'

'Jeez, Mum, so demanding.'

'I'm living vicariously.'

I shake my head at her, heading up the stairs. But when I get there, Mitch is sat on the bed in my old room, reading my letter to Ben.

Chapter Sixty-Seven

Dear Ben,

There are some things I have to tell you. Things I need to own so I can move forward with my life. But they're things that you may not want to know. After all, you left, as well you should have. I neither deserved nor appreciated you - at least, not the way you wanted me to. Not the way you had every right for me to. I wish I knew why I behaved the way I did, I wish I could put it all right, but sometimes, it's just too late.

I've often wondered how much you knew and chose to ignore, versus how much I'd got away with lying about. Like the time I kissed George Newman at his house-warming party after you and I had a row. I justified it by telling myself I thought we were over. Or that George came on to me. I was lying to myself as much as you. I was so hurt by our row, I was so frightened that it meant the end for us, and where most people would fight, something in me couldn't. I pretty much rolled over, accepted my fate.

Except it wasn't my fate, was it. You came back. We talked. It was just a silly row. I'd been so frightened of losing you I made the worst choice. You'd think I'd have learned my lesson after that but there were more lies.

Like the time an old work colleague knocked on my door at two in the morning. I guess I must have mentioned that you were away, working. He'd been out drinking with rugby mates and was hammered. He pushed his way into my house and I didn't resist because I knew him even though I felt uncomfortable. He asked if we could have sex and I said no but he didn't let up. He kept telling me how much he fancied me, how he'd always fancied me. He reached for my hand and placed it on him, he was hard. He told me it was a gift for me and I didn't know how to get him to leave. I told him all about you, I reminded him I wasn't single, he said neither was he and then pushed himself on top of me and though I consented, in as much as I didn't push him off me, I didn't really want to do it. I just felt like I had no choice. We didn't have sex, that much I managed to avoid. But we did other stuff, and I felt cheap and ashamed and dirty. And I felt like I'd let you down. I did let you down. I should never have let him in. I should never have let him talk me into anything. You asked me if I was okay the next day, when you got back. I was in the shower for the third time that day. You must have sensed something. I lied. I said I was fine because, as ever, I'm weak. Always weak.

It was my weakness that meant I couldn't say no to him. My weakness that meant I could never say no to anyone or anything. Like months later, a night out in Dublin. The night our baby died.

I can't believe I'm writing this. I can't believe I never told you. I suppose I just didn't know what to say. I didn't want to have to admit that my actions are very likely the thing that killed it. It had been a heavy few weeks with work dos and the like. I was drinking every day. In some cases, all day. Then I was in Dublin, do you remember? We'd won consultant team at work, we'd got the most contractors out on site. The company gave us an all-expenses trip on a private jet. We were drinking from the second we boarded and it just didn't stop. I was proud of myself for keeping up with the blokes because I am that stupid. We landed, went straight to Temple Bar. I drank pint after pint of Guinness. I'd vomit, then go back for more. I'd chase it with Irish whiskey, knocking them back like an old pro. We were singing and dancing, jumping around. We climbed statues and took inappropriate photos. I kissed a stranger at one point when I lost a game of truth or dare. I made everyone delete photographic evidence because I didn't want you to ever find out. I loved you, more than anything, and that terrified me as much as the idea of losing you. Maybe more.

That night, one of the girls somehow managed to get me back to my hotel room. I passed out in the bathroom and when I woke up, there was a pool of blood around me. I was cramping. They weren't normal cramps, this wasn't like anything I'd experienced before. And it got worse and worse. I thought I was dying, I thought maybe I'd drunk so much something had ruptured. I called one of the girls to help me, she called a doctor. The pain got worse, the bleeding got heavier. By the time the doctor arrived, I'd begun to wonder. He confirmed my worst fear. The one thing I never wanted to happen had happened and then I'd killed it because I was too drunk for its first six weeks. It stood no chance. And I know some people say a foetus that young is no baby, but to me, for a moment, it was. It was our baby. And though I never wanted children, while I waited for the doctor, I fell in love with it. I saw it as a newborn, I watched it toddle, I saw it off to school, I imagined this tiny version of both of us and my heart broke because I'd killed it. And because I knew if I told you, I'd kill you too. You hated how much I drank. You hated the work I did, or at least the culture I was immersed in. And that work, that drink, that culture, had stamped out a life before we'd even had a chance to realise, to talk about what ifs, to make a decision based on facts not forced because of my inability to say no. To walk away.

I will never forgive myself for that. I wouldn't expect you to either. And I suppose that's the main reason I wanted to write this letter. Because I never told you and you had a right to know.

And that is why I'll burn this letter, because I never told you and I have no right to do so now that we've over.

I know the lack of love between us is my fault. I know I pushed you too far. I think the night I lost our baby could have gone two ways. I could have realised what I was doing and stopped it but, instead, I used it as a reason to be angry, to be unavailable, to drink more. I couldn't love you that much, right? If I could let something like that happen, then lie about it. So if that's the case, there was no point trying to keep you. I didn't deserve you. You were too good for me and the day you left was the worst day of my life, but also the most expected. I was vindicated. I was unlovable and you proved it by leaving.

You will never understand how much I regret the me that did that to you.

I loved you, Ben. More than you ever really knew, more than I could ever cope with. I'm sorry it wasn't enough to make me change, maybe in another life.

Yours, always and forever,

Jem. X

Chapter Sixty-Eight

'I thought you were sorting stuff, moving things over,' I say, as lightly as I can. The Moomin envelope is on his lap, the letter quivers in his hands. I want to rip it from him, I want to scream in his face – how dare he read it? How dare he pry? But it's almost as if I can sense how my causing a scene would go. It's like I want to try and keep things calm, not cause a fuss, not cause a fight.

'I can't believe you,' he sneers.

'Mitch, I…' I reach for the letter but he pulls it away. 'Mum wants photos of the room, I just came up to—'

'Why would you keep it? If you weren't happy for me to maybe find and read it some day?'

'I don't know, I just—'

He reads it again, I watch his eyes scan over each word. My mouth runs dry.

'You're not over him, are you?' he says, looking hurt.

'I am. I promise I am.' I sit beside him. I rest my hand on his leg. 'Of course I'm over him. It's you I love, I've told you. I know I'm not always very good at showing it, I just… find it hard. I'm learning, I'm trying to be better. I'm sorry. I didn't mean for you to find it, I didn't think you'd read it.'

'I assumed we had no secrets. I mean, I knew the letter existed, that there were things you couldn't tell me to begin with, but now?

We're basically living together. I love you. I thought you loved me, so I didn't think it would be a problem. I certainly wasn't expecting this.'

He gets hold of my hand, squeezing it too tight so I try and get it free from his grasp. Mum's downstairs, she's happy, enjoying a moment, I want to keep that for her. I kiss his fingers, looking up at him. Submissive. 'I'm sorry, I didn't mean to hurt you. It's stupid. It's all in the past. I'm ashamed. I did some awful things.'

'You did,' he agrees.

'I hate myself for it. I thought writing the letter might help me deal with what I did, accept it even. But of course it didn't. It couldn't possibly. And that's why I need you, you make me a better person, Mitch. I love you.'

'I don't know how I can believe you, Jem,' he whispers. 'I am trying so hard and yet, this is how you repay me. Earlier, you told me you didn't trust me—'

'What? That's not... I didn't. I didn't say that.'

'Pretty much! It's what you implied. With all that stuff about that woman. And yet here you are, keeping secrets from me. Manipulating me. I can see how you're looking at me now, how you're touching me, trying to get me to forgive you by being affectionate. I'm not stupid, you know.'

'I know you're not stupid. I don't think that for a moment. Here, it's fine. Give me the letter. I'll rip it up now. I don't know why I kept it. I'm sorry, here. Please.'

He looks at the letter, slowly picking it up. My heart stops as I watch him decide what to do before he eventually hands it over to me. 'Go on then,' he says, staring, eyes wide. 'Rip it up.'

I fold it in half. My hands shaking. I grit my teeth. I think back to the moment I wrote it, sat in here, weeping as I told Ben everything. I think back to the moment the postman dropped it through the letterbox and I panicked about Ben reading it. I think about bumping into him on the bench about the look in his eye as he left me. Sorrow. Pity. I think about how I felt when the letter came back, that mix of sadness and relief. And how I've kept it in my room because somehow letting go of it was like it was finally the end. Which it should have been. I should have burned it like I intended. And I wasn't strong enough.

So I rip it up. And I keep ripping. Dropping bits and picking them up to rip them smaller. I hold back the urge to cry because now is not the time for self-pity. And when I've finished, there's nothing but fibres and tiny catches of words that could never be pieced back together. I put them in the envelope. I look up at Mitch. 'There,' I say. 'It's done. Gone. Just like it should have been when I first got it back. I should have been able to talk about it with you, tell you what had happened and move on. No more secrets, I promise.'

He stands, slowly, taking the envelope from me, dropping it into the tiny wicker bin in the corner of my room. 'It's for the best,' he says, resting his chin on my head. 'It's for us,' he whispers into my hair and I wonder how he can look at me the way he has yet still want to be with me. Does he love me that much or is this all part of a way to control me? Does he feel like he's got one up on me? 'Now he's gone, we can start our future properly, yes?'

'Yes,' I say, the butterflies gone, my belly now leaden with fear and anxiety.

'Now, go on, take photos for your mum. Show her what we've done. Then come back up here and let me show you how much you need me in your life.'

I force a smile. I take out my phone and standing in the doorway start taking photos. My heart races and my chest feels tight. And I'm not quite sure what just happened.

Chapter Sixty-Nine

'Jem…' says Mitch, startling me awake from a heavy sleep. There's an empty bottle of gin on the side. Mitch had sneaked it up to Mum's room and presented it to me when I finally made it back up last night. I tried to tell him I wasn't up for it, I told him about that time at Leanne's, I made excuses, but he got frustrated at my lack of appreciation, so I drank it anyway. Now, he strokes my hair, perched on the side of our bed, Mum's bed, his breath stale with morning after the night before.

'Eurgh!' I grunt.

'I know,' he agrees.

'Why?'

'It seemed like a good idea at the time. We were celebrating.'

'Celebrating?'

'Our new room. You finally letting go of the past.' My heart lurches. The conversation, the letter, the look on his face, the shame. I wasn't letting go, I was numbing my feelings, just like I always do. 'Thought I'd go and get pastries. Or bacon. Maybe pastries *and* bacon.'

'I don't know if I could eat anything, to be honest. This is why I don't do gin.' I bury my head beneath my pillow as he gets up off the bed.

'Don't be a lightweight, come on, I'll be half an hour. Go get a shower. Get some water on your face, you'll be fine. I'll get your mum a paper too, yeah?'

I nod, realising how much I actually want him to leave the house, to give me a tiny bit of space. How much I want to stand beneath the shower and let water wash all the feelings away. 'Thanks. She'd like that. She loves a paper. Not to read, just to have lying round the house like she's clever.' I'm doing my best to act like everything is fine, like I'm fine.

Mitch laughs, feeding his legs into his jeans, stumbling a little.

'I think I need to stop drinking,' I say, trying to sit myself up a bit, pausing halfway until my head stops banging.

'Don't be ridiculous. We were just having a bit of fun. It's fine. You'll be right after a shower and food.' I freeze as he comes back to me, dropping a kiss on my forehead. I paint on a compliant smile as he jogs out of the room, grabbing Mum's card as he goes. I want to say 'No, don't take hers. Take my card if you don't want to pay for it.' But he's gone, and I don't want to make a scene, and she did say to use it, so I guess it's fine.

I'm staring at the wall, ten minutes later, totally zoned out. I can hear the radio on downstairs, Mum must be awake. I drag my sorry arse out of bed and into my room, looking through my bag for Alka-Seltzer. I pull my old phone out, catching the home button. The screen lights up. There's a message. Shit, I didn't talk to Leanne about visiting. Except the message isn't from Leanne, it's from Ben's number.

For God's sake, leave Ben alone. He doesn't want to hear from you. He doesn't want anything to do with you. And after everything in that letter? I don't blame him. You're now blocked. Move on with your sad, disgusting life.

I scroll up, breath held, and there it is. Picture after picture of the letter I wrote. Each paragraph zoomed in to make it easier to read. All sent last night, to Ben's number.

I hover over a message to him but there's no point if I've been blocked. I look down in the bin at what remains of the letter. I ripped it up. So, Mitch had to have already done it by the time I found him. And yet he said nothing. He pretended like he was hurt, not angry. He made out I was at fault somehow. That he was disgusted in me but prepared to forgive me. Yet, he must have been going through my drawers to have come across it. He said he was moving them into Mum's, not teasing through the contents. Who does that? And did he have any right to make me rip it up like that? I mean, I did it because I didn't want a fight. Like I always do, apologise, back down. Anything I feel, he shifts the gaze and it's my fault.

He had no right to go through my drawers, never mind send this to Ben.

How fucking could he?

I stand in my room, the walls closing in. I'm confused, conflicted, angry, hurt. Frightened. The scene in Cole's car park, Lisa definitely was Mitch's ex. There's now no question in my heart. She was right.

I google gaslighting: *to manipulate (someone) by psychological means into doubting their own sanity.*

And then I google narcissist: *a person with exaggerated sense of self-importance, a lack of empathy, a history of exploiting others for personal gain.*

And I catch sight of myself in the old bedroom mirror that still has stickers round the edge when I decided to decorate it, aged twelve. Twelve-year-old me had such hopes and dreams. Such vitality. She was complex, sure, she'd experienced rejection and loneliness, she'd had to grow up pretty quick when her dad left, but she wasn't nearly as vacant as I am now. She had fight. She had belief. Where did it all go?

Am I that weak that I've missed the signs? How did that happen? I was supposed to be sorting my life out. What the hell have I done?

I wrap myself up in my dressing gown. Mum might know what to think. She'll tell me I've got it wrong, she'll reassure me. Except that when I do get downstairs, it's clear there's something not right. She's sat up but rocking her hips side to side in her chair, her eyes closed.

'Mum?'

'Oh, hey, love, erm, can you get me some painkillers? There's codeine in the drawer.'

'Of course, hang on.' I pull out packs of pills, sifting through until I find the codeine in amongst the steroids and blood thinners. The leftover pain relief from her op, the packets and packets of Halls Mentho-lyptus. 'Here, take these. There's some water.'

She knocks them back, wincing and shifting as she tries to get comfy.

'I've had this pain, down my back, into my groin and across my stomach.'

'How long for?'

'On and off, all night.'

'Mum! Why didn't you say something?'

'I thought it would wear off if I kept moving. I've been sitting up, shifting around. It would ease for a bit, then come back. I just couldn't quite trust myself to get to the drawer, I had paracetamol in my bag here but that didn't really touch it.'

'Do you want me to call someone? Get the doctor out?'

Mum wafts away the suggestion. 'No, no. Don't be silly. I've probably just eaten too much, all that pork belly. Pork never really agreed with me, did it? Even before all this nonsense. It's probably just a kind of indigestion or something. It's fine. Honestly, I'm fine. Just lift my legs up for me, let me try stretching out 'til the tablets have kicked in.'

I do as instructed, watching her tense, then relax as waves of pain seem to peel through her body. 'Are you sure you're okay, Mum?'

'Of course. I'm fine.'

The front door opens and Mitch shouts up the stairs, 'Who's for pastries?' before noticing I'm down with Mum. 'Ahh, there you are. Good morning, beautiful, it's nice to see you vertical. More than can be said for some, eh!' He winks at Mum then kisses me.

'She's not very well,' I say, coldly.

'Oh no. Have you had pain relief? Do you need anything?'

'I sorted it.'

'Great, well done. Come on then, tea? Coffee? That'll help too. What you both having?'

Mum winces a little less than before, then smiles. 'Tea for me, love, please.'

'Erm, coffee,' I say, on the back foot from his sudden return, as if nothing's changed. Which I suppose for him, it hasn't.

He busies himself round our kitchen, making breakfast as he chats and charms. I want to scream out: Why did you send that message? What were you thinking? How dare you do something like that? But I can't, not with Mum. So I just play along as he serves up coffee and croissants. And eventually, Mum's shoulders start to shift back in place, the waves of pain growing further and further between for her.

But my own waves of pain and confusion, each time I think of the letter and the text messages – and Mitch in our kitchen, completely taking over – increase.

Chapter Seventy

I spend the rest of the morning being… compliant. Yeah, that's the right word for it. I've done what was expected of me. Well, mostly. I've smiled and laughed. I've found ways to avoid his affection. I've used Mum as an excuse not to have sex. He didn't like it, said it was my fault that he wanted me. That I shouldn't be so sexy, that it wasn't fair to make him wait, but it was a step too far for me. I can keep the peace, just for now, for Mum's sake, but I've realised how much everything is on his terms. Always. From the moment I kissed him at the park gates and he turned away, to the night he came round with alcohol and we both got shitfaced, then had sex in the lounge. Swiftly followed by him holding back again until in the right time, at the right place, on his terms. His terms don't suit me any more. Everything we do is the way he wants to do things, when he wants to do them. Drinking, eating, going out, staying in. It's all how he wants it. Moving into Mum's room, I mean, yes, that was ultimately Mum's idea, but he started the thought process. Who's to say he hadn't planted a seed with her and maybe that's why she suggested it?

And what about my phone? Was it faulty or was it him? Lisa intimated as much. If I go back over those early dates, that weren't even dates at that point… were the signs there from the beginning? Was he at it from the start? And what for? What did he want from me, from us? He has his mum's house to live in, he has her money. What does he want from me?

My head is full, spilling over with questions and thoughts about these last few weeks, months. Which is why I didn't answer Leanne when she texted to check in, then phoned me twice. I've been quiet again, she'll know something is up. And that's why she's on the doorstep now, both kids in tow, a hamper of pamper presents all wrapped up in a bow.

'Blimey, I thought you'd never answer!' she says, bustling in, handing me Elsie Alice as Harley runs straight into the lounge, launching himself onto the floor.

'Get up, take your shoes off, then say hello nicely, please,' she instructs as she slips her own shoes off and heads straight through to the lounge.

'If Mohammed can't come to the spa treatment, let the spa treatment come to Mohammed,' she says, placing the hamper beside Mum who is beaming at the sight of a full house.

Which is more than can be said for Mitch.

'What a lovely surprise!' Mum pulls her in for a hug. It's been a couple of hours since the tablets and though I can see she's pleased to see Leanne, there's a note of discomfort in her movement again. She's fidgety. 'I didn't know you were coming,' she chirrups.

'Nope! None of you did. Well, I mentioned I might to Jem the other day, but we didn't quite get around to finalising details, did we, chuck?'

'Erm, no. Sorry about that.'

'It's fine. I just wanted to bring some nice bits for you. Hand and foot creams, candles, some nice smelly ones. Face masks, treatments, you know, just stuff to make you feel a bit pampered. And I thought it'd be nice for you to see Elsie, then Harley wanted to come and see you too… though I suspect that may be because he thinks he might get a chocolate biscuit out of it.'

'Oh, he can always have chocolate biscuits from me. Mitch, pop us the kettle on, make Leanne a drink and bring out the biscuit tin, would you?'

Mitch nods, catches my eye and summons me to the kitchen. Compliance kicks in.

Chapter Seventy-One

'What the fuck is she doing here unannounced?'

'I didn't know she was coming, I promise,' I say in a hissed whisper, pulling the kitchen door closed.

'She said you'd talked about it, you must have known.'

'I tried to put her off.'

'Why put her off? What's the matter? I mean, it wouldn't have been a problem if we'd known in advance, would it? Like this though, just turning up, I feel like we've been sabotaged somehow.'

'We haven't been sabotaged.' I can feel myself glare at him. 'She just wanted to see Mum. It's my fault, I knew she wanted to, I just couldn't get myself organised, you know what I'm like.' He looks at me coldly and I realise what I have to do if I want to keep the peace. 'Look, I'm sorry.'

'She's really overbearing too, what's with all the spa stuff?'

'She'll want to pamper Mum a bit, that's all.'

'Is it appropriate? Has she checked if any of those products are okay to use on a woman dying of cancer?' I smart at his description of Mum as he checks in the biscuit tin. 'And there's no bloody biscuits in here. What the hell are we going to give Harley now?'

'It's okay, he'll manage without.'

'Of course he won't, kids don't manage. I'll have to go and get some, won't I? That's how this works. It's fine.' He grabs Mum's card from the windowsill. 'Anything else she might want whilst she's here?'

'No. Look, you really don't have to go.'

'Of course I do.'

'Take my card then, not Mum's.' But he's opened the door and gone into the lounge to be convivial. He makes Mum laugh, he lifts Harley up in the air until his hair skims the ceiling, much to his delight, then he darts out the front door and into his car, tearing off down the street.

I go back to the kitchen to breathe for a moment.

'Crikey, who's driving it like they stole it?' says Leanne, her eyebrows on high alert. 'Is he alright?' she asks, as I make the drinks.

I find something really interesting in the bottom of the tea bag tin. 'Oh, yeah, he's fine. He's just realised we've no biscuits so he's gone to get some,' I say in a sing-song voice.

'Is that all? He came out of the kitchen looking furious 'til he saw me.'

'Did he?' I turn to face her.

'What's the matter?' she asks, instantly, flatly, like her antenna is tuned into something's up.

I swallow, spinning back round to finish what I'd started with the drinks. 'No, no. It's nothing. No, we just had words, that's all. You know what it can be like. My fault really, I should have sorted stuff out with you to come over and then I could have run it by him.'

'Run it by him?'

'Well, you know, tell him. I don't know.'

'You know this is your house, don't you?'

'Mum's.'

'Well, yes, but you're living here too, so it's up to you and her who you have over to visit.'

'Of course it is. He wasn't… it's not…' but I run out of steam because she's watching my every move and I can't keep secrets from her.

'Tell me what's wrong, Jem?' she says, leaning against the worktop. I turn to face her, eyes full of tears, heart clattering. 'Jem? This last week or two, you've gone weird. You're distant. What's the matter?'

'I don't know. I mean, I can't explain it. Something's not right and I don't know exactly what but it's not right and I don't think I can do anything about it.'

'What do you mean? Something's not right. Why can't you do anything about it? Jem, what's going on?'

'Look, I can't talk now, okay. He'll be back soon. But things have shifted, things aren't quite right. Something happened the other day when I took Mum out, before you called when I was in the car with him.'

'I knew it. I could tell by your voice.'

'I couldn't say anything 'cause he was there.'

'What happened?'

I drop into the stool by the breakfast bar. The bar creaks as I rest my elbows on it. 'Some woman stopped me in the car park, told me she was his ex.'

'Who? I thought she lived away, wherever it was he was before he came back.'

'That was Abby. No. This woman was called Lisa.'

'Who's Lisa?'

'That's what he said.'

'Okay…?' Leanne looks as confused as I feel.

'She said a few things, and at first I thought she was talking nonsense, then I wondered about it. Then he told me he'd no idea who she was and I just figured she'd got the wrong person or something but…'

'But?'

I study my fingers. There's so much to say, so many examples I could give that I don't know where to start.

'What did she say?'

'She said he plays games. That he manipulates. That he makes you think you've done something wrong when you haven't.'

'What? Gaslighting?' She pulls out the stool beside me. 'Do you think he has been?'

'I…' I pause because if I say it out loud it makes it true but maybe I need to. 'I'm not sure. I didn't see it that way at all, I didn't even know it was a thing really. I can't believe that's what he's doing, but…' I pause. Mum's chatting to Harley in the lounge. A car goes past and I hold my breath in case it's him, relief washing over me when I hear it drive by. Relief. That's not good, is it? Leanne waits for a moment, presumably waiting until I've worked out what I'm trying to say. Eventually, I manage it. 'Mitch texted Ben last night.'

'What?'

'Photos of the letter.'

'No… no! Why? Why would he do that?'

'He found it, was furious I still had it. Sent it on to him out of spite, I think. I don't know. I only realised this morning and I've not wanted to ask because I don't want an argument.'

'But you have to ask him! I mean, how dare he?'

I pause again, another car. When I know it's safe, I carry on. 'He has this way of spinning things around on me. I don't know, I hadn't noticed it before but when I think back over this last month or so, I can see it now. And this has all happened so quickly, him and I, we've sort of been catapulted into partner status when we should still be in the honeymoon stage, but I've just been so grateful to have his support.

So grateful to get another chance at love, even. After Ben, I thought I'd be single forever, I never thought anyone would be interested in me. And it's so hard, with Mum.' I feel my bottom lip go, so stop, take a breath, I've got to keep it together.

'Oh, love.'

'He keeps saying he's here to help me and Mum. He keeps doing all these really lovely things for us, for her, but it's too much. Too soon. And now he's living here, he's moved us into Mum's room.' Leanne's eyes widen, so I know it's not just me that thinks it's weird. 'I can't fall out with him, it'd break Mum's heart. She wants to see me happy.'

'Are you happy? I mean… you don't look happy to me. In fact, Jem, you look frightened. You shouldn't be frightened of him.'

'I'm not frightened, frightened. I mean, he's not aggressive, he isn't violent or anything, he's just a bit… I don't know. I can't put my finger on it.'

'Controlling?'

'Maybe. Possibly. I guess I've been so distracted with Mum, I just didn't see what was happening and now I feel like I'm questioning everything. I mean, yes, maybe he is controlling.' I bury my head in my hands. 'I didn't see it, Leanne. Why didn't I see it? And Mum loves having him around, she doesn't need the stress of seeing me mess things up again.'

'How is that *you* messing things up again? It's not your fault! Jem, you've got two modes of operation: bumble along with things you're not happy with because you don't want the confrontation, or panic about how happy you are and do everything in your power to ruin it.' She can tell this stings. 'I'm sorry, Jem, but you do. And you have tried so hard to sort yourself out, I know you have. You've had so much on your plate.'

'I didn't think things could get worse.'

'And they don't have to.'

'They already have.'

'So, turn it around, Jem. Take control. Christ.' She half smiles at me, caring. 'You're good enough at fucking things up on your own, mate, don't let some bloke do it better.'

I move away from her. I make drinks. I check out the side window to make sure he's not back yet.

'Jem, you have had a rough time, not just recently, but in general. All those things you put in the letter, they weren't your fault.'

I look at her.

'They weren't. I mean, sure, you have to take a bit of responsibility for some of your choices about some stuff, but we all mess up. We're all a bi-product of what we've lived through. We're all a mess. All of us. It doesn't mean that guy had a right to force himself on you.'

'He didn't.'

'He made you feel like you couldn't say no. That's not okay, Jem. We're all trying our best and often getting it wrong…' When I turn to face her, Leanne's eyes glisten. 'The baby, Jem, that wasn't your fault either.' My bottom lip goes and I bite down on it hard because now is not the time to lose it, but we never talk about it. Not since I came back from Dublin and she looked after me until I was well enough to go back to work a few days later. She reaches out for my arm, lowering her voice. 'For God's sake, Jem. You blame yourself for everything and whilst I'm absolutely not saying you're perfect – like, the tea you made me the other day, it had way too much milk in it.' I cry laugh and she squeezes my arm. 'But this, him behaving that way, it's not okay. It's not your fault.'

And I know she's right but before I can ask her what the hell I do about it, he pulls back up on the drive.

She wipes her eyes and rearranges her face. 'Get out. Whilst you can. Before he hurts you… any more than he already has. And whatever you need me to do to help you sort this, I will do. I'm here for you. You do not have to do this alone. Oh, look, chocolate biscuits,' she says, expertly shifting her tone as Mitch comes into the kitchen with multiple packs and a look of suspicion. 'You really didn't have to go out especially for them.'

'It was no bother. Honestly. Now you go through and sit with Val. Jem and I will bring the drinks through.'

Leanne does as she's told and I smile sweetly, giving him a kiss so he knows everything is fine.

Everything is fine.

Everything is fine.

Chapter Seventy-Two

I'm up in Mum's room, Mitch is in the bathroom. I look over the message from Ben's phone, though it's clearly not from him. Is that his girlfriend? Did he ask her to send it? Has she read it and told him everything? What is he thinking? How does he feel?

I never meant to hurt him.

I look over at the vodka Mitch poured me on the side. He didn't even ask if I wanted one, just handed it to me. 'Your regular evening lubrication,' he'd said.

Why am I still drinking? With everything it did. With everything I've lost.

Mitch switches on the shower, I hear him sing to himself as he washes. Leanne went hours ago and we've spent the rest of this evening just chatting to Mum, before he lifted her onto her bed, tucking her in, chatting with her and making her laugh. And it's so good to hear her laugh, especially as she's been in pain all day, so it turns out. She didn't want to say anything when Leanne turned up because she was so chuffed to see her, but as the evening progressed, it became increasingly clear she wasn't comfortable. I wanted to call the doctors, get them to come out, but she wouldn't have it and Mitch told me not to force it, to listen to what Mum wanted. I only agreed to back off on the basis that I call them in the morning if she's no better. The shower turns off and the bathroom door unlocks.

'We should get a new shower fitted, it's not very good is it, that one?' He ruffles his hair dry with a towel, padding through the bedroom, drawing the curtains closed. 'I'll give my plumber a call tomorrow.'

'You've got a plumber?' I say, aiming, badly, for nonchalance.

He turns to face me, dropping his wet towel on the little purple wicker basket that has Mum's old doll and teddy on. 'Just someone who did some work on my mum's house before I put it on the market.'

'Oh!' I get up, moving his towel, placing it on the radiator. We do a sort of dance as I try to avoid connecting with him in the process. 'I didn't realise you'd put it on the market.' I scurry back to bed, reaching for my vodka before deciding against it.

Mitch laughs. He comes to sit beside me, just a towel wrapped around his waist. The sight no longer excites me. Now, I feel trapped, uncertain, nervous of something kicking off. 'I did tell you this the other day,' he says, shaking his head. 'Blundells came down and whacked a board up. They don't think it'll take long to sell. Eeeh, what am I going to do with you, Jem Whitfield?' He pulls me to him, studying my face. 'You want a top up?' he asks. 'I was going to pour one for me.'

'No, thanks. I don't. I don't fancy it, actually, you can have that one.'

'What? You don't fancy a drink of alcohol, Christ.' He reaches for my forehead. 'Are you ill?'

'I just don't fancy it, alright. In fact, I was thinking I might take a break for a while.'

'A *break*? Ha-ha, yeah, alright then.' He has the sort of smile on his face that suggests he doesn't think I'm capable of it.

'What? You don't think I can?' I look up sharply after I've said it, waiting for his reaction.

'What's up with you? Why so tetchy?'

'I'm not tetchy.'

'You are. You have been since Leanne turned up earlier. Maybe hanging around with her isn't good for you. Does she even make you happy? Has she said something because you've been weird for a few days now? What's going on? Maybe I should get you more vodka. Loosen you up a bit.'

'I don't need loosening up.'

'Are you sure?' He reaches across me, taking a sip of my vodka before handing it to me. 'Go on, have a sip. Chill out. I hate it when you're distant.'

Leanne's words ring round my head. *Get out. Whilst you still can.* And I want to. But I don't know where to start. Maybe I should try the truth, maybe that's the place. When I have the truth, I can justify my asking him to leave. It'd be weird to ask him now, out of the blue. I'd have to justify it. He'd cause a scene. Mum would be worried, stressed even. I don't know how to do this. Maybe I should wait. Focus on Mum… I take the vodka glass from him, draining it in one go.

'That's better,' he says, reaching down to a bag on his side of the bed. 'Good job I've got this, eh? Here, give me your glass.'

He fills it with neat vodka and I knock it back again. Wincing.

'Christ, more?'

Which is when I realise he's been enabling this for weeks. I told him I didn't want to drink when Mum was so poorly and every night we have. Every night we sink a bottle or two of wine, we chase it with vodka or whisky. He always seems to have some in, he's always got a drink. It must make it easier for him if I do too. He pours one for him, knocking it back, before pouring another for me, passing it to me, leaning in to kiss me as I take the glass. I turn to offer him my cheek. 'Who was Lisa?' I ask, before I've even realised I was going to.

His face shifts, he's ice cool. 'I've told you there was no Lisa.'

'I know that's what you said.' I sink my drink again. Wiping my mouth and putting the glass on the side. Alcohol seeps into my legs and chest, I'm detached. Now I've got the courage, I need to hear what he has to say. And remember it. Every last detail. I lean into him, his breath is heavy and alcoholic.

'I love you, Mitch.' I take his hand. Threading our fingers together. 'I want us to be together. But I feel like there's something you're not telling me and I need to know. For us to have a future together,' I say, leaning into him despite everything in my body screaming to run away. 'You know my darkest moments, you've read the letter, you know the truth and yet you're still here. I want to be that person for you. I want to know *your* truth. I want you to feel you can tell me anything, without fear, I'm not going anywhere.' I drop a butterfly kiss on his lips and my stomach thuds to my feet. 'We need to be honest with each other. We need to open up. I think you're not telling me something and I want you to know it doesn't have to be that way. You can tell me anything.'

He shakes his head. His eyes flick to mine, then away. There's a chink, a split in his bravado. There's something there that I can hook on to. Something that will give me what I need to understand who he is and how to get him out of my life as quickly as he came in. And I don't know if I can do this but Leanne's right, I can't spend the rest of my life going along with things as they are because I'm frightened to upset something, or someone. I can't keep making mistakes that affect other people because I'm too afraid to own my feelings. I'm not perfect, who bloody well is, but I am tired of living with self-loathing.

Life's too short.

'What did she do to you?' I ask, leaning into him before I stop and wait.

Chapter Seventy-Three

I've almost given up waiting when he starts talking. His voice is low to begin with, I have to work really hard to hear him. But I listen to every word, I let him speak. I let him take all the time he needs.

'You're right. Lisa is my ex.'

'Okay,' I say, gently, heart now in my throat. 'Tell me about her. What happened?'

He turns his back on me, head in hands over the edge of the bed. I shift to make sure I don't miss a single thing he says.

'She was… controlling.'

'How?'

He lets out a sigh. 'She came into my life not long after Abby left. I had come back up to be with Mum, but the timings are a little different to what I said. I'm sorry… I think I just wanted to pretend none of it had happened.'

'None of what?' He looks up at me from beneath his eyebrows, so I lay my hand on his.

'She made me fall for her and I did, with everything I had. And before I realised what was happening she took over. She moved in to Mum's with me, brought Pip with her, Pip was Lisa's dog, not Mum's.'

If it was Lisa's dog, but they'd split up when we met, how did he still have it?

'She took over. Changed things around. Put her stamp on my mum's house.' I grit my teeth. She took over. Like he has here. 'That's why I really want to sell it. That's why I wanted to stay here with you – there are too many memories there. Too much pain. And I love you, I just want to be with you, I don't want any ghosts. I don't want to feel like she's still watching over my every move.'

I look down at his fingers, still clasping mine. 'It must have been awful, for you to feel this way.'

'I never thought it'd be me. I mean, you do hear about it happening to men, but I never imagined I'd be that weak.'

Weak? 'It can happen to any of us,' I say, trying not to sound too pointed. Incredulous that he'd weave a tale that reflects our own journey so closely. As if I wouldn't notice. Alcohol courses through my veins giving me an odd confidence that I can't let take over. I have to manage this carefully. Damage limitation. For Mum's sake. For my own. 'I'm sorry you felt you couldn't tell me about her.'

'I wanted you to see me for the man I believed I was, not the one she turned me into.'

'Were you afraid of her?'

He takes his hand away now, looking down at his fingers, fiddling with the ring on his right hand. 'Stupid, isn't it?'

'No! Not at all. You were vulnerable, what with everything going on with your mum, and just coming out of a relationship.' As I say this, I almost want to kick myself because the mirror is so bloody clear and up in my face right now.

He nudges me, gently. 'I should have known you wouldn't judge.'

'As if I could!' Oh, I'm bloody well judging. I am judging you hard.

'You know… that's why I had no money to pay for the hotel. Within weeks of being together, I wasn't working because of Mum. Lisa put me on her accounts, we shared everything, she said it was easier that way as she earned the money. Then we split and she emptied everything. That's why the car is in her name too, but it's my car. I was paying for that much at least. Well, I was, until the money ran out.'

'Oh, love. I thought you'd said you had money?' Like all those times you sneered at the fact I had none.

'Did I? I mean, I didn't mean to give that impression. I was probably trying to impress you. But no, Mum had nothing, she left nothing apart from the house. Well, there was enough to pay for a basic funeral and that's it. It was awful. I'd wanted so badly to give her the proper send-off she would have wanted. A beautiful coffin, a wake for all her friends so we could share stories and celebrate her life.' He sniffs, wiping his eyes as he blatantly lies to me. I've heard him say he's got money. I've heard him tell me I'm earning nothing, to let him pay. Fuck, that's why he bought me the phone.

The phone. To replace my other one that wasn't working properly.

How did I not question any of this stuff? How was I so quickly wrapped up in his manipulation?

How on earth do I get out of it?

'I asked Lisa, begged her to let me use some of our money to do that and she wouldn't let me.' He pauses, his eyes full, his bottom lip quivering. 'And when we met, I couldn't believe it. You were so warm, and real. And I saw where you were at, what you had to cope with, I could see which way things were going to go and I just wanted to be with you, let you lean on me. Be the person Lisa never was for me, the person she never allowed me to be. I have so much to give, Jem. Meeting up with you meant I could get out of the house. I could leave it, let her stay there if she wanted to. I took the car, I told her I was. I don't know why she said what she said because it was the last thing I did. I used the tiny shred of courage I had to tell her I was going and taking it.' He closes his eyes.

I want to grab hold of him, point out all the flaws in his story, not least the fact that if he was so frightened of this woman, how did he get the strength to log on to Tinder? How did he have the courage and confidence to be so forthright with me? How can he not see what he's saying?

He continues, 'That was why I couldn't let you kiss me, when we went out to the party for Great-Aunty Vi.'

Oh, right. He had a conscience, did he? 'You were still together then?' I ask, gently.

'I know, I know.' He holds my hand to his chest. 'I am so sorry, I know I lied. I just… I didn't want to do that to you. I was falling in love and I couldn't hurt you. I had to end it with her. You gave me the strength to do that, that's how much you mean to me. I wouldn't be here without you. That night, after I left you, I went home and told her to leave. I gave her a few days to get out but… well, she's still there.' I find that bit hard to believe. The woman I saw the other day didn't seem like a woman happy to stay in a home that wasn't her own.

Oh my God. It's not his home. I bet it's not his home.

'And that's why you're here, with me? Because she wouldn't leave and you had nowhere else to go?'

'It's not the only reason, Jem.' I shift to sit cross-legged before him, suddenly disgusted by the sight of him. 'I promise you, that's not the only reason. I'm here because I love you. Because I want to be here for you and your mum.'

I nod, going over his every word. Aware I still don't know what the truth exactly is but not questioning the feeling in the pit of my belly that says this isn't it.

'She emptied our bank account. That morning at the hotel. That's why I couldn't pay. Jem... I'm so sorry, I just... I'm so sorry...'

He buries his head in my stomach, my hands stroke his hair. And now I realise that the butterflies I felt? Was a kind of fear. The uncertainty about him and us and what was unfolding? That was my gut, telling me something was wrong. And the nerves... that was me, ignoring that self-same gut, just like I always have. And it's like the world's in a bubble. Or I'm in a bubble in the world. It feels dreamlike, I can hear, I can see, I can feel the weight of him on me, no longer exciting, now just, suffocating. Utterly, terrifyingly, suffocating.

Chapter Seventy-Four

Most of the night I lay awake, Mitch beside me, sleeping. I've watched him, the flicker of his eyes, the twitch in his legs. I've seen words play on his lips, though he doesn't make a sound. I've studied his face, wondering how it's possible to fall in love so quickly, then out of it even faster. When he's moved, I've moved, so our skin needn't touch. When he's reached out for me, when I've not been able to escape the weight of his arm resting across my chest, I think I've barely felt it because I'm already suffocating under the weight of realisation.

How could I have got it so wrong, so significantly, so quickly?

How could I have let him come into mine and Mum's life so completely? Was I wrapped up in his charm and how it made Mum smile? Was I convinced because Leanne was encouraging me to be fearless? Was it the sex? The feeling of being adored and wanted, needed, so all-consuming. Am I that shallow?

Is he really that bad?

He's so charming. So generous. He's so tender at times, so loving. He's so supportive of all we're going through, the cooking and cleaning, the taking time to make things nice for Mum. For me. How does that sit beside a man who would look for a relationship when he was already in one? One who would lie, day in, day out? One who would send photos of the letter I wrote to Ben? He knew, he knew what that letter meant for me. He knew Ben hadn't wanted to read it. Why would he send it, knowing what damage could be done? How could I let him do this to me?

Except the more I read up on the kind of person Lisa had said he was, the more I recognise, and come to understand; the more I see how little I have to do with any of this. He doesn't need me; he needs someone that lets him be him. And I will not do that any more.

I don't have much of me left. I thought I was rock bottom before, I had no idea there was more to come. But here I am, still breathing, still standing. Because of Mum, because of Leanne. Maybe... maybe even because of me. He will not take what tiny bit is left.

At six a.m., I creep out of bed because I know I can't sleep, but I don't want to wake him.

I tiptoe through towards the kitchen, but Mum reaches out her hand.

'Love, I was just about to call you.' Her voice is strained, fractured. 'I need you to get the doctor.'

'What's the matter?'

She reaches for a pot she's got by her side, vomiting into it. She spits, she dabs at the side of her mouth, she shifts her hips like she had yesterday, and I see pain etched across her face. 'Please, call the doctor.'

It takes almost two hours for Dr Fairleigh to arrive and in that time, Mum has continued to be sick, just small amounts, but her discomfort has increased significantly. She didn't want to drink anything, I tried rubbing her back but where it would help for a second it would irritate not long after.

'The pain started yesterday,' I say, showing him in to her, glancing upstairs, relieved to see there's still no sign of Mitch stirring. 'She had codeine.'

'How much?' he asks, reaching for her wrist as he studies his watch.

'Gosh, I can't remember. How many times, Mum?'

'I don't know,' she squeaks, then sinks into herself as a wave of pain crushes her breath.

'Maybe three lots, it was helping,' I say, letting her free hand squeeze mine.

'I took some an hour ago, it's not touched it,' she says between breaths and I don't know what labour looks like, but I imagine this is it. Late stages. As the woman pulls away from reality and finds the part of her that allows her body to do what it's supposed to. Do they hear, in that state? Can they say all they need to say?

'She's also been sick.'

I pass him the jug, its contents worryingly discoloured. His face remains poker straight as he says, 'Right.' He digs out a stethoscope from the leather bag he carries, which looks like the ones you get on TV shows, and I didn't realise they really were the ones doctors use when on a visit. He takes her blood pressure.

I crouch down to her eye level.

'I don't want to go to the hospital,' Mum manages. 'I've done the paperwork, it's on the side there. I want to stay here.'

'Mum, let's see what happens first.' But she's gone again, inside of herself, breathing and squeezing my finger before vomiting again. And I see the look on the doctor's face and I feel the pain in my heart and something inside me tells me this is it.

Please let me be wrong. Not now. Not like this.

He turns to me. 'We wouldn't ordinarily administer morphine due to her blood pressure, I think, however…' It's the look in his eye that tells me he doesn't need to finish the sentence. The look that says, I'm sorry, but this is happening. The look that says, there is nothing we can do and we did say it might come to this.

'What's happening?' I ask as Mum breathes through more pain.

'It's very difficult to be certain, but it looks like one of two things, potentially both; I think there is a blockage somewhere, that's what is causing the pain. The hospital suggested that would be the case, didn't they?' I nod. 'However, her vomit would suggest there's also a bleed.'

I drop from crouching to my knees. My head rests on her hand as she tightens her hold, her body rigid.

'The morphine will make her comfortable, if you're happy for me to do that.' I bite my top lip, to stop any sounds coming out because I can't guarantee they won't also be tinged with pain. I just nod, again. And he goes back into his bag, getting the injection ready, doing paperwork, making sure he's noted the batch number, time and location before he takes her hand from me.

Her relief is almost instantaneous.

I watch her melt into her bed, relaxation moving through her body, eyes closed, breath returning to normal. It's that quick. And the relief I feel is almost (but not quite) as equal to the dread I can taste.

The doctor packs his things away, depositing the needle into a small yellow box that he places on the side. 'We should leave that there,' he says.

He checks over her again, monitoring the impact of the drug, before tucking her arm into the duvet and ushering me out of the dining room into the lounge.

Chapter Seventy-Five

Dr Fairleigh invites me to sit down in my own home and when doctors do that, you know it's not good news. He sits across from me in my chair. He leans forward slightly, his elbows on his knees, fingers steepled.

'This is it, isn't it?'

He doesn't answer straight away, but I can tell from the look in his eye. I could tell from the moment he arrived. In fact, I think I knew from when I called him. It was there, in the back of my mind, the truth I didn't want to accept.

'We have to keep her comfortable. That is the most important thing at this point, her comfort.' I swallow. I reach for the tissues that sit by her diary and book, all stacked up neatly in a pile at the end of her sofa. 'I'm going to stay for a while, just to make sure the dose I gave her is sufficient to keep her comfortable. We'll need to get the community nurses over though. Sometime this afternoon. They can fit Mum with what they call a driver.' I look at him blankly. 'It's like a drip that will administer both morphine and anti-sickness on a continual basis.'

'How long for?'

There's a brief pause before he says, 'Until she no longer needs it.'

'But… how? This is all so sudden? She was fine, she was doing really well! We went out the other day! She was eating.'

'And that can happen, we often see an uplift in a patient's energy before things take a sudden change. And we knew something like this would happen. I know that doesn't help you now, but…'

I drop back into the chair, stunned. It's all so surreal. 'I'm not ready… Doctor. I'm not ready. I can't… she can't.'

I stare at the carpet. I search inside my addled brain for some sense of what the hell happens next or a flash of information I can give that might change his prognosis. But nothing comes. 'What can I do?' I whisper, eventually.

He offers a sad smile. 'Talk to her. She can hear you. Keep her company. If you notice any signs of anything changing, or the nurses haven't been, call us.'

'What if she's in any pain again?'

'She shouldn't be. What I've given her should be fine for several hours but I'll organise a prescription for Oramorph too. Are you on your own here? Can anyone pick that up for you?'

On cue, I hear Mitch move about upstairs.

'Erm, that's my boyfriend.' The word sticks in my throat. He's the last person I want here.

'Can he pick up the prescription for you?'

I nod. Mitch comes down the stairs. I catch a glimpse of him as he sees the doctor and my stomach flips.

'What's going on?' he asks, sleepily, checking through to Mum. 'What's the matter?'

'It's Mum, she's…' but I can't finish the sentence and he sweeps me into his arms so I don't have to. I want to push him off, but I also want to hide.

Dr Fairleigh is filling out paperwork. 'Could you collect a prescription for her? If I organise it to be at the surgery pharmacy?'

'Of course, anything at all.' Mitch steps forward like a saviour, he's all chest and arms and look at how helpful and important I am.

The doctor goes off to make some phone calls and check up on Mum at the same time. He gives orders for the community team and reels off drug dosages that they need to bring with them. He discusses another patient and tells them he'll be back in the office in an hour. Then he comes through to me, my hand held in Mitch's, my heart still.

'She's comfortable. The community team will be with you by two thirty at the latest. If you need to give any more pain relief in the meantime, you can give her ten mills of Oramorph as and when needed.'

'As and when? What if I give her too much?'

He shakes his head, gently. 'You won't. It's fine. Just do whatever she needs to be comfortable.'

As the doctor packs up his stuff, I dance around him, lightly, uncertain what to do with myself or where to go. Mitch is busying himself making things tidy, organising the paperwork from the doctor, generally making sure it's clear to anyone who might see that he is very much needed in our house.

But he isn't. We survived years without him. Without Dad. Just the two of us, it's all we ever needed. We can do it again. Well… I can.

Mum sleeps, her breath shallow, her face relaxed. Yesterday she was chatting to Leanne, laughing at Harley, cooing over Elsie. She was in pain, yes, but she was alert. She was aware of what was going off around her and she had opinions. Always an opinion. But now? Now, she lays in her temporary bed, unable to respond when I whisper her name. I hold her hand, her fingers bony, her skin like paper. And it's as though my body has injected pain relief directly into my heart and soul, something to see I survive however long this lasts; I am numb.

Chapter Seventy-Six

'I'll come back later, at the end of the day when surgery's finished, just to see how she is.'

'Thank you.' Mitch hurries through to the front door, opening it for Dr Fairleigh. 'Thanks so much for your help,' he says, gravely. 'We really do appreciate it.'

We?

We appreciate it?

From my bedside vantage point, I watch Dr Fairleigh plod down the drive, medical bag swinging. The house is quiet as Mitch shuts the door and I listen out for Dr Fairleigh's car door closing, his engine turning on. He pulls away. Mitch comes to stand beside me, hand on my shoulder, looming presence. Mum's breath is just about audible, there's something so tiny about her, almost newborn. The bond that knitted us together so tightly for all our years tugs at my gut. She protected me when I entered this world and now it's my turn to do the same as she leaves it. And for the first time in my grown-up life, I know exactly what I have to do.

'Can I get you anything?' asks Mitch, stroking my hair. 'Tea? Coffee? Something stronger?'

I let out a shallow laugh. 'Yeah, that's just what I need, a pint of vodka to wash down the sadness.'

'I wouldn't blame you…'

I look up at him, uncertain if he's being serious. He places his hand behind my head, pulling me into his chest. 'I know how hard this is, I know exactly how you're feeling.'

'Exactly how I'm feeling? How can you know *exactly* how I'm feeling?'

He steps back. 'Because I've been here before. I've sat at Mum's bedside, holding her hand.'

'Right.' I wonder if he even did that. Was he even there when his mum passed? I trust nothing that comes out of his mouth. And whether he was there or not, he won't be here with me. With Mum. I tuck her hand into her side, loathed to leave her but determined to fix this before it's too late.

In the kitchen, I put the kettle on. I mean, I don't actually want a drink, but what else do you do in situations like this? He's followed me through. He stands by the fridge, leaning, watching. 'Why did you send Ben photos of the letter?' I ask.

He looks confused. At least, I'm pretty sure he thinks that's how he looks.

'I saw them, on my phone. It was in my room the other night when I came up and found you with the letter. I probably wouldn't have realised except that Ben's girlfriend texted back. She asked me why I'd do such a thing but I didn't, did I?'

'Why would *I* do that?'

'I don't know. Why would you?'

In the very pit of my belly, so deep I could be forgiven for missing it, there's a sea change. Where fear – mistaken for butterflies – was, there's strength. Where nerves – mistaken for excitement – were, there's…

resolve. It's unfamiliar, but it's stronger than anything else I've felt for weeks, months... years.

'It's not the only thing you've lied about though, is it?'

'Jem, you're tired, you're upset. Your mum's there' – he drops his voice to a whisper – 'she's dying, Jem and this is what's on your mind? I mean, I know grief does strange things but is now really the time to discuss this?'

'No, you're right. It's not.'

'There—'

'You should just go.'

'Pardon?'

Where the assumption I couldn't manage on my own once was, there's fire. And whilst I wouldn't go as far as to say determination, there's definitely det... or determ... and there is no way I am going to watch my mum die with him in this house. Even if that means it's me and her alone, just like it was the day I was born because Dad was away and Mum couldn't get hold of him. She hatched. I'll despatch. If that's what this is, I'm doing it on my terms, not his. 'I want you to take your things and leave.'

'Jem, I know this is a difficult time. I really do understand. We can talk about this another time though. You need me.'

'Nope. No I don't. That's what you wanted me to believe. And for a while, I did. The phone, the taking over here with Mum, the surprises, that was you making me think I needed you. That was you making me rely on you until I believed I couldn't rely on myself. Though, I can't credit you with that achievement. I've never thought I could rely on me. You just tapped in to that. But I was wrong.'

'I'm not leaving.'

Mum takes a heavy breath in and we both stop. She will not die with him here. I watch her through the doorway, my eyes fixed on her chest, waiting to see it move. Which it does. But it's enough to make me certain in what I feel.

'You've got half an hour. If you haven't gone by then, I'll be calling the police and telling them about the money you've been spending out of Mum's account. I'll tell them about your manipulation. Maybe there are a few more things you might like to share with them, whilst we have their attention. I could start, you could finish off, update them on Lisa. If she's the bad guy here, we can kill two birds with one stone.'

He bites the inside of his cheek. He looks out of the window, then back to me. He looks to Mum then back to me again. He fidgets. 'You can't be here on your own with her. You need someone.'

'Mum and I don't need anyone but each other. We never have, not since Dad left. And we never will.' I hiccup, knowing that soon it'll just be me. 'Now leave.'

At Mum's bedside, I take up her hand again, turning my back on him. I'm pretty certain she gives me the very smallest flicker of a squeeze, which clouds my eyes with devastated tears. And eventually, when I hear the front door click shut, I breathe.

Chapter Seventy-Seven

If I'm honest with myself, I'm a little reluctant to call Deni. Her nonchalance hadn't exactly ingratiated her to me but I don't know who else to call. I don't want to put it on Leanne, though not because I'm being a martyr or anything, I just need to manage this my way. By myself. Gently. Quietly. Like any normal grown-up would. I'll call Leanne when I've got organised, assuming Deni picks up this call. It rings as I stare out the big front window, Mitch's car is parked up the road with him sitting in it. I wonder how long he'll stay there ?

'Hello, this is Deni.'

'Deni, it's Jem Whitfield. Hilltop Road, Dronfield. I'm Val's daughter.'

'Ah yes, hello. How are you? I'm due to see you later this week, aren't I?'

I hear a rustling sound in the background and imagine her furiously flicking through pages in the scrappy diary she wrote our next appointment in. I can see Mitch staring. 'Yes. You were. Tomorrow, in fact. The thing is, I wondered if you were able to help me at all?'

'I can try. What's the matter? Is your mum okay?'

'Erm, well… no. Not really. She's taken a turn. It's happened quite quickly. She was in pain yesterday, it escalated overnight. The doctor left about an hour ago.'

'Oh?'

'He's given her some morphine. There's a team coming later to fit a driver and give her some more. They're making her comfortable…' I say that in the same code I now realise the doctor was using. The same code I remember someone saying they might, back when it became talks of palliative, then end of life care.

'Oh. Oh, love. I'm so sorry. But she was doing so well? She was really getting her strength up.'

The memory of Mum ordering me around Coles, buying clothes she'll never wear, picks at my heart. The image of her necking slow roast pork like it was the best thing she'd ever tasted, its juices all around her mouth, it's clear in my mind, right down to the twinkle in her eye. I pack away the sadness I feel, for now.

'There's a prescription at the doctor's for Mum. I don't want to leave her and the community team aren't due until later this afternoon. I wondered if there was anyone near that could collect it for us? I didn't know if you were about doing visits or anything?'

'Actually, I'm due over in Dronfield at lunchtime. I could try and collect it and drop off before then? Now let's see, what time is it now?'

'It's just after ten.'

'Okay, can she wait?'

I glance across to her. 'She's okay at the moment, seems comfortable. I just don't want it to get worse quickly and there not be anything for her here.'

'Well it shouldn't do, if she's had a decent enough dose. Let me finish up here then head over to her surgery. I'll be with you as soon as I can.'

'Thanks, Deni.'

I hang up, placing my phone on the side. I clock Mitch parked outside again but Mum stirring pulls me away from the window.

'Mum? Are you okay? Can you hear me?' Her hand rests on the bed and I slip mine into hers. She definitely squeezes it this time. Her eyes briefly flicker in my direction. She clacks her lips as if her mouth is dry, so I try to sit her up just a little, feeding her a few sips of water until she pushes the cup away.

'Deni's bringing you some medicine up. And the doctors will be back in a bit, with some more morphine and anti-sickness stuff. You're Tom Cruise short of a cocktail.' I smile, then feel my eyes fill before I can stop them. I take a moment, allowing the fear to pass.

'Are you comfortable?'

Somehow, she manages a shallow nod and though there aren't any words, it's the most she's done since the doctor was here, which is an odd relief. Confused tears spill on to my cheeks, finding a route direct to my top lip. I lick the salt and use my free hand to wipe my face. 'Any pain?'

She gives the smallest shake of her head.

'Good. That's good.' Pause. 'That's the last time you overindulge slow roast pork,' I say, and she manages the faintest of smiles.

The house feels big. Overwhelming. The quiet is deafening. The weight of what I know is happening feels crushing. It forces me down, my legs leaden, my neck and shoulders solid. I look around at the dining room with her makeshift bed, wheelchair in the corner. I shift in the wicker chair beside her bed and it creaks like wicker does, which makes Mum raise her eyebrows as if noticing I'm still here.

'Where's Mitch?' she says, her voice so small.

I close my eyes because her eyes are closed too, and I don't know where to begin. Or how much to say. If these are her last days… or hours… however long she has left, I don't want them to be consumed with worry for me. But I also know I've made the right decision and all she's ever wanted is for me to believe in me. Besides, the squeeze of her hand when he left tells me she knows.

'He's gone.'

Her hand flinches. I study her face. A face like mine in so many ways. The same shaped eyes, the same freckle to the left of our noses. Over the years, we've compared photos of me to her at the same age and been blown away by the similarity. We frequently sit the same way. We both pause between mouthfuls when eating, knife and fork on the table, hands clasped together. We both roll our eyes like my nana did. We both fight when we think we're losing. At least, I used to. As a young teenager. Maybe until I was fifteen, sixteen. I think that's when the fight started to fade. And it kept on fading. Until now, I'm thirty-eight and until this morning it had gone altogether.

'Are you okay?' she asks.

It makes me do a laugh cry because how can I possibly be? But I say, 'Yes... I am.'

Her eyes flicker, though closed, then slowly, she opens them just slightly, halfway, turning her head slowly to face me. 'You're stronger than you think. I've always known yet never been sure how to help you see it.'

'I see it now,' I say, resting my cheek on her pillow, our noses touching like inverted bookends.

'You are your mother's daughter,' she whispers.

'Thank God,' I whisper back.

Chapter Seventy-Eight

'Thank you so much.' I take the prescription from Deni.

'It's no problem. How you doing? Can I come in for a minute?'

'Of course. Though haven't you got another appointment to go to?'

'I do. But it can wait.'

I smile to myself because Mum was right. And now it's our turn for her to make us the priority, part of me feels bad for being so cross with her before. Except, it's the tiny part of me that I don't have to listen to any more. The bit that knows I'm flawed and judgmental and make mistakes, the bit that somehow, from this morning onwards, I know won't shout so loud.

'There was a guy outside when I arrived, he asked who I was, said he was worried about you.'

'I'd sort of assumed he might have gone by now.'

'He says he's your partner, you've kicked him out? Is there anything I can do to help?' She's searching out eye contact. Do they have workshops on managing difficult people in end of life scenarios? Probably. 'Do you want him here?'

'No. I don't want him anywhere near me. But I also won't be giving him the satisfaction of calling anyone so he can make out I've gone mad in my grief state or something.' Deni looks concerned. 'It's fine, honestly. He won't do anything. He's many things but I don't think he has that in him.'

'Oh?'

'I think perhaps he's the kind of person who gets his strength from other people's weakness and I just cut all his hair off. I do need to make a phone call though, if you wouldn't mind sitting with Mum for a minute or two?'

'Of course not. Go on, I'll shout if anything changes. Take your time.'

The lock in the back door sticks, like it always does, and I wonder why I was waiting for him to put oil on it when I could have done it myself before now. When I finally unclick it, I step out into the back garden, pulling my coat around me to protect from the breeze.

I wander up the overgrown path that I used to skip along as a kid. I sneak round the back of the garage where I used to sit and smoke Lambert & Butler cigarettes because that's all fourteen-year-old me could find to nick off the old woman I used to cat sit for. I pull out my phone, dialling Leanne's number.

'It's me,' I say when she picks up. 'Have you got a minute?'

'Of course I have. What's up?'

'It's Mum—'

'Oh no…'

'Something's going on, a bleed or blockage or something.'

'I'll come over.'

'No, no, it's okay. I don't need you to. I'm just letting you know. So you don't worry if I don't text for the next day or two.'

'Oh, Jem…'

'I'm okay,' I insist, looking up to the sky as clouds spin past. 'I'm okay,' I say again, because oddly, I think I am. 'Mitch has gone.'

'What?'

'This morning. I asked him to leave. I decided I didn't want him here in this house. Not now. Not ever, actually, but especially not now.'

'Wow… I can't believe you – actually, of course I can. I can believe you did it.'

'I've wasted so many years trying to live and be the person I thought I needed to be and just when I thought I was putting it all right, I made it worse. And part of me wants to say how stupid am I? How could I have done that? But there's a part that's shouting louder.'

'What's it saying?'

'That I'm okay. That I've always been okay. That even when I've been a dick, it doesn't mean I'm not, fundamentally okay.'

Leanne lets out a whistle. 'Finally. The penny drops.'

'I know right, took long enough. I mean, I very nearly messed it right up!'

'Well, I didn't exactly help, did I? Pushing you like that to get on Tinder.'

'You were trying to get me out of myself, you meant well.'

'Yeah, might not bother doing that again.'

'Don't you dare bail out on me now, I probably need you now more than I ever bloody did. Well… by my side though, not carrying me. I don't need anyone carrying me any more.'

'Sometimes you might. And that's okay too.'

'Yeah… sometimes I might. Maybe sooner than I'd like.'

'You know you're amazing. And you will survive.'

'I don't want to have to, Leanne,' I say, letting myself cry properly for the first time all morning. Which may have been a mistake because I sob into the cold air and frighten next door's cat.

'I can be there in a heartbeat, chuck.'

I sniff up. Letting out the sadness and rebuilding the strength. 'No. It's okay. I'm okay, I promise. Just… belt and brace yourself ready for the fallout.'

'I've got casseroles and vodka on standby.'

'Casseroles I'm all over. I think maybe I'll give the vodka a miss.'

'Who are you? What have you done with my best friend?'

'Ha! She's here. She was always here. She just couldn't see it for herself.'

Chapter Seventy-Nine

The funny thing about time is that it can drag. It slows when you want it to speed up. It flies when you want it to slow. It plays tricks. But what I've never experienced before, is when it stops. When everyone around you carries on working to it, appearing, disappearing, living and being and doing what needs to be done at a time like this, and yet they do that whilst you sit, suspended. In a film, I'd be the still one, as those about me blur in a frenzy of busy. So I have no sense of time at all when the next day's dawn begins to chorus and Mum's breaths are getting shallower. Fewer and further between. I've no sense of who I am when tears stream down Mum's face. I don't know where I am when she no longer flickers at my voice. When her hand is limp in mine. I've no connection with the world at all as she breathes in, then out, then in… and, my hand in hers, holding on whilst letting go, she breathes out. And instinctively, this time, I know, without any question in my heart, that she's gone.

Mum's gone.

Chapter Eighty

The churchyard is full. People talk in low voices, kissing one another on the cheek, sharing their sadness. Leanne stands beside me, close enough for me to lean on if I need to, Elsie Alice is strapped to her chest, fast asleep.

The service was strange. Long. I think I want for this all to be over, yet that seems harsh, ungrateful almost. People are here because they care and they come up to tell me that, some more comfortably than others. I bite my tongue with the ones who tell me she's out of pain now, and that she's in a better place. If she'd had weeks, months of pain, maybe I could accept that, but she didn't. A few hours, really, that was all. She's not in a better place. She's away, gone, not here.

I don't say that though; I just agree with each well-intentioned platitude because that's what we're supposed to do. And it is nice to hear the stories some share about how they knew Mum or what a great person she was. I mean, I know that for myself, obviously, but they knew her as Valerie Whitfield, which is different somehow to knowing her as Mum. Nobody else knows her as Mum and it's the one and only time I've wished I had a sibling, someone to talk to about her. Someone else who knew what she was like as a parent. Leanne remembers how bad some of her cooking was, but that's not really it.

God, I miss her.

I glance across to the Dragon's car park. Mitch's car has been there all morning. I half thought he might have turned up in the church, maybe even try and talk to me. As he has each day since she died, via text or voicemail messages, the occasional knock on the door to tell me he forgives me. That we can work through my grief together. That he doesn't blame me for asking him to leave, he understands my pain. That he'll wait outside my house until I am ready for him to come in. That lasted two days, his car was there most of the time, just parked up, watching as people came and went. As the funeral directors collected Mum. When the vicar came round to see me. Leanne said she'd call the police or go tell him herself but I didn't want her to get involved. Sometimes his car would disappear for an hour or two, then it'd come back. He'd sit in the dark and watch me close the curtains and lock the door. Alone in the house.

Eventually, his car disappeared and it didn't come back after a few hours like before. It stayed away for a full day. The next day, he didn't come back at all. And today – unless I missed him – he has at least kept a distance, though I assume he probably stood at the back of the church. I suspect this is less out of respect and more because he's no idea what he'd say if he stood in front of me surrounded by all these people. His weakness is my saviour.

Leanne takes hold of my elbow. 'I need to pop and change her. I'll be super-quick. Then I'll walk with you to the Manor House, yeah?'

'Yeah, thank you.' We had to have cream tea for the afternoon wake. Mum expressly chose it in the list of things I had to organise that she helpfully left in a notepad in her bag. It included where to find the money to pay for her funeral (in a brown envelope at the back of the cupboard she kept her hair stuff in), where to find her birth certificate to register her death (filing cabinet, third drawer down), which church she wanted for her funeral (the same church she was christened in) and where we were to all go afterwards (The Manor House, Dronfield, for a cream tea and much laughter). There was a list of names of people I had to tell and their phone numbers or addresses. There was a tick box by the side of each action so I could mark off each task. Even now, hereafter, she's still organising me.

People come up to me, they shake my hand. They kiss my cheek. Some say they'll see me up at the Manor, others tell me what a beautiful service it was and that they appreciated the invite. I move through the visitors, making my way to the gate to wait for Leanne, and that's when I see him first. Ben. Standing in the very corner of the church gardens, his head bowed as he lays flowers on his own parents' grave. When he looks up, we share a sad smile and I so wish I could run into his arms. Not because I can't cope, but because if I hadn't been such an idiot, he'd be the one standing beside me right now. Letting me lean when I needed to. Letting me stand when I could.

Even when someone comes to say goodbye to me, I can barely look away from him. When I do, to be polite, I look back and see him walking towards me.

Chapter Eighty-One

'Hey,' Ben says, hands stuffed in pockets.

'Hey.'

'Thanks for letting me know, I appreciated it.'

I want to ask him about the letter but now isn't the time. Maybe there'll never be a time. 'I wasn't sure if I should, I know you don't want to hear from me. But you were on Mum's list of people I had to tell and I couldn't not. That's why I messaged from her phone. I wasn't trying to be sneaky or anything.'

'Of course not. No. I'm glad you did.'

'Thank you for coming, I didn't expect you to. I realise how far it is for you.'

He looks to the ground. 'Oh, no, it's fine. I… well, I live back here now.'

'Oh?'

'Yeah. Moved back at the weekend. Was all a bit sudden but it just wasn't right down there.' I have so many questions and none of them are my business. 'So if you know anyone that needs a mechanic, or even just a bit of labouring, to be honest, I'm not fussy, just want to work.'

I smile. 'Of course.'

Leanne's in the background, she spots Ben and me and visibly hangs back. I think I'd rather she came and interrupted, before I get the urge to say anything I shouldn't.

'She was an amazing woman.'

I stick my nails into my palm because of all the people I don't want to cry in front of, it's Ben. 'She was.'

'I owed her a lot, especially after Mum and Dad passed. I thought it was hard when Dad died, trying to be strong for Mum. Without your mum, I don't think I'd have managed. She talked me through it, each and every day. And then when Mum died, it was so soon after, I just couldn't see how to function. I couldn't see myself standing, living, getting back to work and stuff. Your mum, she just quietly, calmly guided me through it all. Honestly, I don't think I'd be standing if it wasn't for her.'

I nod, grateful to Mum, disappointed that I wasn't the one to do that for him. 'She would say you owed her nothing. She liked you.'

'Have you got support? You know? I guess Leanne's around.'

'She is. Just over there, pretending she hasn't seen that we're talking even though she's watching our every move in her peripheral vision.'

He smiles then reaches for my hand and everything in me fizzes. He leans in to kiss me on the cheek and I'm reminded that it's not excitement I want in a kiss, but love. Love and warmth and kindness. It's a kiss that makes me feel steadied, grounded almost. What a thing to walk away from.

'Be kind to yourself, Jem. This is tough, it's big stuff. I don't claim to know how you feel, we all deal with it differently, but I know that it will take time to find your new normal. It's not easy.'

'No.'

'Eat well. And…' He looks to the floor before directly into my eyes. 'Maybe don't drink too much.'

'I will. Eat well, I mean. Not the drinking. I've stopped the drinking, actually. Not altogether sure it agreed with me.'

He studies my face, his hand still holding mine. 'That's good. I mean, I'm glad for you. Must be hard.'

'Well, you know, it gets easier when you realise your blood shouldn't be made up of one-part vodka six parts Shiraz.'

'No.'

'No.' I take a deep breath. 'I'm sorry. For everything,' I say in a half whisper.

He studies our hands, then me for a second. 'Take care, Jem. And thanks again for letting me know.'

He lets go of me, stuffing his hands in his pockets. I want to reach out and take them back. 'Thanks for coming. Hope you get sorted with a job or whatever soon.'

He pauses for a second then turns back and my heart swells. 'Your phone was never blocked, by the way. I wouldn't do that. Just… so you know.'

He slowly turns to leave, pausing again as if he wants to say more but I think I'm glad that he doesn't. Leanne sidles up beside me as I watch him leave. 'Thank God he's gone,' she says.

'Ben?'

'No, Mitch. Look, he's just pulled off.'

'Oh yeah, so he has. Good.' Ben walks as Mitch drives, the pair crossing, probably without realising who the other one is. I wonder what Mitch would do if he did.

Leanne hooks her arm through mine. 'Come on, let's fill our faces with scones and jam.'

'Devon or Cornwall?' I ask, making my way up the path, pausing by the occasional person for them to pass on their condolences.

'Eh?'

'Jam or cream first?'

'Oh, right. I dunno. What would your mum have had?'

'Cornwall. Always. More cream that way.'

'You see, inspiring until the very end,' says Leanne, giving me a nudge.

We walk in silence. I'm aware of people behind me, following us to the Manor.

Eventually, Leanne asks what I know she'll have been desperate to ask for the last four minutes. 'Nice of Ben to come.'

'Yeah.'

'Long way.'

'He's home.'

I feel her jolt at the news but she pretends it's casual. 'Oh?'

'Didn't work out, apparently.'

'But… what about the baby? He's surely not left the baby?'

I shrug. 'No idea. Not my place to ask.'

'Nice to know he's home?'

I think for a moment, pushing the door open to the smell of freshly made scones and Earl Grey tea, just as Mum's list instructed. 'It might have been, if I'd not ruined things. It's mostly just nice to know he doesn't hate me. That much I couldn't have coped with. You go sit over there, I've got people to welcome.'

'Can I get you a drink?'

'Tea. Please. Tea would be perfect.'

Chapter Eighty-Two

They say that people come over less as time goes on. With the exception of Leanne, three weeks on since the funeral, four to the day since Mum passed, I am alone in our house.

I don't really know how I feel about it.

Don't get me wrong, it's been lovely to have food delivered, and people checking up on me. I'm not sure if they're doing it for me or for Mum but each casserole and plated-up roast dinner has been welcomed. I could have given the skate brought over by Mum's best friend Marjorie a miss, but there was something in its nostalgia that made me smile. And it does taste better if you don't microwave it.

But it feels strange to be here alone. And as the weeks pass, I do feel alone. Some people say she's still with me, that she's only in the next room. And I feel bad because I can't reach her. It doesn't seem like she's in the next room, it seems like she's gone. And she's taken a little piece of me with her. I'm not sure I'll ever get that back.

Even now, sat in her chair, it's like she was never here.

Apart from her handbag on the side and her nail file resting on the books she never finished. I considered putting *Hollywood Wives* in her coffin, see if she could take it with her. She'll be furious if there really isn't a library in heaven.

I reach for the nail file. She was the last to use it. I can see nail scuff marks on the grey emery. *Her* scuff marks. *Her* nails. It should probably be a bit gross, and yet it's a reminder that whatever my heart feels right now, she was here. And not that long ago.

A knock on the door gives me a start. I'm not good in the house on my own, that much I've realised. I used to hate it in my own place and that was even smaller than this. This one creaks with every footstep and many times without. I draw back the front door curtain, flicking the porch light on as I open the door. And there he is again. Mitch. A bouquet of flowers in one hand and a bottle of wine in the other.

'Please don't slam the door in my face,' he says, stepping forward so that I can't without shoving the flowers in his face and potentially hurting him.

'I don't want to see you, Mitch.' I push the door gently, preserving some of the heat in the house, making sure I can close it fully if I need to. I look up and down the road, wondering why, on a road normally busy with people going to and fro, there is not a single car around.

'I know you think you don't want to see me, but we had something really special, Jem. And I've given you time. I've given you space, you owe it to me to talk.'

Owe it to him?

'You're grieving. You're not thinking straight and I'm not angry about that. I might have done the same thing had we been together when Mum died. A love like ours, it's so intense, so deep, it's frightening. Especially when you're dealing with the death of a loved one. You probably had conflicting thoughts, those last few days. Not helped by how quick things happened between us, but when it's true, there's no sense in hanging around.'

He's pleading with me. His eyes wide and focused. He leans against the door, his breath heavy with alcohol. I notice his car, up where he'd been parking after I first asked him to leave.

'I love you, Jem. Please, I just want to talk. That's all. See if we can't mend things. You need help. I can help you.'

'I need help?'

'Of course you do. You're broken, and you're bound to be. I mean you were before your mum passed, but of course that's worse now. It's nothing to be ashamed about.'

'I'm not ashamed.'

'Good. That's good. You see, already you're making way to a brighter future. Let that be with me. Let us pick up where we were.' I go to cut him off, but he interjects. 'All that money we spent on your mum's room turning it into a space for us. It's such a waste.'

He has no idea I cleared it out. That I put it back to Mum's room on the day she died. That I moved straight back into my box room because at least that felt safe. And free of him. The memory of how he manipulated and lied. The memory of how good he made me feel and how much I wish he hadn't. The knowledge that he moved in because he had nowhere to go… he had nowhere to go.

'Why are you really here?'

He holds the flowers and wine up. 'To bring you these. To get us back together.'

'Not because you've nowhere else to go?'

'No. Of course not. Jem, I love you.'

I look down at his clothes, crumpled, lived-in. His face is drawn, tired. He's no idea that I've since learned that it was Lisa's house. That I tracked her down on Facebook and she told me she had kicked him out. That his mum lived in a local authority place and left him nothing at all in her will. Not because she was cutting him off – I don't imagine she knew what he was like – but she had nothing. That was the only truthful thing he ever told me: that she had nothing more than a basic funeral. Cardboard coffin, no flowers. No financial legacy at all. He was leaching off Lisa until she got wise to it, then he leached off me and Mum. 'You're living in your car, aren't you? You've come here because you think you can persuade me to let you move back in because you've nowhere else to go.'

'Don't be ridiculous, Jem. I'm here because I love you. I'm here because I believe you made a mistake and I want to help you see that.'

'I think you should leave.'

'Jem. You're being ridiculous. You don't know what you're doing.'

'Mitch, I know exactly what I'm doing. I'm doing what I should have done before, what I was trying to do before you came on the scene. I am sorting myself out. I am taking control of me, of my life.'

'You can't do it without me. You *need* me. You just don't want to admit it.'

I step back from the door, I've never felt so certain about anything in my life. 'Bye, Mitch. If you come back, I will call the police.'

And I slam the door, walk through to the lounge and drop into Mum's chair. And I cry. I cry because I can't believe how strong I just was. I cry because I can't believe how weak I'd been before. I cry because I am exhausted and wrung out and I cry because, bloody hell, I miss her. With every single bit of my being, I miss her.

And I cry because I know without question, that the best way to honour the life she gave me, is to live it to the full, to own my mistakes but not be defined by them, to make peace with myself and others if it's possible. Not to make me feel better this time, but for them, if they want it, so they know I realise what I did.

And to forgive myself, because maybe, looking back, it wasn't always all my fault.

Chapter Eighty-Three

'Morning.' Leanne carries Elsie Alice in her car seat, popping her by the sofa in the lounge. She's sleeping soundly. 'She's been awake all bloody night. God knows why. So bloody needy.'

'Ahhh, poor thing.'

'You say that when you've been up all night trying to get her to cry downstairs so she doesn't wake her brother up on a school night. Andy had to go to London first thing, so I'm flying solo again and I tell you what, I had forgotten how bad this phase is.'

'This too shall pass,' I say, giving her a hug before heading into the kitchen to make tea.

'Indeed. How you doing?'

'Do you want my polite answer or the truth?'

'Always the truth.'

'Middling to shit. I thought I was doing okay, then Mitch rocked up last night and although I handled it, it's just made me realise what a mess I made of things before and how I wish I had a second chance.'

'A second chance for what?'

'To say sorry.'

'Oh, we're not going through that again. I mean, granted, he's not in Cornwall any more, but you really need to let that all go. Stop beating yourself up about it.'

'No, I'm not. I think before, I was saying sorry because I wanted forgiveness, but it's not like that this time. I don't need his forgiveness… I don't even need Kate's forgiveness.'

'You *never* needed her forgiveness.'

'No. But I felt like I couldn't move on without it. Whereas now…'

'Now?'

I pass her a mug of tea and we head back through to the lounge.

'Now, I want to say sorry and own what I did. I want to be honest and just explain it.'

'Who too?'

'Ben, for one. Not about the past, but the letter. And the text messages Mitch sent. I just want him to know it wasn't me. I mean, on that one, it's not that I need his forgiveness as such, I'm working on that for myself. But it kinda is important to me that he doesn't think I'm a total shit. I mean, those photos were a low blow.'

'Ben came to the funeral.'

'That was for Mum. He wasn't there for me.'

'He talked to you. If he didn't care, he wouldn't have made time to speak with you. He'd have shown his respects and then left quietly.'

I blow across the top of my peppermint tea.

'Are you drinking peppermint tea again?' she asks.

'Yeah.'

'What's up with normal tea?'

'Caffeine, isn't it? It's not good for you.'

'It is when you've a teasy baby.'

'Yes, I imagine in those circumstances it's essential. I just decided to give up stuff that was bad for me. So, I'm off caffeine, and I'm thinking about dropping meat too.'

'Are you?'

'And dairy.'

'Bloody hell!'

'Well, I just keep thinking, here I am, trying to get rid of stress. Trying to practise mindfulness, trying to—'

'Don't say trying to be a better person!'

'No, I'm not. I'm lovely as I am; no, just trying to be kinder. Gentler. I feel like I need to roll that out across everything.'

'So long as you don't go getting all hempy on me. Or start lecturing me whenever I eat a cheese sandwich. Or a bacon sandwich.'

'It's fine, I won't. I don't care what you do, I'm just thinking of me. But in a good way.'

'Wow. There's a turn up for the books.'

'I know, right?'

We chat, we laugh, we put the world to rights. She realises she's almost late for Harley's pick-up and legs it, double quick, consumed by maternal guilt. Waving her off, I glance up the road to see if Mitch's – or should I say, Lisa's – car is there, relieved that it's not. Maybe this time he got the message. And if he doesn't, I will definitely call the police.

The house quiet again, I head up to my room, digging through my drawers to find writing paper. The Moomin set is sandwiched between an old magazine and a note from Mum. I pick it up, studying her handwriting. A note to herself, a shopping list with Cole's as the title: *winter dress, midi, polo neck jumper, cardigan, something nice for Jem.* The memory of our last ever shopping trip; a day so clear in my mind, the look on her face, the smile, the laughter, it's like a tsunami wave of grief crashes over my heart as it does each time I'm met with a new memory, a new reminder of who she was and what she meant to me. I breathe slowly, calmly, letting the emotions roll and wave until they settle, as they always do, until I can breathe through them and regain composure. I remind myself that it's precious to have her handwriting. That it connects me to her and I wouldn't ever get rid of it, but as I hold it, I realise it will never replace the conversations we had. The words exchanged, sometimes cross, often full of love. Warmth. Humour, so much humour.

Talking was the thing that saw us through her illness. Talking was the thing that saw us through our hardest years after Dad left. When hormones raged through my fifteen-year-old body, talking was the thing that kept me alive. And she taught me how to do that, how to own what I want to say. She taught me that honesty and authenticity was the only way. It took me too long to fully catch on, to really let go and be okay with all that I feel, but I did. And I did before she went. Sometimes, I wonder if she knew I'd got there, at the eleventh hour. And when I do wonder, my heart is overwhelmed with a certainty, a feeling. And though she is so far away, although she's gone, a voice in my head says, '*I knew.*'

So I pick up the phone and call Ben.

Chapter Eighty-Four

'Thanks for meeting me,' I say, standing up, wondering if I should go to give him a kiss or not.

'It was nice to hear from you.' He sits down. He's not cold, or distant for that matter, but he's buttoned up. At the funeral, he took my hand, today he holds himself close.

'Did you want a drink?'

'Tea. Please. Thanks.'

'Okay, just a minute.'

I go up to the counter to order. I'd thought twice about coming to Ferndale Garden Centre. I've not been back since that day with Mum and Mitch when Mum was poorly and Mitch gave me the phone. I didn't want to relive that memory, yet I didn't want somewhere so important to me and Mum to be tarnished by it either. Facing stuff head on isn't easy, but I think I'm glad I'm here.

'They'll bring it over,' I say, dropping the receipt on the table as I sit down.

'Great.'

We fall silent and my heart lurches. This was a good idea, I know it was, but I'm terrified. 'How've you been? Did you find any work?'

'Yeah, thanks. I'm working down at Clark's Engineering on the machines. The money's alright and I'm just glad to be working.'

'Of course.'

'And how are you?'

'Oh, you know…' I move out of the way for the waitress to set our drinks down. 'Thank you,' I say, pulling my teapot towards me, stirring the pot as I talk. 'I'm okay. Still pushing through paperwork and stuff. There's a lot to do, isn't there.'

'There is. I think that's the worst bit. When you want to cry or scream or shout but you can't because some bank wants you to be a grown-up about accounts and savings.'

'Yeah… Mum was pretty good, left most things organised.'

'Lists?'

'Of course.'

'Of course.'

He sips at his drink, looking around the room. 'Jem, what are we doing here?'

I take a deep breath. 'I wanted to apologise.' I see his body sag a little, which dents my confidence. 'Not because I'm trying to get you to accept my apology and for everything to be okay again. I just feel like before, the letter and grand gesture where I rocked up in Cornwall, it was all misguided. I thought I was doing the right thing, but it was for all the wrong reasons and I want to put that right. If I can.'

'You know, you're not the only one to blame about things between us. This isn't your entire responsibility to fix.'

'I think it's mostly me that was to blame. I was the one that did all those things. I was the one to make all the mistakes. I was the one who lied.'

He puts his drink down. 'I've lied too.'

'What?'

'I know what was in the letter. I read the text message, the photos.' My mouth falls open, my heart stops. 'It's why I came back.'

'But… why didn't you…?'

'I was going to. When I saw you at the funeral, I wanted to say it then but it wasn't the right place. I feel like you've been wearing this guilt, you've been cloaked in it for so long and I didn't know where to start. I didn't know how to make you see this wasn't entirely of your making. I didn't know how to tell you that apologising to me was your first mistake.'

'What do you mean?'

'Jem, do you still have the letter? Have you read it?' I picture the tiny pieces of it nestled in the envelope, cast aside in the bin as Mitch glared. 'No. I don't have it.'

'Can you remember what was in it?'

'Of course I can. I wrote it. I remember everything, I've bloody lived it.'

'You have. But… I think you've lived it from a position of blame. You've decided those things were your fault and you were intent on self-destruct. You always were, and I know why that was. I always understood where it came from but I just couldn't live with it any more. I loved you, I had to walk away.'

He loved me. Past tense.

'Your ex-colleague had no right to come round to our house and shame you into doing what you did.'

'Leanne said the same, but at the end of the day, I could have said no.'

'Could you? Could you really have said no? Did you really believe you had that choice?'

I think back to the night in question, the feeling that I had no choice but to go along with what was expected. And I feel sad for the me that couldn't find the strength to say no. To invite him to leave.

'And the baby.'

I look anywhere but at him because I can't bear to see the hurt in his eyes.

'You had a miscarriage, they happen all the time. Your drinking may not have been the cause.'

'But what if it had been?'

'But what if it hadn't…?'

I reach into my bag, pulling out a tissue to catch the tears before my mascara runs. He places his hand on mine. His fingers are rough to the touch, a worker's hand. He rubs his finger over my thumb before taking his hand away again.

'What if it hadn't, Jem?'

'I don't know. I don't know.'

'You've lived for all this time with the idea that you killed our baby and it breaks my heart to think you'd really be that hard on yourself. But I've lived for all this time knowing there was nothing I could do to help you unless you realised your own demons were breaking you down. I tried so hard, for so long. I wanted my love for you to be enough but I was naive, it could never have been. And not because I didn't love you enough, but because you didn't love you at all. There was no foundation for me to build on. There was nothing I could cling to that might give my love for you weight, or power. And in the end, I had to leave because it hurt too much and I don't deserve that.'

'You don't.'

'Any more than you do.'

I stir my tea, knowing he's right, but finding it hard to feel it.

'Why did you stop drinking?' he asks.

I think about the nights it helped me sleep. I think about the afternoons I'd start early because the sun was shining or there was a celebration, or I was going past the pub so why not pop in for a swift one and a chat with the locals. I think about the insomnia at four in the morning and the banging head at eight. I think about the pains in my kidneys and the lack of funds in my bank. I think about the times Mitch would bring it over and I'd drink it without thinking. I think about the times I drank and drank and drank to excess under the guise of having fun with colleagues or mates. Fun that involved falling into bins and waking up without memories. I think about the reputation I had down the pub, or the comments from friends who'd always joke about what I drank. I think about Leanne, and her occasional nudge of concern over what I was doing, even though I didn't even tell her the full truth of how bad it was. And I think about Mum, and one of her last comments to me about maybe it was time I drank less. And I think about now, how much clearer my head is. How much more energy I have. More money. More me.

'It was a crutch. I never saw it, I didn't give it any thought, but I can see it now. It was like I couldn't function without it.'

'And?'

'Well, I guess you look at some people and know they're an alcoholic. They drink from the second they wake up until they go to bed. They drink White Lightning or cheap rum. I thought I was fine because I didn't do any of those things. I wasn't on a park bench. I can't stand White Lightning.' I try and force a smile. 'I functioned.'

'Functioned…?'

'My name's Jem and I'm a functioning alcoholic.'

He sits back in his chair, stunned.

'I know right. Pretty big, huh?'

'Massive.'

'I think I got away with it for so long because it just looked like I loved a drink.'

'I knew. I saw,' he says, sadly. 'It's why I always tried to steer you away from drinking, encourage you to slow down, but it always felt like somehow I was trying to control you.'

'Probably because I made you feel that way. I remember how you'd say things and how I'd get all defensive, justify my behaviour by pointing out I was a grown woman and could drink as much or as little as I liked. Mum mentioned it a couple of times but gently, carefully, as if she didn't want to make me feel bad for it. And Leanne? I think I managed to hide it from her completely. She had no idea.'

'You're not the first person in the world to drink like that.'

'No. I guess not. I don't really know how it even happened, how it got as bad as it did. It was just a crutch I couldn't escape from. It felt strange of an evening, not to feel numb and disconnected. And I'm not calling that as an excuse. It was a symptom, there were others too. And that's why I stopped.'

'And how do you feel?'

I think for a minute, about the best way to explain how I feel. Through my broken heart and exhaustion, through the weariness of the way I've lived and the challenge of trying to change, for me... 'I feel like I've been given a second chance. Again. But this time I know what to do with it.'

Chapter Eighty-Five

We walk through the garden centre. I watch grown women with their mums and feel a pang of jealousy. I watch older couples picking out flowers together and feel a sense of longing.

We haven't spoken for the last few minutes and I think that's partly because I've said what I needed to, and Ben needs time to consider it. I feel free. My shoulders light. He's right about the situations I've found myself in over the years. I haven't dared let myself off the hook, but I have to, if I'm ever to live the life I want to. I don't deserve to feel the guilt and the shame. Whatever mistakes I've made, I've made. I can't turn back time.

'You haven't asked me about my ex and the baby,' he says, as we reach our cars, Petula parked tidily beside his.

'I didn't think it was any of my business.'

He rests against his car, keys in hand. 'I met her when I first got down to Cornwall. She was the opposite of you, she meditated on the beach and did yoga all day. She sang and made jewellery out of stuff she found. She walked barefoot so she could feel the ground beneath her.'

'Yes… that's quite opposite,' I say, glancing down at my winter boots.

'Then she found out she was pregnant and she was determined to keep it. I wasn't sure but it was her body, her choice. So I supported her. Even though…'

'Even though?'

'Well, it wasn't my baby. We'd been taking it slowly, my choice. I told her it was because she was important to me and I wanted to make things work, but actually it was because I still loved you.'

Loved. Again. Past tense.

'But I stood by her because the father was someone she met at the masked ball in Porthleven. Before me, she was pretty free with her love, her body. She didn't know who the father was.'

'Wow.'

'And even though I wasn't sure I wanted kids, I felt like I should. I didn't feel right just leaving her because she was pregnant. So we tried.'

'Yes?'

'But it could never have worked.'

'No?'

'It just wasn't right. I was forcing something to try and move on.'

'Right.'

'And I loved you.'

My breath catches in my throat.

'I love you.'

I daren't look at him.

'I have always loved you.'

He steps towards me, just enough to fill the space but not so much as we're touching. 'And all I ever wanted was for you to have room in your heart for me, but you didn't. And I couldn't take it. So I left and hoped it might all pass and that I'd get over you. But I didn't.'

I do look at him this time. The man I loved as much as I could became the man I loved more than I knew what to do with, and I crushed it because I was terrified.

'And I don't know if we have a future together because you have your own journey to take and it's early days but…' He takes my hand. 'When you're ready, I want you to call me. I want you to tell me you love me, and I want us to be together.'

'But what if it takes me too long?' I ask.

'And what if it doesn't?' he says.

Chapter Eighty-Six

I watch as his car indicates, waiting for a gap in the traffic to pull out. And as he goes, I let out a long-held breath. The breath that contained the words, I love you, let's be together, because if I can ever say that to him, it has to be right. It has to be when I'm ready. I have to be able to love him. I have to be able to love me.

I take a few breaths, relieved by the letting go of some of the things I've used against myself. I place my hand on my belly, imagining the tiny life it once held and knowing that whether it was my fault or not, it wouldn't have been right for either of us. Not then, maybe not ever. Perhaps fate was at play.

I head home, driving steadily. I go past the end of Kate Pinkerton's road and wonder.

So I turn around and pull up outside the house she used to live in. Her little car is parked on the drive. A Fiat 500. She always loved the little Fiats. We'd drive miles in her little yellow Seicento when she first passed her test, singing loudly to Wham!, laughing as we went.

I knock on her door. And wait.

There are voices from inside. A dog runs to the glass and jumps up. Two slippered feet come down the hallway and there she is, door open. Her face falls from a bright smile to thin-lipped disdain.

'I've nothing to say to you and I'd like you to leave.'

'I know, and I'm sorry, but I really need to tell you something that I couldn't tell you before. Please. This isn't a lame apology, it's just something I should have said when it happened, and though it still doesn't excuse my leaving you in the lurch right before your wedding, I hope that you might see why I did it, even if you don't agree. I wouldn't expect you to agree. I guess I just want to be honest. And then we can both move on.'

She folds her arms but doesn't slam the door in my face and for that I'm bloody grateful.

'The day I should have been at the dress fitting, was two days after I had a miscarriage.' Her face drops. 'I was bleeding quite heavily still, I was also a mess. I'd also been drinking because I was so confused about the baby and what had happened.' She drops her arms, holding the door with one and the frame with the other; her door opens just slightly. 'The thing was, I thought I'd killed the baby with drinking, and maybe I did, but maybe I didn't and either way, it had happened, and I didn't know what to say or where to turn and I couldn't bear the idea of how upset with me you'd have been. It wasn't long after you'd heard it might be tricky to have children, though… I'm happy to see that's not the case. Really happy. It's just that I didn't know how to be honest with you because the whole thing was messed up and I am sorry. I am so, very, very sorry that I let you down. And I know I can never make it up to you and I don't expect you to forgive me or even believe me, but I just wanted to be honest with you. It's overdue, but I can't change that now.'

More release. More weight off my shoulders. More sadness at old me who didn't know how to deal with all the things life was throwing at her. The me who thought she'd been at rock bottom but who'd barely even scratched it.

'I hope you and Greg will be very happy together. I hope you had a gorgeous day. I thought about you, I caught sight of you as you arrived at the church. You looked beautiful.'

On the wall in her hallway, there's a photo of them on their wedding day. She looks dimple-cheeked and utterly in love.

'I'm sorry. I guess that's all...'

I walk down her path back to my car. In the car window I see her still stood on the doorstep. As I open my car door she calls out to me, 'Jem.'

I turn to face her.

'Jackie Collins book club is every third Thursday of the month. The next one's at mine, next week. You'd be very welcome.'

Chapter Eighty-Seven

I bend down behind the telly to flick on the switch and red fairy lights light up the tree. It's probably not entirely as Mum would have had it, not least because I haven't measured each bauble to ensure they're equidistant from one another but still, as I stand back to admire my handiwork, I reckon she'd have approved.

Adjusted a few baubles, but approved.

I can't tell what smells better when I go in the kitchen, the chicken (because who actually likes turkey anyway) or the nut roast. If I'm honest, it's probably the chicken, but I still won't have any.

I jiggle the roasting tray until the potatoes tumble and coat themselves with more oil, browning perfectly. I give the Yorkshire batter a quick whisk to make sure it's still got air in it, determined to get them right. I glance up at the mirror that Mum painted, where once upon a time I'd catch sight of her watching what I was doing, making sure I was doing it right, and I wish with all my heart that she was still here.

Then I head into the dining room and look at the table. Christmas plate chargers are layered with the willow pattern plates and tiny crystal glasses that Mum wanted to give away and I wouldn't bloody let her. Thank goodness for that, because although the plates are small and we may have to pile the food high, I wouldn't have a faux Christmas dinner round at mine any other way.

The clock strikes three and I hear a car pull up outside. A child whoops and screams and I know that the second I open the door, Harley will knee slide into the lounge with prowess and pride. Just as he should do.

'Oh my God, Jem, this looks beautiful,' say Leanne, Elsie on her hip, a bag of toys and nappy stuff slung over her shoulder.

'It does, doesn't it?'

She plants a kiss on my cheek then arranges cushions on the floor, wedging Elsie into them. Harley immediately drops down and starts to play with his little sister like the gorgeous big brother he has become.

'Here's my contribution,' she says, handing me a selection of cheeses and some fizz.

'Lovely, do you want it in the fridge?'

'Nope. I want it in a glass. Madam's outright rejected my boobs now, so I have some abstinence to make up for.'

'But your car?'

'I know right, being a grown-up is crap. Andy's back tomorrow, so I guess I'll just have the one glass and make it last for the rest of the day.'

'I could run you back, if you like?'

'Drunk in charge of two children? Probably best not to.'

'I suppose. Okay, one glass coming up.'

I pull out a flute from the kitchen cupboard, smiling at the Royal Wedding mug, and pulling it out for Harley to have his drink from. 'Did you talk to Kate the other day, when I left you in the Forge? I saw you get up and move towards her,' I call through.

'Yes. I did. It was lovely actually. Feel a bit bad really for being so down on her for so long. She's actually really nice, isn't she?'

'I bloody told you.'

'I know. But I didn't believe you because I couldn't understand how anyone could be so bitter towards you. And I didn't know the full story.'

'Look, you got off lightly, somehow I never managed to shit on your bonfire.'

'No. True. Although you did once wee on my daffodils.'

'Yes. On the same night you force-fed me gin, so I think we're even.'

'We probably are. And drunk Jem was funny, but I think I like sober Jem more.'

'Me too.'

The doorbell goes and I jog through to open it. 'Hi, come in, go through, let me take your coat.'

Kate grins at me, dimples clearly on show. 'Hey, Happy Christmas. I know it's going to be a tricky one this year. I imagine the firsts all are, but I'm so proud of how you're handling it. Here, some Appletiser for you. And some mince pies baked fresh this morning.'

I sniff at the tin, they look just like the ones Mum used to make, which gives me a flicker of sadness before a smile of gratefulness for all the tiny memories that chip in when I'm least expecting them. And for a memory to come from Kate makes my heart swell at how easily we've been able to reconnect. 'Go on through, Leanne's already there. And Elsie.'

'Ahhh, I can't wait to meet Elsie Alice, hey, Leanne, how are you?' They embrace before Kate bobs down to say hello to Elsie. 'You just wait a second and you'll have a playmate won't you, yeah?' She stands up, checking out the window. 'Greg's just bringing Charlie in now. I've sort of left him with the carrier and all the paraphernalia that goes with it. Don't you think it's bonkers how much stuff you have to take around with you?' Kate says to Leanne.

'It's crazy. I'd forgotten how much crap there is. I'd managed to get rid of some with Harley being that bit older. But now, I've got all his stuff and all her stuff and I am an actual pack horse half the time.'

I leave them to chat, helping Greg in with bags and a bottle. 'Sorry for all this stuff. I promise we've only come for the afternoon, this isn't us moving in indefinitely.'

I show him through to the lounge where he greets Leanne and she offers to get them drinks and my heart is almost full with good friends and babies that don't belong to me.

And then Ben's car pulls up on my drive. And he waves shyly at me. And as he gets out of the car, I know that I'm ready. And it didn't take me too long after all. Because when you love yourself enough to love someone else, and you know without question just how much they love you back, what's the sense in waiting around?

The End

A Letter from Anna

Dear reader,

I want to say a huge thank you for choosing to read *The Man I Loved Before*. If you did enjoy it, and want to keep up-to-date with all my latest releases, just sign up at the following link. Your email address will never be shared and you can unsubscribe at any time.

www.bookouture.com/anna-mansell

You have no idea how much I appreciate the time you've given in reading my words. To write and be published is a privilege I take very seriously, and I really hope you've enjoyed this story. Those who've read any of my previous books, may remember from my author letters how much of my earlier books were written at my mother's bedside as she went through treatment for cancer. Some may also know that I then lost her in September 2018.

This book began to come to me in the months after that fact. I remember a conversation with my brother where I said I just wanted her to know we were okay, and that she could go knowing we'd survive, that she'd done her job. I relate to Jem in as much as I too am a fundamentally flawed human being. But I, unlike Jem, realise how this is true of most, if not all of us, to some degree or other. It's so hard to blame ourselves for choices we've freely made without sometimes realising that, in fact, certain experiences may have conditioned our behaviour. It's not about making excuses, but it is about taking responsibility, then forgiving ourselves. To err is human, etc.

With that in mind, I wanted to write about someone who felt they had hit rock bottom, and push them even further, to help them realise just how much they could actually take. Perhaps that makes me sound somewhat cruel, but in fact, it was because I truly believe that we are often so much stronger than we dare to believe.

If you have enjoyed this book, please do leave a review. I'm often found hanging around social media, so feel free to find me there as I love to hear from readers. And if you'd like to hear from me about future books, please do consider signing up to my mailing list, I promise no spam, just book updates as and when they come.

Finally, if you, or anyone you know, is affected by any of the themes in this book, there are support networks available to you. Here are a few links in case that helps:

www.alcoholics-anonymous.org.uk

www.aa.org

www.macmillan.org.uk

www.cancersupportcommunity.org/family-and-friends

www.samaritans.org

Thank you once again for reading. I am truly, truly grateful.
With love, A.x

AnnaMansellAuthor

@annamansell

MrsAnnaM

www.feelthefearandwriteitanyway.com

Acknowledgements

Writing acknowledgements is hard – you don't want to miss anybody out because, like the saying 'raising children takes a village', keeping an author sane when writing a first draft, a second draft, or however many more until it finally comes out into the world, that takes more than a village. A city? A county? A fair gaggle of brilliant people who believe you can do it, even when you're not entirely certain?

To that end, the first person I'd like to thank is my brilliant editor, Isobel Akenhead. Honestly, I've said it before, but she's quite simply brilliant. You know when you know someone gets you, understands what you're trying to say, believes you can say it and only occasionally has to point out that you've a sweary mouth and a penchant for references that may not in fact be understood by anyone outside of a very tight geographic locale. And apologies to her for the amount of toilet humour in my early drafts. I did not intend to turn you into the bad-taste humour police. Tabards!

I couldn't thank Isobel without mentioning some of the other, incredible team members at Bookouture. The longer I write, the more I hear about other writers' experiences, and it reminds me how lucky I am to continue my relationship with the team. They work tirelessly, they're supportive, they understand we're human beings with lives that can sometimes impact on our work, and they treat us all with the same respect, commitment and dedication as each other. Plus they throw a bloody lovely summer party where we all get out of our writing rooms and meet up in real life, and despite my being fundamentally anti-social, it's become an absolute highlight of my year. Particular mention should also go to Noelle and Kim, the very best publicity managers you could hope to work with. I don't know how they do it, but they do. Every bloomin' time!

I'd also like to thank the Empowered Women of Cornwall, a closed group of likeminded women who offer support, friendship and guidance to other women in our beautiful county. When I knew that some of Jem's story would explore gaslighting, I turned to them and invited their experiences to inform my writing. Several of them wrote to me with such honesty, insight and openness, I will be forever grateful for their words and really hope that I've done that aspect of the story justice.

Who else? The brilliant bloggers who read and review our books. There is such a vibrant community of book bloggers across the world, and I've been privileged to have received some very warm and supportive reviews of previous books. These reviews not only make a difference to sales and the profile of our work, but they often come at a time when we're terrified about our new book baby and how it will be received. I really hope that those who've supported my last four books will feel this fifth is worthy of their championship.

Thank you to brilliant writer mates, without whom I'd definitely have lost my marbles by now. Thanks also to my brilliant mate mates, the ones I actually see in real life... apart from the times I cancel coffee or lunch because I'm writing and lose all track of time, reality and human connection. Speaking of human connection, thank you to Him Indoors for a) putting up with me when I'm really not terribly present, and b) working so hard to keep me in the manner I'd like to be accustomed to. I know I still haven't quite managed to buy you that boat in return yet, but if I gave up, it'd never happen, right?

And finally, a great big thank you to my kids. Sometimes, particularly in first draft stages, I think you get the short straw when it comes to mums. Please know that I do the very best I can, I love you endlessly, and will always work hard to be better. Sorry for all the late/burned/inedible teas. But look, I wrote another book! I hope it makes you even just the smallest bit as proud of me as I am of you both.